OUT OF THIS NETTLE

OUT OF THIS NETTLE

NORAH LOFTS

ISIS

LARGE PRINT

Oxford

Copyright © Norah Lofts, 1938

First published in Great Britain 1938
by
Victor Gollancz Ltd.

Published in Large Print 2007 by ISIS Publishing Ltd.,
7 Centremead, Osney Mead, Oxford OX2 0ES
by arrangement with
the Author's Estate

British Library Cataloguing in Publication Data
Lofts, Norah 1904–1983
   Out of this nettle. – Large print ed.
   1. Exiles – Scotland – Fiction
   2. Jacobites – Fiction
   3. Historical fiction
   4. Large type books
   I. Title
   823.9'12 [F]

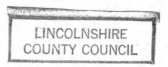

ISBN 978–0–7531–7940–6 (hb)
ISBN 978–0–7531–7941–3 (pb)

Printed and bound in Great Britain by
T. J. International Ltd., Padstow, Cornwall

CONTENTS

PART ONE   The Lost Boyhood 1

PART TWO   The House of Bondage 65

PART THREE The Worldly Hope 225

PART FOUR   The Derelict Kingdom 323

PART ONE

THE LOST BOYHOOD

I hope that I shall not be thought sentimental if I say that I owe my life entirely to my mother. In a sense, of course we all do, but I feel that few women have had the determination, or the skill, to bear a son to a man so crippled in battle that he could move only, and that with aid, between bed and chair.

My father ended his active life at Sheriffmuir in '15, and I was not born until '29. How often she must have despaired. Yet conceived somehow and duly born I was. And if an incredulous eye may have been cast upon the rug-shrouded wreck by the fire and the triumphant woman with the baby in her arms it had only to wait. I grew into an unmistakable Lowrie, beaky nosed, red-haired, thin lipped.

Life had dealt hardly with my mother as it often does, I have observed, with proud people who throw out a challenge. She had been a beauty. There was a miniature that never left my father's pocket for more than a moment, showing her as she had been at her marriage, icily fair, with blue eyes and a regular oval face. She was of Scottish blood though she hated Scotland, having been bred in France. Yet she married my father and came to live at Braidlowrie and had been — I heard it often from her own lips — very happy for a year, despite the climate which depressed her and the people whom she despised.

And then Mar, living up to his nickname of "Bobbing John," decided to bob up on the Stuart side again. The fiery cross went through the glens and up the mountain sides and Edman Lowrie, my father, rode out to fight for his king.

At Sheriffmuir he lost the use of his legs and in the subsequent subjugation of the rebels he lost his lands. The fines imposed took all his fortune and my mother's dowry as well: and as though that were not enough, Braidlowrie was burned so that only the shell of the house and the kitchen quarters remained.

In those kitchen quarters my mother, gently born, softly reared, proud, resentful and unconquered, settled down to live like a crofter's wife. In the formal garden of stone and clipped yews she kept pigs, a goat, a flock of squawking hens. She gathered wood for the fire and when all the fallen and rotten pieces were collected and snapped off she took a saw and felled a tree as need arose. Pride could survive such usage, but beauty was destroyed and I remember her as a tall gaunt woman, with hard eye and a sharp tongue, dressed in old faded clothes saved from better days and a shawl to shield her from the cold which to the end of her life was her constant enemy. Oh, I remember those chill grey dawns and evenings at Braidlowrie, the cold splash of the pig-swill, the seeping of mud through the ill-fashioned shoes, the acrid billows of smoke that poured from the unseasoned timber on the hearth, and I salute my mother. Honour, if not love, was her meed from me.

These discomforts of course I shared, as I did the labours, as soon as I left infancy behind; but the story of the battle and the rebellion and the punishment that followed was told me instead of the charms and rhymes and fairy tales with which other children are entertained. I have tried not to let bitterness colour my recollection of those early days: later on I met many English people, and some were good, some bad, as might be said of the people of any nation: but the stories were told to me bitterly, for my mother, who disliked the Scottish people, hated and loathed the English, and if, on a day when the broth was thin or there was none at all, someone had offered her a saddle of mutton fed on the succulent pastures of England, she would have turned away her head in scorn. Or if, on a wet day, when the snow-water irked her chilblains, she had been presented with a pair of the shoes that the English make so well and told, "Here are English shoes for you," she would have flung them in the speaker's face. So bitter was her hatred. And if I am less bitter I must remember that I did not see Braidlowrie burned: I did not know the galling descent from affluence and honour to penury and obscurity.

Looking back, indeed, I wonder less at her implacable hatred than at my father's imperturbable calm. It must, surely it must have maddened him to see his beautiful, tenderly-nurtured wife tending swine and chopping logs. Her infrequent yet fiery complaints must have cut him to the quick and found a doubly painful echo there. For he, after all, had brought her out of France: he had chosen to fight the losing battle:

5

it was his ill-fortune that she bore as she bore his name. Yet never once did I hear an ill-natured or whining word cross his lips. He sat by the smoking hearth, a rug over his shattered limbs, and unless his hands were engaged in one of the tame tasks that mother found for him he was busy with his books. He had very few. His small precious collection had been consumed in the fire and he depended upon a few stray volumes that had come by chance into his hands. He taught me to read and to count and would have opened to me the mysteries of Latin and Greek but that I was unscholarly and too often busy or tired to pay much heed.

It was never he who told me about the battle or the burning — I sometimes wonder how that story would have sounded with its violence and colour sieved through his mild and reasonable mind. Sometimes, but very seldom, when mother rated me for some task neglected or badly done he would say in his gentle voice, "He's but a child yet, let him be young while he may." I was never grateful for his intervention. It shamed me. I had far rather that mother should consider me an idle and wanton youth than that father should remark upon my tender years. And as I grew I became conscious of a certain contempt for him, so helpless, so resigned, so dependent upon that iron woman, his wife. But later on, much later, grown myself to manhood, I dimly appreciated the quality that was in him, the man who having given all that he had in a cause that he considered just, could sit down in the long afterwards without self-pity, without complaint and without despair. Sired and mothered thus I should have been other than I am.

At what age I was when the legend of Braidlowrie first laid hold upon me I cannot remember, but it was well established by the time that I was twelve. I used to pause in my tasks to stare at the blackened walls, the blank windows that looked like the eyes of dead men, the tragic crumbling chimney stacks and dream of the house as it had been, proud and strong, beautiful in its strength and its completeness. Lights would shine for me from those windows, the dead chimneys smoked, music sounded as the pipers went round the table where the silver dishes gleamed. Mother, restored to the beauty of the miniature, sat at the table in a silk gown that showed her white shoulders and there were rings on the hands that had never known ill-use. And there was a man in the picture somewhere, I knew that though I never saw him, the man who had restored Braidlowrie, the man who had given beauty for ashes and made the desert blossom like the rose. Myself.

In the lengthening spring twilights I would stand with a bowl of chicken food or a pail of swill in my hands and dream my youthful dreams . . . and then a hungry sow would thrust her snout against my knees, or mother would call, "Colin, Colin, will you be all night there?" and the lights and the music would fade. The blackened chimneys reared themselves against the slatey sky, and the wind moaned before the coming night. I would hasten over the remainder of my duties and then go thankfully to the kitchen where mother was dishing up porridge or broth from the black pot that swung from the soot-encrusted hook. The faint light of the home-made dip showed me the ravages that time and hardship had made in her beauty and a heaviness would settle on my heart. Nothing brought home to me the insubstantiality of my fancies as that did. Never, never would she sit at the table with her face glowing beneath the light of twenty wax candles in branching silver sticks.

Then suddenly one evening that thought failed to do its dismal work on me. My whole dream was not rendered ridiculous and pitiable because of mother's face. There were other women who could face the light of twenty candles . . . and for one of them, whom I neither knew nor cared either then or for many years after, but for one of them should my dream take shape. I might not be able to restore Braidlowrie into the semblance of my mother's stories of it, but the walls I could rear, the garden I could clean and garnish, the chimneys I could cause to smoke and the rooms I could inhabit. That became my self-appointed task in life. And now that I was looking forward instead of backward nothing could make my heart quail before the task. I never again felt that destructive desire to laugh at myself. I am glad that I passed that stage before I learned that laughter is the most destructive thing in the world.

I had no friends in my childhood. That was only natural. The families with whom my parents would have been friendly were isolated in their poverty just as we were. Unless one could afford a horse visiting was out of the question. There were children aplenty in

Crosslochie, but mother set her face against my associating with them: and even if she hadn't I had little time for play. As I grew older I began to do willingly the tasks that mother had forced upon me as a child, for it was easier for me to do a job, even though it taxed my strength to its limits, than to see her going about it. I killed my first pig when I was twelve. Tammie, the old man who usually did jobs like that for mother, was unable to come because the stiffness in his joints had come upon him. Mother said, "I'll do it myself then." I saw the white come around her nostrils as though an invisible hand were pinching her nose.

"When?" I asked. She hesitated for an instant, and then, with a shrug at her own weakness at delaying, she said, "This afternoon."

While she was out of the kitchen I sharpened the knife on the doorstep. I worked until the edge and the point were glittering sharp. Then I went out to the pen where the pig destined to support us that winter had been fattening. The throat of a pig is loose of skin and very tough: and there is a lot of blood in a pig. I was sick three times before it was over and I could go to mother to ask her aid in lifting the heavy carcase on to the skinning board. But that was another weakness finished with. Mother never had to kill a pig again.

My pleasures, and by that I mean my relaxations from menial labour, were snaring and fishing. In these I was encouraged by mother because my catches made a welcome change from the salt pork that was our staple meat diet. I was fishing when I got acquainted with Janet Thatcher.

I'd known her by sight and just to speak to in the
road almost since I could remember, for the Thatchers
lived at Crosslochie in a little house that respectable
people pointed scornful fingers at. The family had a
very ill name. Fran Thatcher, Janet's father, had been
hanged for sheep-stealing and there were those who
held that that was the least of his crimes. The mother
was a slut, grown so fat these many years that only the
old people could remember her passing through her
own doorway. It was a matter of speculation among the
least serious of the young folk how she would be got
out for her own burying. One day, no doubt, Ellie and
Janet, her daughters, would be just such hulks of
shapeless flesh, but when I was a youth, rising fifteen,
they were both shapely pieces and pretty enough. The
hair that escaped from their shawls wasn't blown into
rats' tails like other girls', it danced in little curls that
seemed to have a life of their own: and on a misty day,
or one of soft rain, it was as though the tendrils had
been hung with pearls. Mother would have been angry
with me if she had known that such things had taken
my eye, but who can choose what his eye shall see and
what miss? Ellie was a little frightening. She scorned
boys, and often took a very high hand with men. You
had to pay a little more than was easy for you to sleep
with Ellie, they said, and it was no good calling her
"whore" afterwards, for she only laughed and shook her
curls. She was crafty and secret too, so that she was
never caught in her misdoing, and once, when Alec
Slanty's wife went after her to scratch her face for
making free with Alec, she said, "Would I be having any

truck with a little runt the like of that one? He's boasting I tell ye." That didn't sooth Mrs. Slanty much as you can imagine. Janet was younger and milder, not so set up with herself, though that might come, and lots of the boys in Crosslochie had their eyes on her, both for her own prettiness and for the name that Ellie had brought on the house.

I gathered all this information in bits and pieces, for though mother hated that I should have anything to do with the village people a certain amount of contact was unavoidable, living as we did. And although I hadn't gone so far as to thrust myself on Janet's notice I had eyed her. For I was at an age then to begin to wonder what lay behind the jokes and the half-spoken things, and the love stories in the books that father pored over. There seemed to me then to be a great gap between the mere physical action that you could watch between cock and hen, between boar and sow and the kind of poetry that such a thing became when it was between, say, Romeo and Juliet. And there was the story of Jacob working seven years and then other seven for Rachel because Leah for some reason wouldn't do.

You will understand that I was young and that my lonely, isolated life forced me to puzzle things out for myself. And as I look back upon it now, after knowing so many and so various women, it seems that my puzzled boyish interest in this question proves that it is a fundamental matter. I mean that so many things have to be thrust upon you from outside, this came from within. Mother had impressed upon me that although I was poor and worked at lowly tasks I was born a gentleman and that any intimacy with the lads of Crosslochie must not pass a certain line. Left to myself I should never have thought of that, for instance. Interest in politics too had been thrust upon me. But interest in girls and their bodies and the feelings that they might evoke, that had come of itself. That was concerned with being a man, not a gentleman, not a Jacobite. Therefore I say that it was real.

When Janet Thatcher paused by me where I sat on the burn's bank and asked in her clicking Scots tongue, which mother so detested, whether my catch was good I was immensely flattered. I forgot for a little time that I was Colin Lowrie of Braidlowrie and was just like a village boy whom she had deigned to notice. She sat down beside me and toyed with my amateur, home-made tackle, and when at last I made a catch she was just as pleased (and more obviously) as I was myself. She asked whether I often fished there and I told her yes. We made no appointment, but when I went next day, which was unusual for I seldom fished two days running, she was there before me. I had courage enough that day to look at her. And I have honesty enough now to admit that I was proud on that day to see that she compared poorly with the girl in father's miniature who had become for me the symbol of female beauty. Janet was coarse. The colour on her face and the texture of her skin were apple-like, firm and hard. Her eyes were black and bold; and the hair that I had so admired from the distance was like a horse's tail, springy because it was wiry. But the whole effect was pleasing and I was like a man who says,

"This is not the dish that I should choose, but it will do." Poor Janet! It is a shame to describe her so. She did much for me. But description, unless it is honest, is useless, and to limn myself as an indiscriminating lout would be to deny almost sixteen years of my mother's teaching.

My priggishness was punished! By the time that we had met four times I was mad for her. I wanted to run my fingers through those springing curls, their wiriness forgotten. I wanted to put my lips to those black eyes under the shining lids, bold though they might be. I wanted . . . I wanted . . . I had no idea of what. And I was as helpless in the face of my desires as if I had been deaf and dumb and impotent indeed. We forsook the burn's bank and walked in the woods where the new larch leaves were burning a bright green flame and the wild cherry trees shook down a shower of snowy petals on us: and we talked about fishing and setting snares and fattening hens and farrowing sows. Truly, looking back I could laugh, if the memory did not call up an unwilling sigh.

What would have happened I do not know. I might have blurted out some unmistakable gaucherie and so broken down the bonds of friendliness that bound and yet divided us; or she might have grown impatient and led me along the road that I do not doubt she had travelled before. But our small personal drama was swallowed up in the more general affair that has gone into history by the simple name of "The '45."

I should need the skill and the pen of Homer fitly to describe to you what that year meant to us who had been broken in the '15. For the first time in my life there were comings and goings at Braidlowrie. Secretly at first, and then openly, men came along the moss-greened path between the overgrown yews, past the garden beds where the pigs rooted and the hens scratched. From walking in the woods with Janet I would return to find a stranger smothering his coughs as he sat by the smoking logs, talking and listening to my father. I heard for the first time the catchword, "Lowrie knows." And I learned that my father was not by everyone considered the helpless meek puppet that I had deemed him.

I forgot my puerile hankering after Janet Thatcher's flesh. I was swept bodily into the dizzy stream of Jacobite feeling, Jacobite plans. A new light came into my father's face, new vigour into his mild voice. For the first time in all my sixteen years I heard him say, "Had I but the use of my legs!" And that not to my mother to whom such words should have been addressed twenty times a day, but to a black-bearded stranger who had ridden up on a borrowed horse that would, he declared, be returned when it had carried him in triumph to London.

The Prince landed. The fiery cross went round. I was afire to join the Jacobite forces . . . and then mother would not let me go. Of all the people she alone had remained unmoved. Or should I say that she was moved to scorn and bitterness, to Cassandra-like prophecies, to bitter mirth? We had fared so well in the last rising, hadn't we, no wonder we had a taste for it! Ah, the edge on her voice as she said that. Did we think that thirty years of settled rule had undermined the Hanoverian dynasty? What was this but the last feeble effort of the dispossessed?

And with every one of her jibes a little snake of hatred for her reared its head in my breast, because she said what the rest of us only feared in silence. Finally, when I said that I *would* go and looked to father for support, she flung herself down on the broken bricks of the kitchen floor and put her arms around my thighs. I was amazed and disconcerted to see that her eyes were full of tears that gathered and spilled over the lids to lose themselves in the furrows of her face. She swallowed twice and then said in a voice that I had never heard her use before, "Colin, do this for me. Stay quietly here and I'll never ask you anything again. I'm an old woman now, an old woman before my time, and I have lost everything that makes life sweet to women. In thirty years I've never had a moment's peace, nor a pleasure, no, not so much as a new gown. All that is left to me is my son and this bit of roof over our heads. If you go and the venture succeeds, you may never live to see it. If you go and the venture fails, we'll lose our roof. Leave it to the grown men, Colin, that are too set in their ways to heed the voices of their women."

I had never seen her cry before, not even on the day when the pigs had the sickness and lay down to die all together.

"But mother," I said, protesting, "the Prince has called for me, and I'm big and strong. Think of the rewards that will be ours when he is King of England."

15

"When he is king let him remember your father. He shall not have what is mine despite . . . despite . . ."

A spasm passed over her face, the voice was strangled in her throat and from her knees falling sideways she dropped to the floor. Behind me sounded my father's voice.

"Lift her to the settle, lad, and splash water in her face. And you bide here if you anyway can. She has had much to try her and is not so strong as she appears. One young man more or less will not affect the cause."

I said hotly, breathless with lifting mother, "If every young man thought like that, father . . ."

"Every young man is not the only son of his mother and she a widow," said my father. I recognised the words from the bible story and was a little taken aback. Did father count himself then already dead?

That evening, after mother had recovered, I went out, and because I had been defeated in the greater thing I was driven to assert myself in the lesser. I went down to Janet's house and asked her to come out. She came to the door barefoot and would have me go in while she put on her shoes and her shawl. It was with a pleasing feeling of defiant excitement that I stepped across that threshold. What I expected to see I scarcely knew, but there was nothing to mark it off from any other house in the village. The fat old woman sat by a fire of glowing peat holding the ends of three pieces of coloured ribbon that Ellie was plaiting. Both women looked up at me and smiled as though I had been a regular visitor. Mrs. Thatcher made some remark about the weather to which I muttered a reply. Ellie finished the plaiting and took the ribbons away.

"Sit ye doon," said the fat woman, pointing to Ellie's stool. "Young Lowrie isna it?"

I nodded awkwardly.

"It'll be a grand day for ye're feyther if yon business in the Sooth land goes forrard right, willna it?"

"I suppose so," I said.

"Aye. Ye'll no be coming to see the likes o' us thin." She peered at me through the little eyes that could scarcely see over her fat cheeks, and then, perceiving perhaps that I was acutely uncomfortable, she changed the subject abruptly.

"Give me ye'r hand, young Lowrie and I'll speir the future for ye."

I thrust out my hand and she took it in one of her own, fat and dirty, like an old cushion. I watched her face in the red peat glow and saw interest and a kind of excitement leap into those little eyes. Up till then I had been merely embarrassed, but now something waked in me too, and I found myself waiting for her to speak with a suppressed eagerness.

"Well," she said at last, "Janie'll get little good of you, my bonnie lad, nor any other woman I'm thinking. Ye've got the oddest hand and the craziest that iver I laid my eyes on. There's water and blood and water again, and mair blood. There's gold here too, ill-gotten some of it. There's journeys and far countries and queer people."

17

She paused and I thought she had done, but she held my hand firmly, and continued to stare at it. After a long pause she said,

"This rising will alter ye'r life though ye willna be in it. And ye'll come at last to ye'r journey's end, but not the road ye think to. That's all I can tell ye."

"You've told me the most important thing," I said.

"What's that?"

"About the rising," I said breathlessly, for already in my mind the masons and carpenters were busy on Braidlowrie, the broad acres were back again and the pipers were going about the silver-laden table.

The old woman began to laugh. Her fat cheeks shook, her eyes were quite buried. "Ye mustna mind an old woman's babble," she said at last, husky-voiced from laughter. She cleared her throat and spat into the heart of the fire. The spittle hissed. Disgust shook me. I hated the thought that my hand had laid in hers. Janet returned then with a bright ribbon in her hair, and the shawl slipping down over her shoulders. I eyed her through the shadow that her mother cast. After tonight, I thought, I would not see Janet again.

And then to us, waiting anxiously, there came the news of stirring battles: of clansmen, armed only with the blades of scythes fastened upon poles, cutting the heads from the British infantry, the legs from the cavalry. There came a Friday in December when the Prince reached Derby, and London was stricken with panic. Never had the dark days seemed so short and light, never had the cold seemed so trivial a thing. Next year

. . . next year . . . what wouldn't we have of warmth and comfort . . . next year? Only my mother remained sceptical.

But before the year turned, the Prince was back over the border and Cumberland, with more than double the men, was in pursuit. It was like being on a see-saw then, hope and fear, hope and fear again. Time after time I begged mother to let me go. "Never," she said, "never." When I persisted she said at last, "And don't think to go like a thief in the night, for I shall follow you wherever you go. Though you march in the midst of a thousand men I will seek you out and stay your hands. You shall not strike a blow that might bring the name of Lowrie to English ears again."

It had obsessed her, that notion that we must preserve our poor security even at the price of honour; and at last, knowing that what she said was true and that she was capable in her frenzy of shaming me before men, I gave over pleading and resigned myself.

The line of battle surged ever Northwards and in April, when the wild cherry trees were thick with buds just breaking into a foam of green and white and the larch trees were bright again, the forces met at Culloden and all our hopes were shattered. Never more, we knew in our hearts, would the Stuart standard be raised. Never would the broken be restored, never would the crushed be lifted. Gone forever were the broad acres and the pipers.

The knowledge spread like the knowledge of death, cold, insiduous, inescapable.

And the subjugation that had followed the '15 had been as nothing to this. Men rode from the field of battle to the coast and took ship to any land that would shelter them. The flower of the Scots nobility fled like thieves in the night, never, some of them, to look upon their native land again. The sky was darkened by day and made livid by night by the burning of the great houses that were sharing Braidlowrie's fate. To us on the quiet hillside above Crosslochie, heavy with our own disappointment and despair, horrible tales came creeping. How the wounded after Culloden had been heaped together and made a living target for the six-pounders. And the men who died thus were the very ones who, after Preston, had carried the English wounded upon their broad shoulders and given them brandy to keep the life in them! Could any Scotsman remain cool at that memory? Thirty-five of our refugees who had taken shelter in a hut were burnt alive at Cumberland's order. And those were men who on the retreat from Derby had so conducted themselves that none could point to a single instance of rapine or disorder; Glencoe men who had mounted guard at Oxenfoord so that their enemy, Stair who had ordered the massacre, might come to no harm. Noble hearts all of them — at the mercy of the Butcher.

And then all suddenly there were English soldiers at Crosslochie and the cry was going up, "Where is Glenranald?" What avail the bloody murders, the lustful punishments, the burning, the rape and the exile if he, the youngest, the most gallant, the most famous of the Jacobites escaped?

"Where is Glenranald?" He had been seen at the fore-front at Culloden, a dripping sword in his hand, urging on his men with voice and example, accounting, it was said, for twenty English in half the number of minutes. His horse had fallen at the moment when the Scottish ranks, overborne by numbers, had broken, and he had not been seen again. He was not among the dead or wounded. Where was Glenranald?

Twelve English soldiers and their officer came early to Braidlowrie and searched the house. We stood, mother and I, in the kitchen, like dumb things, and father sat like a statue while they ran their swords through the straw of the mattresses, through the panels of the wall, through the very rug that lay across my father's legs. Not a corner was left unsearched, but in the end they went, grumbling and discontented. For we had not seen Glenranald, knew nothing of him but his fame. My mother, straightening the house again with vicious movements, and relighting the fire that they had watered in order to search the chimney, turned to me and said,

"You see what we were saved from? There will be no "Lowrie knows" about this. And to make the more sure of it you will bide on the place till this is over. No more cony snaring, and no more fishing. I want you in my sight. Glenranald is doubtless in the district and doubtless they will find him. But you will be nowhere about. Mind that."

No way to speak at such a time to a thwarted boy whose blood was being roused every minute by some new tale of fury. The afternoon found me walking in the

Boarswood, my rod in my hand, my snares in my pocket, my soul athirst for some stirring thing to befall me. And what befell me was a soft step behind me and Janet Thatcher's voice saying, "I havena seen ye this lang time, Colin." For I had been mindful of my resolve made that evening when her mother laughed and spat in the fire.

"I've had much else to think of," I said shortly. But she fell into step beside me, and I looked at her with a distaste that was in exact measurement with the desire that I had once felt for her.

"The red-coats are speiring everywhere for yon Glenranald, Colin. And they've their eyes on ye'r feyther."

"How should you know that?"

"Ellie heard it. She's got freends among the English."

"She would have," I said fiercely. For wasn't it just like that family to welcome in the murderers and to lie with the rapers for the cursed English silver?

"I hae na truck with them, Colin," Janet said. Her voice was very small.

"Oh no?" I said sneering.

"Na indeed, I've had na truck with nabody since the day I spoke with ye, by the stream. Ye remember?"

"I remember," I said, wishing that she would go away and leave me to my thoughts.

"Whit's wrang with ye, Colin? D'ye na like me any mair?" Such a pleading voice.

"I like you well enough. I've been very busy. I'm busy now. I've a lot to think of."

"I'll not disturb you."

We walked along in silence, steadily climbing the slope of Boarswood between the larch and birch trees.

Presently I drew a snare from my pocket and with an exaggerated care stooped to set it. While I was crouching there with my head down and my hands busy Janet gave a little cry. I sprang up and looked in the direction in which her eyes were staring. And there, at the foot of a great tree, half hidden from the path by a tangle of low bushes, was a man. He lay on the ground with his back turned towards us and I could see at a glance that this was no ordinary loiterer asleep in the wood. It was a fully armed Highland gentleman either dead or swooning. A voice in my mind cried, "He is Glenranald," and another replied, "Lowrie knows."

Softly, as though the peaceful wood were suddenly full of enemies, we crept around the bushes and kneeling one on either side turned him gently upon his back. His face was deathly white and there were blue shadows round the sunken eyes and the pinched mouth. I loosened the thongs and buttons of the fine green jacket all mucked with blood and mire and fumbling within the soft cambric shirt and chamois jerkin laid my hand on his breast. His body was warm, I noticed that first, and then, under my fingers, felt the faint distant flutter of his heart.

"He's not dead," I said, looking up at Janet who stood staring down at the man.

"I'm sae glad," she said with genuine feeling in her voice. "Whit can we do for him?"

A great wave of bitterness came up and hit me. He needed brandy and warm blankets and bandages for his wounds, to say nothing of a doctor's attentions. He needed a soft bed for his poor body, and nourishing food, and peace and careful nursing. And of all these, I Colin Lowrie of Braidlowrie, could offer him just nothing. Nothing. Not even the shelter that I could have given a homeless dog. I remembered the thorough searching that Braidlowrie had undergone that morning; I remembered Janet's words about my father's house being under observation, and I groaned.

"Colin," said Janet. "Do you see the roots of that tree how they stick oot? A little digging would make a hollow wheer he could lie sheltered anyway. Attend ye to that whiles I rin doon to Crosslochie. There's brandy in the hoose if they didna drink it all the night and I'll bring some rags to put on his wounds. I'll be gone no longer than half an hoor."

Holding her skirts close by her knees she rounded the bushes, regained the path and was gone like a shadow through the trees. I found a stout branch and began to hollow out the widest space between the upstanding roots of the ancient tree. The deepest cave I could make, however, would only just take a man's body to mid-thigh; his legs would be exposed still unless we covered them with brushwood. I gathered a pile in readiness and then, waiting Janet's return, I set to work to investigate the extent of his injuries.

There was dozens of minor cuts and scratches and three serious wounds. One at the base of his throat, a gaping hole that would have taken an egg, one in his

24

arm, a clean cut that had exposed the bone, and one in his thigh — I judged that to be a pistol shot, though I had never seen one. It seemed miraculous that a man so wounded should have got so far from the battle-field, and I thought it unlikely that without skilled attention he would ever get the better of the wound in his throat. I was thinking of that and wondering if this were indeed Glenranald when Janet stood beside me again. I had not heard her coming. She bore a basket on one arm and her other hand was pressed to her side. She was speechless from running, and although the chill of early evening was already deep in the wood there were drops on her forehead.

She fumbled in the basket and brought out a silver drinking flask, the kind that officers carry. Loot, I thought, taken from the body of some dead or dying Scotsman and given by a drunken English red-coat into Ellie's hand. And all to serve a Scotsman's need, I reflected grimly as I took off the top and filled it to the brim. I dribbled a little, a drop at a time between the stiff blue lips. Some ran down over the stubble on his chin, but from the gasp that he gave I gathered that a little at least had gone down his throat. I waited a moment and then tried again.

Meantime Janet was tearing a white petticoat into strips. Coming closer she saw the hole in the man's throat and recoiled with a little cry. But there was spirit in her, for as I looked up she came forward and said firmly, "That should be washed first."

"We've no water," I said, overcome anew by the sense of our inadequacy and helplessness.

Stooping, she lifted her skirt and with fierce little hands tore a large square piece from the petticoat that she was wearing.

"The burn is just above us. I'll soak this." She was back, breathless again, before I had got the third small measure of brandy into the man's mouth, and with firm gentle hands she swabbed out the wound with the dripping rag. Then, clumsily, we bound on the strips of linen. All this time it had been like working on a dead thing; and when, just as we tightened the bandage upon his leg wound which we had left until last, the man groaned, we both started as though someone had spoken from the path. He groaned again and I saw the eyelids flutter though they remained closed.

I bent down near his ear and said clearly, "It's all right. You're with friends."

There was no sign that he had heard me. Suddenly I was aware that twilight was falling and panic seized me. Suppose I had been missed and had been followed — even by mother!

"We can do no more at the moment," I said. "Help me to lift him into the hole, then we'll cover his legs with this stuff and come back tomorrow."

As gently as we could we laid his head and the upper part of his body under the hollow root.

"Puir man," said Janet," "it's a cold bed." She took off her shawl and tucked it around him, like a mother with a baby. The thought made me remember her mother.

"Your shawl will be missed," I said.

She looked up with a smile.

"Nathing's ever missed in our hoose. I doubt if they'd miss me. They'd not bother, anyway."

We piled the brushwood high over the outstretched legs and then studied our work. You might have passed within a yard of him and never guessed. It looked like a heap of rubbish drifted by the wind to the foot of the tree.

"I'd best go up and cross the burn and down on the other side," I said. "No one must guess."

"D'ye think it is Glenranald himself?"

"I do. And if not it's some poor soul in a like case," I said. "Will you come up tomorrow about the same time?"

"I will, Colin, and I'll bring some things. Good-bye." Something remained to be said.

"Good-bye Janet. And Janet, you're a grand girl. I like you full well."

She laughed a little as she rounded the bushes. Then we went, quiet and cautiously, separate ways to our homes.

For one unnatural moment I caught myself envying Janet her home after I got back to my own. I tried to imagine a home from which one could absent oneself for an indefinite time and have to offer no explanation: whence one could purloin a flask of brandy and a petticoat without being noticed: and to which one could return without a garment with which one had set out.

My mother was looking over the half-door of the kitchen, and that light of frenzy that always appeared in her eyes when she was talking about the English or the Prince or the Jacobites was shining strongly as she asked,

"Where have you been?"

"Setting snares on Boarswood."

"All this time?"

"All this time."

"Did you hear what I said to you this morning?"

"Yes mother."

"And you disobeyed me?"

"Yes mother."

"Is that all you can say?"

I couldn't say "Yes mother" to that, so I launched into the most feasible explanation about the length of my absence which I hoped would distract her and also serve in future if I were late again.

"They're going through the lower woods so thoroughly, mother, there was no sense in setting snares where I usually do. I went right up Boarswood, almost to the burn. I saw no one and no one saw me, that I can swear. And it was no more dangerous and a great deal more useful than hanging about the steading all the afternoon."

"That," said mother fiercely, "is not the point at all. I especially asked you not to go off the place for any reason at all. We all know . . ."

Father said mildly, "Can we have supper now?"

Mother turned with a face of thunder and snatched the pot of broth from the hook. There was silence until father said,

"I trust there'll be something to reward you for your long climb tomorrow, Colin. A good rabbit stew would be fine."

For an instant I thought that there was just a shade of hidden meaning in his words and in the glance that went with them, but I dismissed that as fancy. What could father know or guess at? Nothing, of course, nothing. And it was no new thing for him to support me a little in the matter of absence.

We had finished supper. Father was reading, mother's wheel was whirring and I was busy putting bands on a new wooden bucket that I was making for pig-swill when there was a rattle of muskets outside. The top of the kitchen door was thrown violently open and six eager, inquisitive faces appeared. The expression of disappointment that fell on them all told clearly enough that they had expected to find Glenranald warming himself at our fireside. None of us said a word. The officer in charge — not the one who had visited us in the morning — reached over and unlatched the lower half of the door and strode up to where my father sat.

"We must search this house again. Glenranald is known to be in this district. Reports have come in that he has been seen coming this way."

Father inclined his head in a manner that said, "Search and be damned," and bent over his book. The officer called and three of the men followed him in. There was nothing much to search; the kitchen where we lived, a backhouse where wood and stores were kept, two bedrooms that had been part of the servant's quarters; that was all that was left of the house. The men who were left outside routed about in the sheds, we could hear the grunts and squawks of the pigs and hens as they were disturbed. Naturally nothing was found. The officer, angry at this failure, paused by father on his way out and said in a voice that was like spitting,

"We know that this man is about here and we know where your sympathies lie. Don't think to fool us."

Father never even raised his head. The soldiers marched out leaving the door open, and as I closed it mother said,

"You see. They'll have us yet, innocent as we are."

I went to bed with a heart of stone and a head of flame. How, in the face of this suspicion and this power, could I, could we, hope to save the man who lay under the brushwood?

All the next day I thought about him, the refugee whom I called, in my mind, Glenranald. It irked me sorely that there was nothing that I could take to contribute to his comfort and well-being. Raw eggs, I thought, were nourishing, but that day mother collected our eggs as usual and there were four. Even one would be missed from four. There was no brandy in the house, nor had there been since I could remember, and I certainly dared not take any of mother's linen or garments for bandages. My one hope was that Janet would not fail me and that she would be more fortunate than I.

When I had fed the pigs in the afternoon I put down the pail and walked away. I expected to hear mother call me at any second and when I was at last out of hail from the house I was trembling with excitement. I could not be sure what I should do if I heard her voice asking, "Colin, where are you going?" Had I the courage to defy her to her face? I was afraid not. And if that seems puerile in a youth of sixteen years I can but defend myself by thinking that I only knew my mother.

Janet was waiting for me beside the path behind the bushes. I paused to look at that snare of mine which was, of course, the only one that I had set on the previous afternoon. Pray God there might be something in it, a furry brown alibi. And for once God was kind and there was. I laid it beside the path, reset the snare and joined Janet. She showed me the contents of her basket — fresh linen, eggs, milk and broth so good and strong that it had set into jelly. I was grateful, but there was impatience and bitterness in my gratitude. It was not right that a Thatcher of Crosslochie should be able to offer so much and a Lowrie of Braidlowrie so little. It was not right that Glenranald should owe his life, should he escape with it, to goods gained by such means.

We bent over the sick man who lay as we had left him but was a trifle less shadowy of face. To our surprise he opened his eyes immediately and looked at us calmly. Then he said in a voice surprisingly strong for one in such a case,

"Then I didn't dream it."

"What?"

"That someone was tending me."

"We're doing what we can and God knows that that is little enough."

"It will serve," he said.

We fed him with brandy first, and then with egg beaten into milk with a twig. He must have been a strong man, for we could see the force of his life rushing up visibly to meet such encouragement. Presently he said in that astounding voice which seemed to my fancy to have a bugle call in it,

"You're very good to me. Who are you?"

"I'm Colin Lowrie, and this is Janet Thatcher," I said, since Janet seemed to be leaving the talking to me.

"Not Edman Lowrie's son?"

I nodded.

"So I got as near Braidlowrie as that?"

"Yes," I said. "Were you coming there?"

"I had hoped to."

"Well, be glad that you didn't. We're being searched twice a day for you . . . you are Glenranald?"

"I am. So they're searching for me, are they? I guessed as much. Is there a reward out for me?"

"A thousand pounds," said Janet. "It's written up large in Crosslochie."

"Holy Christ! A thousand! I'd hardly have thought the English would have gone above a hundred for me." He laughed as he lay there on his back in the mire. Then he grew serious. "That means, my children, that you take your lives in your hands when you bring me this excellent brandy. Did you realise that it is treason to 'receive, succour or comfort' such as me? Your life especially, young man, wouldn't be worth a farthing dip if they caught you. You'd better be gone."

"I'm safe enough," I said with an assurance that I didn't feel. "I come and go by a different way each time. And I've my snares for an excuse. No one would suspect Janet. She has friends among the soldiery."

"Ellie has," said Janet quietly.

"Oh yes, Ellie," I amended. Then to Glenranald I said,

"How long will it be, do you think, before you can move?"

"Not long. I've no bones broken so far as I can discover. It's loss of blood and lack of food that brings me so low."

But I could see that talking had exhausted him completely and he lay limp while Janet applied the fresh linen and placed the jellied broth by his side. It was only his courage that made him speak so strong and cheerily.

"We'll come tomorrow," I said, when we had made him as comfortable as we could, refolding the shawl and re-arranging the brushwood.

"Have a care to yourselves and run no risks," he said.

We kept him hidden for a week. Towards the end of it there were two days when I dared not leave the house because there were soldiers prowling about between Braidlowrie and Boarswood. However on both days Janet went and came over in the evening on a pretext of buying eggs and whispered to me that he was doing fine. On the day after that we were searched again, and then perhaps suspicions were lulled, for when I climbed on a bit of wall to survey the land my path to the wood lay clear and, as far as I could see, unwatched. Janet had whispered to me that Glenranald had asked her to bring him if possible some old clothes, the rougher the better, something that would serve as disguise. I was determined that in this at least I would do my part. The spring had come and I could spare my greatcoat. By the time I needed it again in the autumn this affair would have blown over and I could admit to having given it away.

It was made of sheepskin, that coat, fleece turned inwards, and I had had it six years. It had been made full big and it was only during the last winter that I had made any pretensions to filling it. It would cover him grandly. The only trouble was the difficulty of smuggling it out of the house. Mother was already so angry with my absences that for four days she had not spoken to me: but I was certain that if she saw me going out in my overcoat at the back-end of April the silence would break most unpleasantly. However, during the morning I was able to hide it in an out-building, and when in the afternoon I joined Janet by the bushes I was glad that I had something to offer, for her butter-basket was so full that she could hardly squeeze her fingers around the handle. The week's rest and food, makeshift as both had been had effected a great change in Glenranald. He sat up shakily as we approached him and smiled. His eyes went hungrily to the basket from which Janet hastily produced meat, bread, butter and cheese — food that made my own mouth water, so good it looked, so appetising compared to the thin broth and porridge that we ate at Braidlowrie. Janet must have caught some thread of what I was feeling, for she said, and there was apology in her voice,

"We've niver had sic' food, or sa much in Crosslochie befair. Ellie is doing grand."

"Ellie *is* doing grand," echoed Glenranald, biting hard upon a bread roll. "And who is Ellie?"

"Ma sister," said Janet, and her eyes, meeting mine across Glenranald, pleaded, "Please don't say anything about Ellie." Later I wondered many times at her meekness. After all why should she apologise for Ellie who had provided, unknowingly, all these things?

Glenranald licked his fingers and then said briskly,

"Well, I shall set out tonight. They're combing the woods now. Last night there were voices and lights on the path yonder. It only needed that there should have been a dog and somebody would have been a thousand pounds the better off. It's full time I flitted. I want to get to Nairn."

"But they'll be watching there. Too many have gone that way."

"Maybe. But two miles beyond Nairn there's a little cove, and there're fishing boats there that come in and go out again with other cargo than fish. That's been arranged."

"And after that?" I asked curiously.

"After that, lad, there's France, and behind that the whole of Europe where there's always work for a good sword, you know."

I thought — he'll never be able to come back. And I thought of Braidlowrie, and how I should be feeling if I had to turn my back on it, never to return. Poor as it was, wretched as life often seemed there, it was home. It held my roots. I looked round at the woods where a few pale leaves were powdering the branches: I remembered the primroses up on the banks of the burn: I thought of the harebells in August . . . all little things and things that seem to matter less, alas, as one grows older. I was heavy with the thought of his exile. And yet he, who was to be exiled, was laughing at the clothes that Janet was unfolding, one by one. They had all belonged to Fran Thatcher, he who was hanged for sheep-stealing, and were calculated to make any man laugh. Moving so stiffly and so weakly that the thought of his setting out on foot for Nairn was the thought of folly, he stripped off his own mud-spattered, blood-stiffened garments and put on the queer shapeless things that had been Janet's father's. Finally I took off my sheepskin coat and said awkwardly, "It'll keep you warm at night."

No one would then have recognised our gallant gentleman.

Janet slipped the silver flask into one pocket of the coat and a packet of food into the other.

"Now I can wait until dark," he said, and dropped down into the hole that I had dug with a gasp of relief. But he gathered his breath again and said in that same strong voice,

"Words are poor things at a time like this, but I must speak my thanks. God bless you for the services you have done me these last days. What is left of life for me is due to your care and courage. God send that you get back safely this one time more and aren't suspected. I thank you. God bless you both."

I had been stamping down the loose mould over the spot where we had buried the garments, the sword, the dagger that he had discarded. The pistol, still in its leather jacket, he had thrust inside his coat. I trod heavily once or twice more and then cast a handful of brush over the place before I looked at him and said,

"There was little enough we could do . . . and Janet has done most of that. But we were glad to do it, and proud. And we wish you very well on your journeying."

There were tears in Janet's eyes and her mouth was unsteady. I realised that she had grown fond of our foundling, as I had. He held the hand of his sound arm towards us and shook hands with us in turn. As he did so I had a strange moment of vision in which I saw, from the outside of myself as it were, the three of us standing there under the tree on the verge of parting, set for our different roads. Then Janet took up her basket and with last farewells and backward glances we pushed past the bushes that had shielded him so well and stood on the path.

By this time the tears were running down Janet's cheeks and, hating to leave her so, I said,

"Come up to the burn, Janet, and see the primroses. Then you can walk as far as Breckny with me and go home by the church."

I took her basket from her and she dried her eyes on the edge of the shawl which she had picked up and hung over her arm.

"He's not fit for footing it that far," she said at last, "and I fear for him. There'll be danger enow I'm thinking before he gets to Nairn."

"We can't do anything about that, Janet," I said.

"I knaw. And perhaps 'tis as well that he's leaving the night. Daft Wullie has twice met me and speired what it was I had in my poke."

My heart gave a lurch.

"What did you tell him, Janet?"

"Only "nathing for you the day, Wullie." Ye see I often give him bits and pieces, so he hangs roond me like a dog."

"Did he follow you?"

"Na. He laughed and kicked up his heels and rinned awa'. Only any day he might take it into his head to come after me, ye ken and then I couldna come. So it's as well I'll not have to go again."

"Damn Daft Wullie. It's a pity he can't run foul of a red-coat who'd put out his light for him."

"Oh, there's no harm in Wullie, Colin. It just made me uneasy to be asked whin I had all those things in my basket. That's all."

We stopped by the burn for a little while and gathered primroses into Janet's basket. Suddenly she said,

"Wheer's France?"

"Over the water to the east of us. It's a big country."

"I'd hate to be rinning to it and niver coming back, wouldna you, Colin?"

"My mother always speaks well of it," I said, "but yes, I'd hate to be leaving Scotland."

The mention of my mother made me think of the time. Almost in silence we hurried to Breckny Pool and our paths parted.

38

"Whin'll I see ye again?" Janet asked wistfully.

"I'll come down to Crosslochie," I said, and I meant it too. Whatever her mother was, whatever her sister, Janet was a gallant girl and had been more than a friend to the cause. We had something in common now. I gave her her basket and she ran off smiling.

Mother was waiting for me at the gap in the wall where there had once been a gate. The period of disapproving silence was over. She laid hold on my arm with a grip like iron.

"Where have you been?"

"To look at my snares."

She eyed my empty hands.

"You're lying, Colin. Where have you been?"

"On Boarswood. I came home by Breckny."

Still holding my arm she dragged me, with strength I never dreamed she possessed, into the kitchen and slammed the door.

"Now," she said, "we'll end this. For the last week you've driven me almost mad. Always out, where we haven't known, and coming back with excuses that wouldn't deceive a child. For the last time, where have you been?"

She stood close to me and glared at me with such fury in her eyes that big as I was I was frightened. Father said, as though to explain this display of feeling,

"The soldiers were here again this afternoon, Colin. They asked after you and took it very ill when we couldn't say where you were. They didn't believe us."

"Then you know what it's like to have *your* word doubted," I said rudely. "I have been on Boarswood. It isn't my fault that I've nothing to show for it."

"Then why, if that is true, couldn't you tell us where you were going? It's the secrecy, the mystery . . . I can stand no more of it. And I tell you, Colin Lowrie, sixteen years old you may be, but unless this mystery is explained to me I shall keep you in this kitchen by force if necessary, until this country is quiet again."

"All right, I'll tell you," I said. "I've been going to Boarswood to see and to walk with Janet Thatcher."

Mother took a step backwards from me as though I had announced that I had the plague. She was quite speechless for a moment though her lips moved oddly. Then she said, and all the old fury had gone from her face, leaving it set and white like stone,

"Is that true?"

Seeing that I had done myself harm rather than good, and had not ended the scene as I had hoped to do, I nodded wearily.

"Yes, I can see that it is."

Walking backwards with one hand stretched behind her she reached her chair and dropped into it like one stricken with sudden weakness. But there was no weakness about the voice in which she said,

"I suppose I heard aright. You did say Janet *Thatcher.*"

"I did, mother."

"Then the end has come. It isn't enough that we should be beggared, that you should work like a crofter's son and that I should slave like a swineherd's wife. No! Now you must so far forget yourself as to go walking with that girl."

"There's nothing wrong with Janet, mother."

"Nothing wrong! A gallowsbird for a father, a sloven for a mother, a whore for a sister. Nothing wrong with that is there? Indeed no. A fit mate for a Lowrie."

"I'm not talking of mating with her, mother. I walked with her on Boarswood. The two things are not the same."

"There's little difference when the girl is one of that brood."

"You're wronging Janet," I said. "What her father was, what her mother and sister are is no affair of hers."

I turned instinctively to my reasonable father for confirmation, but for almost the first time found none. He regarded me gravely.

"Why did you tell us this, Colin?"

"Because mother asked me."

"And you told her the truth?"

"Yes father."

"Then it must stop. You hear me? It must *stop*! Low as we may be brought, to the level of crofters and swineherds" — he looked at mother — "we have never yet consorted with the Thatchers of Crosslochie or their like. Never a one of that family has been truthful or honest or decent. It would well suit Jessie Thatcher, and her daughter too, I have no doubt, to bring things to a pass where that brassy-haired baggage would either be mistress of Braidlowrie or stand to wag her bastard in your name. No, don't interrupt, hear me out, Colin. I well believe that such thoughts are far from you, but you must believe me when I say that there is nothing else in the minds of such wenches. Your poverty won't protect you from them. In poverty they live and die, but poverty with a Lowrie would be honour to a Thatcher and I cannot have you duped by a bright eye and a handful of yellow hair."

For the second time that day I had a mental vision of myself, overgrown and gangling, with clumsy shoes, and large wrist-bones protruding overfar from the sleeves of my home-spun jacket. My face burned — not so much at his words as at the realisation that I had been fool enough, if such a trap were really laid, as almost to walk into it. I felt that my old desires for Janet were written large on my face. Well, I had drawn a pretty hornet's nest about my ears and there was only one thing to do about it — tell them how Janet had helped me and with what. I tried to begin with dignity.

"You may have no respect for Janet," I began, "and in that you wrong a fine girl, but you might have a little for me. There's been nothing between us except . . ."

"I'm glad to hear that," interrupted my father. "I know that young blood is hot and young heads feckless but the thought of you and that trollop . . ."

"Will you listen?" I bellowed, for I thought of that little trudging figure with the heavy basket, that wild dash back to Crosslochie for the brandy, the shawl, those little coarse gentle hands swabbing out wounds that sickened her with a piece of torn petticoat. "Will you listen while I tell you that trollop as you call her has in this last week saved . . ."

I broke off in a panic, for the top of the kitchen door was thrown open, and turning, expecting to see the gloating face of some spying English red-coat, I saw the trollop herself, wide-eyed, open-mouthed, leaning over the half-door waiting for the breath to speak.

I flung open the door and dragged her into the kitchen.

"They've not taken him?" I cried.

"It's not him, it's you. You must get away at once. Daft Wullie, he followed, he's told them everything. Half are after Glenranald by the road you told him to take and the rest are after you. Make haste."

"Get going," said my father, "any of our name in this is a dead man."

Mother gave a scream that rang through the kitchen and drew a metallic note from the cooking pots on the shelf. Then she fell back in her chair, stiff and white.

"What of you?" I said to Janet. "You'd better come with me."

"Oh, don't fash yerself," she said, dancing with impatience. "Ellie'll speak for me. Two redcoats — with her all afternoon — drunk. They'll swear I was there. Take the West road, it's clear. And take this . . ." She pushed into my hand a little canvas bag, heavy and warm, and with "God keep you, Colin," she was gone into the gloaming.

Father was half lifting himself in his chair, raising his body by the pressure of his hands on the arms. I said,

"Good-bye, father. Don't fret for me, nor let mother. I'll be all right. God have you both in his keeping and forgive me for bringing this on you. Good-bye."

I shut the kitchen door behind me, ran across the yard, vaulted the wall and fled like a hare towards the west. I had no food, no money and no greatcoat. I was in a worse case than Glenranald, except that I was whole, and there was no price upon my head — as yet, I thought as I ran.

Through four long nights I ran and walked, walked and ran through the darkness. The three intervening days I hid myself, one day in a strawstack, one day beneath a bridge, and one day in a tree in a wood. I was casting round in a semi-circle all the time, trusting to my instinct and my sense of direction to bring me at last to the sea.

I am blessed with a sense of direction that is quite as special a gift as second sight or water divining. I'd discovered it myself in childish play, long years ago, and I practised often for the fun of it. I would fix my eye upon a certain tree or chimney, or a white stone in the distance, close my eyes, twirl round until I was dizzy and then turn and stop with my face towards the given object. I never failed. I could feel the trees, the chimney or the stone pulling all the time at my mind. And now I could feel the sea. So though I had begun running inland and journeyed only in the darkness I had followed the pull of the sea, and sure enough in the dawn of the fourth day I came out on the coast.

In all that time I hadn't tasted food and though I had rested through the day-time I had run and walked as hard as I could at night, scrambling through brambles, plunging through burns, panting up hills, pushing

44

myself a path through desolate woods. Not a word had I spoken to a creature.

Now, on that morning when I pushed my way through prickly gorse bushes on to a common that ended in the grey sea, I was past thought, past caring what became of me so long as I could find food and a shelter of some kind. Myriads of muffled bells rang in my ears, my knees sagged as I walked, and the gnawing in my stomach had passed from the realm of discomfort into positive pain.

There was no question of laying up that day. Risky as it might be I must find some place where I could eat. But was I to beg? Even then the thought appalled me, partly by its humiliation, partly because I felt that to beg was a sure way to bring notice, and maybe suspicion upon myself. And then, only then, I remembered the bag that Janet had forced into my hand. Fool, I thought, there may have been a good oatcake in it all this time! I drew it out, and so famished was I that my first feeling upon opening it was of disappointment. It wasn't oatcake; it was money. Quite a lot of money, there were several broad silver pieces in the stream that poured into my hand.

I looked at it. Janet had no money of her own. Either she had taken it, or she had borrowed. In either case it was almost certainly Ellie's money — and how earned? Four days ago I should have loathed the touch of it in my palm. I should have imagined the traffic in lust that lay behind it; the stuffy little room where it had changed hands — passed from hand to hand how lately engaged? But that was over. A whole phase of my life

45

had closed. I realised that as I slipped the stream of coins back into the bag. The English soldiers had, all unwittingly, fed Glenranald and financed me. Confusion to the English. God save the King!

I trudged along beside the sea, not looking at it for to do so increased beyond bearing the dizziness that beset me in waves almost as regular as those of the water. By midday I could see chimneys and the smoke going up into the sky. It seemed to my light-headed fancy that the houses came towards me and grew up around me until at last I was in a street and the scent of people and smoke and fish attacked my outraged stomach so that it was all I could do to stand upright and preserve an ordinary appearance. I must do so, for there were several people walking or loitering about. Quite soon I realised however that no one took much notice of me, by which I gathered that this was a sizable place where a stranger was no novelty. An unknown face in Crosslochie would have arrested every walker and drawn people to their doors.

I walked along, sometimes putting out my hand to steady me as I turned a corner, until at last I saw an open door beneath a swinging sign and a bench set out under the eaves. An inn. I crossed the threshold and dropped down on to a settle that stood just inside the door. If the place had been full of red-coats, if Cumberland himself had stood by the barrels in the corner, I could not have gone another step. An untidy woman with a baby in the crook of her arm came and asked me what I would have. Brandy, I told her, and something to eat. She watched me as I drained the little

mug and set to work on the rye bread and fat bacon
that she brought me, and although I tried to eat slowly
and casually my avidity must have been obvious, for she
said, propping one shoulder against the wall for
comfort and looking down on me,

"Feed you cruel bad on ships, don't they?"

"Yes," I said. "Do you get many sailors here?"

"A few. But the *Evening Star* is nearer the harbour ye
see and maist goes there, to their sorrow."

"How to their sorrow?"

She did not answer immediately. She stood quite still
looking down at me and there was something in her
face that reminded me strongly of Janet. Not a
resemblance of face so much as of expression. But the
brandy on my empty stomach was working havoc with
my wits and I could not consider the matter seriously.
When presently she leaned down to me and said in an
urgent voice, "Don't go to the *Evening Star*, pretty
boy," I thought I was falling asleep where I sat.

"Eh?" I said. "What's that?"

"Don't go to the *Evening Star*. Lisbet stands by the
door and smiles and the lamp shines on her hair. She's
pretty, oh, she's bonnie, but what help is that when
you're out in the *Firebird* with Lovick? Tell me that."

Was the woman raving, or had delirium come upon
me?

"You're such a bonnie boy yersel'. I never could
resist the red hair."

She stretched out her free hand and fingered my
hair, all tangled as it was from lack of combing and

from a night spent in a stack. I shifted my head nervously and said,

"I wish you'd explain more. Who is Lovick and what is the *Firebird*?"

She settled herself on the seat beside me and a strong smell of dirty baby rose to my nose. Still looking at me with lustrous dreaming eyes that made a strange beauty in her grey face, she said, "If I tell you, will ye no go there?"

"Well," I said, with no inner intention of making a promise, "I'll not go, if you explain this mystery."

"Lovick is captain of the *Firebird* and he has so bad a name. Oh, the shameful things they tell of him! He's verra short of hands, so tonight Lisbet will stand at the door of the *Evening Star* and the lamp will shine on her hair. The bonnie young men will step within, but they willna step out. It's carried out they'll be and put aboard the *Firebird*. So don't go to the *Evening Star*, you with the hair like a flame."

Doubtless, I thought, the woman is mad, and she pays overmuch attention to other folks' hair and little to her own, but in her madness there has been a sign for me. I know now of a captain who is short of men.

By this time the brandy, the food, the joy of having a bench beneath me, and perhaps in some small degree the soothing, brooding presence of the slipshod woman, combined to make my desire for sleep overwhelming.

"Can I sleep here until evening?" I asked. "I can pay for a bed."

A sly avid look came into the woman's face.

"Of course," she said, and rose from the bench. Opening a door at the far end of the room she motioned me to follow. Along a dim, unevenly paved passage she led me, up some rickety stairs and into a little room that smelt of stale bodies and airlessness and damp. God knows that life at Braidlowrie had not bred me to any ideas of luxury or even refinement, but I had realised when I went into Janet's home and I realised it anew now that my mother through poverty and hardship had preserved a certain fastidiousness in her household arrangements. Our rooms were always aired and speckless, our coarse linen clean.

Still, I was in no state to be particular. I wanted merely to stretch myself flat, put down my head and lose in the blessed tide of sleep all consciousness of these last days and nights. The woman left me and I closed the door. Within a second I had kicked off my shoes, loosened my coat and was wallowing on the bed. Oh, the ease of that first moment of relaxation! I was being borne away on a wave of darkness, deep as the burn at Breckny Pool, soft as the massed heads of cowslips, when suddenly the door opened, and the slipshop woman without the baby and with her hair tumbling loose to her shoulders came in and stood by the bed. I had half-opened my eyes at the sound of the door but now, thinking that she had come in on some errand of her own, I closed them again and the pool-dark, cowslip-soft wave rose for a second time to engulf me. From its very heart it seemed that arms were encircling me, a soft damp mouth came down on my lips. With a sigh I was yielding myself into the dark

49

embrace when, afar off, as it were, a voice sounded, that same brooding voice, dreamy, melting with endearments. The woman's voice, and the arms and the mouth were hers too. The dark wave turned to one of scarlet flame. I scorched in it. The sudden hammering of my heart must have been audible to her. I lay paralysed, like a hare when someone treads near its form. And the paralysis solved the problem for me. My closed eyes, my still body, the deep breaths that I drew to combat the suffocation of my racing heart convinced her that I slept already. She shook me gently. I sighed. And then I slept indeed. I did not even hear her going or the closing of the door.

When I woke the room was inky black and I lay for a little while wondering whether it were evening, or early morning, or whether perhaps I had slept on into the second night. And now my body, fed and rested, woke to a sense of danger. Famine and fatigue had vanquished for a little the consciousness of the danger of pursuit and capture; but now I cursed my folly at having entered a house at all, at having spoken to anyone, at having risked alienating the woman. The thought of her confused me. I must go from this room, get down to the public part of the house quickly and then watch my chance to slip away. I groped in the darkness for my shoes and forced them over my sore swollen feet, buttoned my jacket and smoothed my hair with my fingers. I longed for a wash. The sharp splash of cold water on my face would have cleared my brain, but the room boasted neither jug nor basin.

50

That blessed sense of direction that had brought me to the sea served me again. I found the door without difficulty, and holding my hands on either side like a blind man I made my way down the stairs and along the passage. The room where I had broken my fast was dimly lighted but empty and at its end the door stood open on the street and liberty. I laid some money on the bottom of an upturned pipkin and stole out of the place.

For about five minutes I was exhilarated by my good fortune in not seeing the woman again. And behind that there was the deeper if less immediate satisfaction in having got this far in safety, in having reached the sea, found a port and learned the name of a captain who would be likely to take me on without too many questions. But my high spirits did not last. The loneliness and strangeness of these alien streets pressed upon me disquietingly. Before some of the shops and houses lamps were hung out or lanterns stood on the cobbles, and the feeble light that they made served only to emphasise the darkness of the shadows which were full of menace to me, used as I was to the familiar emptiness of the night around Braidlowrie.

It was raining too, a thin cold smizzle of rain that made the walls and cobbles shine where the light fell on them. Soon a film of damp discomfort lay upon my clothes, my face and hands. I longed for the comfort of my sheepskin coat, and that set me wondering how Glenranald had fared, and from that it wasn't far to thinking about myself. I began to pity the boy who had been driven from his home, who was walking in the rain the desolate streets of this unknown town, whose sole hope for the future lay in finding a man with a reputation so evil that none who had any choice would take service with him.

I thought, too, of my mother — of that white set *dead* look which had come upon her face — of that last cry as it shivered through the kitchen. What would her feelings be when she regained consciousness to find me gone? And would the English vent upon her and upon my helpless father their rage and disappointment at finding me flown? Ought I to have stayed and faced the consequences of my action?

Almost I turned back then. But I thought even the English could not find a case against two people so obviously innocent, who had been in their house on the very afternoon when Daft Wullie discovered the secret. There could be no excuse for using violence on them. And short of using violence there was nothing the English could do to hurt my parents, while me they might legitimately hang. And probably would unless I gained the *Firebird* and that quickly. The instinct of self-preservation reared its head once more, and I set out determinedly for the quay.

A little stone jetty ran down into the water and several boats were moored to iron rings in its side. It seemed lighter here away from the close-packed houses and I could see the boats bumping gently against the stones as the water moved them. Further out tiny unsteady lights, rising and falling, marked where the ships rode. One of them was the *Firebird*: but how should I know her, or knowing, reach her? I stepped out on to the jetty, and immediately withdrew my incautious foot. For at the end something had moved, and in moving disclosed to my eyes two lanterns, one dying out, the other just kindled. He who had moved had been stooping over them, lighting the new one.

"Well, Johnny boy," he said, and the voice was English, "I don't think Bonnie Charlie will be this way tonight, but you can't be sure of nothing in this blasted country except this — ing rain. So hold the lantern high in their faces when I asks them their business. And the rest of you just *try* to keep awake, will you?"

And now my horrified eyes could make out the dark shapes of three, four, six soldiers, all with muskets, standing on guard at the end of the jetty. One of them picked up the lantern and waved it in another's face.

"Aha, Chunky, I can recognise you. And that's more than your own dad would, I'll be bound."

Laughter and some scuffling followed this sally and another said, "You save your bastard talk till you see Charlie Stuart, and that on't be tonight. He wouldn't face the rain!"

So this was the vaunted English wit, was it? I shrank back into the shadow of a wall and ground my teeth. The glimmer of an idea came into my mind. What had the woman said about the bonnie young men who walked into the *Evening Star* and were carried out to wake on unpopular ships? Were they drunk or drugged? They couldn't be questioned either way. And there was nothing incriminating about my appearance, was there? Just an awkward, half-grown youth in rough peasants' clothes. Did I look like a possible hand? Should I be worth drugging? And was drugging painful? Or did they just club the "bonnie lads" on the head? Never mind what they did. Here was I at the edge of Scotland where I had forfeited my life, and the one way out was guarded and watched. I must do something.

Just along the front, to the left of the jetty, was the *Evening Star*. I identified it by the lights that shone and the noise that issued from it. I must go in and take my chance. I walked towards it and then stopped irresolutely. More soldiers might be there. Lisbet's hair under the lamp-light was hardly an attraction that they would miss. I turned and walked in the opposite direction. Then I stopped again. This was no good. This running to and fro through the night like a homeless dog was getting me nowhere. I must think of some plan and stick to it. And since I could think of no other I decided to go back to the tavern and try by peeping in at the window or the door, to ascertain whether it would be safe to enter. I retraced my steps.

A ragged curtain was stretched across the window, but it wasn't quite wide enough. Moreover the top sagged between the two nails by which it was fastened. The gaps at the sides afforded me no view of the interior so I rested my hands on the sill and stretched up, endeavouring to peer over the top. I had just got myself into position when a man, coming suddenly out of the doorway, lurched sideways, caught his foot in mine, reeled, clutched my middle and brought me down on top of him in the slimy mud of the roadway. He began to speak in a thick, furious voice, giving vent to words unknown to me, but which I guessed then, and was assured later, were curses of a particularly choice quality.

I struggled to my feet first and he pulled himself up by clawing my knees, my waist and shoulders in turn. Then he towered above me, a huge man, both tall and stout, with sea boots on his legs and a greatcoat with a tiered cape and a collar turned up about his ears. It was too dark to see more than things that could be identified by their shape. He did not let go his grip on my shoulder: he tightened it and shook me to and fro, like a dog shaking a rat, until my head wobbled and I was sure that my neck was dislocated.

"You scurvy-ridden, louse-eaten little bastard, what are you gaping in that window for? Waiting to trip somebody with your great feet I suppose. Can't you speak? Open your mouth and answer me, or by God I'll make you."

I voiced the only reason that came into my dazed head.

"I was looking for Captain Lovick."

"Oh, were you indeed. And what in hell do you want with him?"

"I heard that he wanted hands. And as I want to go to sea I wondered if he'd take me on."

"And why do you want to go to sea?"

"I don't quite know. I just want to. My father was a sailor. I suppose it's in my blood."

"And that's a lie if you never tell another. Sailors' sons know better than that. Only fools and folk with somebody after them want to go to sea. Which are you?"

"A fool, I suppose, by your reckoning."

He took a tinder-box from his pocket and, after several fruitless attempts resulting in more swearing, succeeded in kindling a light.

"There's a lantern down by the doorstep there, if you haven't put one of your hoofs on it. Hold it here and I'll tell you which you are."

I groped round, found the lantern and held it while he lighted it. I was acutely uneasy. I had, of course, no idea who the man might be, and although his manner and his words were rough there was something about his manner of speaking that made me think that here was no ordinary sea-faring man. He might almost be English — perhaps an officer disguised in order to spy about a place where refugees were likely, sooner or later, to appear. As the light strengthened and he lifted the lantern so that it shone on my face I looked at him, making a great effort to keep the terror and apprehension out of my face and succeeding in looking defensive and defiant I have no doubt.

He looked at me for a long moment, and I was not at all reassured to observe a change come over his face. An expression almost of pleasure lightened the lantern-lit face. And his voice had changed too when he said at last,

"No fool. So who's after you?"

"Nobody."

"All right then. Walk out to the jetty there, take the second boat from the end and row out to the *Firebird*. She's — let me see — yes, third from the left. There, did you see the light that dimmed just then? Smoky lantern. Lot of lousy lazy bastards on that old tub. Tell the soldiers on the jetty that you're going to join Captain Lovick's crew of choice rats and see what they say."

He took his hand from my shoulder. I had heard the mockery in his voice and now my sole aim was to get away from him. Never mind the *Firebird*, never mind anything except to be alone again. Better starve on the moor or in the woods than to be snared like this, a helpless cony in a trap.

"All right," I said with what boldness I could muster, "second boat, third light. Thank you."

Turning sharply I took two paces away from him and then ran for my life. But swift as I was that huge and not entirely sober man in the great sea boots was swifter. How he could run! I was scarcely past the opening to the jetty before he had his hand on my shoulder again and had jerked me to a standstill.

Desperate by this time I struggled madly, kicking him on the shins and aiming unskilful punches at his enormous chest. He put a stop to that with an effortless blow that sent my head snapping back and made my knees buckle under me. He kept me upright by the grip on my shoulder.

"You stupid little fool. I suppose you want the soldiers to come and ask what's going forward. Come on with me and keep your mouth shut."

He dragged me along the jetty and paused by the guard.

"You remember me, I think, or I wasted a hogshead of tolerable Madeira. This is a new fellow of mine who has taken more than is good for him to celebrate his signing on. Who's on your list tonight?"

The soldier reeled off a list of names. I heard the Prince's, said mockingly, and Glenranald's — so they hadn't taken him yet — and then, "Colin Lowrie, aged sixteen, big for his age, red-haired, speech almost English."

An uncontrollable tremor shook me, and the man who held my shoulder said loudly, "He's going to spew! Here, get out of the way." He gave me a push that sent me reeling past the sentry, and then he turned back and said easily,

"Well, if you catch one of them you'll be rolling in your own coach. I think my men are asleep. Jab 'em in the guts, will you?"

The soldier obligingly leaned over the side of the jetty — above the second boat I noted hurriedly, but before he could bring his musket into action two heads appeared.

"Oh, hullo," said the big man, "had a nice snooze? Well, wake up now. And you get in. Clumsy lubber. My God, you'll have to learn to be nimble!"

I stumbled into the boat; he followed me. The two men began to ply their oars and I was out of Scotland.

"And now, Colin Lowrie, aged sixteen, big for your age, red-haired, tell me why of all the chuckle-heads that call themselves captains do you want to go to sea with Lovick?"

Ever since we had dropped into the second boat I had guessed the big man's identity, and a profound depression had descended upon me. Rough-tongued and brutal I thought, a big ruthless bully, there'd be little comfort in life on his ship. And now he knew my secret. I ran my tongue over my stiff, dry lips and said,

"I heard that he was short of men."

"You didn't by any chance hear why?"

"No," I said discreetly.

To my astonishment the big man broke into a laugh of pure amusement and the two fellows at the oars tittered in company.

"You think I'm Lovick, don't you my bright boy. Well, that's where you're wrong. Fanshawe is my name and I'll tell you here and now that you're mortal lucky to have run into me. Lovick is in that stinking dive and he's striking a bargain with that crafty bitch and her father that several watery-bowelled fools are going to be sorry for before they're much older. The *Queen of Sheba* is a cranky, cross-grained hussy but she's heaven compared with that bloody *Firebird*. What do you say, lads?"

Both the men thus addressed said, "Aye, you're right there, sir," promptly and with feeling.

"And now that you know what you've missed, let me hear what it was that nearly landed you in Lovick's clutches."

"I told you. I want to go to sea. I've had a . . . I've had a quarrel with my father."

"Who gave a description of you to the English soldiers. Boy," he said disgustedly, "have sense! The idea that they might send you back to him nearly made you jump out of your hide, didn't it? Don't try to pass a cock-and-bull story like that off with me. Why, the name Colin Lowrie nearly made you wet your breeches, and if I hadn't been there to give you a shove even that mutton-headed Englishman would have seen it. Come on now, here's the *Sheba*, and if you want to come aboard you'd better spin your yarn quickly."

So, without mentioning Glenranald's name, or the name of any place, I told him the story, making it sound as though I had merely taken pity on a wounded man, and not admitting to any political knowledge or feeling whatsoever.

"Ummm," he said when I had finished, "Lowrie, eh? There was a Lowrie once, but a good way from here that was, who was up to the neck in that other shindy. Edman was his name. Maybe you never heard of him."

"I've heard of him."

"Well, your speech may be nearly English, but your caution is the real Scots kind. Anyhow, here we are."

The boat had come to rest under the loom of the *Sheba*, and one of the oarsmen stood up and grasped a dangling rope. Envying the big man's agility, I followed him over the side and stood for a moment watching the faint lights of the harbour while he gave orders to a man who came to meet him. Then he led me below.

To my Braidlowrie-bred eyes the cabin which we now entered seemed furnished with the utmost comfort and magnificence. The walls were panelled with walnut wood, polished to the surface of satin, and pleasing to the eye with its freckled grain. Benches of the same wood, upholstered in brown velvet, ran all round the walls, and in the centre a table, clamped to the floor, bore silver-covered dishes, flagons and a horn cup with a rim of silver. Two corners of the cabin were glassed in: one of the cupboards thus formed was full of books, the other held a number of trinkets, little figures of brown and green and yellow and black stone, each kept in place by thin splines of wood nailed to the shelves. There were two hanging lanterns in cases of bright metal, and at the opposite end from the door by which we had entered a curtain of brown velvet covered either another doorway or a bunk.

All this, of course, my eye took in in a moment of time, and, then, turning, I faced the man who had befriended me. I had noted his size before, but he looked larger here within the narrow limits of the cabin that he had done on the front or on the open sea. His face was in keeping, large but not fat, weatherbeaten and somewhat lined, and lit by eyes of a peculiarly brilliant greyish blue. His hair which he wore rather long and swept back from his forehead was brown and curly and in contrast to it his thick fair eyebrows looked curiously pale. His mouth was thin and crooked, with a twitch in the corner that broke readily into a grin. But these catalogued features do not describe the face that I studied under the yellow lantern light on that evening so long ago. For me, searching his face for clues to his character, since upon this so much of my future depended, the general expression of his face was more important and I imagined that I could read intelligence and impatience and a kind of scorn into it. Not, I decided, the face of a man to be lightly crossed, even though he was looking at me then with kindliness.

"Well?" he said, questioningly, and I shifted my gaze quickly and shuffled a little uneasily. "Are you hungry?"

"I think I shall never be not hungry again," I said truly.

"Wait till you get outside one of Africa's egg messes and then see how you feel," he said, smiling. Then he went to the door, and inserting his first and second fingers into the corners of his mouth he blew upon this natural whistle a blast so loud and piercing that it must have been heard all over the little ship and beyond.

In answer there came the rapid scuffing of bare feet upon bare board and in at the doorway there came a figure the like of which I had never seen before. It was like a cylindrical bale of coloured cloth perched upon two thin black legs that ended in enormous bare feet. Two equally thin black arms emerged from it and the top was surmounted by a thin black face with wildly rolling eyes, like a shy nag's, white teeth filed to points and a thatch of black nobbly curls just powdered with white.

I had never seen a black man before though I'd heard of one in a play that father once read to me. Othello was his name and I'd certainly never imagined him anything like this. I'd thought that a black man was as like a white one as a black pig or hen is like a white one.

"Africa," said Captain Fanshawe, "have you anything hot besides this?" He pointed to the food already on the table.

"Cook egg mess in one minute, Marsa."

"Very good. Cook plenty, and some bacon, too."

"New bacon come on ship 's'morning. Cook that or old bacon?"

"New, you jackass. And on your way up just tell Mr. Barker, that if we don't soon get under way he'll have nothing but old bacon from here to St. Crispin's."

"Yes, Marsa," said Africa, grinning wide, and vanished. But Mr. Barker, whoever he might be, had already saved himself from this fate, for as Africa's scuffing footsteps died in the distance the ship shuddered and ducked, her rocking motion became less gentle. We were under sail.

The egg mess, when it came, was a mass of beaten eggs, puffed up, brown and crisp on the outside, yellow and succulent within. I had never tasted an omelette before, and seldom since have I tasted any to compare with those that the black man made. And never, even of his, was one so good as the one I ate that evening. There were strips of crisp bacon alongside it; and when, having watched me clear my platter, Captain Fanshawe lifted a cover and offered me some of the smoked ham that he himself had been eating, I was forced, reluctantly, to refuse.

"It's very good of you," I began at last awkwardly, "to treat me like this. I'll learn all I can as fast as possible so that I can be useful, and not a dead loss."

He studied me oddly for a while and drank deeply before he replied.

"You can be useful, all right, my young friend, if you set about it the right way."

And once more, as when the woman had looked at me in the inn, I was reminded of Janet. All three of them, the young girl, the slipshod woman, the big man, had looked at me with speculation, with approval, and with a sort of hunger.

And now, I thought, you must be dreaming. Or the events of the last few days have fuddled your brain. Janet and the slattern at the tavern, yes, possibly, but this other is palpably fancy.

PART TWO

THE HOUSE OF BONDAGE

I learned a great deal during my first days aboard the *Sheba* but little that I had expected to. I mean that I gathered but scanty knowledge of seamanship. But of other matters I learned much. Indeed only a very stupid person could have lived in close proximity with Captain Fanshawe without greatly increasing both the range and depth of his knowledge. Politics, geography, trade, classical literature, history, that brilliant, inquisitive, sardonic mind took interest in them all. He could describe what he had seen, and what he had thought with equal ease. Yet he was not forthcoming about himself, and it was a mystery to me why a man of such learning, such sophistication, indeed such natural elegance of mind, should be content to remain the captain of so insignificant a vessel, doomed always to the company of common men, afloat and ashore. To be sure, his life in many respects was not unenviable. He lived with a degree of comfort: on board the *Sheba* his word was law. His trade with the West Indies — we were bound at the moment for St. Crispin's — was lucrative. He carried luxuries such as tea, silks, clothing and trinkets from London, and wool and hides from Scotland to the islands, and brought back sugar from Barbados, rum from Jamaica, tobacco from St. Crispin's.

He carried letters and executed commissions. Occasionally he took passengers. It was an interesting business, but it was such as men like Lovick and others whom I had heard described were capable of engaging in with equal success. He was built for finer things.

Coming now to the point of my story that I am, I must in common justice remark the man's fine qualities. In an age of brutality he was humane; men were happy on his ship, fed well and properly used. I heard curses aplenty on the *Sheba*, and if he were kept waiting, or annoyed in any other way, he would threaten his crew with unspeakable things, but no man was ever flogged to my knowledge. And he was not served the worse for that. He was the first and almost the only person whom I ever heard deploring the slave trade, and he almost invariably referred to Barbados as "that Hell of an island" because the conditions of the slaves were held to be worse there than anywhere else. Africa was apparently a piece of human salvage from some such Hell. And the blackamoor's devotion to the captain was a touching thing to see. He was, moreover, a grand navigator, for the *Sheba* was indeed the cranky cross-grained hussy that he called her and in a heavy sea her behaviour was incalculable in the extreme. But he coaxed her back and forth over the Atlantic as one might lead a cow to pasture. I've known him stand eighteen hours on end at the wheel during a hurricane and in the seventeenth crack a joke with Africa about the quality of the soup which the black man carried up to him. He was a grand man. And looking back, though I recall one angle of our acquaintance with discomfort,

I am yet ashamed of that discomfort, wondering whether perhaps the feeling does not brand me as a prig and a fool, still immature. I think not. For we live each by his own light, and coming sometimes ignorantly upon some new thing we have only our own delight or our own repugnance to guide us: and although I admit freely that Captain Fanshawe was right by his own light, I must admit, too, that I was right by mine.

We had seen the Canaries drop into the sea behind us, and so far every day had been a new delight to me, so long as I did not think about my parents or Braidlowrie. Or perhaps I should say "about my parents," for my feelings for Braidlowrie and I had come to terms. My exile, I had realised, was not the end of my dreams for the restoring of my house, it might well be the furthering of them. Out in the world I had more chance of making the money I needed than I had while feeding pigs and snaring conies in my home place. I was indeed so sure of my mission in life that I was ready to see in almost anything a stepping stone towards its attainment. It was a surety that I never lost completely. During the chances and mischances that befell me so plentifully in after years my confidence was often shaken, but never quite overthrown; hope slept for months and years on end, but that it did not die is proved by the fact that at the slightest fortune it leapt again, lively and devouring as ever. So I settled my mind about Braidlowrie, and I thought as little of my parents as possible, and I enjoyed being on a ship in the middle of the boundless sea, I enjoyed the sunshine, the good food, the novelty of the life. And I enjoyed the company of the captain. But this last was a tainted enjoyment.

From the first my position had been that of a guest rather than a refugee. I ate in the cabin with the captain, either before or after Mr. Barker — they were seldom, almost never, off duty together. I slept in a tiny cabin, no more than a cupboard adjoining the cabin where we ate. I had no duties. I wandered about, picking up scraps of knowledge from everyone, from Mr. Barker who taught me about the compass, to Africa, who with less success tried to teach me simple cookery in his cluttered smelly galley. And if the captain hadn't looked at me as Janet was wont to look, if he hadn't sometimes laid lingering fingers upon my hair, my cheek or my shoulder I should have been perfectly happy. But he did so look, he did so tentatively caress me, and even my ignorance was subtly alarmed.

One evening when from the deck or through the portholes one could see the colours of the sunset melting and spreading upon the oily sea, when afar off the little waves curled lazily, breaking without foam, the captain, at the end of the meal that we had been sharing, whistled for Africa, who came running. Taking a key from a chain that he carried in his pocket he handed it to the Negro.

"Bring us a bottle of the brandy that Mr. Everett gave me that time we fished him out with the boat-hook. You remember."

"Oh yes, Marsa, I 'member. That was funny sight, him splashin' 'bout, callin' Gawd to help an' you tryin' to hook him like he was a big fish." Africa's face split into a grin as he recalled the diverting scene. To my surprise the captain did not smile in reply, he spoke quite curtly to Africa, "All right. Don't stand there talking. Fetch the brandy quickly and bring the key back."

Africa's face resumed its habitual melancholy expression.

"Run all time, Marsa," he said as he hurried through the doorway.

He came back very quickly, the key dangling from one thin crooked little finger, both hands clasped almost reverently about a large, lop-sided bottle of greenish glass. He set it on the table, and stooping to the locker beneath the bench took out and placed beside it two beakers blown from glass so fine that they looked like the cups of some exotic flower. Africa did not speak, the sharp note in the captain's voice had utterly crushed him. With a backward glance like that of a chidden cur he stole out, shutting the door softly behind him. Captain Fanshawe carefully replaced the key on the chain and the chain in his pocket and then poured the brandy into the flowerlike glasses. He held one towards me almost ceremoniously.

"Everett's father was one of the best judges of liquor of his day. He left this to his son, who was an old man when he gave it to me. I should like to think that it was some of the first brandy ever bottled. You know they didn't bottle things until they discovered how to use cork, sometime in the last century. This is a tipple that a good many crowned heads would be glad to have under their noses."

I said, diffidently and with truth, "It's rather a waste to give it to me, you know. I've only tasted brandy once before; I didn't enjoy it much."

"Taste that and see what you think. As for waste, I'm the best judge of that, young Lowrie. Or shall be." He said the last three words slowly and so softly that I barely caught them.

I lifted my glass and drank. Truly this brandy was as different from the stuff I had drunk from the mug under the brooding eye of the woman at the tavern as Africa's ox-tail soup was from mother's onion stew. It was silk on the tongue, fire in the throat and spring in the veins. Before I had finished half my portion I was aware of living, just living as I had never been before. Later on I came to know this intense concentration of consciousness in the moment as the beginning, the only worthwhile moment, of the process of intoxication. If one could only hold it! If there was only some liquor made that could raise one to that state and then stop, so that subsequent quaffing did not bring on lack of awareness, drunkenness, oblivion and reaction. Of course I did not think like that then, I was only aware that the sunset colours of the sea were trapped within the golden-brown wall of the cabin; that everything had a glow; that I, Colin Lowrie, was alive, facing across the table the man who was my friend; that life and hope were quick and strong within me, and that in the glass that stood before me on the cluttered table was something rare and fine which I was lucky ever to have tasted. I drank again, liquid sunshine, with the sting in it that this strange new sunshine had: silk and fire and the thrill of spring. There was flush on my cheek before the captain said suddenly,

"Do you know ought of women, Colin?"

I felt the flush darken into heat.

"I've barely talked to more than three," I said. "My mother, and a girl called Janet who helped me grandly with the matter I told you of, and . . . and there was a woman in the tavern, she told me of Lovick."

He drank deeply, drained his glass, refilled it and drank again before he said,

"And do you remember her simply because she gave you information?"

I managed to say steadily, "No. I suppose I thought of her when you asked me that because after she had shown me the bed she came and lay beside me, with her hair down and her blouse undone."

"And did you take her? But of course you did."

"No. I was almost asleep. I did go to sleep and when I woke she was gone."

"And this Janet?"

"Oh, Janet was a friend of mind. Once there was a time when I — when I —" (the biblical phrase popped into my mind suddenly from nowhere) "when I lusted after her, I suppose. But something happened to change that."

I thought, as I listened to my own voice, that I must be drunk to be talking so.

"And that's all you know of the pleasures of the flesh, is it? So much the better."

He had been drinking steadily during this conversation, and now there was that about his speech and look that convinced me that he, too, was intoxicated. For one brief moment that drew me to him. It was fine to be here, man to man, drunk on sunshine in the short afterglow of the sunset. But he leaned towards me and said in a strange voice — as though his words came only after an inward struggle,

"The Easterns have a motto, Colin. 'A woman for use and a boy for pleasure.' I agree with them. That is why I held the lantern in your face that night on the quay; and that is why I brought you here."

Inherited knowledge: instinct: pure speculation. Which was it that made the whole thing clear to me, even as I muttered something about not understanding? Suddenly the scene which so short time ago had stood etched with the sharpest pencil of reality, became unreal, fantastic, terrible. There was the captain's face distorted by a sly avidity and a horrible kind of tenderness. There was the fading light in the cabin as though the walls were giving up the light that they had stored. There was the lop-sided bottle and the flowerlike glasses. And then the scene, all set for fantasy, became a background for fantasy so extreme that even my protests smacked more of incredulity than of conviction. Sickness of a kind I had never dreamed of came upon me, even my skin was sick. There was no dignity about either of us. He was strong, but I think that he was not exerting his full strength, and I was tough enough to hold my own for the moment that his madness lasted, though to deal unkindly with him who was always so kind to me increased my nausea tenfold. Quite suddenly he stepped backward from me, and drawing out his handkerchief mopped at his face.

"Dans la nature sont tous les gouts," he said quietly, "and you, of course, have a right to yours. But I'd rather not see you more than necessary in future."

I tried to say, "I'm sorry," but no words came, only a gulp. I hurried out of the cabin, feeling obscurely in the wrong.

After that, except for passing glimpses I saw no more of him. I fed with the men and spent my time with them when I was not brooding in my cabin. But I heard him often, rending the air with curses, threatening all and sundry with horrible fates. The men acknowledged among themselves that the captain was in a more lastingly surly temper than usual, but they seemed not to connect my sudden ejection from the main cabin with the cause of this ill-temper. Or if they did gave no sign of it, any more than they had shown any surprise or curiosity at my sudden arrival on board.

I wondered then, and have done since, whether they were aware of his peculiarity and accepted it as a corollary to his other unusual qualities; and whether they had seen a similar little drama enacted upon the *Sheba* before. It was fortunate for me that nothing was said or hinted, for my mind was in such a state of chaos, and my nerves so frayed that I should have attacked anyone who annoyed me — and naturally should have had the worst of it.

But there was even worse to bear. One after another, almost as though deliberately, the men would come out with some story that threw into prominence some good point of the captain's character. Mr. Barker, for example, chose just this time to interrupt a lesson in navigation in order to tell me how, and from what, Africa had been saved.

"We was watering down by a creek that runs through a swamp down in Viginny," he began in his slow ponderous voice. "And the captain had come ashore, just for to stretch his legs. The casks was filled and we was just embarking when out of the thicket bursts Africa — only of course we didn't know his name at that time — with two great dogs and six men at his heels. He was just at his last gasp, mark you, and the foremost dog was just making a spring for him when the captain whips out his pistol and shoots it through the heart. It drops and Africa with it. T'other comes on. Captain is ashore again by this time singing out to us: 'Ready with them oars, lads,' and aiming at t'other dog as he runs with his second pistol he shoots that too and slings Africa over his shoulder. The head man of the six, him with the musket, aims and fires and hits the captain in the thigh. But he runs — and I don't know no man what can run better — and reaches the boat two jumps ahead of 'em and clambers in, Africa and all. 'Now swim for him, ye so-and-so devils,' he shouts, and taking my pistol empties it into the one with the musket what is just ready to shoot again. Gets him fair and square too. That was how we got Africa, and a pretty sight he was too. Lashed to ribbons his back was. He'll tell you, and I've never known him caught in a lie, though with a nigger naturally you can't be too sure,

76

that it was all because something was missing and they were sure he'd got it. So they strung him up and give him a dozen and said, 'Where is it?' Not knowing he can't say, so they give him another dozen and so on. Eh, 'twere a grand rescue and a wonderful run. And the wound in his leg would've felled a lesser man."

There were other less spectacular stories too. There was the man who had been smitten down with Yellow Jack and looked like dying because none of his mates dared go near him. A funny little man with queer speech told me that tale. "Captain said, 'Lily-gutted sods you, doon't you know that St. Peter has list like pay-sheet and until your noomber's called naught can kill you?' Must have believed in tale too, for he went in to fellow and tended him till fever came up in black vomit. Aye, and think, when t'voyage were doon, Alfred Scates as were still weak as kitten and had nut tooched tackle, nay nor coiled rope all through journey, he did have pay same as t'oothers. 'Tis true as God's aboov. Ask Alfred Scates else." The sing-song voice was reverent, and from what I had heard about ships and the men who commanded them I did not judge the reverence ill-placed. Alfred Scates would have gone overboard from any other ship. As for the pay, God's eyeballs! as Fanshawe himself was fond of saying.

These stories played havoc with my self-esteem and added incalculably to my misery and bewilderment. I began to see myself hopelessly in the wrong. And I was like a man steering without chart or compass on a night when there is no star to guide.

I missed the captain's company, too; missed terribly the long, desultory conversations, almost monologues on his side; missed the kindliness, the strange oaths and the stories. At night, when but for the man at the helm the ship would seem deserted, I used to hang over the side and watch the wheeling stars and listen to the wind singing softly or shrilly through the shrouds, and I wondered. Once or twice I was on the verge of . . . but what matter? I did nothing. Only I mooned about, sadly regarding the remains of the idol of my boyish worship, having it built up almost daily before my eyes by some word or story, and then having it smitten down again by memory's relentless hand.

But this state of affairs did not last long. A certain "end-of-voyage," feeling grew in the very air. The sailors began to talk of the pleasures of St. Crispin's, the chickens and the fresh fruit they would eat, the wine they would drink and the women they would find. (There wasn't much that I didn't know, in theory, about women, by this time.) I was beginning to wonder what the immediate future held for me, and had resolved in my mind to offer Captain Fanshawe my passage money, for pride's sake, and to disembark at St. Crispin's. I should have preferred a bigger island, but I was eager to end this uncomfortable phase.

I've thought since, that if what happened was not enough to cure a man of fore-planning, nothing ever would be.

One morning, early, while the air was still cool and so heady that I went about gulping it in in order to get enough of it before the sun climbed high enough to drain out all the refreshment from it, the look-out sang out that there was a ship ahead of us, lying low in the water and, he thought, showing signals of distress. The captain hurried up with his glass and, after corroborating the look-out's report, altered the *Sheba*'s course so that instead of passing just to the north of the other vessel we gradually drew up alongside. It looked a sorry sight, so low in the water that it was almost awash: and all the canvas being furled, it had a skeleton look as well. There were a number of men aboard, huddled together on the side that stood slightly higher out of the water, and they waved repeatedly. Faint calls came over the water as we drew nearer.

"They've no boats, sir," said Barker.

"So I see," returned the captain testily. "Stand off now, she's ready to go under at any moment. Lower our boats and bring the men off."

The *Sheba*'s two boats were lowered and manned, and we watched them speeding across the gap of water which might not be lessened with safety because of the disturbance that the sinking of the ship — she was bigger than the *Sheba* — would cause.

The first boatload returned. The foremost man to step on to the *Sheba* was a small, swarthy fellow, decently dressed in a suit of dark clothing and a loose greatcoat. He had a small pointed beard, a scar across his chin and gold rings in his ears. He hurried up to Captain Fanshawe and stretched out both his hands.

"Portuguee," he said, withdrawing one hand to point at his own chest, and then, with a tap on Fanshawe's arm, "English. Good friend."

"Came along just right for you, anyway. What happened to you? Where are your boats?"

He rapped out the questions sharply and eyed the Portuguee and the rest of the boatload with no great favour. The little man shook his head and smiled.

"No English much. Enrico tell." He looked round, but Enrico was apparently not among the strange assembly of figures bunched together on the *Sheba*'s deck and Captain Fanshawe had to wait for the explanation until the first boat had made a second journey and the wreck was cleared. Enrico was a giant. He made that huge man, our captain, look ordinary. The Portuguee captain had, I thought, taken an exaggeratedly good view of Enrico's linguistic abilities. He made wonderful grimaces and threw his hands about and stamped a lot, but though I had crept close and listened carefully I could make out only a few disjointed words: rogues, boats stolen, powder and shot gone.

The little captain had stepped back a little as though to allow Enrico's hands full play, and then suddenly, while Fanshawe stood looking into Enrico's enormous face, trying to make head or tail of this jabber about rogues and boats and powder, the Portuguee threw back his coat, whipped a knife from his belt and with a roar like a charging bull's dashed forward. Simultaneously every one of the men whom we had rescued drew a weapon and made a rush for the nearest of the *Sheba*'s crew.

In less than a moment from that first cry hell was loose upon the deck that had just been swabbed clean.

There wasn't an armed man among us. The captain who had been at breakfast was still in his shirt sleeves, and had only his heavy brass telescope in his hand. The two men who had been swabbing deck raised their iron bound buckets, the rest snatched up any weapon that lay to hand, but it was hopeless from the start. I saw Enrico raise his broad curved knife and plunge it towards Fanshawe's chest. Actuated by some primeval passion that felt like exultation I let out a yell and dived for Enrico's knees and got them in a grip that I had seen boys use when practising throwing one another on the green at Crosslochie. Fanshawe's blood spattered down on the back of my neck as Enrico's hand withdrew the knife. I saw the curved blade again, scarlet now, aimed this time at my heart. I ducked and it took me between shoulder and collar bone. I felt it go in and tear out again, saw the blood stream down my shirt: but it wasn't painful then, it was maddening. I threw myself bodily at him again, like a cat springing at the trunk of a tree — and about as effectual. I might have unbalanced a smaller man, though even that would only have delayed the inevitable end. Enrico simply staggered back a step, seized my throat in his hands and dashed me to the deck. As I fell I could see, upside down as it were, the captain raise his telescope and bring it down on Enrico's ear, and Africa fling himself into the fray armed with the shallow iron pan in which he made his egg messes. Then my head hit the deck, and for me the fray was over.

I struggled up out of darkness into darkness and was immediately conscious of horrible pain. The wound in my shoulder was like hot coal, my throat was so sore that it was agony to swallow and my head was one enormous bruise. Still, I was alive. Of how many more of us could that be said? I lifted my head an inch or two and swallowed hard. Immediately I heard Africa's voice.

"Is you wakin' Marsa Colin?"

"Hullo, you're there, are you, Africa? I've had a crack on the head and missed everything. Have you been awake all the time? What happened? Where are we? Are any of the others here? What about the Captain?"

Africa burst into loud sobbing. "They done killed marsa captain, they done kill ever'body 'cept me an' you an' Mis' Barker. An' do you know what fo' they didn' kill us? Oh — oh — oh — you know, don't you, Marsa Colin? They's sell us, that what they's do. Oh Lawd God, take mercy 'pon this poor black man. Got a hole in his leg Lawd, and his blood run fast, make it run faster Lawd. Save Africa from going back into bondage, please Lawd God, please."

His words, and the really pitiable earnestness of his prayer, sent such a chill of horror through me that it was a moment or two before I could say,

"What makes you think so, Africa?"

"I knows so. I knows that Portuguee captain. He sell things he steal. Steal ever'thing. Oh, why didn't the Lawd let me see him first. Then I cry 'Pirate' and marsa captain needn' die." He choked and then demanded in a loud wild voice,

"Oh Lawd, why wasn't that my time for empty the slop water?"

The Lord vouchsafed no answer to this reasonable question, and Africa went on sobbing in the dark.

For the first few moments my thoughts were all upon my personal loss in this affair, my wounds and my uncertain future. But coming up through them, like a fish from the depths of a dark pool, rose the thought of Captain Fanshawe. Dead. Never again to laugh, or joke or swear, never again to wrestle with the kicking wheel. And we had not spoken a friendly word since that night just out from the Canaries. The thought wriggled in my mind like a red-hot wire.

"Who killed the captain, Africa?" I asked at last.

"That big damn elephant man same as set on you. When he chuck you the captain split his head with that glass an' the big man knife him. Oh dear, oh, they's sure sell me. I done mighty damage with that pot I makes the egg mess in." A little note of pride crept into Africa's tearful voice. I hadn't even that much consolation.

"Mr. Barker hasn't come round. Is he much hurt?"

"He sure is mighty bad," said Africa, who despite his efforts with the cooking pot seemed not to have missed many details. "He almost suttinly die. If not he not wuth much at St. Crispin's."

"For that matter I've got a nasty wound myself, and I heard you mention your leg. Perhaps they couldn't sell us even if they wanted do."

"Ours is on'y flash bites. You'll be wuth fifty pounds, they say. Old man like me not wuth much anyway. Some free nigger'ull buy me, and that sure is the wust of all."

Africa's mind, like a tethered goat, went round in a circle. And his fear was infectious. He had been a slave. And though outwardly there was a difference between us, since he was black and I white, I had heard enough about white men being sold to the islands not to draw any great hope from that difference. Plenty of white men had gone that road after the '15, and plenty more, no doubt, were on their way.

For one odd, uncomfortable moment I wondered whether, after all, I had come all this way voluntarily only to fulfil the fate that would have been mine had I stayed in the kitchen at Braidlowrie and awaited the coming of the soldiers. Perhaps the King of England *had* been chosen and anointed by God, and perhaps punishment *did* await those who would not accept him. Perhaps that was why the rebellions had failed, why my father had lost the use of his legs, why I lay here now.

But that was nonsense, because to bring me to this pass it had been necessary for a Portuguese pirate to lose his ship, and for many — alas how many — good men to lose their lives. The hand of God could not be seen in that, surely. That was attributing the Almighty with too much political interest and I put the thought away. I was here because that Portuguee was a damn crafty little sod, and because the sight of men on a sinking vessel had made Captain Fanshawe's humanity overcome his caution. That was all.

And being here I must plan some way to escape before the fate that Africa regarded as inevitable could come upon me. I would offer the Portuguee the money that Janet had given me. It wasn't much, not nearly the fifty pounds that they had priced me at, but it would be obtained without difficulty, and it was sure.

In darkness and inactivity time moves slowly. Africa wept again and then slept. There was no sound from Mr. Barker. Thirst added itself to my torments and became so extreme that at last I felt that I could have borne all my afflictions if only I could have a cup of water, greenish and brackish and full of queer floating things as it had by this time become.

Presently Africa woke again and spoke to me. We talked a little, not much, for we were too sunk in misery to have much to say. Suddenly he said, "Mis' Barker dead too."

"How do you know?"

"I heered his ghost go past me. Ain't no good layin' here with a corpsie. Deading powerful catchin'."

I did not point out to him that a very short time before he had been praying for death.

Presently there was a sound of creaking hinges, an oblong of light appeared and the darkness in the hold changed to grey. A man's legs began to come down the ladder, his body and head came into view. He stepped lightly off the last rung but one and came and looked down on us. Over Mr. Barker's body which lay in the furthest corner he stopped, peered closely and then turned it over with his foot.

"Dead," he said. Then to us, "You can come up. And don't try any nonsense." His English, though clipped and careful, was perfectly good. Enrico's hand-signs and stuttered words had been part of a scheme to gain time.

I pulled myself to my feet. My head reeled, my heart shook my very eyeballs, but I caught the side of the ladder and stood swaying until the first bad moment had passed. Then the man hustled us up the ladder and at last we stood blinking on the deck in the bright sunshine of mid-afternoon. We had lain in the darkness for more than twenty-four hours.

A half-hearted attempt to clear the deck had been made, but the blood-stains still showed clearly. Drawn by a morbid fascination I looked towards the spot where the captain had stood at the moment when I fell. That was his blood. Over the side, near where he had fallen, his body had been thrown. And so many others. The men with whom I had eaten, men who had shown me things, men to whom I had talked. Men who were going to have so fine a time among the flesh pots at St. Crispin's, fleshpots themselves now for the hungry fish. And the sea, the sun, the sky, even the ship, unchanged.

The Portuguese captain stood by the man at the wheel. The man who had fetched us led us towards him. Far way, on the line where the sky met the sea, lay a smudge of shadow. Hurriedly, before the captain turned, I asked, "Is that St. Crispin's?" The man nodded. I felt in the inner pocket where my money lay. Time was short, shorter than I had guessed. God send that I might strike my bargain. And Africa, what of him? I looked at his face, drained grey with terror, at his horny bare feet gripping the deck and hardly able to support his trembling shanks. Then something hardened in me. He was old, I was young. Five years ought to see him out of the bondage of the flesh. By biblical reckoning I had over fifty years to go.

The captain turned and came towards us. His pointed black moustaches curled up towards his eyes like a cat's, his small black eyes were bright. He had the air of a man well pleased with himself. And he had every reason for self-congratulation. By a simple and not very risky trick he had gained not only a new ship but a marketable cargo. Hides and wool and manufactured goods, no doubt he had by this time checked them all: and no doubt Africa and Mr. Barker and I figured at the end of the long list.

He looked at us and asked a question in a language that I did not understand. The man who had fetched us gave him an answer and then together they looked at us. Over Africa, when they had poked and probed and peered into his mouth, they shook their heads. They regarded the wound in my shoulder, and then the captain snapped his fingers, dismissing it.

"We're very thirsty," I said. My tongue rubbed against the sides of my mouth like leather rubbing against wood. The man translated my complaint and then fetched two small measures of the green water I had been dreaming of. The pair gabbled on in their own tongue. When my mouth was moistened I asked, "What are you going to do with us?" I hesitated to say, "Are you going to sell us?" because I had just a hope that Africa had fabricated that story out of his own foremost dread, and in that case, if they hadn't thought of it I didn't want to suggest it to them.

Instead I said, "I have a suggestion to make to the captain. Will you translate for me?"

Speaking slowly and allowing the man whom the captain called Carl, to translate each sentence, I said,

"I am not a servant or a sailor. I am a passenger on this ship. I am on my way to St. Crispin's. I will pay you to put me off there."

"He would like to see your money," said Carl.

With the innocence of the utterly inexperienced, with the guilelessness of the completely honest I put my hand into my inner pocket and brought out Janet's bag. Carl promptly snatched it and handed it to the captain who emptied it into his palm, studied the coins carefully, put them into his pocket and tossed the bag overboard.

"Enough, no!" he said emphatically, "but will do. St. Crispin's, yes." Carl elaborated, "He says it isn't enough but he'll take it and put you off at St. Crispin's."

Africa, who had been listening and watching, now flung himself down on his knees and clutched me around the waist with his long scraggy arms.

"Take me too, Marsa Colin. Buy me off too. 'Fore the Lawd I's serve you for the rest of my days. Don't let this poor nigger be put back into bondage agin. Please Marsa Colin, I begs you."

His anguish was terrible to see. I said,

"I'm really sorry, Africa, but you heard what he said, there isn't really enough for me. If I had any more I'd do it, honestly I would . . ."

It was impossible to watch him and remain unmoved. Great tears poured down his face, he beat his woolly head on the deck and trembled as though with ague in every limb.

"Listen," I said, "I've just thought of something. Will you translate again, please," I said to Carl.

"This old nigger isn't worth very much, you can see that for yourselves, but he's very much afraid that you might sell him at St. Crispin's. He is old, and not very strong, but he is the best cook I've ever known. He was Captain Fanshawe's cook, and though he said he'd had several he said not one had been as good as he is. Couldn't you keep him and let him cook for you? Will you just try him? Let him make you an egg mess. Have you ever had an egg mess? Do, please, just try him."

In my eagerness I had gone close to the captain so that I was pouring out my plea straight into his face. He put out a slim dark hand and pushed me back a little. He listened to Carl's translation of the last sentence and spoke and shrugged.

"The captain says," said Carl, "that our cook is not as good as could be wished. This nigger may make an egg mess for us to try."

Africa had stopped his howling and stood blinking and sniffing while these speeches were exchanged. Then a curious light broke out on his face. He darted across the deck, stooped and fumbled round and stood up again with a look of triumph on his face and the iron pan in his hand. He made straight for the galley, and as no one showed any further interest in me I followed him.

The galley which even in Africa's day had been no model of neatness, was now indescribably cluttered. The cook had not washed anything since the ship had been taken. The fire was out and I helped Africa to relight it and to deal with the dishes. All the time he was fuming with impatience and grumbling to himself.

"All the better," I told him. "The longer we are the hungrier they'll be and the hungrier they are the better they'll like it."

"Ain't never seen me make egg mess, has you?" he asked at last.

"No, I never got so far." For though Africa had always welcomed me into the galley and had shown me simple things he had been very secretive about what he considered his special dishes.

"Now," I said, when the fire was burning and there was space to work in, "this is your chance. Get to work and make the best egg mess you've ever made."

"I can't do that, Marsa Colin," he said, suddenly glum.

"Why on earth not?"

"'Cause these eggs isn' fresh. Fresh eggs blow up better. These eggs is old and flat."

"Never mind. You do the best you can and I'll take it in and explain that you can do even better with fresh eggs. Come on now, get to work."

He clamped his pale tongue firmly between his pointed teeth and frowned fiercely. I watched him crack the eggs, beat them, and stand the bowl aside. The frying pan, which had escaped the washing, he rubbed round with a cloth dirtier than the pan itself could possibly have been. He put a piece of fat into it and set it on the stove. Waiting for it to heat he beat the eggs again. When the fat was smoking he lifted the pan, and deliberately gathering a mouthful of spittle — and where that came from God alone knew, my mouth was still dry — he spat into the middle of the pan. I thought of all the egg messes I had eaten and my stomach heaved sickly.

"Not hot enough," he said, and set the pan back and went on beating. After a moment or two he repeated the performance, was satisfied with the resulting crackle and sputter, poured in the yellow stream and let it settle. Then he seized the knife and with a dexterous twist of the wrist turned the mass upon itself, and there was the egg mess, just as it came to table, crisp and brown without, yellow and succulent within.

When it was ready I went into the cabin. I hadn't been inside it since that fatal evening and as I stepped into it a welter of feeling came upon me. Mourning, regret and hatred of the little swine who now possessed it, and mourning again.

Within thirty hours the small beautifully tended cabin had become filthy. The table was littered with bottles, tobacco ash and the remains of meals. The little figures in the cupboard had been disturbed — probably in an attempt to assess their value. There were great gobs of spittle on the polished floor. Distaste, and a weariness that was the result of emotion and weakness, almost floored me as I took in the scene. The captain, Carl and another man were lolling upon the benches with glasses in their hands.

"Africa has made an egg mess and it is ready," I said. And then, playing desperately for Africa's sake, I eyed the cluttered table with disgust.

"I will call him to set the board properly. It is only fitting that the captain should be properly served." Would that appeal to his vanity? Yes. When Carl translated the sentence the little man looked at me with interest and straightened his back. Properly served, God! Wouldn't I like to properly serve him!

"Go and set the cabin table, properly, like you used to." Trembling and apprehensive Africa obeyed me. Once inside the cabin, however, and ignored by the occupants, he set to work swiftly and unobtrusively. I handed him the warmed plates and the egg mess and within five minutes the three ruffians were seated at the neatly appointed table, and the captain was dealing out portions of the egg mess, which hadn't, I reflected sadly, improved by this delay.

Despite the throbbing of my head, despite the nausea I had felt when Africa spat into the pan appetite had wakened in me. As soon as we had found ourselves on deck again I said to Africa, "I'm hungry, aren't you?"

"Shan't never be hungry no more till I knows," said Africa dolefully.

"Well, we can hope," I said. And I found myself indeed truly hoping that the little Portuguee would take kindly to Africa's cooking. Life on a pirate ship was not what one would choose, perhaps, and he might find that his new master was less kindly than the old, but it would be preferable to organised slavery in the islands.

I thought so, at least, and Africa seemed to agree with me.

"Shall go over the side, Marsa Colin. That's what this old nigger'ull be driv to do."

"Well, wait," I said again, "and hope for the best. We'll soon know. Was there anything else to eat in that galley?"

"Make egg mess in one minute, Marsa Colin," he said so eagerly that I felt ungrateful for saying,

"No thank you, Africa. I don't feel like egg mess. I'd like some bread and cheese."

He scuffled away and returned with two great hunks of the bread that he had baked on the day before the disaster. The flour had been near the bottom of the barrel and there were several sharp bits and alien bodies on the loaf, but we were hungry and munched at it steadily. It was dark when we finished.

I remember sitting there in the gloom and thinking how haphazard our captors were. Nobody thought to watch us, or feed us. If we had taken it into our heads to jump overboard there would have been no one to prevent us. Not that anyone but a determined suicide would have jumped overboard in that shark-infested sea. In the pirates' eyes of course we were unimportant — an old nigger and a youth — I realised that. But it rankled that the captain had taken my money and not offered me any supper. I ought to have been invited, though God forbid I should, to have shared Africa's egg mess in the cabin.

The thought had hardly gone through my head when Carl appeared, looking about for us. When he saw us he ended Africa's suspense at once by saying in his careful English,

"The captain has decided to keep the black man as cook. He should attend to the table now. The captain also wishes to see you below."

Africa grabbed my hands into his two big bony ones. "Gawd bless you, Marsa Colin. Gawd bless you. Africa pray fo' you day and night long's he got breff in's body." I wondered idly later on what God Africa prayed to, or whether the nightly prayers were so disturbing as to merit the answer they received.

"You see," I said, disengaging my hands, "it's going to be all right and the better you please the captain the better you will fare. Come and clear the table now."

Down in the cabin the meal was finished and the punch bowl was on the table. The third man was stirring it with an ebony-handled silver ladle. Two bottles of Everett brandy stood by the bowl — they hadn't been long in finding that! The sight of those greenish, lop-sided bottles took away all the vicarious pleasure that I was feeling over Africa's fortune. It was Fanshawe's brandy, it was his punch bowl, his ladle and his cabin. This little rat had gained it all by the foulest means, taking treacherous advantage of another man's kind-heartedness. But because he was in possession, and because I was out to save my own hide if I could, there was I regarding him civilly, taking the seat he pointed out to me, saying, through Carl, "You will never be sorry that you decided to keep Africa."

I ought, I knew, to have picked up one of the bottles suddenly and brained him. Then Carl and the other man could have sent me to join the honest men at the bottom of the sea. But whom would that benefit? Not Fanshawe whom nothing could ever hurt or help again. Certainly not myself. That moment's thought brought home to me something that not the burning of Braidlowrie, not the failure of the rebellion, not even the fight on the deck had done — the helplessness of weak right in the face of armoured wrong.

Without giving the matter any thought I had always acted upon the assumption that ill-fortune was the outcome of wrong, or at least foolish, doing. Only as lately as during the voyage when I thought about my parents I had been comforted by the thought that since they had not known anything about Glenranald and had been in the kitchen watching the soldiers renew their search at the very moment when Daft Wullie was spying on Janet and me, they would be safe. It had taken me almost seventeen years to learn that fortune, good or ill, is entirely divorced from ethics. Captain Fanshawe, an intelligent, honest and kindly man, had been ousted from his ship, banished from life itself, by a crafty, dishonest little rat of a pirate simply because wrong happened to be armed and right, for the moment, defenceless. And now, although it was right that I should attack him I wasn't strong enough to do it. I sat down, leaned gratefully against the panelling behind me and accepted a glass of the surly man's punch.

I put it down near me on the table. I didn't intend to drink it. They had taken out those very flowerlike glasses, and one was already in fragments on the floor.

They had just kicked the pieces aside. Their behaviour was much like that of pigs in a flower-garden — and that made me think of the pigs in the garden at Braidlowrie amid the broken statuary and ragged yews. I thought, in the light of my newly acquired cynicism, of my father and mother. I thought anew of the first occasion upon which I had seen those greenish bottles and flowerlike glasses. Misery mounted in me steadily while the captain, Carl and the other man talked and drank and laughed. A swelling rose in my bruised throat and I discovered to my horror that I was very near to tears. I, Colin Lowrie, to break down before this treacherous scum. I snatched up my glass and drank hurriedly.

Carl refilled it when it was empty, and said with the air of trying to be polite to a stranger, "You will like St. Crispin's. It is a pleasant little place." He turned back to the table and spoke in his own tongue. All three of them laughed. Later, I knew why. Just then I didn't even wonder. For the punch was warm within me and soon I was conscious that my hard tight misery was melting like the last snow in the warm rains of April. I sat and waited for the moment of clarity and confidence that had come upon me once before in this cabin.

And suddenly it was there. I felt that uprush of consciousness, of being, of strong life. It banished everything but its own warm glow. I was Colin Lowrie, alive and young. I had escaped from the slaughter. I had made my bargain with the little rat across the table. It was through my idea that Africa was now happily pottering about his galley. All these things meant something, were omens. Just as my body was guided by its peculiar sense of direction, so my life was drawn towards some magnet that lay in the future. I was going on and on.

I even seemed to increase physically. My wounded shoulder hurt me less and my head steadied. If it had occurred to me then to pick up the bottle and set about the captain I have no doubt that I should have done it. But it didn't. Fanshawe's words, reported by the little man in the story of the Yellow Jack, flashed into my mind . . . "St. Peter has a list like a paysheet and until your number's called nothing can kill you." I believed that at that moment. It explained everything. Fanshawe and the rest of the crew, every man aboard the *Sheba*, save only Africa and me, had been called at once. And in that moment, just on the verge of intoxication, I tapped a secret source of knowledge and was sure that it would be a long time before I was called.

But the moment ended. The fumes crept about my brain, dimming the ecstasy that had been of their own making. My hands and feet receded from me. I grew sleepy. The three men in the cabin had been drinking more steadily than I and had gone back into some discussion that caused the surly one to bang his hands on the table and to gesture with his glass. There was nothing to keep me here. I said to Carl,

"I think I'll go to bed."

He said, "Good night" and the other two looked round and grunted.

I went to the little cabin that had been mine: my refuge, I recollected, from the man whom I should never see again. Even that thought failed to move me at that moment. There were some things in the cabin that gave evidence of someone else's occupation of it. I didn't care. I bundled all the things together and put them outside the door. I climbed into my own bunk and was asleep as soon as I had stretched myself flat.

When I woke it was daylight and the motion of the ship had stopped. I dressed carefully, smoothing my hair and clothes, wishing that I had other than the rough garments that I had. A new phase of life was beginning. What St. Crispin's held for me I could not even guess, but whatever it was I wished that I could have gone to meet it clad in clothes that would have given a good impression. I had never thought much about clothes. At home they hadn't mattered greatly. The shattered glory of Braidlowrie had cast a protecting shadow over our rags: here it was different. But though no one knew it I must not forget. I was Colin Lowrie of Braidlowrie. I was born a gentleman. I was a Jacobite, as much an exile in an honourable cause as the Prince, or Glenranald, always supposing that they had attained to exile. With thoughts like these I bolstered myself to face the vast unknown world that lay outside the *Sheba*. Much encouraged I presented myself, without invitation, to the cabin for breakfast. I even found myself scorning the cluttered table, littered as it was by the dishes of those who had breakfasted before me.

There was a mirror in the cabin and for almost the first time I studied myself carefully in its dim surface. I regarded with shocked disfavour the amount of reddish down on my cheeks and chin. It was a disgraceful badge of boyhood. I must shave, that was the first, the most essential thing. Then I realised that since I had last studied my face — in mother's mirror — I had aged a good deal. The resemblance to my father was now pronounced and unmistakable. The same red hair, the same thick red eyebrows that made a bar above the blue eyes. His, too, was the beaky nose, oddly fleshless in a face that was not thin. I noted these things with detachment and found myself wondering why the look of me had been so attractive to that woman, to Janet, to Fanshawe when he held his lantern to study it. To me it was not attractive, it was a tanned and younger edition of my father's face, and it badly needed the attention of a razor. Could I borrow one before I went ashore?

Wondering this I left the mirror and turned my attention to a ham that stood on the table. I had almost broken my fast when there was a sound of voices outside. Carl came in first and held the door open, respectfully, I thought, for a stranger who came in, followed by the captain who was wearing a hat and carrying a stick as though he had already been ashore.

The newcomer was a short, sturdily built man with a deeply browned face and a neatly trimmed beard of black, freely speckled with white. He wore a coat of some thin pale silky material and from its front a frilled shirt foamed upon his breast. His thick but shapely legs were encased in a pair of well-cut breeches of pale supple leather and ended in riding boots with coloured tops and tassels. I took special note of his clothes because I had that very morning become aware of the defects in my own wardrobe, and my first study of him, though it lasted only a moment, was full of envy.

The three of them spoke together in the captain's tongue and then Carl, turning to me abruptly, said,

"Stand up and take your coat off."

Something in his voice annoyed me, so I deliberately broke off a piece of bread, filled my mouth with ham, chewed, put in the bread and chewed again before I said,

"What for?"

"Mr Standish wants to look at your shoulder."

"Is he a doctor?"

"No, but he knows a greal deal about wounds." I swallowed my last crumb, stood up, slowly removed my shabby homespun jacket and exposed, not without shame, my torn and bloody shirt.

It was the same shirt in which I had fled from home, my only shirt, In the old days on the *Sheba* I had washed it frequently and dried it in the sun, but I had had, naturally, no time to launder it since Enrico's knife had gone through it. The whole of the sleeve and front were stiff and brown with blood. Because of this, and because the stranger was so elegantly dressed, and even more because of the authority in Carl's voice, I would not offer my shoulder for inspection, but stood still on the far side of the table. There was a little pause. Then the man whom they called Standish strode round the table. Calmly and deliberately he tore at the hole which

Enrico's knife had made so that the whole of the sleeve was loosened and fell down stiffly over my elbow. I opened my mouth to protest and then closed it again on a bellow of pain for his stubby fingers were probing my wound. The raw edges opened and the blood began to run again. I pushed him away violently.

"Damn you, whoever you are," I said in a voice sharp with rage and pain. "You've hurt me, and look what you've done to my shirt."

He turned back and said in English, "The wound is nothing, but I do not care for his temper."

The captain, not understanding, smiled placatingly.

"What the hell has my temper to do with you?" I demanded, mopping at the blood that was trickling over my chest. He turned to me and with a cat smile said,

"I've just given a matter of thirty-five pounds for you, that is all."

For a moment I was so staggered by surprise that I was speechless. Then rage took me. I put one hand on the table and vaulted over it, straight to where the little smiling captain stood. I saw the smile change to terror as my hands closed round his throat. I forced his head backwards and sideways. If it was the last thing I did I would break his neck in the way in which I had killed fowls in the old days, or put a snared rabbit out of its pain. But his neck was tougher than hen's or rabbit's and Carl and Standish, recovered from their first surprise, hung one upon each arm, like terriers from a bull's nose. I jabbed out my elbows, I aimed blows with my feet at their shins. If I could only hold them off until that satisfying click told that the Portuguee's spine had given way I didn't care what happened after. It almost happened. But they were heavy men, they were pulling in opposite directions, and though I had the strength of three men in my fury I had, too, a wounded shoulder. My hands shifted a trifle. The Portuguee snatched his opportunity and brought up his knee. I fell back against the table doubled over with such pain as I'd never known existed. The two men who were holding my arms fell back too and for some moments there was no sound in the cabin save the heavy breathing of the four of us.

In that space I regained my senses. Violence could not serve me because I could not be violent enough. I must try reason. Thank God the man Standish spoke English! Standing upright again with no little difficulty I turned to where he was standing wiping his face and palms upon a fine lawn handkerchief.

"Look here, Mr. Standish," I said, "I don't know what this pair of rogues have told you, but they've deceived you anyway. I'm not for sale." Those simple words stopped me, denying as they did something so fantastic that it needed no denial. It was like saying, "I'm not dead." I shook off the feeling of unreality and looked earnestly into his face. "This little swine by a trick took the ship on which I was a passenger. I'm the only white man left alive. They want me out of the way, that's only natural. But I gave him money and he promised me a passage to St. Crispin's. It was a silly thing to do, I see that, but I've never had dealings with a rogue before. He can no more sell me than I can sell him. I'm not a Negro and I'm not a criminal. I'm a Scots gentleman coming out to St. Crispin's upon business of my own."

Standish tapped his excellent teeth with a carefully tended thumb-nail, and returned my stare for a second.

"And what exactly is your business, young man?"

"I don't know yet."

"I *see*. A secret errand? And with whom?"

"That is my affair."

"Pardon me, mine. You see Captain Barlesci has taken my money. It would be very awkward, not to say embarrassing, if, when we go ashore, someone — shall we say the Governor himself? — is there to meet you. You see it is very much my affair."

All this time Carl had been gabbling away in an undertone, translating what was being said. Standish now swung round on his heel and spoke urgently to the captain who once broke off this conversation to say to me,

"Damn rogue. All lies."

Apparently he made his tale good, for without more ado Standish turned to me and said crisply,

"Have you any papers that prove that you are a Scots gentleman with any business in St. Crispin's? If so produce them. Barlesci here will then return my money and the affair will be closed."

"Any papers I have are again my own affair, Mr. Standish. I question your right to demand them." And though I tried to speak boldly my heart had dropped into my stomach, for here I was indeed nobody, and the rogues had me in their hands.

"We'll soon see," said Standish in a reasonable way. He spoke to Carl and Barlesci and the three of them set about me in a business-like way, searching my pockets, diving into the recesses of my clothing, and, of course, finding nothing. Carl went into my cabin next door and searched there.

When he came back empty-handed both Standish and the captain looked frankly relieved. The former said quietly,

"It looks very much to me as though, if you are what you say, a Scots gentleman," and oh the scorn with which he repeated that unlucky phrase, "that you left your own country in such a hurry that you neglected to bring even a change of clothing with you. I should make my guess that you're one of those Jacobites. Probably that other captain had orders to sell you anyway. So put on your coat and come along quietly. I detest more than anything a scene in public."

"I shall not come quietly," I said hotly. "I am a free man. None of your truck with this little bastard can alter that. Why, if there was any law or justice in these parts he wouldn't dare bring a stolen ship into a harbour at all! You may have given him money but you haven't bought me. I shan't come with you. I shan't work for you. So you'd better ask for your money back — and if he won't part with it I'll help you get it."

Standish sighed wearily. "Your tales are so different that I don't know which to believe. I won't believe either of you. All I know is that I was offered an able-bodied young man for thirty-five pounds, I've parted with the money and I intend to have my purchase. I didn't come here for the sake of an hour's argument and a struggle to get my money. I bought you because at this moment there happens to be a serious shortage of labour in the islands. Doubtless there will shortly be a good supply of Scots gentlemen, after the trials in England are finished, but that doesn't relieve the moment's necessity. So let's have no more nonsense. Put on your coat, if you want it, or come without."

The complete cynicism of this speech, his almost amiable indifference to the moral aspect of the case, dumbfounded me. It was obviously nothing to him whether Barlesci were a pirate or an honourable man. He just wanted a labourer and considered that he had bought one, and that was all. It occurred to me that though, in this cabin, I was worsted, outside I might get a hearing. There would be men ashore, surely, who would be able to judge impartially, men who wanted neither my price nor my labour. I would appeal to them as soon as my foot touched the shore. I picked up my coat.

"Very well," I said.

Barlesci had recovered and was smiling again. He took a bottle in his hand and offered Standish a drink, but he brushed it away with a gesture that said plainly that he had no great liking for the captain's company and had wasted quite enough time over this business. Barlesci swallowed the tot himself and followed us up to the deck. He gabbled a little to Standish who nodded with testy haste and then we dropped over the side into a smartly painted little boat with a red and white striped awning over the rear seats. It was rowed by two Negroes, naked except for loin-cloths of the same red and white material. I sat down and looked about me.

The *Sheba*, as I looked up for a farewell glance at her, looked different. All her paintwork had been renewed in a different colour, and the worn and battered effigy of the Ethiopian queen which had been her figurehead was gone and in its place was fitted a swan's long neck, narrow head and swelling breast, new and gleaming white. In bright straggling letters the word *Swan* had been painted on her prow. There were other alterations too, but I had gathered the main idea and was no longer interested enough to note them. It was enough that the *Sheba* had been blotted out as though she and those upon her had never been. I turned my attention to the harbour.

St. Crispin's is a small island, shaped like a roughly made oat-cake out of which a child has taken a bite. That bite is the harbour, a natural semi-circle with horns of land coming out on the north and south. The coast shelves so sharply that ships can anchor within two or three minutes' rowing of the shore, and since this means a great saving of time and labour in the loading and unloading of vessels, Josepha, the port that lies round the harbour like a necklace, does more trade than many ports four or five times its size. I learned later that St. Crispin's has another natural advantage in being of volcanic origin which gives it extremely fertile soil, easily tilled and almost extravagantly productive.

Despite my distress of mind and uncertainty of outlook I looked towards the port eagerly. We were there in a very short time. A landing stage faced with hewn stone ran sheer into the water. At intervals short flights of steps broke its smooth surface and near each flight were rings set in the stone for the securing of boats. The Negroes rowed to the base of one of these flights and Standish, not holding me in any way, said, "Up you go."

I wondered at his trust until I reached the top of the steps where I was stopped by a man, neither black nor white, a kind of smutty colour who just barred my way until Standish close behind me said, "All right, Amos. A new man of mine. I'm taking him across to the plague office."

A six foot breadth of wooden paving divided us from a door with an awning projecting above it. With a hand on my elbow he propelled me across the planks, through the door and a bare lobby and into an inner room where two white men sat smoking at a table.

"Morning, Sheridan, morning Last," he said briskly. "Just run over this fellow for me, will you? He's perfectly all right, but I suppose these formalities must be considered, eh? He's got a wound in the shoulder."

The younger of the two men rose languidly and came towards me. "Strip, please," he said in a weary way as though he had repeated the words many many times.

Now, I thought, is the moment to make my stand.

"Listen," I said, "I'm *not* his new fellow. I'm a private person whom a little scoundrel of a Portuguese pirate pretended to sell to him. I didn't belong to the man; how could I? I'm a Scotsman and as free as any of you here."

107

"He's one of those Jacobite fellows," said Standish, without haste or heat. "I've just given thirty-five pounds for him and before God I regret the necessity that made me do it. A bad bargain. Such an intractable, argumentative . . . why, I'd as soon have a Koromantee . . ."

"He'll calm down," said the elder man. "Come on now, Scottie, be sensible. You've lost the toss, you may as well be agreeable about it."

"But you must listen to me," I said, with that frightening feeling of unreality assailing me again. "I was an ordinary passenger on a ship called the *Queen of Sheba* with Captain Fanshawe. A man, a pirate, named Barlesci took the ship by a trick and killed everybody except me and an old Negro. Then he took it into his head to sell . . ."

"What is all this garble about Sheba and Fanshawe?" said Sheridan jocosely. "I always thought it was Sheba and Solomon. Ha. Ha. Come on now. Will you strip or must we help you?"

Even as I began to remove my coat I ventured upon one last appeal.

"Can't I make you understand that a crime is being committed? This man may be under a misapprehension that I'm doing my best to remove but he has no right to bring me here and call me his man. I'm nobody's man. I'm a free Scotsman."

Sheridan rose, even more languidly than Last had done, and came round the table, propping his behind on the edge of it.

"Listen," he said, and his air was one of patience with a fool. "We don't give a damn who you are. If you

108

were God Almighty and you landed in St. Crispin's while there was plague at Port of Spain, plague in Barbadoes, plague in Jamestown, you'd have to come in here and get a clean bill from Last and me. We don't want any stories told to us, all we ask is for you to take your things off and let us get on without wasting any more time."

I stripped; and tried to stand impassive while they peered and poked into my armpits, my groin, behind my ears, between my toes and fingers.

"Sound as a bell," said Last, "and not such a bad bargain, if I may say so, Mr. Standish. A fine pair of shoulders." He flicked his hand over my back. Sheridan went back behind the table and began to fill in a paper.

"Very quiet in here, isn't it?" asked Standish conversationally.

"Just now, yes. We were busy earlier. And tomorrow or next day there's a cargo coming in from the Gambia. Jellybags passed the old *Flying Fish* about three days out and he got in yesterday. A fast tub, his."

"You'll be busy enough then. Don't let anything in you shouldn't."

"Trust us, sir. There you are." He handed the paper across the table to Standish, who without a glance thrust it into his pocket. That action brought home to me a sharp sense of my position, of the futility of further protest. I wasn't even to handle my own bill of health. It went to my master — as though I were a dog! The fate from which I had tried to save Africa had overtaken me.

I cannot rightly convey the complete misery of that moment, the sense of helplessness, of injustice, of impotent rage, of unwilling belief in the incredible. But I still fought against the sinking of my heart. Above all things now I needed courage. I must remain, in my own eyes at least, a free man, a Scotsman, a Lowrie. I was not a poor helpless, ignorant timid Negro, torn out of a mud hut, shipped he knew not where. Nobody should own me.

Perhaps something of my thought reached Standish, for at the door of the lobby he stopped and jerked his finger over his shoulder to the room we had just left. He said, without gloating or rancour, but calmly, as one stating a fact.

"I let you say all you wanted to in there, didn't I? And you saw how they took it, didn't you? Well, believe me, that's just how everybody else will take it. You can go along into the Square if you like and shout that you belong to yourself, but if I come along and say differently, and show Barlesci's receipt and this bill of health made out for one man of mine, nobody will believe you, nobody. You're not alone. There's several like you in the islands. I've got two old '15 men up at my place at this very minute. You might just as well settle down and take it quietly and not make things rough for yourself. We've got methods for taming rough customers — don't forget that."

"But those others you speak of had a trial. Rightly or wrongly they were condemned. They're called indentured labourers. I've heard of them. And they're indentured for a certain time, ten, fifteen, twenty years. After that they're free."

"And who comes poking round, do you think, to know whether their time is up? And who would listen to them if they got up and announced it? Nobody. They're lifers and they know it. You're a lifer too, and you may as well know it. I'm a patient man, understand that, but I've used all the patience that I have to spare for you. So come along and don't madden me."

There was a hitching rail just to the left of us and by it there was a light split-cane carriage with large wheels painted red. Two sleek mules with polished hoofs and pom-poms of red and white on their bridles stood dozing in the sun. Near their heads was an old Negro with a fuzz of white hair. His pose was as somnolent as theirs but he was not asleep, for as we came through the doorway he sprang to attention, unknotted the reins and stood with a smile on his face, the very picture of willing service.

"Get in the back," said Standish.

I looked about. There were several people in the street; men clad much as he was in light suits and wide straw hats. There were coloured women of shades varying from ebony to biscuit carrying baskets or bundles on their heads. There were white women, too, each escorted by a white man or attended by a little black boy. Surely among them all there must be one person with some idea of law and justice. Upon this hope I made my final stand.

"I'm not going with you," I said and went to walk on. Standish, still cool and calm, stretched out his arm and took my shoulder, the wounded one, in a grip of iron. I struggled wildly. The white-haired Negro threw down the reins and wrapped his arms around my knees. I began to shout. The mules, startled by the sound, pranced madly. One of the men passing ran to their heads and held them. Unable to move I ceased wrestling and saved my breath for shouting. I roared out my protest, disjointed words and phrases. I cried that I was a free man, being taken off against my will, against the law. Standish shook me so that the speech bubbled from my lips like water from a shaken bottle.

A large crowd had gathered by this time but not a soul interfered or even asked a question. Scenes like this were a commonplace to them, but I didn't know that then. Finally Standish hit me heavily on the mouth, a knock-out blow.

"Heave him in, Abraham," he said. The Negro tightened his grip on my legs, heaved, and I fell into the body of the carriage, dazed, sick and for the moment, beaten. Standish climbed into the seat of the vehicle, took the reins that Abraham gathered up for him and waited until the old man had clambered up beside him.

"Another of these tiresome Scotsmen," he said to the crowd at large.

"I wish you joy of him, Jimmy. I hope he was dirt cheap," someone called. And another added. "You should stick to Koromantees, old man." Several people laughed. The man who stood at the mules' heads stepped back. Standish shook the reins and we rattled away.

112

I lay in the back of the carriage as it bounced and sped over the rough road through scenery that I should at any other time have enjoyed, so new it was, so lovely, and I touched the depths of humiliation. Why, oh why, had I ever run from Braidlowrie? Better a thousand times to have swung from the gibbet in the company of noble men whose only crime was their failure, than to have come to this — a slave.

I tried to realise that I belonged to this little dapper man just as his clothes did. I was on a level with Abraham and the mules. I thought of the place to which we were speeding behind those nimble heels, and realised that there were men there, two men, who had been slaves for thirty years. Thirty years! In thirty years I should be forty-six, almost forty-seven years old. My life would be behind me — and nothing done save the tasks imposed upon me by this Standish for his profit.

Unbearable thought. My life was my own. My energy should be directed towards my own ends. I wanted to make money, to rebuild Braidlowrie, to assert myself. It was incredible, incredible that this thing should have happened to me. But there, just ahead of me, was the stumpy little figure, holding the reins between his fingers, encouraging the mules by clicks of the tongue or almost caressing touches of the long whip, and he was credible enough — and he was my master. For thirty-five pounds and by the custom of this queer country, and by his own implacability and calm he was my master.

I hated him. I hated him even more, I think, because of that calm: because he had explained to me outside the plague office the futility of protest: because he had not been ruffled by the affair in the street though he had warned me on the ship that he detested scenes in public: because he had not even troubled to hit me until he was forced to: and because he had hit me once, just once, heavily but without spite. All these things were evidence of his assurance, his superiority, his scorn.

His voice broke in on my musings.

"Hi, you there at the back, I don't know your name. What is it?"

"You'd better give me one," I said out of my hatred. "People often re-name dogs they buy."

"So they do. Well, I shall call you Scottie. What I was going to call to your attention was the fact that we've just turned on to the Springhill Plantation, my place. We shall be home in a few minutes now."

I made no answer. The word "home" called up so much that even if I had wanted to speak I couldn't have done so. I did look about me, though, and saw the apparently limitless fields stretching away on either hand, full of green plants, evenly set out, about as tall as a man. And working among the plants were men, and women too, short and tall, none very fat and varying in colour, though less variable than the women in Josepha. Some were bareheaded, others had twists of red and white calico or broad green leaves on their heads to protect them from the sun. And there were two, both working near the track, who were trousers and straw hats something like Standish's own. He pointed towards them with the whip.

114

"See, those are your compatriots, Scottie! They still feel the sun more than the others so I give them my old hats. I shall have to find you one. I don't know whether I can spare this yet."

He took it off as he spoke, and regarded it earnestly, twirling it on his hand.

"Yes, it's seen its best days. Here you are, you can have it now."

He tossed it backwards to me. His old hat! God, how I hated him.

He no longer needed the hat for the bare sun-beaten track had run into an avenue of some trees that gave off a pleasant scent, and the bright light became a deep green shade. It curved slightly and then I could see a long low white house with a roof that projected far beyond the walls and was supported by pillars. Vivid splashes of colour resolved themselves as we drew nearer into flower-beds full of bright blooms. I saw one mass of colour move away as we approached and stared at it puzzled, not realising that I was seeing a peacock for the first time. We drove near enough to the house for me to distinguish the flowering creepers that twined about the pillars of the veranda, then we turned sharply to the left, rounded the house and drew up in a neatly sanded yard. The house flanked one side of the square, stables and outbuildings defined the others, and from one corner ran a path, at the end of which I could see a little street with mud-plastered cabins on either side. The slave quarters. My future home.

Abraham leaped down and took the reins from his master.

115

"Take a look at Belial's near front shoe, Abraham. Seems loose to me," said Standish, and then, seeing me in the back of the carriage, he added. "You can come with me for a minute. And bring that hat. It'll be gone in a flash if you aren't careful. Half my people are Mandigoes and can steal with their toes. Though God knows why, their hands are bad enough."

He started to walk away as he was speaking. I grabbed the loathesome hat — which after all I might need — and scrambling down followed him up to the back of the house. He opened a door and revealed a room, neat and tidy and furnished like an office with a heavy desk, a massive carved chair and a bare bench. Seating himself in the chair he took a cigar from the box on the desk, lighted it with care, drew several breaths of smoke and exhaled them and then said,

"Sit down. We may as well get ourselves straightened out at once."

I sat down. He put his elbows on the table and regarded me seriously.

"Now see here. I've stood quite a lot from you, one way and another. Just now you were unpardonably insolent when I asked your name. If it had been anyone but Abraham who is meek as a sheep, with me, I should have had to fetch you a damn good crack with a whip. But we can't have any more of that. I'm ready to believe that you've had a rough deal and there's no doubt that you feel pretty raw about it, but that sort of behaviour isn't going to make things any better for you. Get into your thick Scots head that you've been bought and paid for, that if you don't work willingly there are ways of

116

making you, that it will pay you to be civil and willing, and you'll find it's not so bad. It's quite possible to lead a tolerable life at Springhill, and that's more than could be said for a great many plantations.

"And mark this. I happen to be an easy-going man up to a point and I hate unpleasantness. If you're going to make trouble I shall simply sell you to a neighbour of mine who enjoys nothing more than to watch a good flogging before breakfast. He'd give fifty pounds for you this minute for the pleasure of putting a hot coal on that saucy tongue of yours. That is a literal fact. God's blood, I should like to have seen his face if you'd made him half the scene you made me this morning, or said that about buying a dog. It's a damn lucky thing for you that I happened along this morning when that little yellow Barlesci was looking for a billet for you."

He broke off to pull at his cigar and I took advantage of the moment's respite to say, as levelly as I could manage,

"That's your side of it, Mr. Standish, but I wish you'd try to put yourself in my place for a moment. Suppose you had taken passage on a ship and parted with all the money you had in the world, and then were sold to the first person who happened to pass. Wouldn't you make a scene? Or would you settle down to be civil and willing? Just think of that happening to you, and help me. I know you've parted with your money, and I daresay that yellow swine told you a feasible story, but do please believe me that my story is true. It's a terrible thing to have happened to a free man. Let me go. I swear I'll pay you back as soon as ever I'm able. I'll make that my one object in life. You don't seem an unreasonable person, surely you can see the injustice you'll be doing to keep me here."

He was quite still for a moment, and a wild hope shot through me that my appeal had really reached him. I had looked straight at him during the speech and put into it every bit of earnestness and urgency that I was feeling. After a moment he spoke.

"You're asking the impossible, you know. I have a plantation and I must have hands to work it. I needed another man, you came along. I paid the price and brought you here. Yours may be a hard case, but it's not the only one. I don't buy white men as a rule. I don't approve of it to tell you the truth, but as I told you there's a severe shortage of labour. There's plague in the Sugar Islands and the planters there are paying ridiculous prices for men, so we go short. But even with black men, if you sit down to go into the matter of right and wrong you'd go crazy — I should at least. They don't ask to leave their homes and come here to work on the plantations: nor do they ask to be born into slavery, as they are, every day. I just don't think about it, see? I'm not going to look on you as somebody who's had a hard deal, that'd make me uncomfortable. To me you're Scottie, able-bodied white man, who cost me thirty-five pounds, and can work in my fields. While you do your work you'll be fed and housed and clothed and treated properly. Now I don't want to hear any more, you understand? You're here and you're mine, and that's all there is about it. Don't make any bile over the inevitable. And you'd better forget all that about the

Scots gentleman. It'll eat into you else. Abraham will show you where you live and so on, and for today you'd better rest that shoulder. That's all."

That was indeed all. There was no point in saying anything further. His attitude was so clearly defined, and so reasonable in its complete lack of reason, that the spirit was taken out of me. And I didn't like the sound of the neighbour. Quite meekly I picked up the hat and went to find Abraham.

So for the moment I settled down to become one of the domestic animals on the Springhill Plantation. In a very short time my resentment at being there at all was leavened by thankfulness that I *was* there and not at some of the places which I heard described. Many of Standish's neighbours considered him to be deplorably lenient and constantly prophesied that one night he would be murdered in his bed. I discovered that below the froth of the prosperity, the severity, the autocracy of the planters there ran a dark restless tide of fear. It coloured the whole state of slave owning. Slaves must be kept, they were necessary, but they must be kept in abject subjection because they were both feared and hated. Even at Springhill the least thing that might be construed into insolence or slackness was instantly and severely punished. It was the inevitable outcome of a society based upon an essential injustice in a place where black so heavily outnumbered white. But at Springhill there was a certain superficial humanity at work. We were driven hard, but we were not killed with labour. We were fed roughly but adequately. We were not punished without cause, or simply to intimidate. We were given consideration when sick. Consequently the worst threat that could be made was the threat of being "sold away."

Nevertheless it was a hard and brutalising life, and naturally for white men who had known other states, other climates, who had had their personal hopes and ambitions it was worse than for Negroes, who, so long as they were fed and housed properly, seemed as happy as animals would be in similar conditions. I never found a Negro in whom the mere fact that he was a slave roused mental anguish.

I was put in a cabin with the two other white men, the relics of that earlier rebellion. I appreciated that after a time and marked it to Jimmy Standish's credit. For we were able to talk together and to preserve some kind of cleanliness in our cooking and living arrangements. A state of appalling filthiness prevailed in most of the native cabins.

My fellows at bed and board were known as Mac and Fergus. I never heard their other names. Perhaps they had forgotten them themselves. Perhaps Jimmy had named them as he had me. They were always considered a pair: the crisis of their lives and the ensuing thirty years had been identical: they had worked together at Springhill, shared the same cabin, eaten the same food, been constant companions for hard on twenty years of that time, yet I never knew two men more unlike one another.

They were both old men when I knew them. Mac, who looked the younger, said that he was sixty-four;

120

Fergus reckoned his age as fifty-nine, but he looked seventy. Mac was of middle height, thick-set, square-headed and bow-legged. He had a profuse dirty white beard that swept down over his chest and reached the top of his trousers. He was surly, bitter and bad-tempered, at once proud of his ability to do a day's work, and carefully sparing of his energy. I found his bitterness quite understandable! It was Fergus who puzzled me. He had been much above average height, but field work and living in a low cabin had bowed his shoulders, so that he looked a very frail old man. He was so thin that when he chewed his food every muscle and bone in his face clean up to the temple could be seen moving. When he lifted his arm, or bent his leg or took anything in his fingers, sharp cracks like little pistol shots testified to the rheumatic condition of his joints. On wet days life must have been agony to him. All through the damp "sorting" season, when the tobacco leaves were pliable enough to be handled, he moved about with difficulty, creaking and cracking, but never once abandoning his work. He was very experienced and willing and although no one would have judged from his appearance that his work could be of any value he was one of the best hands at Springhill. I think that Jimmy Standish, in his casual way, was rather fond of Fergus, he sometimes gave him delicate food easier than the regulation rations to eat. He gave him the best of the cast-off clothes, and the razor which was the old man's most cherished possession had been Jimmy's too.

Although later on I was glad that I had been put to live with these two, at first I hated it and thought of it as a refinement of cruelty. For the first weeks I could hardly bear to look at them — old men, nearing the end of their earthly span, who had had no lives of their own, except once long ago, when of their own free will they had done that which had imperilled their freedom forever. Did I see in them a picture of my own future, my own age? Soon, very soon, despite Mac's toughness and Fergus' uncomplaining doggedness, they would be too old to earn their keep any more. What then? Would they be given their freedom so that they might starve, or would they eke out their remaining days on a little grudging charity?

For this, I used to think, looking at them in the twilight at supper time, had their fathers got and their mothers borne them. Was it for this too that I had come into the world? Surpassingly bitter thoughts. It made me share more than willingly in Mac's hopeless, resentful, cynical view of life. My arrival was bad for him. It stirred up the embers of his misery. Seeing me, young and lusty, doomed, as he thought, for the path that had been his own, roused much the same feelings in him as the sight of him, at the far end of the hated journey, did in me. Together we railed at the English, the slave-owners, Whittle the overseer, and Treacle the foreman, at fate itself. Fergus must have found us a pleasant pair to live with, but he never complained or checked us, nor did he share in the conversations. He sat with his pipe — often cold and empty — between his teeth and either meditated or dreamed or put clumsy patches on his clothing. One evening, however, during one of our tirades I felt his eye on me, and at last he put out his thin veined old man's hand, and laid it on my knee.

"It isn't often," he said mildly, "that I interefere or give unasked advice, but, laddie, it goes to my heart to see such misery in you. What's happened to you, you could neither help then nor mend now. All that remains for you is to be patient: and if in His own good time the Lord in His wisdom sees fit to let this cup pass from you, you'll be glad that you didn't waste time in rebellion, and if He doesn't the sooner you learn to drink it the pleasanter it will taste."

Mac rose with a grunt from his place by the wall,

"The Reverend Mr. Fergus-Love-Your-Enemies is noo gang ta mak a bid for ye'r soul, Scottie. Mind him weel, mark wheer meekness has gotten him. I'll awa to Jacko's and see hoo he's progressing wi's still. There's a brew mair to ma taste."

He lumbered out, and through very embarrassment I longed to follow him, but Fergus still had his hand on my knee, so I didn't move. He withdrew it presently and tucking his long arms round his thin body, sat motionless and quiet for some time. He was silent so long that I was driven to speak.

"I often wonder," I said, a little shyly, "what it is that makes you so different, so different from Mac and me, I mean. You're an old man. At an age when men look to be reaping the reward of their labours and to settle down in peace and comfort and honour with their children and grandchildren about them, you have

123

nothing. You work all day long for the food you eat and this miserable shelter overhead. One day you won't even be able to earn them and then you'll be like an old horse or a toothless dog. And yet you seem happy and resigned. How can you be?" I demanded, my voice rising in passion. "Don't you ever think 'what have I done to deserve this?' And what did you do? You fought in a cause that you believed in, and you lost a battle. It isn't fair or just. If there were a God in Heaven He'd see that it wasn't just. He'd do something about it; we're brought up to believe He can do anything. But I don't believe there's a God in Heaven, or He wouldn't have let the *Sheba* be taken, and one of the best men ever I knew be killed by one of the worst. He wouldn't have let me be sold, or you, or Mac, or indeed any of these poor creatures out there. Think, Fergus, think, of Tessimadi where they have floggings every day just because Oldfield loves cruelty. Think of that nigger we heard of who was castrated just because Cartell had a coloured mistress who preferred a man of her own colour. Don't talk to me about the Lord, Fergus, talk to me about the Devil who surely rules this world."

My voice broke with passion. I sat breathing hard, aware that my violence and blasphemy had relieved me quite a lot. I had an obscure feeling that in defying God like this I was issuing a challenge. To vindicate Himself he should send Standish in to say that he had done wrong in buying me and would free me at once. I would, I felt, if someone challenged my very existence so.

124

Fergus said nothing for a long time. I thought that my outburst had shaken and silenced him. But presently in that same mild voice which seemed to come from a long way off he said,

"You think too much about this poor flesh, Colin lad. Injustice, and cruelty, and the triumph of force there has always been in this world, and always will be. I'm not denying that. But it's only the flesh that suffers from these things. No man, no cruelty, no force can shut a man off in spirit from communion with his Maker. Yon nigger that you speak of — he'll lose some pleasure maybe, and some trouble too — but his soul isn't injured. And God has to do with souls, not bodies. You should always remember that. We don't understand His ways. No man can see why Christ, God's Son, had to die the way he did. Wouldn't it seem to you that for a regiment of Michael's angels to have come down from Heaven and taken away the nails and trodden the crown of thorns underfoot would have been a better and quicker way to save the world? Every man who ever saw it or heard of it would have believed in Christ's divinity then. But in time that would have been just a story. And now, at this time would it be any comfort to you, Colin, to know that seventeen hundred and forty-six years ago one man was saved from a painful death, and you suffering as you are? No. But to know that one man faced death without flinching, endured pain by choice so that he might understand it and defeat it, that has been a comfort to many."

"It doesn't comfort me," I said with stubborn truth.

125

"Maybe not, because you look at it wrong. You say why should this happen to me? Then you look about a bit and add, or to Mac or Fergus, or to any of those who suffer? There's no answer to that. I know. I wasted a lot of time looking for it myself. Listen, I'll tell you something that I've told no one, not even Mac. I wasn't always what you see. I was a man of substance with a fine little estate in Appin. My parents were both drowned crossing a loch in a storm and at twenty I was my own master. I had two passions, gaming and wenching. You spoke just now of my children and grandchildren; no doubt by now I have many. But they don't bear my name. Marriage would have interfered, I thought, with the fine time I was having. I meant to marry one day and settle down, but meantime I enjoyed myself. I've seen France, aye and Italy. For nine years I lived as I pleased, minding neither God nor man. Then I joined Nithsdale's men — more for the adventure and the thrill I thought fighting would bring. I was taken with him and the rest after Sherriffmuir. I learned that my value in the world was less than that of many a horse I had owned. A sobering thought, Colin.

"Twenty-seven pounds I made in the open market at Barbadoes. I did nearly ten years there on a sugar plantation working for a Dutchman who was a devil incarnate. You can't tell me anything about injustice, lad, or sheer fiendish cruelty. For two years I was in Hell, literal Hell. Personal and vicarious misery was my portion every night and every day. I wear a shirt now no matter how hot it is because my back is no sight for anyone with bowels in him — and yon Jimmy Standish is one of those."

"I should consider him," I muttered. Fergus ignored me.

"But that isn't what I set out to tell you, except that it proves that I know what you and Mac feel when you talk that way. At the end of two years of Hell there was a little slave rebellion in Barbadoes. There were a lot of Koromantees there then — people have been careful of getting too many of that breed together since. They're good workers, splendid fellows almost all of them, but they are savage and intractable too. They seem to be indifferent to pain, intrepid, cast in the old Stoic mould. I've seen some of them die, quite horribly and quite unmoved. They always head rebellions. I joined this lot. We were put down and punished with frightful savagery. The masters had, for once, the excuse that they had been badly scared. I was flogged, pickled in brine and flogged again. And I saw things better not described, things I try to forget.

"When I was coming round from my second dose, weak and light-headed, I had a moment of vision. I'd never been a Bible reader or anything like that, and my state of mind was as far from being religious as any man's could well be, but the voice that called to Saul on the road to Damascus telling him that it was hard for him to kick against the pricks spoke to me and in almost those very words. I lay there in a filthy hut and I heard a voice as clearly as I hear yours now. And I realised that none of this misery mattered a scrap. My lot had been cast. It was for me to bear it with what courage I could muster, and to wait. In the eye of eternity and omniscience what did seventy years amount to? Nothing. Did it matter whether I was a comfortable gentleman living on his ancestral lands or a slave, toiling on a sugar plantation? Naked had I come into the world and naked should I leave it. Did it matter whether my flesh were whole or broken? It was but a temporary lodging anyway, destined to be food for worms. Cherish it as I might I could not prevent that final dissolution. But the spirit, which I had clogged with self-indulgence during my good fortune, and warped with bitterness during ill, that was an immortal thing, destined to return to God who was its source. I realised then, Colin, that God is a spirit and that the flesh is so little to Him that He could look unmoved upon the martyrs at the stake, upon His own Son on the Cross, knowing that it was only for a moment.

"I can't describe to you the content and peace that came upon me. I was not a slave, an exile, a defeated and thwarted person any more. I was a scrap, a flicker of an immortal light — what happened to the candlestick that held it for a moment was less than nothing — and it has been so ever since."

I sat silent for a little while. I was trying, honestly, and with my whole heart, to gather the significance of what Fergus had been telling me: trying to apply it to myself: trying to be convinced. I might as well have tried to convince myself that I was eighty, or that I was black, or insane. I wanted to say to him, "You admit that you were light-headed, that would explain the voice. And all the rest of it is an attempt to console yourself, the only way of escape left to you from the misery that you were enduring. Because life is so brief why it should be tolerable. Because we come naked and go naked is a reason for gathering around us as much as we can while we have the power. You are being like that bird we hear of that hides its head in the sand. You blind yourself with thoughts of immortality just as Jacko and Mac blind themselves with the corn brew. And for the same reason — that the naked facts are too horrible to bear. And you are doubly enslaved because you are resigned." I wanted to say all this, but I couldn't. I looked at him. All the light had gone now and there was only the red glow of the ashes of our supper-fire to see by; but I could see the delicate face, patient, almost happy. Any attempt even to shatter his peace would be a more cruel thing than anything that a slave owner could do to him. I said instead, "Thank you, Fergus, for telling me all this. I wish I understood it better. I will try."

He smiled and said nothing and presently Mac returned bearing a gourd carefully in his gnarled hands.

"See here," he said, "Ah've brought ye a taste o' Jacko's corn brew. Man, it's graund. He's gotten the trick of it at last. It has a kick like a mule."

His voice was thick and jovial. He offered the gourd to Fergus who refused it. "It gives me a head that nearly drops off when I stoop and I'm setting out all day tomorrow."

"Confusion to tomorrow, and God rot the setting oot," said Mac, raising the gourd to his own lips. "Here

129

lad, ye tak a taste. Forbye only the good Scotch 'tis the best Ah've swallowed."

I looked from one to another of them. Drunk on corn brew? Drunk on godly belief? Which? I had no choice. Unable to imbibe the one, I must turn to the other. I took the gourd not knowing that the decision was momentous and drank so long that Mac, looking at me with comical dismay, said,

"Here, go steady. 'Tis not ye're mither's milk you have there."

Sometimes we discussed the possibilities of getting away. I always opened this subject, for though I quickly saw that at Springhill we were favoured above the average I could not resign myself to the thought that I must stay there until some miracle or accident set me free. I might wait all my days. And there seemed to me, in my ignorance, no reason why a white man should not walk into Josepha and persuade some kindly captain to give him a passage in exchange for his work, or failing that, to stow away on some outward-bound vessel. There was, on the face of it, nothing to prevent it. Certainly we were watched at work, but only sufficiently to see that we were working to the limit of our powers. At supper time and during the darkness we were unguarded. The plantation was not walled in, how could it be? It had a boundary of many miles. What was to prevent me, or all of us, from stealing away? Nothing that I could see, except the fear of failure and subsequent punishment.

I often, in the early days, put these ideas before Mac and Fergus. And they, opposed upon so many questions, were unanimous about this. It could not be done, and anyone fool enough to try it was making a rod for his own back.

"Every free white man in St. Crispin's," said Fergus positively, "is a potential enemy of men like us. Go into Josepha if you're lucky enough to get so far. Your clothes, your hands, your hair, all cry aloud. The first white man you meet will come up and say, 'You're Jimmy Standish's new fellow, aren't you? What's your errand here?' They're all in league. And every ship's captain is in league with them, otherwise he'd find no market for his wares. In an island this size everybody knows everybody else's business. You may not think it, but practically everybody knows you. Jimmy's friends ride past with him and you're working. 'See that red-headed fellow,' he says. 'He's my latest purchase. Got him from so-and-so. Cost such-and-such. Isn't settling down too well.' I warn you for your own good. Take that red hair of yours ten yards over the Springhill boundary and your back'll suffer."

"A hat would hide my hair," I said foolishly.

"Aye, and who's hat?" asked Mac. "Yon hat is better known than ye are. Ask yersel', man, who else would be gang into Josepha in yon breeks, wi' na shoon to's feet and wi' Jimmy's hat on's head. Nabody but a rinaway. Ah knaw lad. Fower times in ma first year did Ah try it. All telled Ah wasna absent twenny-fower hoors."

"Did you ever try it?" I asked, turning to Fergus.

"Twice, in Barbadoes. The first time the very first planter I met, a man I'd never set eyes on, tied my wrist to his stirrup and brought me home that way. The second time I got into a town and thought I was well hidden in the crowds. But I was in the lockup before I'd drawn breath almost and when my Dutchman came to claim me I had twenty lashes at the public whipping post, like a law-breaker. As I was. The first law for slaves is, 'Thou shalt not run away.' I'd not advise you to try it, lad."

Nevertheless I brooded upon the subject and the more I brooded the more it seemed to me that with a little luck the thing could be done. It ought at least to be tried. If a man were more than an ox or ass he should prove it by behaving unlike them. That my stall was comparatively comfortable did not make it less a stall.

"I chose my time carefully. I waited until the hoeing season came and the transplanted bushes were high enough to make it necessary for the overseer to approach the spot where a man was working before he could see him. If I were not missed at the general turn-out at dawn, and if my place were not immediately seen to be empty, it might give me a little start.

An old Negro, past field work and employed at odd jobs about the place, included among his duties that of cutting our hair. To save himself from receiving over-frequent visits from us he used to crop it closely, almost to the skull. I went to him and said, firmly but placatingly, for he was an autocratic barber at the best of times,

"Don't cut mine quite so close, Pluggy. A little hair is a protection from the sun."

132

"Got a hat, ain't you? he said peevishly. "Can't give no 'vidual 'tention. Can't give no fash'nable haircuts. Be back 'bout nex' week yammerin' fo' 'nother cutting."

But despite this unhelpful attitude he did cut my mop in slightly less drastic fashion. By the end of the week, I thought, it would be neither so long nor so short as to attract attention.

Next I applied, through the overseer, for a pair of fresh trousers. The pair I wore, the pair in which I had left home, were by this time, despite their strong home-spun texture, a mere mass of fluttering rags that had been torn by brambles until they were only just past my knees.

"I can't understand," he said, regarding me coldly, "why Mr. Standish pampers you fellows so. Why can't you wear the red and white clouts like the niggers do. We might have a few less airs and graces then. I wonder that he doesn't get a tailor in to measure your arses."

The overseer was the great draw-back at Springhill. Perhaps Jimmy, distrusting at heart his own lenient measures, engaged him purposely as a counteracting influence. He wasn't purely white. I'd never seen an Indian then, but later on I recognised in many an Indian half-breed those yellow eyes, dirty buff skin and ill-assorted features, and above all the sense of inferiority that seemed to gnaw at Whittle all the time. And he came, I knew then, from the mainland, which supports my theory. He detested Mac and Fergus and me simply, I think, because we were white, and he never let pass an opportunity for administering a rebuke, a jibe, or a glancing blow of the crop which he always carried. Secure in our belief in Jimmy's essential humanity we did not fear Whittle quite as we might have done, and I, at least, drew a certain pleasure in looking him boldly in the eye whenever he spoke to me, or I to him.

He was an ugly man, a mass of bad proportions, a large head on a thin neck, lumpy body with spindly limbs, enormous hands and feet, all knobs and hollows. He appeared to have one ambition, and that was to grow a beard like Jimmy's. But for some reason his chin wouldn't grow one. He'd go about for weeks at a time with an inch of grubby looking stubble that never lengthened. Then he would grow disheartened and shave it off. In his presence Mac's magnificent growth seemed to acquire a life of its own, seemed to bristle and flaunt itself. He hated Mac most of all. In our cabin he was always referred to as Tottie Samson. Mac invented the name years before my arrival.

Some days after I had made my request he brought me a pair of Jimmy's old white duck trousers. My heart fell when I saw that they had been roughly hacked off at the knee. "Freedom for the limbs and privacy for the —" he said as he flung them down for me to pick up. I knew as he said it that he had cut them. I cursed as I stooped. The short legs made them almost as conspicuous as my own ragged pair. He caught me a cut with his crop on my seat as I bent over.

"Say 'thank you,' you ungrateful little bastard."

"I intended to thank Mr. Standish next time I saw him."

"Thank me, here and now."

"Thank you," I said, "sir."

He couldn't very well haul me up in front of Jimmy for a fraction of a pause before "sir," so he flicked me again, snarled and went off.

Night by night after that I watched the waning of the moon. At last it was a mere sickle of silver with its horns towards the west. I shaved myself carefully with Fergus' razor, stored part of my ration in the pocket of the mutilated trousers, shook out the jacket that I had not worn since the day Jimmy brought me to Springhill. At sunset, after I had handed in my tools, I did not go to the cabin but stole out over the pasture behind the slave quarters, took cover in a tobacco field and began to steer for the road. I had only been along it once but Josepha was pulling at my mind like a magnet. If my arm had been long enough I could have put out my finger and touched the plague office. I found the road and crossed it in order to walk in the shadow of some trees which grew on the other side and stepped out briskly. Running I thought unwise.

My heart was beating frantically from excitement. I could feel that backward-glancing, hunted look come into my eyes again. I remembered it — a feeling of strain — from my earlier experience of running away. I compared my chances now with those of that time. If I were taken now I should hardly be hanged; for if, as a raw recruit, I had been worth thirty-five pounds, today, an experienced field-hand, I was worth double. But though the penalty of failure was less so was the chance of success. In Scotland I was running in an open space, and most of my enemies were behind me, here I had only Josepha to make for, and all men were my enemies.

Presently the trees ended and the ground on either hand was covered with tobacco. This was the Tessimadi plantation. I felt an inward shiver as I thought of all that I had heard about that place. There was a strip of long lush grass along the side of the road and there was nothing between it and the tobacco plants of the fields. There was little cover, so I skulked along near the edge of the fields trying to go swiftly, and carefully at the same time. I left Tessimadi upon my right. The house, and the drying sheds, the stables, the outbuildings and the slave cabins, I passed them all, solid shadows upon the velvet surface of the night. I could see the little lights and the glow of the fires at which the slaves were cooking their evening meal. Tessimadi lay so near the road that I could even hear the music that came in snatches from the house. Oldfield was holding one of his parties. I cursed him as I hurried past.

The grass was soft under my feet and the edges of the tobacco leaves brushed my cheek and shoulder with little soughing noises as I hugged their shelter. Presently, with a suddenness that paralysed me I heard, just ahead of me in the darkness, a snorting sound. I darted into the tobacco field and stood rigid. I dare not penetrate far lest the rustling betray me to whoever, or whatever, was there in the gloom. The shadow deepened and took shape. It was a man on horseback. He was riding on the grass, or else the dust in the road was so thick that there had been no sound of hoofs and if the horse had not snorted I should have run into him. He passed: but just as I was drawing breath again there was a rustling near me, something cold touched my bare shin and as I drew back a dog's menacing growl rose from under my feet, a dog's sharp teeth were driven into my shin. With difficulty I restrained a cry of pain and terror, and doubling my fist brought it down on the creature's nose with all my power. It gave a cry through its nose, like a little whistle, but it held on. I took hold of a nearby plant to steady myself, and with my free leg dealt it a heavy kick in the ribs. It let go and drew back, snarling and yelping. The rider had halted his horse at the sound of the first growl and now called in an arrogant voice, the voice of one accustomed to exacting obedience,

"Come out and show yourself, whoever you are."

I stood perfectly still.

"Seize him, Patty, good dog," said the voice and I braced myself for another attack. But the dog was wary of me and merely exchanged the yelping for a shrill bark.

"What the devil is it then?" asked the dog's master. I heard the horse turn and plunge into the field, not two rows from where I stood. Encouraged by support so near at hand Patty came on again. Should I bear another bite without retaliating and hope that she would draw off and her master believe that only some small animal was in the field, or should I meet the attack half-way? I hesitated and was lost. The teeth met in my leg again and did not unclose. She growled through her clenched teeth. I kicked her. She growled.

She was a grand dog, a courageous, persistent dog, but no friend to me. I put down my hands and seized her throat in a last desperate attempt to loosen her teeth by throttling her. She turned like a snake, let go my leg and sank her teeth in my fingers. As I withdrew my hand she held on and swung from it. Simultaneously the horse burst through the plants and the rider, leaning down, had me by the shoulder.

"What the devil are you doing, skulking about in there?"

I said, as boldly as I could,

"Call your dog off at once, sir. She has my hand still." Clearly he had expected some recalcitrant Negro to begin mopping and mowing. He was taken aback.

"'Lease him, Patty. Good dog. Guard! Now will you explain your business?"

"I was taking a short cut when your devil of a dog set about me. Such a dog ought not to be loose on the road."

"Had you been on the road she would have passed you. Your position in the field, your silence when she attacked you, invite suspicion. What is your name?"

"For that matter what is yours? Leave go my shoulder if you please."

"Oh no. Not quite so fast. We can't have people skulking about in tobacco fields after dark and refusing to state their business. A short cut! Whoever heard of taking a short cut through a tobacco field with a good road within three yards. You're coming up to Tessimadi, so that I can have a look at you."

"I most certainly am not. I did not accost you. The boot is on the other leg. There is no crime in walking through a field if that is the shortest way. Let go my shoulder." His fingers shifted, but only to a firmer hold. I thought, God — I'll be missed and Jimmy will be in Josepha before me. I can't stand here arguing with this fool. I twisted out of my jacket, leaving it in his hand and was off, through the plants, and on to the road. I had reckoned without that devilish dog.

"After him, Patty!"

This time the seat of my trousers. Once more the hand on my shoulder. A stunning blow with the butt of a pistol and I was being dragged, despite my struggles and protests, back up the road to Tessimadi.

There were lanterns swinging between the pillars of the veranda and behind them every window on the front of the house was blazing with light. A Negro ran forward from the shadows to take my captor's horse.

"Never mind the horse, he'll stand. Hold this fellow a minute."

The Negro held me, all too closely, while the man alighted, and then, taking the back of my neck in a vice-like grip, he shoved me before him and up the shallow steps into the house.

"I thought as much," he said, as the light fell on my bare feet and shorn trousers. The hat had been lost in the struggle.

"Jimmy Standish's red-headed Scotchman that was such a bargain! I say, Oldfield, I say, all of you, come here!" I used to call that way to mother when I came back to the steading with a good catch by rod or snare.

They poured through the wide double doors at the end of the hall, men and women, a party of them, all finely clad and all agog with interest. Oldfield I recognised; Mac had pointed him out to me with a few enlightening words and curses one day when he had visited at Springhill. He came bustling forward, a thin yellow-faced man, riddled with malaria.

"Cartell," he exclaimed, "my dear fellow, we had given you up. What have you got there?"

"Jimmy Standish's red-haired fellow. Caught him in a tobacco field just down the road. And do you know the swine had the insolence to ask me my name when I asked him his. Can you beat that?"

Somebody tittered and somebody else said, "He's bleeding all over the rug."

"Here, get on to the tiles," said Cartell, giving me a push. "Don't worry about the blood, ladies. He has plenty to spare; cool his head. Patty got him. Good Patty. And do you know what the first thing he said to me was? 'Call your dog off at once, sir; she has my hand.' That's the kind of rubbish Jimmy encourages. He'll be sorry for it some day, mark my words."

"Where is Jimmy?" someone asked.

"He'll be here presently," said Oldfield. "And what a delightful surprise for him. It'll be like the shepherd who had the hundred sheep and one strayed. I make no doubt he'll carry him back on his shoulders."

"Are you speaking of my father?" asked a clear acid voice from the back of the group by the double doors.

Oldfield coloured beneath his yellow. "I'm sorry, Miss Avril," he said. "I'd forgotten that you were there.

And you even must admit that your father's ideas are slightly peculiar."

"I might admit it, Mr. Oldfield, but only to myself."

She had worked herself forward until she was near the front and I looked at her with interest. I had never seen her close at hand before though Fergus had once pointed out a flying figure on horseback and said, "Miss Avril that is. Poor lass, she's homely." Looking at her now I saw that Fergus' idealistic eye and kindly heart had dictated that term. She was the ugliest young woman I had ever seen. Her forehead was so steep and narrow and her chin so thick and broad that her face was like an inverted pear. Black eyebrows met above small black eyes and the smudge of them spoiled the eyes that might have been her best feature, for they were bright and lively looking. In figure she was like her father, thick and sturdy, and her dress of stiff plum-coloured silk entirely failed to lend her dignity while it accorded ill with her sallow complexion. A homely lass indeed. But not without character. In front of that crowd who were gloating over me with an intensity out of all proportion with the occasion, an intensity that showed how deep was the feeling of enmity between the slave and those he served, she came forward and said in that loud clear voice,

"I think something should be done about that leg and that hand. He's losing a lot of blood, and dogs' teeth are often poisonous."

"I agree, Miss Avril. I think the wounds should be cauterised."

141

There was a note of gloating in Oldfield's voice. Through the throbbing of my lacerated flesh a premonitory pang made itself felt. My whole being drew itself together into a tight knot of resistance and I found myself supplicating a power that I no longer wholly believed in for strength, for endurance, so that I should not cry out and gratify these gloating spectators.

With the air of men bestowing charity Oldfield and Cartell offered to "dress" my wounds themselves. The rest of the party crowded, chattering, through the double doors. It was plain that my recapture had lent an unusual zest to the evening. The music began again.

The two men pushed and dragged me through another door and into the kitchen quarters, where in one large room with an enormous fire at either end, a number of people were busily engaged, basting the joints that hung on the spits, piling fruit into dishes, preparing mounds of vegetables. A stout Negress in a voluminous apron was supervising all these activities. Oldfield pushed away the cooks and the cooking apparatus from the more distant fire and himself heated the iron. Half swooning with horror I watched it grow redder, saw him withdraw, felt the heat of its approach. If I can bear this I shall never mind anything again. Drive the top teeth into the lower lip so that any sound may be muffled. Not to call out when the iron meets my sizzling flesh. If mortally possible not to faint or groan. You think too much of this poor flesh, Colin lad. God has to do with souls not with bodies. Does it matter whether my flesh is whole or broken? It matters now. Oh God, it matters now. There is nothing, nothing in the whole world but this agony. No soul, no mind, nothing but this scorched and tortured flesh.

Oldfield was disappointed. Never were wounds so thoroughly cauterised! But he had no sport. I bore, in that first instant, an eternity of pain, then I fainted.

They must have left me then, for when I came to myself I was in the corner of the kitchen and the stout Negress was pouring water over my head while another, younger one was endeavouring to open my mouth so that she might force a spoon between my lips. But my upper teeth had penetrated the flesh so that the canines rested on my lower teeth. Before I could unclench them the old Negress hissed and instantly they were both on their feet, tending the joints by the fire. Through the open kitchen door came Oldfield, Cartell, another man and Jimmy Standish. I scrambled to my feet and stood weakly by the wall. Jimmy came over to me. His face was set and serious. For the first time I found myself unable to meet his eyes and stared down at the plump short legs in the fine breeches of russet coloured silk. I saw him shake back the ruffles at his wrists before he lifted my injured fingers. Then he looked at my leg. Finally, with the cat smile he looked into my face and said, "You must prove everything, mustn't you, Scottie? Who bit your mouth?"

"Not Patty," I mumbled.

He turned to Oldfield, and his smile was more heartless than ever as he said smoothly,

"They brand runaways, don't they? Thank you for sparing me the job. And thank you, Cartell, for catching him. I'm much obliged to you. Now where is Patty? She should be congratulated too." He turned away and then spoke to me over his shoulder.

"If Mr. Oldfield will allow it you may wait here and come back with me. Will that be all right, Oldfield?" Calmly and coolly as ever he went away. I didn't hate him this time.

Directly he had gone the two Negresses dropped their work and turned back to me. The little one took a bottle from her apron pocket and held it to me. "You can drink properly now," she said, in a voice that made me think of velvet. The older one went over to a cupboard and rumbled about in it for some minutes. When she came back she had a little pot in her hand.

"Ah uses this when Ah bu'ns mahseff. Smudder it on liberal. An' on yo' mouf as well. Aunt Iley's ointment that is, an' pow'ful good stuff fo' killin' pain."

I dipped into the black and pungent paste and smothered it on liberally as she had directed. It did take some of the agony out, and no doubt for a surface burn, such as a cook sustains frequently, it was invaluable, but my severed nerves and muscles were beyond the comfort of potions. I applied myself to the bottle, gasped as the rum burned its way down my throat and before long was experiencing the solace, the numbing quality of the spirit.

"Yo' may sit in mah chair," said the fat one, "an' bineby when Ah has gotten dis dinner offen mah han's Ah will give yo' sumfun to support yo'seff."

She pulled forward a substantial chair, the only one in the kitchen, and I sat down upon it, watching the dinner being dished and carried through into the front

THE HOUSE OF BONDAGE

of the house. I forced myself to take interest in the proceedings, noting the dishes, counting the cooking pans, apprising the skill and nimbleness with which the fat woman worked, the authoritative tone she used to her underlings. I must occupy my mind and keep the surface of it occupied, so that I could withstand the dreary thoughts that attacked it, my failure, the present pain, the certainty of punishment to come.

When the dinner was served the fat woman and the rest of them, all except the little Negress with the velvet voice, went out to "catch a breff of air." With nothing else now to look at I studied the girl carefully. I realised for the first time that a young Negress can be very graceful and pretty.

This one was slim and rounded and her frock of coloured print, with its sleeves rolled above her elbows and its front covered by a white apron, emphasised the lines and curves of her figure, the neat round waist, the prominent pointed breasts, the straight back. Her black crinkly hair was drawn into a knot high on the back of her head, so that the clear line from which it grew was visible at forehead and nape and over the ears. The ears themselves were pierced and had little studs of gold in them. My mind gave a leap. Oldfield, as well as Cartell, was reported to have a coloured mistress. Was this the one? It was possible, but of course I had nothing to go upon save the gold in her ears, the extra clarity of her speech and her general desirability. It was over the last that I now brooded. She was prettier than Janet, smaller, daintier, and being all the same colour she

escaped the suggestion of bucolic coarseness which
Janet's red cheeks had always given her.

I didn't speak to her because I could think of only
two things to say, "What is your name?" and "Are you
happy here?" And in both these, as I tried them over, I
detected a tang of patronising curiosity. So we were
silent until she said,

"You haven't been at Springhill long, have you?"

"How do you know?"

"Because you wouldn't try to run away if you had."
There was the most intense conviction in those simple
words. She smiled, and I watched with pleasure the way
in which her full lips curved back from her even white
teeth.

"What's your name?"

"Colin really, but at Springhill I'm called Scottie —
because I come from Scotland, you know."

"I see. I suppose that is why you were so brave just
now."

"Why?"

"Because the Scotties are always brave. I've heard
Mr. Oldfield say so. He won't ever buy one. He says,"
she wrinkled her brow in the effort to recall the phrase,
"that they break before they bend. Or should it be the
other way? Anyway he won't have them. Why are there
so many of you?"

"We've been having a war in our country, and a lot of
bad luck."

"You're young, aren't you?"

"I'm eighteen."

"Oo, younger than me. I'll be twenty soon."

"What's your name?"

"Poppy."

"I like that."

"I like yours, too. And your hair."

I couldn't think of anything else to say. It became more difficult every moment to sit there, concentrating upon things outside myself when really I wanted to roll upon the floor and scream and groan. The comfort of the ointment and the numbness from the rum were both wearing off. Daggers of pain ran from my limbs to my brain. I wished I were dead. When Poppy said suddenly,

"I wish I was at Springhill," I dragged myself out of an abyss of pain to say,

"I wish you were, too," but the words were almost automatic.

The cook and her satellites returned to the kitchen and I was relieved to see them. I had fought against my inner wretchedness as long as I could. Now I sank into myself and under cover of the renewed noise and bustle, groaned and whimpered.

I thought that the utmost length of endurance had been wrung out of me, but when one of the Tessimadi Negroes came running some hours later to say that Mr. Standish and Miss Avril were waiting for me and I stood up hastily, I found that the muscle in my leg had stiffened. Every step was excruciating. I hobbled round to the front of the house which was all a-jostle with departing guests, calling to their attendants, soothing restive horses and exchanging bantering chat among themselves. Jimmy, who had arrived late, had come on his big cream-coloured mare, and was waiting just behind the cane carriage in which Miss Avril, with a lacy wrap over the unbecoming frock, was seated beside Abraham.

"Come on," said Jimmy to me, "walk between the carriage and the horse."

"Oh, surely you'll let him ride, Jimmy," said one of the men, mockingly, "he's got a bad leg you know."

Jimmy gave his cat smile. "I'm committing this apparent brutality, Dodder, in order that his leg shouldn't stiffen. It's the truest kindness. Good night, Oldfield, and many thanks for an agreeable evening. And thanks again, Cartell, to you. All right, Abraham, off you go."

I longed for the moment when the darkness should swallow us. The humiliation of that moment remained with me for the rest of my life. So many of them, all well fed, well mounted, or in good carriages, well clad, well pleased with themselves, all smiling at Jimmy, whom they liked although they teased him, all staring at me, as limping, ragged, swollen mouthed, I got into position with the mare's nose at my shoulder and began to hobble away.

I thought of the distance up to where the Springhill road began, and the distance of the rough track after that, with every step sending a special pang through the constant grind and ache in my leg. I tried walking on the toe only, keeping the muscle contracted. It was better for a while, but it brought on an appalling cramp in my instep. Before long the sweat was pouring off me, and my breath was coming in sobs. People passed us, cantering lightly along the sides of the road, shouting final farewells to Jimmy and Miss Avril. Hell!

We turned off the public road at last, and once inside the Springhill boundary Jimmy shouted to Abraham who drew up.

"Get into the back," he said briefly. "At this rate we shan't be home till tomorrow. Get along now, Abraham."

We bowled rapidly along the familiar road and stopped before the house where a solitary lantern hung by the door.

"Get along to your quarters. I'll see you in the morning," said Jimmy. I gathered my last remnant of strength to say,

"It was very good of you to let me ride."

"I was in a hurry, damn you."

I set out on the apparently endless journey that led to the cabin, Mac's "I told you so," Fergus' commiseration, and their unanimous, unspoken, but obvious certainty that badly as I fared now, I should feel far worse tomorrow.

But although the next day was one of long-drawn-out pain and fever, the first of several, not another word was spoken about my escapade. Whittle complained of my slowness and caught me several spiteful whacks with his crop, but no formal punishment came my way. Slowly the hole in my calf healed, leaving an irregular pit lined with puckered skin. One of my burned, bitten fingers healed completely, save for the scar, the other stiffened and became useless. It did not cause me much inconvenience for it was the third finger of my left hand, but I grudged it.

Gradually the memory of the experience sank into the background of my mind, and only revived when I was tempted to repeat it. Presently all that remained of it were my scars, my hatred of Oldfield and Cartell, and my memory of Poppy. I began to regard stealthily the black girls at Springhill, hoping to find there, close at hand, one with that grace, that youth, that appeal.

Quite soon I found, or persuaded myself that I had found her. She worked in the laundry and her name was Cassie. A cold and bare description of one's first, initiating love. "She worked in the laundry and her name was Cassie." Nothing there to fitly herald her arrival in my life. And indeed there was, at first, nothing in it, save the cold bare fact. No one ever set about such business in a more literal, unromantic, deliberate way. I wanted something to compensate me for the misery of my life, for the long hours of oxlike labour, the dull stretches of boredom in the cabin, the lack of freedom, the dearth of hope in the future. And I had glimpsed the possibility of pleasure as I had looked upon Poppy and found her desirable. She, or her like, had been sufficient to serve Oldfield who was rich and free and powerful, why should I scorn or neglect so possible a source of pleasure and interest?

I began to look about me at Springhill the moment I was free of pain. I, who had hitherto looked upon the Negresses with dull eyes that saw merely fellow slaves, now began to look upon them with calculation. Which one was comely, which approachable? The latter class was vastly in the majority. Outcast though the white workers were they had still the magic talisman of a white skin. I discovered in those few days that almost any woman at Springhill was willing to look upon me kindly, to respond to any greeting with more than its fellow. But of them all Cassie was the most desirable.

Her mother, who also worked in the laundry, was a half-caste, fruit of some miscegenation that had given her a pale skin but had not removed the stigma of slavery. Cassie's father was unknown at Springhill but he was probably a full blooded Negro for Cassie was much darker than her mother though less flat of nose and thick of lip than others of her colour. I began looking at her as I passed and found that she returned my gaze with interest, catching my eye and then turning away with a half-smile. When I spoke to her one evening as she was coming out of the laundry and I was leaving the tool shed, she was pleased, and smiled, touched her hair with one nervous hand and pleated her apron with the other. We arranged, with little preamble, to meet after supper in the shrubbery at the end of the vegetable garden.

"Out of this nettle, danger, I pluck this flower, safety." I had heard those words from my father's lips many times. They occurred in one of his favourite plays. And now, out of the wilderness of nettles that life had become, and to which I had added my own special plant of ill-placed and deliberate lust, I was fated to gather a flower of delight and passion, and, later on, the flower of wretchedness that passion becomes when its little hour is run. It even seemed, to my heightened fancy, that someone, long since, in planting that shrubbery of . flowering trees and bushes, had all unwittingly made a little Eden in which the old scene could be played.

She came to me, sleek and shining, with scented oil on her hair, wisdom in her eyes and hunger on her lips. She restored to me something that I had lost when Jimmy had said "A new man of mine" that day in the plague office. I went into that shrubbery a resentful, beaten boy for whom the future held nothing but a dull round of hard work and frustration; I came out knowing that there was just one place on earth where I was master, where being a slave didn't matter, where a slave might be equal with a king; knowing too, that the future held, with any luck, innumerable occasions upon which I could both give and receive pleasure. Once again I remembered Fergus' words. "You think too much of this poor flesh, Colin lad." Then here was an opportunity for the flesh to repay me a little of what I had suffered through it.

That was the first of many meetings which brought, when the first clumsiness and awkwardness was past, an ever-increasing pleasure.

Knowing Cassie also opened another door to interest for me, in that it took me out of our cabin into the life of the black quarter. I got to know Jacko who was always experimenting with his home-made still and turning out varying brands of corn-brew. Jacko was one of the Mandigoes of whom Jimmy Standish had said that they could steal with their toes as well as their hands. There was always some evidence of his skill somewhere about his person or his cabin. And he was always ready to swop the proceeds of a theft or of his still for a slice of fat pork.

Twice a week, on Tuesdays and Fridays, we were served with about a pound of fat pork apiece. Most of us seized this ration eagerly for it was the main variant in a monotonous diet of meal and potatoes. On Springhill these things were rationed generously, and we had fruit occasionally; but pork came only twice a week and the Negroes looked forward to it like children. I found it quite easy to resist. I had tired of pork before I left childhood behind, and this was much fatter than that which we had eaten at Braidlowrie. I think the climate had something to do with it, too, for though I was working as I had never before worked I found my appetite far more fickle and I was always glad to trade my share of the meat for an egg, a melon, a bunch of onions or a gourd of corn-brew or any other of the unlikely things that Jacko was capable of producing.

He lived in a filthy shack which he shared with a very musical Negro named Timmy and two women, Madda and Sylvy, who were their wives according to the loose ideas of matrimony that obtained in the cabins. They had a crowd of piccaninnies, and seemed, miraculously, I thought, to be able to distinguish which were their own. Madda was half-sister to Cassie, so we were always specially welcome in the shack, where, for that matter, hospitality of a kind was very free.

Timmy owned a banjo which he treasured far more dearly than he did his Sylvy or his offspring, though, in common with most of the blacks, he was kind and indulgent to his family. The banjo, however, was his comfort and joy and for hours on end in the soft early darkness after supper he would sing to its accompaniment. And gradually, one by one, all the Negroes within earshot would steal up, darker shadows on the night; and squatting down, just within or just outside the cabin, they would sway on their haunches and join in the mournful crooning.

With very few exceptions the songs were all on the same theme, the hardships to be endured in this life contrasted with the pleasures to be expected in the life to come. A few, a very few, were a variety of love songs verging on the bawdy.

"Hold Up Yo' Heart" was a great favourite, and a good example of the former kind. The mellow strumming, the minor voices, the hollow drumming of hands or feet to the rhythm, combined to make the sing-songs things to remember.

Hold up yo' heart
Towards de sun,
An' ply yo' hoe
Till day is done
An' dere'll be rest
Fo' ebbery one.
Hold up yo' heart
Poor nigger. Poor nigger.
Hold up yo' heart

Poor nigger.
Hold up yo' heart
An' keep it high,
An' think of Hebben
By an' by.
Yo' won't be hoein'
In de sky.
Hold up yo' heart
Poor nigger. Poor nigger.
Hold up yo' heart
Poor nigger.

That was certain to be repeated four or five times at every sing-song. The most decent and the most popular of the love songs was known as "Keepin' dem Sheep." Once started they found difficulty in ending this one. It went on and on, a thing of endless repetition.

Jacob worked fo' his gal,
Keepin' dem sheep, keepin' dem sheep,
    keepin' dem sheep,
Jacob worked fo' his gal.

Adam worked fo' his gal,
Hoein' dat garden, hoein' dat garden,
    hoein' dat garden,
Adam worked fo' his gal.

Dis man work fo' dis gal,
Totin' dis load, totin' dis load,

> totin' dis load,
> Dis man work fo' dis gal,
>
> Pleasure all de same,
> Keepin' dem sheep, hoein' dat garden,
>   totin' dis load.
> Pleasure all de same fo' Jacob,
> Pleasure all de same fo' Adam,
> Pleasure all de same fo' dis man.

They always started off with Jacob. I wondered why, since Adam was first. But as they went from Jacob to Adam and back again, worked on to "dis man" and then went back to either Adam or Jacob it didn't matter much. I used to wonder, too, where the songs came from, who made them, how did they spread? Some, no doubt, were indigenous to certain plantations, but there were others that seemed almost universal. Sometimes, from my place by Cassie's side, I sang, or beat my foot to the rhythm, and I learned that these primitive people had discovered the secret of the value of rhythm for dissipating weariness. I have gone to Jacko's cabin at times when I was too weary to walk, far far too weary to take Cassie away to one of our quiet places, and after an hour of Timmy's strumming risen up invigorated as by a night's rest.

I found myself swinging my hoe and stripping leaves, even making the holes to take the seedlings to the chopped metre of Timmy's songs. It was a not negligible ease to labour. And Cassie gave me ease of body and mind, just as Jacko's corn-brew eased another part of me, which would rise up now and then because of this same ease. Unless Jacko had made a bad brew, which occasionally happened, or the latest still had been discovered and raided, or my own hunger had driven me to consume my trade pork, I seldom went to bed completely sober. Fergus took his courage in his hands — I could see that some minutes before the words came — and remonstrated with me. But I rounded on him quite fiercely and forced him to agree that since life had so little to offer of comfort and nothing of promise it was best not to despise the paltry gifts she allowed us. I passed into a state of quiescence that had in it some of the seeds of happiness.

So the sorting season came again, humid and harassing. Fergus went creaking about with his head on one side and his face drawn with pain. After the sorting came the sales and after those the distribution of new clothes, seeds for those of us who had energy enough to cultivate little gardens, and rum for everybody. Two days were given up to the wearing of new clothes, and eating and drinking and singing and then we went back to work preparing the beds of deep sifted soil and wood ash in which the tobacco seeds were sown. I had started my fourth year at Springhill.

Just after the holiday, always known as "The Thanking Days," things began to go wrong between Cassie and me. On two separate occasions I had waited in vain for her at our meeting place; and going at last to the cabin where she lived with her mother and three other women, and then to Jacko's, had failed to find her in either place. The first time it happened I sidled up next morning to the laundry door and stole a word with her.

"What happened last night, Cassie? I waited a long time, then I went on to Jacko's, and your cabin. Where were you?"

She had come to the door straight from the wash-tub, and there were silvery flakes of foam on her hands and arms. At my question she gave me a sidelong glance and then, picking up the corner of her apron, carefully wiped her hands as she said,

"Ah just was vurry busy, Colin."

"Oh," I said, leaping to the conclusion, the welcome conclusion, that she had been working. "I see. You were here. I didn't think of that." She dropped her head slightly and looked at me under her lashes and said with eagerness,

"Uh-huh. Ah wuz wukkin' heah."

"Well, can you come tonight? I'll wait. I don't mind how long I wait if you'll come."

"Shoulden think Ah'll be late attall tonight. Ah suttinly will be theah."

She gave me her sudden smile, which was like the glint of sunlight that sometimes shoots from the edge of a dark cloud. I clasped her warm damp hand in mine and darted back to my work. Once or twice during the day I remembered that sidelong glance, the eagerness, and the downheld head, but chiefly I thought of them dotingly. She had so many pretty ways, and just then I found every gesture and turn of her head delightful.

She came to the shrubbery that evening and we made up for lost time.

But on the second time that she failed to meet me, after waiting a long time I crept across to the laundry. It was all in darkness and when I tried the door it was locked. Something prompted me then to return to my cabin and go to bed. I could wait then till morning and if Cassie should say that she had been working I should know that she was lying. But I didn't want to catch her out in a lie. I admitted that to myself as I stood there miserably planning my next move. I wanted to know where she was, with whom and why. I ran as hard as I could back to the meeting place, hoping against hope that she was there. But there was no Cassie in the dark hollow, where by breaking off low-growing shoots and twigs we had made ourselves a little green-roofed shelter. I ran on to the cabin where her mother showed surprise at seeing me.

"Shore, Ah cal'kated Cassie wuz wid yo'. Ain't seen her all ev'ning."

"Perhaps I've missed her," I said, and went, without much hope, to Jacko's.

He had just sampled his latest brew. Pluggy, the barber, Abraham, Timmy and he were seated round the fire with the red light shining on their teeth and eyeballs. Jacko welcomed me vociferously.

"Come in, Scottie," he said, "an taste dis excullunt corn-brew. You's lookin' a trifle down in de mouf."

"You can't see how I look in this light," I said, on the defensive at once. "You all look like a picture of hell."

159

"Mebbe we does, but dere ain't no corn-brew in dat place liken dis corn-brew. Ah'm tellin' yo' dis corn-brew is excullunt."

He handed me the gourd. I tasted it and confirmed his verdict.

"It is good, Jacko. You get better and better. Give me some more, a good lot more. It's pork day tomorrow."

"Shore is. News of dis corn-brew get about an' Ah knows one nigger wid a full belly tomorrow."

He laughed his rumbling throaty laugh.

"Where're Madda and the children and Sylvy?" I asked.

"Dey's gorn to de preachin'," said Jacko. "Madda vurry displeased wid muh. Ah 'ngaged mahseff tuh go wid her, but den dis corn-brew wuz hollerin' tuh be tried, so Timmy and muh stayed tuh home. I's cal'kated yo' knew about de preachin' seein' Cassie ain't."

"I'd forgotten," I said; but I remembered that Cassie's mother was "all smarted up" when I'd called there. Cassie wouldn't be at the preaching though, she was no more interested in it than I was.

"Ain't no need fo' muh tuh go tuh de preachin'," Timmy said with the utmost complacency. "Dat Sylvy she pray fo' muh most ebbery day. Reckon she prayin' fo' muh dis 'dentical minnut. Ah ain't suh mad about de preachin', and Sylvy she ain't suh mad about de corn-brew, so us wuks in vurry well. Same's one holin' an' one plantin' at settin' out time. You-all'd care fo' li'l tune, huh?"

He stretched his long arm back into the shadows behind him and found the instrument which he laid on his knee.

"What you-all wishful Ah sh'd play?"

"'Ain't Got Time,' would be very suitable, in view of what you were saying just now," I said. Timmy struck an experimental note or two and then slid into the tune. Pluggy and Jacko drained their corn-brew, settled their feet and threw back their heads the better to give tongue.

Ah'm suh busy wid de wuk oll round muh,
Ain't got de time tuh talk wid God.
Oll dem fellas preacher tell us 'bout
Dey had de time tuh talk wid God.

Ah'm suh busy wid de hoe an' de plant stick,
Nebber got time tuh talk wid God.
Shan't get tuh Hebben, nebber get tuh Hebben,
Ain't got de time tuh talk wid God.

Less mah woman an' mah deah ole preacher
Takes de time tuh talk wid God.
'Splain up de case of dis busy nigger,
Ain't got de time tuh talk wid God.

Tonight I did not join in the singing. I sat there thinking about Cassie, and suddenly it struck me that she might be with someone else. I repulsed the thought because I felt sure of her, but it came back with renewed force. There was a legend, I remembered, I

161

suppose it existed on every plantation where black and white were gathered together, to the effect that though the love of a white man was a thing to covet because it gave "style" and was evidence of a girl's attractiveness, it was not to be compared, from the point of view of pleasure, with that of a black man. That legend was repeated every time a coloured mistress fell from power because of unfaithfulness with a man of her own colour. And a surprising number of them did so. The Negroes cherished the legend among themselves perhaps as a deterrent to their women, perhaps as a sop to their own vanity. Dispossessed and less than the dust as we are, said the legend, we still have this. I remembered this now. Was Cassie, at this moment, lying beneath some big buck who was giving her something I couldn't? I had to know.

I got up, set down my gourd, thanked Jacko for the corn-brew and promised to see him tomorrow when the pork was given out, and went into the night. I was ashamed to go again, openly, to her mother's cabin but I was drawn towards it as by a magnet. I hid myself on the other side of the cinder path and watched. After a short time I heard voices and saw Cassie's mother and the woman who shared the cabin come home. They had been to the preaching.

"Iff'n dat Cassie ain bin home an' mended dat fire we's get cold welcome," I heard one of them say. And from the expressions of dissatisfaction that arose after they had entered the cabin, I knew that Cassie had not been home.

162

I settled down in the position that I had once found so difficult to adopt and which now came easily to me, crosslegged with my elbows on my knees and my hands cupped beneath my chin, and I waited. There was a heavy dew, and my clothes grew clammy. Presently everybody in the slave quarter was indoors and quiet if not asleep. Somewhere a baby woke and wailed and somebody hushed it. The silence grew deeper. A dog barked from the courtyard, and far away, from Tessimadi perhaps or Claremont, another answered it across the dividing darkness.

The corn-brew was working in me and I grew heavy. I stretched myself across the path and waited, lying on my back. So many, many stars. "Peepholes into the golden glory," one of the nigger songs called them. A pretty thought, but for me meaningless. My failure, despite my most desperate efforts, to follow Fergus' flights of imagination, had convinced me that belief in a spiritual world was a thing that you either had or hadn't, like a sense of music, or direction. And I hadn't it. Until I had arrived at Springhill I had given the matter little thought. I had been brought up in the Catholic faith, but the Catholicism at Braidlowrie had been like the gentility, a thing of memory rather than actuality. Still it had suffered. Since I had been at Springhill, however, I had considered the question of religion very earnestly. It mattered to me in my present state. For if this life were only a transitory thing, a preparation, an ante-room to "golden glory" then Fergus was right in thinking and saying that what happened to you in it didn't matter. But if you felt, as I most assuredly and miserably did, that this was all of life that you could be sure of, then it mattered damnably. And it mattered, it mattered, it mattered, that Cassie hadn't met me and hadn't yet come home.

And then, admitting that, I was ashamed. How far had I fallen, that I, Colin Lowrie, son of a long and honourable line, should be lying here on the cinder path outside a slave cabin waiting to find out why a black girl had failed to meet me.

Suppose Mrs. Thatcher had prophesied this on that evening when I was so proud and scornful. How I should have sneered, and laughed. I had an impulse to get up and go away while there was still time, and never to look at or speak to Cassie again. But infatuation, with a dash of curiosity, kept me chained and I lay and waited and listened.

At last I heard a bird fly up with a startled cry from the Big Pasture, the meadow where the riding horses roamed and grazed. I got up and going carefully over the shifting cinders of the path, reached the end and stood by the gate that led into the pasture. A foot-path led from there to a similar gate at the far end, and beyond the farther gate was the house where Whittle the overseer lived. The moon had risen during my vigil and the dewy grass of the pasture shone silver. It was beautiful, unearthly, but I had no eye for its beauty. For hurrying along, keeping to the foot-path and holding her skirts high above the damp grass that bordered it, was Cassie. Cassie coming by moonlight from Whittle's house!

Her eyes were on the path and she was quite near the gate before she saw me leaning against it. She dropped her skirt and her hands flew to her breast in the ancient, traditional gesture of a startled woman. She stood still and looked round like a frightened animal, then turned and was half-way across the meadow again before it dawned on me that she had not recognised me and was just terrified of the waiting figure. I vaulted the gate and flew in pursuit, yelling, "Cassie, Cassie, it's only me. Don't be frightened."

I saw her glance back over her shoulder, run another step or two and then stop. I caught up with her and twisted her towards me so that the moonlight fell on her face.

"I was waiting for you," I gasped. "What have you been doing?"

She said, hysterically, "Oh. Oh. Oh. Oh deah. Ah thought yo' wuz a ghostie. Oh Colin. Oh deah. Shore Ah wuz skeered. Ah's niver been suh skeered in all mah days. Oh deah."

I could see her hands and face twitching. I forgot my suspicions, my long waiting, even the fact that she had come from Tottie Samson's. I remembered only the Negro's great fear of the supernatural, remembered that this was my little Cassie. My arm went round her and I held her without speaking until she stopped twitching.

"There," I said at last, as if speaking to a child. "It's all right now, Cassie, isn't it? You aren't scared any more. You're all right with me, aren't you, Cassie?"

She smoothed her skirt and her hand went up in that way I knew so well, touching her hair.

"Ah doan mind wid yo'. But Ah doan like dis moon. De shadders leap out at yo'."

"You shouldn't be out as late as this," I said. "What have you been doing?"

"Ah bin washin'. Dat man ain got no feelings. Keepin' muh washin' way into de night."

"Is that truly what you've been doing, Cassie?"

"Shore. Ah's bin washin' up at Mistah Whittle's house ever since de landry shut."

"Why didn't your mother go? She's a better launderer than you are and Tottie is particular about his linen."

"Oh, shore, Colin. Ma is shore better dan muh. But Ma, she got oll set tuh go tuh dis preachin'. Dat's why Ah go."

"Then I think you might have let me know."

"Niver had no chance. Mistah Whittle he send fo' muh dreckly de landry shut."

It was possible. Even as I obeyed the impulse that made me reach for her hand I despised myself because her story was so possible. But by that time the hand lay in mine: a hot, unsteady little hand, and dry.

I said gravely, "Cassie, this hand hasn't been in water since the laundry closed. Come on now, tell me the truth. Why have you been to Whittle's? Or shall I guess?"

She pulled her hand from me and put it, with her other one, over her face.

166

"Ah didn' want yo' tuh know," she said in a low shamed voice.

"Why did you do it?" I said.

She brought her hands down from her face and stretched out for mine, pulling down on them in her earnestness.

"Ah couldn' help it. Dat's de trufe, Colin. Ah didden want tuh go. 'Fore Gawd I didden. Ah hate Mistah Whittle. Ah's niver even look his way."

"And this isn't the first time, is it, Cassie? There was that other night when you said you'd been working late."

"Yes," she said, "and some udder times. Ah just didn' want yo' tuh know, Colin. Doan hate muh. Shore I couldn' help it. Didn' have no choice, 'cept tuh be sold away."

"Did he tell you that?"

"Yes. Vurry mad at muh he wuz, vurry mad at muh, caze Ah didn' want no truck wid him."

She began to cry. I wanted to put my arms about her and say comforting things, but the thought of Tottie kept my hands where they were, clenched at my sides. To have touched her then would have been like drinking from the same glass as Tottie, using his handkerchief, sharing his bed. I could only say,

"Don't cry, Cassie. I quite understand. And if you really don't like him, it shan't happen again. I give you my word for that."

Tears brimmed her eyes as she looked at me, amazed.

"Your word. Yo' can't do nothin'. Ain't nothin' Ah can do mahseff. Ah'm only a black nigger gal, an' though you appear tuh forgit it you's only poor white slave. Ain't no chawnce we's do nothin' agin Mistah Whittle."

"Blast Whittle. He doesn't own us. I shall go to Jimmy. He's boss. And I'll persuade him to tell Whittle to keep his filthy paws off you if I have to crawl on my knees to get him to do it."

Cassie gave a strangled cry.

"You's get muh sold away iffen yo' does dat. Doan yo' do dat, Colin. Ah'll get sold away an' nebber see you' no more. Dat's what been bodderin' muh."

"You won't be sold away, Cassie. I won't even mention your name. I shall just explain to Jimmy that I want my girl to myself. He'll understand that."

"An' yo' ain't mad at muh?"

"I'm not a bit mad at you, Cassie dear. I quite see that you couldn't help yourself. Come on now and get to bed."

"I'se dat glad yo' know, now," she said, walking with lightened step beside me to the gate. "Dat's been a heavy burden on muh soul."

"You should have told me before. And, Cassie, I'm trusting you to tell me if it happens again. I shouldn't like —" I hesitated on the brink of speech so brutal but after all it was vital to me and I wanted her to understand. "I shouldn't like to have you just after Tottie Samson, Cassie. If I found out after I'd never get over it. So please remember that. This, if I can manage it, will all blow over, but if anything of the kind ever happens again I've got to know. Is that clear?"

"Yes, Mistah . . . I mean yes, Colin," said Cassie meekly. And that involuntary, misplaced word assured me that she was impressed.

I left her at the door of her cabin and crunched off over the cinders towards my own. I realised as I lowered myself beside the protesting Fergus, that the situation was horrible, and that everything was in Whittle's favour. But even so I was relieved to find that almost four years of bondage hadn't made me meek. I was still capable of going up to the house and asking, or if that failed, demanding, to see Jimmy. And I knew too, that if Jimmy failed me, as he well might do, that I was capable of attacking Whittle himself. He might flay me afterwards, but I'd have his blood first.

My pleasure in my own capacity for indignation was probably priggish, but it is not until a man is in a position where he has nothing to depend upon except what is within him that he appreciates the strength or deplores the weakness of that last defence. I was a slave, without rights, without court of appeal. I was barefooted and my hands were horny as hoofs. I had lived for almost four years on a diet nicely calculated to conserve strength without producing spirit. My clothes were my master's cast-offs. But I was white and I was whole and sane and capable of speech. There was that in me which could drive me into Jimmy's presence and make an effort to convince him.

At the end of the day we all took our tools back to the toolhouse and stood or hung them in their proper places. Tottie Samson, or the foreman, Treacle, supervised this performance, and some degree of supervision was certainly needed, for the Negroes were most lackadaisical about property. Perhaps it was because the hoes and the planting sticks, the spades and the axes were not their own, but I had noticed a similar carelessness over their own private tools and utensils. Even under Tottie's eye some things would be thrown on the floor, or left outside.

The tools disposed of, the rations were given out through a hatch in the wall of the storehouse and then the long line of weary workers shuffled off through the twilight to make their fires and cook the supper. Tottie mounted his horse, held all ready by Abraham, and galloped off across the Big Pasture.

On this particular evening I waited until the rations were served and Tottie's horse had cleared the gate at the end of the cinder track. Then I turned, hid my ration behind the mounting block and went to the laundry. Cassie wasn't there.

"Can you let me have a little hot water to wash my face and hands?" Cassie's mother pointed to a tub from which she was baling suds, and put a piece of strong lye soap into my hands. I washed thoroughly, damped down my exuberant hair, thanked her and went across the courtyard. I tried the door of the office first, almost praying that Jimmy might be there so that I could find him without fuss or bother, but the office was dark and empty. I went along to the kitchen door.

The cook, a buxom young Negress whom I knew because her cabin was just across the path from ours, was in the kitchen with her hands in a bowl of flour.

"Hullo, Daisy," I said. "I want to see Mr. Standish about something very important. Is he in do you know?"

"Shore he's in. I heard him not two minutes ago bawling Phoebe's head offen him caze he let dem discanters get low. Phoebe'll be back'n minnut and yo' can ask him." Phoebe, despite his name, was a big buck nigger, the aristocrat of the coloured population at Springhill — the butler.

He soon appeared and Daisy repeated my request to him. He regarded me dubiously.

"Vurry onusual thing for a field hand to be boddering the master just on dinner time. Where's Mistah Whittle an all?"

"My business is with Mr. Standish, Phoebe. And it's important. Will you go and ask him if he'll spare Scottie a moment, or will you show me the way and I'll ask him myself?"

"You'll kindly behave same's any udder field hand and not go obtruding into the house. Wait there whiles I ask him." If one thing were needed to strengthen my determination not to be like "any udder field hand" it was that, coming from Phoebe. I waited with what patience I could muster. Phoebe returned and said pompously,

"The master is in a intense hurry, but he will see you for one minnut. Come this way."

I followed him along a corridor where underfoot the rugs slid on the highly polished floor and into a room which to my unaccustomed eyes seemed very brightly lighted. So bright that I had to blink and screw up my eyes before I saw Jimmy who was standing before the hearth with a glass in his hand. He was holding it towards the light and then sniffing at it speculatively. Without noticing me he addressed Phoebe.

"*Is* this the Everett, Phoebe?"

"Yes, sah. It is."

"Well, I doubt it. I doubt it very much."

The sulky look that comes easily to a spoiled Negro appeared on Phoebe's broad black face. He was the butler, he had said it was Everett, and that should be enough for anybody. I looked towards the table, expecting to see the lop-sided, greenish bottle, but saw instead a heavy cut-glass decanter with a silver band round its neck and a silver label hanging from a silver chain.

Jimmy tasted again, and sniffed.

"I think you're wrong again, you old dunderhead. This is good, but I don't think it's Everett. I suppose I shall have to come down and see for myself. I wanted Everett specially. Mr. Oldfield and two friends are coming and he would know in an instant."

"That's Everett sah, shore is."

I went another step into the room.

"If you would allow me to taste it, sir, I could tell you in a moment whether it's Everett or not."

"What the devil . . ." Jimmy began, turning sharply, "ah, yes, the Scots gentleman, of course. So you're a

172

judge of brandy, are you?" Phoebe looked at me as though his eyes were going to start out of his head.

"No," I said bluntly, "I am not. But I cut my teeth, so to speak, on Everett and I think I should know it again. May I try?"

Jimmy handed me a glass without a word. I tasted. Silk on the tongue, fire in the throat, Spring in the veins? No. Nevertheless a sudden doubt assailed me. Fanshawe's Everett had been very old. Perhaps this was of the same make but of a different time. I might be wrong and cover myself with shame. Odd as it may sound I dreaded to do that. But no, if this were kept a thousand years it would never be the same. It lacked something. I set the glass on the table.

"That's not Everett to my mind," I said firmly.

Phoebe swelled. Even his pursed lips bulged. Jimmy said,

"Nor to mine. Bring a bottle of the Everett, Phoebe. Bring the *bottle*, mind."

Phoebe stalked away. Jimmy lifted his coat tails and lowered himself into a chair. He did not ask me what I wanted and I waited for him to speak, so there was silence until Phoebe returned.

"Now two glasses."

Phoebe, with another glare at me, set two glasses before his master and retreated. Jimmy poured out two measures of the brandy and shoved one towards me.

"Try that."

I thanked him and took up the glass. This was Everett. I felt its peculiar quality as soon as I swallowed the first sip.

"That's more like it, isn't it?"

"This is Everett, all right," I said. Swallowing hastily I added, "I wanted to see you, Mr. Standish, about some thing rather awkward. It may not seem much to you, but it means a great deal to me."

"All right, out with it."

"It's about Mr. Whittle . . ."

Jimmy's manner immediately stiffened.

"If it's a complaint, Scottie, you must understand that Mr. Whittle does nothing without my approval, so I can't . . ."

"Well, it *is* a complaint," I said, "and I reckon Mr. Whittle didn't ask your approval about this either. It's about a girl. As far as such a thing can be said in the circumstances she belongs to me. She likes me and I like her. Now I find that under threat of selling her away, Tottie Samson is making her go up to his house and . . ."

"*Who* is? What has this to do with Mr. Whittle?"

I realised what a slip I had made and could have bitten out my tongue.

"I'm extremely sorry. That just slipped out."

"You mean that that is what you call Mr. Whittle among yourselves? What was it? Say it again."

"Tottie Samson," I mumbled.

"And why do you call him that?"

"I don't know. It's just a name."

"I'll lay it's got a meaning, too. And I'll lay you know what it is. Come on, what is it?"

"'Tottie' I can't explain. But Samson had a lot of hair, you know — and you've seen his efforts to grow a

174

beard, like yours, sir, haven't you? So we call him Samson. Only among ourselves, Fergus and Mac and me. It amuses us, and we're rather short of amusement."

"It amuses me too," said Jimmy, stroking his own growth thoughtfully. "So you object to sharing your girl with your overseer. Is that it?"

"That's what it amounts to. She objects too."

"I see. Well, Scottie, since everything has to be explained to you, I'll explain this. Mr. Whittle, despite his deficiency of beard, is a very capable and trustworthy overseer. So long as he serves me as well as he has done, I have no objection to his taking his fun where he can find it. Plantation life offers little opportunity for amusement, as you so truly remark."

"There are other girls," I said.

"And other men. I suppose that if I began to interfere in a matter like this, I should have a constant stream of visits from disgruntled field hands. And I shouldn't have an overseer very long either. You see that?"

"I see."

"There's another thing too. Why did you pick on Cassie?"

"Cassie?"

"Don't play the innocent, Scottie. Of course it's Cassie. We aren't all blind, you know. You picked on Cassie because she's the comeliest little piece around here at the moment. And no doubt Mr. Whittle thought so too. He doesn't know Everett from corn-brew, but I don't doubt he's a judge in other departments. I'm rather surprised that the complaint has come from you. I wonder he hasn't warned you off. You should think yourself very fortunate that he doesn't mind sharing with you."

I thought — I should just like him to mention it to me: but I said nothing. I realised that it had been hopeless from the first. Cassie was quite right, there was nothing we could do. Realisation of my own foolish presumption came over me in a sick wave. I looked into a future without meetings in the shrubbery, for I could not share Cassie with Whittle, and since he was the overseer and I the field hand, his she must be. Must she? I'd kill him first!

"You'd better get out of the house before you burst," Jimmy said mockingly. Then he added, without change of voice, "As my overseer Mr. Whittle's amorous adventures are outside my province. But I will ask him, as my son-in-law to be, to strengthen himself against the charms of little black girls."

I ignored the promise, though it was the very thing that I had come to beg for, and thought only of the threat in that mocking sentence.

"You're never going to let him marry Miss Avril," I blurted.

"Dear me, Scottie, you haven't got a claim there, too?" he said, to my intense amazement.

"He's not good enough. Why, he isn't even white," I said. He raised his brows and stuck out his lower lip. "It's not for me to say that I suppose," I faltered, "but there it is, and if I were her father I shouldn't think he was a match for Miss Avril."

"Well, that you see is all a matter of opinion. And in this case the opinion is neither yours, my haughty Scots gentleman, nor mine. My daughter is a very headstrong young woman and has reached years of discretion. He'll be her husband, not yours nor mine. The business has a practical advantage too. I can't hope to live forever, you know."

"It'll be an ill day for Springhill when he steps into your shoes," I said.

"He may have grown a beard by then," said Jimmy lightly, rising as he spoke. "And I think you may set your mind at rest about the other matter. Good night."

I went out of the house quickly, but once outside I dawdled about, thinking. Jimmy's whole attitude puzzled me. His standards were so queer. He didn't care much for Tottie, that was quite clear to me. Yet he was allowing his daughter to marry him. He had been considerate to me, hearing me out and giving me a measure of his best brandy; yet he had taken obvious pleasure in throwing "Scots gentleman" in my teeth and in making me believe for quite a long time that if Tottie wanted Cassie he must have her. Most surprising of all he had asked me that question about objecting to Miss Avril's marriage.

And why did she wish to marry Tottie? Had no one else asked her? And was that because she was so dreadfully unattractive? Surely she could have found a husband without difficulty. She was Jimmy's only child and heir to Springhill. She couldn't love that yellow-eyed sprawling ape. Why had she thought of it? And now, Good God, now, he would be master of the plantation and all who worked upon it. We'd all suffer, and we three white men would suffer worst of all. The very sight of us was bad for him. What a prospect!

I got back to the cabin. Fergus was smoking and Mac was picking his teeth with a long thorn. That reminded me that I had left my supper behind the mounting block. I was too disheartened to go back for it. I was too disheartened, even, to tell them the news. In my mind I framed the shattering sentence, "I heard tonight that Tottie is going to marry Jimmy's daughter." I framed it, but the thought of how Mac would rage and prophesy disaster and how Fergus would be philosophical and say don't worry about the future, dried the words on my tongue. I went off to meet Cassie. For her, at least, I had a scrap of good news.

Two days later everyone on the plantation knew about the match. The sewing girls had been set to work upon the wedding gown. Tottie strutted like a peacock and made yet another abortive effort to grow a beard.

Everywhere in the cabins the news was received gloomily. Tottie the overseer was bad enough, but Tottie the prospective son-in-law and heir was far worse. And yet, such is human nature, Negro nature especially, the actual wedding-day was made the occasion for the wildest rejoicing.

It was arranged to take place just after the first spring rains which were a sign for the seedlings to be planted. Two days were given up to the festivities. For a full week beforehand relatives had been arriving and the house was full to overflowing. The wedding was on Thursday and on Wednesday evening the clergyman was fetched from Josepha, and Cassie and a number of other girls sat up half the night making garlands to hang from the ceiling of the dining-room where an altar had been set up, and decorating the house with fresh flowers.

Everybody seemed to forget that it was Whittle, the hated Whittle who was marrying his master's daughter. It was a wedding, a full dress, extravagant wedding, and that was all that mattered. The only dissentient voices were in our cabin, where Fergus said,

"It's a mercy that her mother didn't live to see the day. Though I doubt very much whether it would ever have happened then."

"Did you know Jimmy's wife?"

"Aye. She was a very sweet lady and she died untimely. They were very devoted. They used to walk about hand-in-hand and laugh. We often saw them. He's never been the same since she died. There's been a lack in him. Jimmy doesn't really care about anything any more. That's why yon Tottie has got such a hold. Jimmy's kind enough, but only because it comes easier to him."

"And I suppose he's letting this happen because it's easy, too."

"That's the only reason I can see," said Fergus. "And we must hope and pray that Jimmy Standish lives to be a very old man and keeps his legs and his wits."

I had expected philosophy from Fergus. This proof that he, too, feared Whittle's rule was disquieting.

On the wedding-day everybody of note in the island was at Springhill. The lawns in front of the house were like flower gardens with the plumes and dresses of the women, the bright coats and breeches of the men. The Big Pasture looked like a horse fair. All the girls of Cassie's age had been given new dresses of flowered print and small frilly aprons and little caps. They were to serve the guests. The rest of us, apart from unharnessing and watering the horses, had no work to do that day and long before noon had gathered in the Little Pasture, where, in a trough of hot ashes, whole carcases of pigs and oxen had been cooking since the night before.

Discounting the cause of the celebration I was forced to admit that it was one of the merriest scenes that I had ever witnessed. The sun shone clear and bright, throwing up the contrasts of colour, catching the white teeth and eyeballs in the crowd of black faces. Every Negro who owned an instrument of any kind had brought it with him and the first twittering notes of any tune was a signal for a chorus of voices to rise and almost drown the music.

It was on this day, just before the meal was started, that I first saw the Reverend Tobias Missletwaite — he who was always known as the Preacher. He lived in Josepha, at least he had headquarters there in a small wooden church which served the coloured population of the town. But in mid-week he went on visits to all the plantations where his presence was encouraged. He held meetings, performed, if permission from the owner was forthcoming, the marriage ceremony, baptised babies and buried the dead. He wasn't welcome everywhere. Oldfield wouldn't allow him to set foot on

180

Tessimadi, Bavister had driven him violently from Claremont. They believed that his ministrations wasted time and that his doctrines were subversive to discipline.

He was allowed to visit at Springhill and usually called there about once a month. I had never seen him because I had never felt any desire to go to the preaching, but I looked at him now with interest. He was a small, thin, dried-up man, far past middle-age, yet with something sprightly and active about him that denied advanced years. He was shabbily dressed in a suit of very worn black cloth and his clerical bands were frayed and yellowed from much washing. His wig was old-fashioned and so ill-kept that it looked as though it were made of grey wool. He was much loved by the Negroes, and there were many babies called Tobias after him. Both Madda and Sylvy had named a boy Tobias, which was very confusing in that already confused household.

This morning, as I watched him, he walked slowly towards the troughs which had just been opened and took up a position in front of them. The babble of talk which had renewed its volume when the savoury odours of the baked meats arose died down as he raised his right hand. In a thin old voice which yet held an astonishing carrying power, he said,

"My friends, before we eat, let us pray."

Those of us who were sitting struggled to our feet. A few who had begun drinking early rocked a little and clutched at nearby shoulders, but with few exceptions I saw that the large horny hands came together, the black

181

eyes closed and the woolly heads bent forward. They looked like a lot of children praying for the first time. There was something very touching about it. I wondered how God felt, looking down on those meek heads, and knowing that these were weak, harmless, childlike people who had never had anything, not even the common freedom to come and go as they wished. The thin voice carried to the ends of the Little Pasture and arrested my attention.

"Oh Lord, source of all mercies, giver of all good things, who by Thy holy presence didst bless the marriage feast at Cana, look down we beseech Thee upon the union which we are gathered together to celebrate today. May it be happy, hallowed and fruitful.

"Thou knowest, Lord, that in this fair land there are many unions that are made without Thy blessing and against Thy law. Thou knowest too, for all things are plain in Thy sight, which of these are due to force of circumstances and which to wanton lust. We beseech Thee that in the former case Thou wilt not withhold Thy blessing, and that in the latter the sinners may be brought to wisdom and repentance.

"Finally we ask, Lord, that the day may come and that right speedily when Thy Word shall be known, Thy Law obeyed on earth as it is in Heaven, so that ignorance and superstition and oppression may be known no more beneath the sun. All this we ask for the sake of Thy dear Son, who on his earthly pilgrimage was poor and lowly and who took His chosen followers from amongst the toilers of the earth. Amen."

A murmur, like the sudden boom of bees, swept over the field. It was the many-tongued echo of his "Amen." After it there was an instant's silence, and then, shaking off gravity as though it were a dark cloak, the slaves began their repast. Eight of the older men, of whom Fergus was one, began with long keen knives to carve the meat. Women hurried round with baskets of scorchingly-hot roasted potatoes flecked with ash. Soon every set of jaws was working, and except for their noise there was silence in the pasture.

I sat there wishing that the Reverend Tobias had stayed at home, or at least contented himself with asking a blessing for Tottie and his bride. For the rest of the prayer had stung me. I realised at that moment the drawbacks of a strict upbringing which cultivated a conscience that might go out of action for long months at a time but could chatter and nag again when stimulated as mine had been by that prayer. It was chattering now. Was I one of the wanton sinners? Had those rapturous hours under the fragrant puff-ball trees been wrong? The idea of marrying Cassie had never once crossed my mind. No doubt I could have done so. Jimmy would have laughed maybe, but he would have given his permission. Therefore, not having been driven into unhallowed union by the force of circumstance, I was, in the eyes of men like the Reverend Tobias, a sinner and had made Cassie a sinner too.

I split open my second potato and watched the steam rise from its centre. I was feeling much as I had felt on the night when Fergus talked with me: that I was wrong, but that I couldn't help it, that I preferred to be

183

wrong. If I let this chance prayer, to which, in courtesy, I had been bound to listen, take hold of me I should seek out Cassie, suggest that we should be married and arrange for the preacher to perform the rites the next time he came to Springhill. And ever after, in the eyes of God and man I should have a black woman for my wife. Well, what of that? So far as I could see I was doomed to Springhill or some other plantation for the term of my natural life, and no one whom I should ever meet would see anything strange in the union. And I was fond of Cassie. My conscience, speaking clearly after its long silence, said that there was just this one thing to do.

But the voice of conscience was not the only one speaking. Reason would make itself heard. After all, I was the victim of circumstances that had existed before I was born. By this time I should have been picking myself a bride from one of the houses around Braidlowrie, from Strangcaundle, from Frasersmote, from Blythlanger. My father and hers should have been talking of settlements, my mother and hers discussing linen, and the pipers should have been practising the wedding music. Force of circumstances had taken me to the bed of bare earth under the puff-ball trees. And as the familiar names of my countryside rang through my memory I knew that I should never marry Cassie, nor any other woman who couldn't face with honour the light of twenty candles in silver sconces on the table at Braidlowrie. A sudden turn of fortune's wheel had landed me in the mire; another, equally unforeseen, might deposit me where I should have no need for

Cassie. Neither my own conscience, nor the eloquence of others, was going to make me do something that I might regret. I had not deceived Cassie. She had never shown any sign of expecting more of me than I had given her. And who was the Reverend Tobias to be a judge? I bit into my potato.

The afternoon was given over to slumber and the processes of digestion, but in the evening all the musicians gathered together at the end of the Little Pasture where the troughs still gave out a gentle heat, and even glowed as a breeze caught them. They began to play, not songs but throbbing, almost tuneless rhythms that caught at the feet. No one, however leaden-footed, however heavy-hearted, could have gone from one end of that meadow to another without breaking into a jig. I have known ignorant people to say, "Oh, but the slaves are so happy, they're always singing and dancing." That is not proof of happiness, but of the potency, the irresistible rhythm of their primitive music. Even I, standing still and lonely by the gateway, found my toes twitching. I found the scene extraordinarily interesting. I watched the leaping and writhing, the darting forward, the swift retreats and found it difficult to believe that these were the same bodies as those that dragged home at the end of a day's work almost too weary to collect their suppers. Old Pluggy was crouched over a drum, his thin hands coaxed a rumbling note from the ill-made instrument; there was a look of intense, withdrawn concentration upon his face. He looked a very different person from the surly old barber that I knew.

185

These were, I thought, no more a people in bondage. They were happy savages, enjoying their reaction to the primeval call of the music. I knew that here, in the heart of St. Crispin's, I looked upon the heart of Africa. Why had it happened? Why could a handful of white people, bent upon their own profit, hold all this wealth of energy, of bone and muscle, in fee?

Suddenly, as I stood there thinking, a light touch was laid on my arm. Turning swiftly I found myself staring down upon the Reverend Tobias Missletwaite.

"Good evening," he said, and now that he was no longer addressing a crowd all the power had left his voice and it was the thin pipe of an old man.

"Good evening," I said.

He looked at me closely, from my bare feet to my cropped head, and though I managed to stand still I was conscious of a desire to wriggle like a shy child beneath his scrutiny.

"You haven't been here long, have you?"

"A mere matter of four years," I replied harshly.

"Really? So long as that? How much longer have you to serve?"

"Well, look at me. I'm hale and hearty, sound in wind and limb, I suppose I'm good for another fifty years or so."

"Dear, dear," he said gently. "Would you mind if we sat down, old limbs tire easily you know. Thank you. Now, if you won't think me unpardonably curious, tell me — aren't you indentured for any given length of time?"

"I'm not indentured at all. I'm what Jimmy Standish calls a lifer."

"And why is that? There was a murderer at Claremont who was sentenced to twenty years. You can't have done worse than murder. Why, you must have been quite a boy when you came here."

"I hadn't done anything," I said. "I was unlucky enough to be on a ship that a pirate called Barlesci captured. He simply sold me for thirty-five pounds."

He looked at me in silence for a moment, probably weighing up the likelihood of my story being true. He must have had so many stories told him as he went from plantation to plantation. There was hardly anything that he couldn't have believed.

"Is that so indeed?" he said at last. "I've heard of similar cases. They all illustrate the need for a strong central government in this part of the world. A crying need. What with wars and rebellions and mixed nationalities and piracy nothing is safe. But of course we are so remote and so long as trade continues to flourish little else matters, or so they think. These indentured labourers now, so often, so very often, they are not set free when the time comes. I am perpetually writing to his Majesty's ministers about the injustices that occur. It was over the matter of that murderer at Claremont that Mr. Bavister and I fell out. He hadn't the slightest intention of freeing the man. It is a source of great sorrow to me that through trying to call the attention of those in England who should know of them to these crying scandals I so often lose opportunities for what little good I might do amongst these poor lost creatures."

He sighed.

"Well, my case needn't worry you at least," I said. "Even if you wrote to England about me they'd only say, 'Serve him right.' You see, my father is a well-known Jacobite and I got mixed up in the last rising and had to run away. This is what I ran to."

"It's a very sad story. Still, there is one thing to be glad about. Mr. Standish is far more humane than his peers generally. Haven't you found that? He permits me to visit here, for instance. I shall think over your case, though. Maybe I might see something that could be done. I've had much experience. Not, I must emphasise, that you should build any hope upon my activity. That might lead to disappointment. Would you mind explaining to what extent you were mixed up in that rising?"

I told him briefly about Glenranald.

"So you really committed no crime at all, only a kindness. And you were how old? Sixteen? A mere child. Another massacred innocent." He sighed again, then moving his hand towards the dancers who had flung themselves exhausted upon the ground, he murmured, "And those, all massacred innocents."

"It passes my comprehension," I said, "how anybody, even a clergyman, can reconcile all this sort of thing with the theory of a just and loving God. I can't. That's why you've never seen me before. I never go to the preaching."

"I can't reconcile it either," he said quietly. "I so frequently see things happen when it seems that God must take a hand — things no ordinary decent man could watch without protest. And I haven't the spiritual insight that some people have. I just go on from day to day because even if what I teach is as false as I sometimes fear it is *I still* feel that a belief in Christ is to be preferred to superstition. And I *know* that the hope of heaven is a great comfort to those who have little to hope for in this life. And we are definitely told, aren't we, not that evil does not exist, but that it does, and that we must overcome it. And so, often despite myself, I go on. The way of the realist is very hard."

There was something so sincere and simple about his words and the glance of his wrinkled old eyes that I suddenly pitied him. After all he had devoted his life to a cause and didn't seem, in the latter days, to have the comfort of complete faith as compensation.

"At any rate," I said firmly, "you bring light and comfort into a number of lives. The people at Springhill — and no doubt other places that I can't speak for — think the world of you. And the women who go to the preaching *are* better mothers and wives, now I come to think of it, than those who don't."

"My dear lad," he said, his face brightening, "you can't imagine how you please me. Nothing could be pleasanter hearing. Now Satan, behind me! I'm not going to be flattered into sin at my time of life. Well, there are several other people with whom I must have a word and this lull seems a favourable opportunity. I must confess that if I walk about when that music is

189

playing I find myself moving in a most unseemly manner. Just give me your name, will you, and I'll see what can be done."

For the first time at Springhill, where I was Scottie to everyone but Cassie and Fergus, I gave my full name.

Cassie had evidently been watching, for as the old man said good night and walked away, she came sidling out of the shadows and put her hot hand on my arm. The bright pale dress and cap shone in the dusk.

"Well," I said, "have you finished?"

She nodded.

"And did you enjoy looking at the fine dresses? Did Miss Avril look nice?"

I asked these questions, not because I cared, but because Cassie had been talking excitedly for days beforehand about what people would be wearing and how grand Miss Avril's gown was to be. I expected her to embark upon an animated description, with no little envy in it. But she only said dully,

"Nice enough."

"You sound tired, Cassie. I expect you've been running about all day, and you were up half the night. Poor little thing. Shall we get away from all this noise and sit quietly somewhere?"

"Ah'd like dat. Ma nor de udders would be in de cabin. Shall us go dere? Ah's got sumpun Ah wants tuh tell yo'."

Tottie, I thought, damn him to Hell. Last night while Cassie was supposed to be working up at the house. A last fling before ordinary good manners demand that he spend a few nights with his ugly bride.

190

We reached the cabin, and Cassie, still in silence, set about mending the fire. When the flames were leaping she rose from her knees and stood before me, her hands hanging down, the picture of dejection.

"Oh, all right," I said with impatient pity, "you needn't say it. I might have known it was no good going to Jimmy. I'll have to think of something else."

"Ain't dat," said Cassie glumly. "Ah's gonna have a baby. Dat's a pleasin' prozpek ain't it?"

My first feeling was of shocked surprise, though why it should have been I didn't know. It was natural enough. We were both young and there had been many meetings under the puff-ball bushes. And negro women were unusually prolific. A very large proportion of their babies died in infancy, otherwise there would have been no need to import slaves from Africa, for plenty were born. So we might have expected this, even sooner. Nevertheless I was surprised. My second thought was of Tottie. Would this be my baby, or his? I put the question to Cassie who turned out her palms helplessly.

"Ah woulden' know," she said.

"You don't want it, do you, Cassie?"

She shook her head emphatically.

"Then isn't there anything you can do? Perhaps your mother, or Madda . . ."

"Ah's done plenny. Old Suzy she most kill muh wid dat brew she make. Ah doan mind fo' mahself, but Ah do hate do notion of habbin' a slave baby. Ah doan wanta make no baby fo' Mistah Whittle to hab. Old Suzy she laff like anything when I tell her dat, but dat is a fac'."

"I hate that idea too," I said. "I suppose we ought to have thought of that before. But I just didn't."

"Ah did," said Cassie, dropping down on to a stool. "Ah bin dis way afore, but old Suzy she wukked better dat time. Ah's vurry miser'ble."

I said helplessly, "Don't be miserable, Cassie. I'm very, very sorry about it myself. It's all my fault. But I don't see that there's anything we can do now. Do you?"

Cassie sat still for a time, staring at the fire. Then she rose from the stool.

"Ah thinks Ah'll try old Suzy agin. Dat stuff most wrench out mah innards but Ah'll try just once more."

She looked tired and sick and unhappy, and I thought — God alone knows what that old woman puts into her concoctions — and it came to me to say, "Don't take any more of her muck, you may hurt yourself." But I didn't say it. The horrible words "slave baby" rang in my ears still. I didn't want any part or lot in bringing a slave baby to Springhill, to outlive Jimmy, to taste Tottie's tyranny. I said nothing to stop Cassie as she moved to the door.

But old Suzy failed agin, and before long it was impossible for me to look at Cassie without being reminded. I got so that I couldn't bear to be with her and when a meeting was unavoidable I used to stare past her at the trees or the sky or the ground by our feet, anything rather than let my eyes rest on the thickening figure, ripening into motherhood, a state that should be proud and honourable but which in this case was horrible and shameful.

The shame was actually all in my mind. Illegitimate babies far outnumbered the others upon all the plantations. Slave marriages indeed were empty formalities even when blessed by the owner's permission and hallowed by the preacher's ministrations. Husbands and wives were separated, sold apart as casually and naturally as male and female animals might be. And breeding between those who had bothered with neither formality was regarded just as naturally.

Cassie at least escaped the censure that would have been hers in other communities. And I, of course, was not regarded as having any "duty" towards her. Having no rights, I had no responsibility. Nobody cared whose baby it might be. And although for a brief, uncomfortable quarter of an hour after that prayer on Tottie's wedding day, I had toyed with the idea of marrying Cassie, this event did not revive the idea. If by marrying her I could have made the child that was coming free, I would have done it, and I should then have welcomed the baby gladly, but there was no question of that. If I could have spared Cassie anything by the same means I would have done it, but there was no question of that either. All I could do was to hope that the child would die quickly: and that I did, with all my heart.

For a month or two life went on as usual. We took the seedlings out of their beds and planted them in the ridges of the great fields. Fergus could transplant a thousand a day. He took a great pride in that, it was proof of expertness. Mac never averaged more than six hundred, and he mocked at me, when, inspired by Fergus and stung almost against my will into competition, I boasted of attaining at last an output of eight hundred in a day.

"What for? Can ye tell me that?" he demanded. "What ye don't set oot some ither puir bastard will. An' what isna done the day will wait the morrow. Furthermore ye that work so fierce are no freends of ye're ain kind. Stir enow to avoid Tottie's crop and Treacle's whip and no mair. Else they'll be haverin' one fine day why it is that everybody doesna plant a thousand."

"He's quite right," I said to Fergus. "I hadn't thought of it that way."

"Is your mind easier when you dawdle or when you speed along?" asked Fergus in an impersonal voice.

"I thought, and knew that when I was hurrying, counting as I worked, driving myself along row after row, I didn't have time to think. No time to brood over being a slave myself, or over having begotten a slave who would be doing this in the long years ahead.

"When I speed along," I said.

"Well then," said Fergus.

But I had caught the essential logic of Mac's protest and contented myself, after that, by digging deeper holes with my plant stick, by pressing the soil down around the young shoot with extra care and so not exceeding six hundred or six hundred and fifty a day, which was about the average. When work was finished and the demand for physical energy no longer a brake upon the processes of thought I used to go along to

Jacko's shack and drink corn-brew and listen to the singing. Madda had had a baby soon after Miss Avril's wedding-day and sometimes, under cover of the singing, I used to watch her with it. All day, while she worked in the fields, it would lie, quiet and uncomplaining, in the corner of the field, wrapped in an old yellow bit of blanket. But in the evening it seemed to come to life, and would gurgle and croon and butt its little curly head against her great black bosom as she suckled it.

A slave baby, with God knew what tasks and miseries ahead of it, yet at the moment a happy little scrap of humanity and Madda's joy. And no doubt Mac's mother had loved him, and Fergus' and my own. Yet if they could have known, if they could have looked down the long years and seen us here, fed and housed and worked like beasts, could they have rejoiced, even that a man child was born? Could anybody, in this world where everything was so unjust and uncertain, rejoice that any new life had come to be the sport of this injustice, this uncertainty?

Sometimes, if the corn-brew were scarce or weak and I was still sober, the sight of Madda and her baby set me thinking so bitterly about the one that was coming that I had to leave the singing and rush out into the night. Minute for minute and pang for pang I paid for those stolen hours at the end of the vegetable garden.

Day by day the sun grew hotter and presently the tops of the tobacco plants were crowned with clusters of pale pinky-purple bloom. Picking these off, so that the leaves might the better spread and thicken, was the

195

best job of the year. There was no back-breaking stooping to do. And this year the heat tried me less, my skin no longer scorched and my head swam less frequently.

Upon one morning, some little time before noon, I had worked up to the end of a row, mechanically nipping away and dropping the purplish petals. Before turning at the end and beginning the new row I stopped to tighten the piece of string that held up the remnants of my trousers and as I did so my attention was attracted by the sound of wildly galloping hoofs. I stepped from the soft hoed soil of the field on to the edge of the hard track and looked along the road. It was the merest curiosity, the kind that grows upon men to whom nothing ever happens. To know that someone had arrived in such a hurry at Springhill would entertain the vacant mind all day with a flock of speculations as to what his errand might be.

I was not prepared for what I saw. Jimmy's big cream-coloured mare was racing up the track as though the devil himself were riding her: and hanging down from the side nearer me, with only an arm looped through the rein and one foot caught in the stirrup to prevent his body from trailing on the ground was Jimmy. At every one of the mare's strides his body swung out and then in again, striking the mare and frightening her to further speed. She was past me before I had a chance to stop her. That didn't matter greatly, for Tottie, mounted, had ridden to the field's edge a little nearer the house and as the mare passed him he put his piebald horse alongside, galloped a little way with her, reached for the reins and brought her to a standstill. It was the only time that I had seen him perform a neat and finished action.

All the fieldhands within sight or hearing dashed to the spot and I ran with them. They were lifting Jimmy down when I reached him. His face was a dark violet colour and there were blobs of foam at the corners of his mouth. A stroke, I thought, Jimmy has had a stroke, and for an instant my heart stood still. The mare stood panting and heaving and trying to jerk her head away from the terrified looking darky to whom Tottie had given the rein.

"We must carry him up to the house," Tottie said. He hesitated for a moment, looking round, perhaps for a gate or something that would serve as stretcher. There was nothing. "I'll take his head," he said then, "you, Scottie, take his feet."

Fear gave me courage.

"What about a doctor?" I asked. Tottie stared at me. "Oh yes, of course. The doctor. You, Ebenezer, get on my horse and go into Josepha for a doctor."

Ebenezer looked wildly round. His eyes popped with fright.

"Shore, Massa. Ah dassen mount dis animal. Ah on'y deals wid de mules."

Tottie looked round. That's right, I thought, take your time, let Jimmy lie out here in the broiling sun while you pick somebody else who can't ride. And then, on the edge of the field I saw Mac, and the expression on his face startled me.

"I'll go," he shouted, pushing through the group. "What doctor are ye wanting? And how will I find him?"

Again Tottie hesitated. Mac misinterpreted the hesitation, though it was all too plain to me.

"Canna ye trust me with yon spavined animal? Man, I was in Briersley's Horse. I'd tak him safely to Jericho. What doctor do I ask for?"

"Doctor Hopgood," said Tottie. "His house is just opposite old Missletwaite's church. If he isn't in they'll send you somewhere else."

Mac looked from the piebald horse to Jimmy's mare and back again.

"I suppose this is fresher," he said regretfully; and in one beautiful movement was mounted, turned, and started off along the track.

"You, Ebenezer, take the mare up to the house. Now, Scottie, take the feet." He put his hands under Jimmy's shoulders and after snarling, "The rest of you get back to your work," he gave me the word to go forward.

It was not very far to the house but Jimmy was a heavy man and twice we had to lay him flat so that we might gather our breath and renew our hold. It was a very undignified journey. At last we saw the garden beds and the pillars of the house and stooping over some of the flowers was Miss Avril. She dropped the blooms she was holding and ran towards us like a lapwing.

"Oh. Is it an accident? What's happened?"

"Keep calm," snapped Tottie. "It's nothing probably."

"It looks like stroke to me, Mrs. Whittle," I said.

"Shut your mouth. What do you know about strokes?"

Jimmy's daughter went before us into the house. "Bring him in here," she said and flung open a door. We followed and laid our burden on a wide low sofa covered with pink brocade. The ugly purple colour was still in his face, but he was alive, for with every breath his lips puffed a little, like the lid of a kettle just on the boil.

"Isn't there anything we can do?" asked Miss Avril in a terrified voice.

"Nothing," said Tottie. "I've sent for the doctor."

"He'll be such a long time," she said tremulously.

"We can't help that, but we can keep calm," he said unkindly.

"And we might," I put in, since neither of them had suggested it, "loosen the things at his waist and neck and put some cold water on his head."

"An amateur apothecary," said Tottie unpleasantly. Nevertheless he fumbled at the throat of Jimmy's shirt and untied the wide silken band that girded the stout waist. His wife said,

"Of course, I'll get some water. And perhaps Lyddy might know something."

"Better to wait for the doctor. We might do harm," said Tottie. I knew then what I had guessed all along, that Tottie wanted Jimmy to die before the doctor reached Springhill. Everything that he had done had been done slowly and unwillingly, even sending for the doctor had been my suggestion. I looked at him and he looked at me. For a fraction of a moment our eyes met over the supine body of our master, and our thoughts were perfectly clear to one another. I could read his hope, he my fear.

"I don't think we need you any more. Get back to work. And tell Treacle to come up here to see me after the noon spell."

I turned back once after I had left the house and saw that Tottie had pushed aside the pink curtains and was looking out of the window. He was not looking at me. His eyes were riveted upon the outer world, the lawns, the flowerbeds and the green tobacco fields. His eyes were pleased and dreamy as he surveyed the inheritance which was trembling into his hand.

Sick at heart I sought out Treacle the half-caste foreman whose colour gave him his name. This day's work might make him foreman, and Tottie master.

During the course of the afternoon the doctor arrived upon a lathered horse. Mac wasn't with him. He was probably making the most of his brief liberty staring at the sights in Josepha or trying to cadge a drink at a tavern. It would be altogether against his principle to hurry back. When I joined Fergus in the cabin at supper time he was still absent, and Fergus wore a worried air.

"I do hope he hasn't done anything silly," he said, blowing at the roots of the fire. "If some kind-minded person has given him a drink he'll likely hang about till he's locked up. I've brought his supper and I hope he'll be here to eat it. He'll be in trouble else."

"We'll all be in trouble," I returned bitterly, "if anything happens to Jimmy."

"That's true," said Fergus and busied himself in separating the two rations he had brought from the storehouse. "Maybe we'll hear something later on. We'll hearken for Daisy coming back from the house."

Daisy was the cook at the house and lived with her man and a rabble of children in the cabin just opposite ours. There was little need to "hearken" for her arrival for it was always loudly heralded by a stream of strident abuse directed at one or another of her family who had let out the fire, neglected to take in the washing, forgotten to fill the water bucket or let something happen to the baby.

Tonight, however, though we sat for a long time by the door of our cabin we heard nothing of Daisy. Nor did Mac arrive. The thick darkness that came after sunset gave way to starlight. The circling smoke that kept away the mosquitoes rose from the fire and lost itself in the night. Fergus and I spoke now and again but a mood of silence was on us, and we were both listening. Occasionally a bird might be heard, or a dog barking, otherwise a curious quiet brooded over the cabins. Not a note sounded, no one was singing, not a voice was uplifted in greeting and there was none of the coming and going on visits that there was on other nights. Everybody was at home, waiting to know whether marsa was going to live or die. I remember thinking how much hung upon that single life. It was like a string upon which our fates were threaded like beads. No single life should mean so much. No one man's death should have the power to darken so many lives. We were less happy than animals, who may any day lose a good master and gain a bad one, for we had the extra misery of dread and anticipation. And anticipation and dread hovered in a cloud that could be felt over the whole plantation.

Presently there was a step on the cinder track and Daisy's voice was heard.

"Mah chillun." Then, as the children poured out to meet rebuke, or to share the scraps that she had brought with her from the kitchen, her voice rose again,

"Mah chillun, lift up yo' voices in a sorrowful cry, let de deep cry of desolation be heerd. Mourn, mourn fo' de best marsa ever seen under de sun. Weep fo' him dat is no more."

All along the cinder track the negroes came dodging from under low doorways and took up the mournful cry, "Ahhh, Ai, Ahhh." The women wept and the wordless litany was punctuated by their sobs. The sorrowful wave of sound rolled up towards the winking stars. It was one of the most moving things I have ever heard.

We stood there listening for some moments, then Fergus turned back into the cabin and I followed him.

"Well, Tottie didn't have to wait long," he said quietly. "He's master now. God help us all."

Outside the wailing "Ahhh, Ai, Ahhh" echoed, although it did not hear, the prayer.

Even after the wailing had at last died down and all the cabins were quiet, Fergus and I sat by our replenished fire and waited for Mac and speculated about the future. Once I said, voicing a sudden thought, "Do you think he's got away?"

"Who? Mac? Never. He'd no money and no clothes, and he had Tottie's piebald nag that everybody in Josepha knows. I should say he's drunk and in the lock-up. We'll see him tomorrow or the day after and Tottie will have a warm welcome for him I don't doubt."

But next day, amid all the sombre comings and goings at Springhill the piebald horse was brought back by a stranger. Daisy, at the end of a long day preparing funeral bake meats for the morrow, stopped to tell us that she had heard in the kitchen that Tottie's horse had been found tied to the hitching post near the waterfront, and that though Tottie had sent Treacle to search and inquire at every likely spot in the town no sign of Mac had been found.

This news caused the wildest excitement, for just as every unsuccessful attempt to escape struck a blow at every slave's hope, so each rare successful venture kindled a vicarious joy. I shared the excitement. That night I almost forgot that Jimmy was to be buried next day in my speculations over what had become of Mac. I tried to imagine what he had done after calling at the doctor's house, and tethering the horse to the post. Had he met someone like Fanshawe who had sympathy with slaves? Had he seen an opportunity to stowaway? Had he been stolen? Or had he, knowing that Jimmy mightn't live, thrown himself into the harbour rather than face Tottie Samson's rule? Anything seemed possible in this incalculable country. And I remembered the look on his face when he had offered to ride into Josepha. It had been, for one instant, like the face of a gambler who picks up the card for which he was waited for a long time. Perhaps Mac had. I hoped so.

That evening and the night, and the day of the funeral passed and still nothing was heard. Wherever he was we wished him luck, and envied, without grudging, his escape. We never heard of him again.

They buried Jimmy Standish by his wife, under the shade of the scented lime trees where the lawns ended. All that evening there was the mourning in the street of the cabins and the sound of the saddest songs. "Rest Yo' Soul in de Redeemer, yo' weary bones in de clay." "Pray Soft fo' de Young Angel." And perhaps saddest of all, "How can us manage now?" Over and over these three were repeated. We two white men stayed in our cabin, for as in times of rejoicing, so in times of sorrow, the Negro and the white express themselves differently. And although "How can us manage now?" was a question urgent to us as to them we did not feel like singing it, even to the most dirge-like music.

For a short time, a matter of two or three weeks, things went on as usual. Tottie and his wife moved into the big house and Treacle moved into the one across the Big Pasture. That was the only immediate change. Then one night, calling in at Jacko's with my port ration, I found Madda and Sylvy in tears. They didn't wait for me to ask what was wrong but burst into noisy lamentations at once. The preacher had been forbidden to come to Springhill any more. Madda rocked to and fro over her baby.

204

"An' now," she moaned, "dis poah chile of sin ain gonna be baptisaled. Lookit de li'l robe on him an'all, an' de blessed names oll ready. John Mark he wuz tuh be, after de 'Postles."

"Well," I said, with intent to comfort, "you can still call him by those names."

"Ain de same at oll. Ah can call'um how Ah like, but nobuddy 'cept de preacher can't put de blessed water on an' washen de mark of sin offen dis chile's forread. An' now de preacher ain' coming no more. Dat's like a dark night an' de one last star go out."

There was such genuine misery on her face and in her voice that I was moved to wonder whether the Reverend Mr. Missletwaite's teaching hadn't done more harm than good. Women like Madda had quite enough to distress them without worrying over baptism, infant damnation and marks of sin.

"Don't fret, Madda," I said. "God will know that it isn't your fault, or the baby's; that you'd made the robe and everything. Tell me, when did this happen? Have Mr. Whittle and the preacher quarrelled?"

"Shore hab," said Sylvy, who had been silent quite long enough for her fancy. "We's all at de preachin' and de preacher 'ngaged in de openin' prayer when Mr. Whittle come bangin' in. Preacher look up to see what makin' sich a 'sturbance an' Mr. Whittle say, 'Come on, outen dat. Take yo'self offen dis place an doan nebber let me see yo' face no more.' Preacher say de Amen as cool as a water melon and we all get to us feet. 'Den yo'll share in de sin of dem udder men dat make their slaves walk in de dark,' preacher say, 'only your sin'ull be de greater in dat yo' did hab fo' many years a good sample to show yo' de right way.'

"'Yo' get offen dis place an' sabe yo' preachin fo' dem dat likes it,' Mr. Whittle say. Den he turn to all'v us and say, 'You all get to yo' homes an' see iffen yo' can't get sumpun useful tuh do.' So we all come away an' den he an' de preacher hab some more talk. Den we see de preacher ride away wid his head down like he wuz sorrowful. Iffen dat had on'y waited till after de baptisal Ah coulda borne it better."

"Dis," said Jacko sagely as he took my pork and measured out some corn-brew "am de end of de wedge what show where de wind am blowing." I realised from his neat and tidy aspect that he had gone to the preaching to see the child baptised, though he had said no word to betray the fact.

"Where's Timmy?" I asked, tasting the corn-brew which was not quite up to standard.

"He'm gone tuh see old Suzy," Jacko explained. "Since de baby cain hab Chrissen charm put on him Timmy tuk de notion dat one of de old ones would do. Old Suzy 'bout de on'y party round here dat remember dat sort."

Even as I marvelled at the instant and instinctive rebound towards the beliefs of an older day, Timmy entered. In his huge hand he carried a tiny bag slung on a piece of dirty twine.

"Old Suzy awful mad at yo', Madda, and at Jacko and muh. She allus wuz dead agin de preacher. Now she say we's go creepin' back. Come to think of it, Ah ain so shore dis a good charm. She laff a lot when she make dat bag."

He stood still with the bag swinging from his hand, and I saw the expression of bewilderment and consternation upon his face mirrored in those of Jacko and Madda and Sylvy. It would have been funny if it hadn't been so pathetic.

"Did yo' give her dem presents?" Jacko asked.

"Shore Ah did. She gotta mighty lotta stuff in her cabin. Dere's five babies wuz tuh be batisaled. Ah specks dere's five famblies been tuh her wid presents. Ain so shore we all ain got bad charms stead of good. Ain so shore dis baby better wear it."

"If it were my baby," I began, and then stopped suddenly as it dawned upon me that soon, very soon, there would be a baby of mine. I pulled my thoughts back. "If it were my baby I should throw the thing in the fire. It looks quite filthy enough to give the child the plague. Why can't you get out of your heads all this twaddle about charms and marks of sin? He's a nice little baby and if you look after him properly his body will grow up all right, and if you bring him up right he'll be good enough. Neither the preacher's words nor old Suzy's charms can do him either harm or good."

"You don't believe in nothing," said Sylvy reproachfully. "You ain't nebber seen de light."

"Yo' shudden talk dat way 'bout charms, neider," Madda added. "Ah's seen good charms an' Ah's seen bad charms. Mighty pow'ful ones. Ah think, Timmy, dat old Suzy laffed caze she like de presents. Gimme de charm. Us'll try it."

She fastened the dirty string round the creased little black neck. The baby smiled.

"Dat's a good sign," said Timmy, much relieved. All at once I was aware of my alien race, my different colour. Quite possibly now, if anything happened to the baby, they would attribute it to my suggestion of throwing the charm into the fire. Mere friendliness could not really bridge a gulf so deep of different blood, different upbringing, different outlook. I said good night quickly and went out. Anyway I had my duty call to pay to Cassie.

Now that her body reproached instead of enthralling me I found her company tedious in the extreme. We had nothing, apart from the bed under the puff-ball trees, in common, and nothing to talk about. Tonight, certainly we could talk about the preaching being stopped, and I told her, at great length, about Madda's baby and the charm.

The last link between us had broken when Cassie's attitude towards the coming baby underwent some inexplicable change. Something obscure and primitive had come upon her so that she had forgotten all her bitterness about having a slave baby and was simply looking forward to the time when it should be born and she could hold it in her arms. She was always full of chatter about the dress she had made for it: about her desire that it should be a boy: about what names she would choose for it. As soon as I had finished telling her about the charm I could see that her mind was busy with plans for similar preparations against evil on behalf of the coming child.

I left her that evening with a sense of appalling loneliness. Here was I spending my life, all my best years, among creatures only once removed from a state of savagery. And the one man of my own kind and colour was cut off from me by the barrier of his resignation and philosophy. I felt suddenly that I missed Mac. We had at least been able to understand one another's grievances: and the two of us could hold our own even in Jacko's cabin. Not that I would have wished him back. For he had left Springhill at the most fortunate moment — before the blight of Tottie's rule set in.

Two days later Madda waited for me at the door of the tool house. Her gang, which was working in a different field from mine, was just moving off and she dared only linger for a second.

"Cassie's time came on early dis morning," she said hastily. "Old Suzy's dere."

"Has the baby come?"

"Just coming when I left. Suzy say dat'll be a boy. Oh, oll right, oll right, Mr. Bossy Treacle, I's coming."

She hurried away and fell in at the end of the line. It was very kind of her to have told me. Treacle would catch her a flick with his whip for lingering.

That evening, as soon as work finished, I hurried to the tool house and then pushed my way well to the fore of the line by the hatch of the storehouse. Pluggy was handing out the rations and saying in a monotonous chant, calculated to forestall complaint,

"No, dis ain' gonna be pork night no more. Pork once, on Toosday in future. No, dis ain' gonna be pork night no more. Pork once, on Toosday in future. No, dis ain' gonna . . ."

It sounds a small thing. Now, with many good meals between me and the memory of that evening, I realise how trivial it can sound — "Pork once, on Toosday in future." And even at that moment it meant less to me than it did to the others because I used it mainly to trade with. To the Negroes who loved the fat pork, it had all the features of a minor tragedy. As they turned away with the measures of meal that were to last until next evening they muttered among themselves.

"Marsa Standish nebber cut de pork in harbs not eben dat time when de horn-worm got at de crop."

"Ah's bin heah all mah life an' we's allus had pork on de Fridays."

"We's gonna be like dem poah scraggy niggers over to Tessimadi. Oll skin an' bone, dat's what's we's be."

Suddenly, behind Pluggy's grey head and the bags of meal in the hatchway, Tottie Samson's yellow face appeared.

"Quit that muttering and move along there. And you, Pluggy, stop that bawling. They can see there ain't no pork tonight and that'll do."

The muttering died away instantly, and did not begin again until the Negroes were among their cabins and out of earshot of Tottie. I hurried into our cabin and laid down my meal. Usually I made the fire in order to save Fergus the stooping, but tonight I went straight round to Cassie's place. Old Suzy had gone and the other women were outside on the cinder path jabbering about the pork ration. Cassie was alone, crouched on a stool by the fire, and in the curve between her breast and her knees there rested a tiny bundle.

Her face lightened as she saw me.

"Ma wuz gonna fetch yo' after supper," she said. "How did yo' know?"

"Madda told me this morning. Are you all right, Cassie?"

"Ah's fine. An' it's the boy, Colin. Ah's changed mah mind 'bout de names. Ah think we's call him Scotland. Dat's de name of de place, ain it?"

"It's the name of the place, Cassie. It'll sound funny for a little boy."

Her pleased look vanished.

"Ah thought yo'd be pleased wid dat name."

Oh, my God, why must I hurt her now?

"Now I think of it I do like it, Cassie. I suppose I'd got used to the other names. Can I have him for a moment?"

She got up and laid the little bundle in my arms. I stooped so that the firelight fell on the child's face. It looked incredibly old and melancholy. It was a pale clayey colour and seemed to have no nose, only wide flat nostrils. At first the eyes were closed but after a moment they opened and revealed a milky, unfocused stare. The tiny weight of him, and the warmth made me feel faint. I said irritably to Cassie "I suppose you've had a fire here all day. This cabin is stifling," and went across to the door.

The heat of the day was already draining away and the first stars were pricking through. The women were

211

still a little way up the path, talking in low, grumbling tones. I held the baby close to me and gave my thoughts their freedom. Was this mine, or Whittle's? How could a man tell? Suppose I was responsible for calling this little scrap of humanity out of the peace of non-existence into this world of slavery. Not voluntarily, not because I wanted a son, or had anything for him, but idly, accidentally, blindly. Perhaps that look of melancholy was due to some strange foreboding of all that he would have to endure before he reached the end of the road upon which I had set his innocent feet. Hunger, perhaps, and weariness and lack of freedom, the lash and the slave cabin and the scorn of luckier men. And perhaps there would flow in his blood some drop of the Lowrie strain, heritage of a free people which would irk him, as it irked me, making bondage a weariness to the spirit as well as to the flesh. Unendurable thought. Was it mine? Was it mine? Was there any way of knowing? I touched the puckered little brow with one calloused finger and the edge of the shawl fell back. I could just make out there was fluff on his scalp. What colour? I couldn't see out here in the dusk.

I called over my shoulder to Cassie.

"He's got some hair. I didn't know they had hair so soon. Is it black?"

"No. Dat's just like yours. Dat's why Ah thought of Scotland. Dem udder names would of done if . . . if Ah wuzn't sure."

So he had the Lowrie hair. And there was the blood of my fathers in him. Yet, though the miracle of

212

which I dreamed should happen, and I should be free, *he* would belong to Tottie, a slave's offspring, a chattel.

Something seemed to crack in my head. My mind cried, "I may seem of all things the most driven and helpless, but in reality I am God. I made this and I can destroy it. No son of mine shall be a slave." I pulled up a thick fold of the shawl over the shapeless little mouth and nose and laid my hand firmly upon it. Loudly, still speaking over my shoulder I began to tell Cassie about the pork ration imitating Pluggy's monotonous chant, describing Tottie's face coming through the hatchway. "Like a tortoise out of a shell," I cried. "Like a tortoise out of a shell."

Anything, anything to drown the thought of what was happening under my hand. The little body jumped once, convulsively. Queer little sounds came from it, but I only spoke more loudly. It seemed an hour before I dare push back the fold of the shawl.

I walked back to the firelight and said in a voice that hurt me — like strangling — "Cassie, I think something's happened to the baby." She snatched him from me and leaned down to the firelight.

"He'm dead," she said incredulously, and then, growing wilder and wilder, "He'm dead. Dead, dead! Mah baby's dead!" Her cries reached the ears of the women who were on the path, her mother rushed into the cabin and the others followed her until the place was full to overflowing with pushing, screaming, gesticulating women. Nobody noticed me and under cover of the confusion I stole away.

I turned away from the cabins into the Big Pasture and once there I flung myself face downward on the grass and cried. I had done the best, the only, the inevitable thing . . . But I remembered the tiny weight of him, and the warmth and the puzzled, unseeing stare. And there was the memory of Cassie. "Rachel weeping . . . and would not be comforted."

I lay flat on the grass and the dew fell cool and heavy, drenching my thin shirt and ragged trousers: and I cried for the last time of my life. I emptied out there upon the wet grass all the tears that there were in me. I wept for Cassie who would know the ache of empty arms, hunger for the blind searching lips at her breast. For Cassie whose nine months' burden and labour had turned in a moment to a lifeless bundle in a shawl. I wept for myself, for my wasted youth and blighted future. I wept for the life that I had snuffed out as one might a candle. And yet, would to God, I thought, that my father had done as much for me.

After a long time the tears ceased and I got up. There was a moon again as there had been on the night when Cassie came from Whittle's house and I frightened her. I stared at it. Blank, cold, horrible face, staring down unmoved on all that met its gaze. I hated it that night. I hate it still. Under its wide white beam I stole around the back of the cabins so that I might avoid passing the place where Cassie was mourning her dead. I reached the cinder track again near Jacko's cabin and stooped low to enter the doorway.

"Jacko," I said bluntly, "I haven't any pork, you know why. But if you've any corn-brew give me a drink. I'll make it right with you on Tuesday."

"Shore," said Jacko in his deep soft voice. "Come right in, man. Ah doan want no pork. Ah's lorst several babies mahseff. Yo take a good pull at dat, an' forget your bodders." He looked at me with a world of sympathy and understanding and kindness in his eyes. My heart swelled again. Dear Jacko, expert thief and slave — so far better a man than the master who grudged him enough to eat! Oh God why doesn't the world collapse with horror at its own iniquity?

Madda had evidently forgiven me for my scepticism about the charm.

"Git yo' music, Timmy," she said, "an play, 'Pray soft fo' de young angel.' Dere's mighty consolation in dat song."

"No," I said harshly. "If you must play, Timmy, play something loud and merry."

"Shore," said Timmy, "you am feeling bad. Cain think right at dis minnut of no merry music."

"Go on then. What does it matter? Play what you like!"

Timmy cast me a look of compassion. Then he fingered a note or two and all four of them broke gently into song.

"Pray soft fo' de young angel what has just put his wings on. Gotta learn a lot in Hebben. . . ."

Little red-haired son of mine I wish I could believe that there was a Heaven for you, with a cradle and a mother's love and sunshine and other children to play with. Down here you might have had them if I had held my hand, but they would have been only a prelude to Hell.

I sat and got drunk.

From Daisy, who got her information from Phoebe, that expert listener at doors, came news of changes at Springhill. Apparently Jimmy, for all he had a fine house and good horses and grand clothes, had left but little money and this his son-in-law attributed to the slack way in which the plantation had been run. He was going to change all that! Those of us who were able-bodied were going to work much harder. The old and feeble who had been parasites were going to be sold off or turned adrift. The second pork ration had already gone, and now the allowance of meal was going to be reduced. Springhill was going to make Whittle's fortune as Tessimadi had made Oldfield's.

From the same source came rumours of bitter differences between Tottie and his wife. I quite believed that these reports were true. Miss Avril had loved her father and Tottie's ways were not his. Besides, could anyone, even an infatuated woman, live long with Tottie and not come to hate him? And their differences had not stopped short at angry words. Phoebe had listened, horrified and inactive, while blows were struck and things were thrown. God send, I used sometimes to think, that he might strike her in my presence! But it never happened, of course. I was a field hand.

About the changes, at least, Phoebe had not drawn upon his imagination. They, and many others, came to pass.

One morning we were all lined up in order. Tottie came down the line with his crop in his hand, Treacle with a sheet of paper and a pencil, at his heels. Starting with Fergus Tottie tapped him on the shoulder. "Stand out." Fergus stepped from the line. All the way along he went, picking out the old ones. Pluggy, Abraham, Sinda, David, and others whom I scarcely knew. For each one who stood out Treacle made a mark on the paper. Old Suzy was the first on the woman's line, and after her an almost sightless old woman named Aggie, another who was bent almost double from rheumatism, Madda's mother, and many more.

The rest of us then lined up at the tool house and went off to the fields. I took a good look, a farewell look at Fergus as I passed him. The calm, faraway expression of his face broke up into a smile and he slightly raised one hand. Heavy heartedly I set about the interminable hoeing.

"What will become of them?" I asked Jacko as I drew level with him.

"Dey'll be sold to folk's as am just beginnin', or to poah whites or free niggers what'll beat de daylights outa dem. Dat happen when you get old."

I hoed on past ten plants thinking of Fergus and then something happened in my stomach and I was sick. It was happening all over this part of the world. It wasn't only Fergus. Oh God! But why call upon God? Did He care? Was He being sick on His pearl-studded throne?

But for Fergus, anyhow, I needn't have worried. Within ten minutes he entered the field, hoe on shoulder, settling his almost brimless hat, Jimmy's last gift, over his eyes. I left my row, after a careful, stealthy look around to see whether Tottie or Treacle had yet entered the field.

"Reprieved," said Fergus with his faint, sardonic smile. "Tottie remembered just in time that I'm one of the few who can plant a thousand a day."

"What about the others?"

"Some are going to be sold cheap to people who can't afford good labour, and the rest, I suppose, will live on the charity of their friends and relatives. They're cut off the ration list anyway. God pity them."

His hoe descended. "You'd better get back, Treacle was just behind me."

His hoe bit into the soil, even, efficient strokes. Even after that little interlude he wasn't wasting time, or being slovenly.

Gradually, after that day, step by step and stride by stride the atmosphere upon Springhill changed. Less food, more work, more bullying. And by the strangest irony of fate there came next year a boom in the tobacco trade. The habit of smoking became more widespread and there was a blight in Havana. Tottie decided to clear more land for the spring planting. He went down to Josepha and bought four new slaves, big strong Koromantees who knew no English but chattered together in their own Gold Coast tongue and wore armlets and necklaces of teeth and berries. He sold Jimmy's cream mare and bought two new mules and with this much extra labour set to work to get an area of woodland under cultivation in time for the spring. We chopped and dug and finally hauled out the stumps that were too deeply rooted to be attacked by spades.

We discovered that although in Jimmy's time we had seemed well-fed, actually we were then living upon a nicely calculated minimum. The decrease in rations, the halving of the meat and the slight reduction in the meal allowance had made an almost incredible difference to our well-being. And there was now, just when our need was greatest, no time to attend to our own little gardens. We began work as soon as it was light and ended in the darkness and were too tired to do anything but creep into bed as soon as supper was eaten. There were no more sing-songs in the cabins, no more drinking of corn-brews in Jacko's shack.

I should have sworn that I was hardened to anything by this time. I had reached my full growth and every muscle in me was fully developed and hard; but stump-hauling left me dizzy and heaving and there were others in worse case than I, men who fell in their tracks, tangled in the ropes that bound them one to another and to the stump. Pulling, with a rope around your waist, against something that does not, perhaps for a full half hour, give an inch, jars every nerve and bone in your body. Even my jaws used to ache at night from the pressure of setting my teeth as I took the strain.

And Tottie or Treacle was always there to exact the final, the impossible ounce of effort: to belabour straining back and quivering limb with whip or crop.

Before the rough ground was half cleared I was planning madly to get away. Anything would be better than this. My life had not been calculated to encourage sentimentalism but I can truly say that in addition to my own woes of hunger and overwork and stripes to bear, I was afflicted by the misery all round me. It hung like a veil of smoke over the whole plantation. Old Pluggy, begging, like a homeless dog, from cabin to cabin: the blind woman, Aggie, who was found, dead of starvation on the waste ground behind the cabins: Fergus who had never shirked anything, being beaten one morning when his rheumatism made him slow: these things hurt me more than the hauling and the gnaw of hunger. I couldn't bear the sight or sound of this suffering. I must make another attempt to escape and hope rather to be killed than retaken.

I often wondered why I didn't kill myself. Why I didn't turn the knife that severed the flat cake of corn meal and water against my throat and perish in my blood. I thought of it many times. No more hunger or weariness or blows, no more pity, no more rage. But there was importance in being alive. Something might happen. And sometimes when I woke from dreams of Braidlowrie, though my heart was sore when I found myself waking where I did, I knew for an instant that while there was breath in my body there would be hope in my mind. To kill myself would be to hand Barlesci and Jimmy Standish and Tottie a victory. But I would make another attempt to escape.

It was madness of course: the madness of the desperate or the demented. But at the time I thought I was acting most sanely: that I had learned from my earlier attempt: that this time I stood a chance. Even now I can look back and feel a pang of reminiscent, sick despair for the young slave who thought that he could get away in Tottie Samson's clothes; who was arrested in the street at Josepha; who was claimed by an outraged master; who had robbery as well as attempted escape to answer for, and who paid for his folly in a puddle of blood at the whipping post outside the Springhill stables.

One of the new Koromantees wielded the scourge. He had been appointed to the post of flogger because he was big and strong and savage and hadn't been there long enough to have made friends whom it would irk him to flog. Tottie looked on, and for an eternity of twenty minutes, took full and exquisite revenge for all the moments of baffled hatred that I had given him in Jimmy's day. And he was well within his rights. I *had* stolen his clothes. I *had* run away. It was perfectly fair, according to the standards of the place, that my blood should be spilt and my flesh tattered in payment for the double crime.

Next morning, raw and bruised and aching, wincing at every movement, I was back at work with my lesson well learned. There were a thousand chances to one against ever getting away. The punishment for failure was savage and immediate. The risk was too great. I settled down.

Of Cassie during this time I saw nothing. The light bond between us had broken with the ceasing of my desire. Within a month of the baby's death she was taken into the house in some capacity or another and shortly appeared in a silk gown with flounces and gold rings in her ears. And who should blame her? That was her way of escape and it was better than mine. There came a time when, seeing her flaunting by, I did not even remember the hours in the shrubbery, or the evening when she had cried about Tottie, or the moment in the cabin when in one movement I had snuffed out the life that we between us had made. Life was damped down now into a smouldering furnace. Bestial labour, constant hunger, ever-present fatigue, careful avoidance of anything that might give offence. Slavery.

The cleared land was planted and the crop gathered. More land was cleared. Miss Avril grew old suddenly and had no more fine dresses, she used to walk through the pastures with a little dog at her heels, plain, neglected, the woman who had served her purpose, regretting I am sure the headstrong impulse of an injured vanity that had driven her into Tottie's arms. Cassie grew stout suddenly and was superseded by Madda's eldest daughter.

Season followed season. Fergus died one night in his sleep. Waking at dawn and stretching out my hand as usual to rouse him I found him stark and cold. I was glad, more glad than I had been of anything for years. Life lately had been a misery to him, and to me to watch. I buried him myself in the slave plot by the light of a borrowed lantern and dropped the worn-out husk of him into the ground with much envy and little sorrow. His work and his misery were ended. But so, cried something in my unresigned mind, was his life. To this end had his whole life dwindled, here ended his philosophy, his kindness and his faith. Even in death there were the dark marks of Treacle's whip upon his fleshless body. Man that was made in God's own image. Faugh!

I had been at Springhill ten years when war broke out anew between France and England.

PART THREE

THE WORLDLY HOPE

At first sight it would appear that the war which was to be known as the Seven Years' or the French and Indian War would have but little effect upon us who were so far removed from the countries concerned. Sometimes, indeed, I have been told, European countries would be at war and their colonies preserve the most friendly relationships. But just at this time the rivalry between France and England had reached a point where blood-letting was welcomed by everybody and upon the mainland of America and in the islands disturbances soon arose.

St. Crispin's had been originally a Spanish settlement, one of the earliest, though not important because of its small size. The French had taken it from the Spaniards and done a great deal to make the harbour the busy centre that it was. Some time during the Huguenot wars the English had taken it and had held it ever since. But now that war was once more afoot everyone expected that the French would make a bid for its recapture.

But even that, at first, did not appear to concern us, the slave population of the island. There were soldiers in Josepha, they would do any fighting that was to be done. And we had but little interest in the result of such fighting. Timmy — he who had played the banjo in the days when there was spirit enough in us to desire music — had once been owned by a Frenchman in Martinique and made no secret of his desire that the French might take the island.

"Eben de wust Frenchman am better to wuk fo' dan Mr. Whittle," he said with assurance. "Ain no Frenchman woulden let de priest bury yo' or marry yo' or baptisal yo' babies. Bery good de priests wuz in Mart'nique, bery pow'ful too. An' French marsa am good. Dutch wust, den English an' French am best. Ah's be bery glad to see dem lilies wabe ober dis place."

I thought suddenly of my mother who had always said that the French were a civilised race. But I did not share Timmy's hope. I was too dejected in spirit to care who owned me. Even a humane and civilised nation would have its exceptions and we might fall to one of them. Also, it had been borne upon me these last few years, the avarice for profit, combined with the absolute power that was the slave-owners' prerogative, was bound to have a detrimental effect upon any character, however fine. Jimmy Standish had happened not to be greedy and had a squeamish side to his complex nature, therefore life had been tolerable under his rule, yet he had not hesitated to enslave me or to call Mac and Fergus "lifers". Slavery debased those who owned, as well as those who were owned. I had no hope.

Before long the war impinged upon our lives. There was a great deal of coming and going among the planters. Tottie rode into Josepha and was absent for two days. On the morning after his return we were lined up again as we had been at intervals for the winnowing out of the old and inefficient. This time, however, it was the youngest and strongest who were asked to stand out and the others who were sent off to the tool house.

Tottie then mounted his horse, and from this elevation addressed us. We had doubtless heard, he began, that England and France were at war and that the French were attempting, amongst other things, to capture this island. Should they do so we should be the ones to suffer. The French were the worst and hardest masters in the world. Moreover they belonged to a religious body called Roman Catholics who believed in human sacrifice. Any one of us who had a child might expect, should the French succeed in landing, to see that child's throat cut and a priest drinking its blood. Furthermore every French slave owner had his private mark which was branded into the thigh of every slave he owned.

I looked round for Timmy as Tottie said that, interested to see whether his disbelief would be shown in his face. But Timmy was not with us. Perhaps Tottie knew of his sojourn in Martinique and refrained from including him. Tottie was no fool.

He went on speaking and every word was calculated to raise terror in these ignorant people, so that, even in the confusion of a siege, they would not take advantage of any relaxation of discipline but would throw in their lot whole-heartedly with their master's. From that point of view it was a good speech, and it was not Tottie's fault that he had in his audience a man who had been reared a Catholic and whose mother had lived in France.

Our names were then written down upon a roll and the list read over. As each of the oddly assorted names was called its owner stepped forward and received a length of the red-and-white striped calico that, wound into a breech clout or made into a skirt, was the uniform of Springhill. Then we were marched into an empty drying shed where a meal, the like of which had not gladdened us since Tottie's wedding-day, was set before us.

Jacko, who had pushed his way to my side, filled his mouth with fried pork and potato and said, through the barricade,

"Ah hope dis war go on fo' twenny years. Maybe we's get food like dis oll de time. Maybe we's get guns too. 'Course you hassen got no babies, but soon's marsa say dat bit 'bout dem killin' de chillun Ah knows dat Ah could hannle eben one of dem guns. Dere nebber wuz sich a fighter as dis nigger gonna be."

I looked at his wide innocent face, with a streak of grease from his breakfast making a slow way down his chin and a pang went through me. Deluded, deliberately misinformed, he was ready now to fight for those who, having battened upon and ill-used him, had found another use for his strength. Common men, ignorant men had been used like that since time began. For a moment he stood before me, a symbol of all those who, urged by the sheep-dog Terror, had willingly galloped into the slaughter-house. And then he was just

230

Jacko, enjoying an unusually good breakfast again. I thought of our rising. At least all those who rose had had an interest in the cause and the result of it. That was how wars should be. At this moment the masters should be carrying the weight of this affray,

"I guess we won't get near a gun," I said. "They'd never dare arm us." But at the same time hope reared a timid head in my heart. And when, fortified by our meal and clad in our new cotton clouts, we set out for Josepha, I stepped lightly. Something was happening at last.

There were twenty-four of us Springhill men and at the gates of Tessimadi we were joined by thirty of Oldfield's. Oldfield himself, ageing now and a cripple from gout, rode beside the file. I remembered the pleasure with which he had "cauterised" my leg and fingers, and I hoped that gout was the most painful affliction of all those the flesh is heir to.

The slaves sang as they walked. It was the first time that some of them had ever been off the plantations since they were born or taken there. To go into Josepha was in itself a holiday.

The whole force of the defence was concentrated in the port, for it was the only accessible place along the coast line. Our first job was to build, of beams and stones and loads of moist soil, mounds upon which the cannon were to be mounted. Then, to link these mounds, we erected breastworks behind which the defenders might shelter to repel attack. It was heavy work and hasty, but not so hard as stump hauling, and it was a change. I worked just hard enough to escape notice but without enthusiasm. Let the French come. Nothing that they could do would be worse than what Tottie had done of recent years at Springhill. And in the confusion . . . Hope, or if that be too strong a term, speculation, awakened in my mind, burrowing up through layers of despair and indifference like a shoot through layers of last year's leaves. In the confusion, if I kept my wits about me, I might see a chance, which, boldly taken, would alter my whole life.

I listened eagerly to every careless word dropped in my hearing and learned that the cause of all this activity was the news brought in by a fast vessel of French ships sighted between St. Crispin's and Martinique, heading in our direction. I remembered the conversation in the plague office on the day of my arrival and wondered idly whether Jellybags, whoever he might be, in his same "fast old tub" were still acting as scout.

Lookouts, stationed upon the flat roofs of the highest of the white buildings, kept watch through their glasses: but for the first day and a half after our arrival at Josepha their vigil was unrewarded.

In the midst of all this labour and suspense we were not allowed to forget our slavery. Tottie, with his list in his yellow hand, checked our numbers several times a day. We of the striped breech-clouts were kept together: the Tessimadi men, distinguished by their yellow calico, were kept apart from those of Claremont who wore green. Time was, I reflected, when we of Springhill would have stood out from the rest by virtue of our sleek condition, but that time was past. We were all alike, lean, scraggy and scrofulous. The slaves from other plantations of which I had never even heard were similarly isolated and counted and overlooked. The general apprehension and confusion had not undermined the sense of ownership.

In the burning hours of the second afternoon alarms were suddenly sounded. The lookouts had seen sails on the horizon. Immediately the soldiers in their bright coats, who had been lounging about and spitting as they watched us hauling and pushing and heaving, were all attention. The cannon were already mounted and now supplies of powder and fuses and balls were carried up to the platforms. An officer went round from gentleman to gentleman as they overlooked their slaves, spoke for a time and passed on. He paused by Tottie and I sidled into a position where I could overhear.

"In the event of a landing, which is improbable, but just possible, what is your opinion about arming the slaves, Mr . . . er . . . Whittle?"

Tottie drew a few lines with the toe of his boot in the loose soil that we had scattered upon the hard roadway of the waterfront.

"I should be against that, even as a last resort," he said, finally.

"That seems to be the general opinion," said the officer. "Still, it might be as well to pick out a few absolutely trustworthy men with the idea in view. Our force is able and well-disciplined, but as you see, small."

"That," said Tottie rather hotly, "is not our fault. We pay our dues and they should cover the cost of adequate protection. Slaves are for work, not fighting."

"It's rather late to complain now," said the officer, even more hotly. "If the dues had been raised a penny and the permanent force increased you'd have talked revolution in an instant. You islanders are all alike. Short-sighted and distrustful of your own men."

"I'd trust my men with every gun in your armoury."

"Then why oppose arming them?"

"A matter of principle," Tottie said. The officer snorted and passed on. I saw him put the same question to Cartell, and saw him shake his head. Of course, they were all afraid. Oh God, I prayed into space, let them give me a gun. Let Tottie trust me with a gun. Two minutes would be long enough. I remembered the heavy old musket, rusting in the corner of the kitchen at Braidlowrie. There'd never been powder for it, but I knew the feel of it, the way it worked. And I had an aim that had been acquired from catapults and bows and arrows, home-made and faulty every one of them. I could account for Tottie, in two minutes, with a gun. God let him pick me.

We were forced to work with redoubled speed. All through the sweltering heat of the late afternoon and the brief twilight we toiled to raise the earthwork breast high all along the curved line of the waterfront. Gradually, as though they were growing out of the sea, the sails and masts and then the hulls of the French ships appeared. Around us all was confusion. In addition to the activities of the soldiers and the slaves there were the terrified townsfolk endeavouring to remove every portable article from the shops, warehouses and houses that faced the harbour. Women and old men and children staggered away with bundles towards the landside of the town. Night came down like a curtain upon the coloured scene, but beneath it the town stirred still; lanterns and voices and hoarsely shouted orders testified to the wakefulness of Josepha.

Next day, withdrawn with the rest of the slaves, I watched my first battle. At first it was like watching a play. The tall ships came up gracefully, dipping and tacking until their bright cannon had the range of us. We watched three balls, directed with exquisite precision, destroy in three minutes the platform for one of our cannon that it had taken us eight sweated hours to build. Stones and beams and close-packed earth flew in all directions and the cannon dipped and slithered, ending with its harmless muzzle pointing to the sky.

The platform must be repaired. But that meant working within the range of the French guns, and many Negroes, terrified as they were of their masters, rebelled at that. It was with difficulty that twenty of us were rounded up and driven to the work. The rest, with the cunning of the weak in this world, scattered amongst the deserted warehouses and shops and houses, or melted away to return to their plantations, the evils of which were at least familiar.

Other shots found the buildings along the front and tore through the white walls as though they were made of paper like the houses in Japan about which Fanshawe had once told me. Our guns, or our gunners, were inferior, or else the sun, coming up dazzlingly behind the French ships, confused their aim; for although our cannon thudded again and again, not a

235

shot at first found a mark. The balls ploughed up the water of the harbour and that was all.

The haze of the smoke rose and thickened so that over the harbour presently the sun was dimmed and it was strange sometimes to look inland and see the white buildings and the green trees fresh and bright. Then, under cover of the smoke, the boats began to be lowered from the ships and filled with men. They began to steal across the dividing water. One cannon, ours, upon its reconstructed platform, flashed and boomed and one shot fell amidships of a boat. The ends of it flew up in splinters, among the flashing spouts of water and then, as the water settled, we could see bodies and bobbing heads and bits of shattered timber rise to the surface and float. Another shot from a ship hit the platform again and the gunner, fuse still in hand, rolled down the little mound and fell at my feet in a welter of blood. At that, interest, which had kept me watching, gave way to caution and I took cover behind the earthwork.

Small parties of soldiers now took up exposed positions along the edges of the stone wall that went down into the water, but the French boats — and they seemed numerous and swift as mosquitoes — scattered around the half-moon of the harbour and avoided the guarded steps. The heavy booming of the cannon was supplemented by the rapid rattle of musket fire; the almost play-like deliberation of the earlier phases of the battle gave way to confusion. The air was dark with smoke and full of shouting, officers rallying men, men yelling themselves into a frenzy of battle lust, screams of wounded men. And amid it all I heard the shout that told that slave-owners were slave-owners still. "All slaves withdraw. All slaves withdraw."

I ignored it, but the few slaves who had sheltered behind the breastwork at the same time as I took refuge, rose and ran obediently to the shattered buildings across the roadway. I saw Oldfield hobble into the line behind the earthwork and start to load the heavy little pistol which was all that he could manage in the way of weapon. Then somebody thrust a warm musket into my hand and said, "Aim low." I picked up the pouches of powder and shot which he had dropped beside me and was engrossed in loading the unfamiliar weapon when something hard was rammed into my ribs. I whipped round, thinking that the French had landed in another part of the line. But it was Tottie who stood behind me with the muzzle of his gun pressed into me.

"Put down that musket and get into your line."

I looked at him; saw the resolution of fear in his eyes; saw his finger on the trigger. I dropped my weapon and went the way of the other slaves, back into the buildings. But the others had followed those who had gone earlier and the big fruit warehouse in which I found myself was empty save for scattered fruit, barrels and wicker baskets. I turned my back upon the fighting and fished about in the debris for whole fruit. After all it was not my battle. Any allegiance that I might have owed to England had been cancelled long ago. I was Colin Lowrie, son of a Jacobite. I had been watched for at the ports of my native land, accurately described so that I might be taken and hanged. Now I was not going to stay in this dangerous place, nor was I going to follow Jacko and the rest of them back to Springhill. I was going to take shelter and when the town was taken I was going to make my own bargain with the French, if that were possible. I began fumbling in my mind for the French so reluctantly, yet perhaps so fortunately, learned from my French-loving mother.

Just then a cannon ball crashed through the building to the left of me, a shower of masonry and powdered plaster poured down. A brick hit me violently on the head and as I stood reeling I saw an English soldier dart into the building, kneel down and take aim. But a shot from outside carried away half his head and he fell backward, his musket rattling on the cool stone floor of the warehouse. I ran forward, picked it up and then began to thread my way out of the ruined building, making for the road that ran along the other side, the street where I had made my last attempt to free myself from Jimmy Standish on that morning all those years ago.

I came out about midway along the curve of the road. At the end further from the harbour some horses, left there by their masters, were tied to the hitching post and stamping-mad with terror. Racing towards them, pausing now and then to shoot at a pursuer who gained too quickly, were the gentlemen who had feared their slaves too much to arm them. Serve them right, I thought. And then I saw Tottie. He was running on my side of the road. A French soldier shot at him and missed. Tottie ran on.

He was level with me as I raised my musket and just past me as I fired. In that second, years and years of impotent hatred were re-lived in my mind, no less bitter for being telescoped into a little space. Fergus being flogged, dying with the marks of the whip upon him: the old slaves being denied their ration: the semi-starvation, the blows that we had taken while our limbs were jarring at the taut rope: even the old affair of Cassie: all these were behind that simple crooking of my finger. I got him full between the shoulders and he fell forward. The soldier just behind him ran on.

I jumped a pile of broken wall and rubble and seized Tottie round his waist and dragged him into the comparative seclusion of the warehouse. I didn't even bother to make sure if he were dead. With fingers shaking from excitement I ripped off his trousers and put them on, still warm from his body as they were, over my hated breech-clout. As I tightened them about my waist I felt my lips curl back as a dog's do when he snarls. The breech-clout had been the final ignominy, which Jimmy, from some lingering sense of fitness, had never thrust upon Mac or Fergus or me. Tottie had been delighted when the last pairs of Jimmy's cast-offs, preserved with anxious care, had by their raggedness made it imperative for Fergus and me to apply for others. He had flung the lengths of striped cotton at us, together with assurances, which weren't needed, that the pampering days were done. Now my own legs were decently covered while his knobby limbs stuck out, grotesque and naked.

Under the trousers he had been wearing a belt of brown leather, greasy from use. I unstrapped it, intending to wear it to support the trousers, which, tighten them as I might, were too big for my waist, slender from hard work and under-feeding. But as I drew it clear of the body the weight of it told me that this belt had another purpose. It was indeed an elongated purse. I peered into its pouches. Golden guineas, broad silver crowns, more money than I had ever seen in my life before. I strapped it about me, and then, to hide it, donned the coat with the hole and the powder burn in the middle of the back.

Next I measured my feet by his. No good. Tottie's feet were enormous at the end of his thick shanks, but my own, from going barefoot so long, were bigger. Never mind, if things went as I planned and hoped I could have boots of my own.

I found a handkerchief in the coat pocket and taking it in my hand like a flag of truce I stepped into the street again. The noise of the firing had lessened and the smoke haze was shredding out on the breeze that often swept over the island in the late afternoon and early evening. For a moment or two the street was empty, save for the bodies lying as they had fallen, with pools of blood widening in the dust about them. Then suddenly I heard French voices and out of another warehouse further along the road I saw three French soldiers, each with a cluster of bananas in his left hand and a musket in his right, step into the street. I held the handkerchief high and went to meet them. I drew a deep breath to steady myself and then said loudly, in the best French I could muster,

"Welcome. Please speak to me. I haven't heard a French tongue in ten years."

They weren't even surprised. Perhaps they remembered that St. Crispin's had once been a French possession. They asked me a few questions as we walked along abreast, and I found the French words crowding back into my memory so that my answers were prompt and, I suppose, satisfactory. The offered me some of their bananas and took me along to the Square in the middle of the town, where, over the Governor's big white house, the French flag was already being run up.

Two officers stood at the top of the shallow steps, talking. They had their swords in their hands still, but as we approached one of them slid his into the scabbard and drew out his handkerchief. He pushed back his hat and dabbed at his forehead. Slowly, as though by deliberate imitation, the other repeated the actions. It was as though they indicated by dumbshow that the fighting was at an end. For them that might be true, but I felt that for me it had only just started. The three Frenchmen who had met me had seemed friendly enough, but they were only common soldiers, without influence or power. What would those in command make of my story — supposing that I was permitted to tell it? They might take the view that technically I was a slave and must share the fate of the other conquered property. Something in me hardened at that thought. I had not come thus far to be thrust back again to the level of Jacko and Timmy! And it was better not to wait.

All day I had been forcing things and so far had done well. I would continue to solicit Fortune, rather than wait for her to turn to me.

"Take me to your officer," I said to the soldier nearest me. He consulted briefly with his fellows and then began pushing through the men who were rapidly filling the Square, until we reached a gorgeously attired young man who listened to the soldier's hasty, blurting explanation of me and my request to see an officer, then turned and swept me from head to toe with a scornful glance and languidly inquired what I wanted, and whether I thought that the French had nothing else to do than listen to individual stories from people whom they didn't know.

"But it is important to me that somebody listens *now*," I said urgently. And I longed, with a fierceness that almost sickened me, for a chance to speak in my own tongue. I could be so much more lucid and convincing if I hadn't to confine myself to phrases which I could translate.

"I'm a Scot," I said desperately. "A Jacobite. I was sold without justice and without reason. I hoped that the French would befriend me. The Jacobites and the French were always friends."

"Oh, Scot," he said without interest. "Jacobite. I am not interested in that." He turned away with a final gesture of hand and shrug of shoulder that dismissed me from his presence and from his mind.

The little common soldier looked at me helplessly.

"I can do nothing," he said. "I must return."

242

One more minute — I thought — and I shall be just a unit in a disorganised slave community. I had a moment of panic, as though I had stood poised on the edge of a precipice and was now slipping. I mustn't slip.

"One moment, just one moment more," I said, and laid my hand on his little square shoulder. "Isn't there one Scotsman with all you French? Hundreds of Scotsmen found their way to France, and good fighters every one of them. Isn't there one here?"

He thought for a moment, and then the blankness of his face broke into a look of understanding and determination.

"Come," he said simply and together we hurried across the Square, separated sometimes by the press of people but not for long. We reached a side door of the Governor's house where a guard was already posted. My little guide spoke to him hurriedly and then said to me, "I can come no further."

"What do I do now?"

"The one you must see is within."

"And how do I get inside?"

He raised his shoulders. Suddenly I remembered the belt. I fumbled in it and brought out the first coin that met my fingers — a guinea. I pressed it into the little soldier's hand.

"Thank you," I said, "you have done your best." He jerked his thumb to the guard.

"For him too," he hinted. I fished out a second coin.

"Ask for le capitaine and do not be deterred," said my friend. And as he hurried away the guard pocketed his coin and stood aside.

"The door at the end of the passage," he said and took up his place again, wooden and immobile.

I made my way dizzily down the passage and opened the door at the end of the passage. If this fails and someone else says he isn't interested I shall die of sheer despair, I thought as I turned the handle.

There were two men within, bowed over a table of maps and papers. They looked up startled. One was just a face. But at the sight of the other my whole inside gave a great jump. An April afternoon, the clean, unperfumed scent of cherry blossom in the air, my sheepskin coat coming warmly from my arms, Janet crying. Even as these things shot through my memory I assured myself that it couldn't be. Coincidences didn't happen in real life, only in the old plays that father read. But even as I so rebuked my leaping fancy my mouth opened and I cried, without any breath left to cry with, "Glenranald! Glenranald, do you remember Lowrie?"

He left the table and came towards me and we met with an impact that sent us into one another's arms. He clasped me, held me away so that he could kiss me, French fashion, on either cheek, clasped me again. The other officer stood watching this demonstration with interest and surprise.

"Louis," said Glenranald, forgetting his French in his excitement, "this is the Lowrie I've told you so much about. The one who saved my life."

"Je ne comprends pas," said Louis patiently. Glenranald ignored him and turned back to me.

244

"Where have you come from? What have you been doing?" His eyes had fallen upon my bare feet with the out-sticking prehensile toe that comes of walking barefoot in soft soil.

"They didn't *sell* you?"

"I was sold," I said slowly, "ten years ago. But the English were only indirectly responsible."

"Because of me?"

"In a way. But it's a long story."

"Well, thank God in His mercy," said Glenranald, with an emotion that went oddly with his hard lined face and brilliant uniform, "that now at last I can do something for you."

"If you'll just speak for me," I said unsteadily, "and not let me be sent back to Springhill — you've no idea what it's like here — every man's hand is against a slave — it does something to you — breaks you. Another rebuff just now and I should have collapsed. And then it was you!"

"Thank Heaven. And you've nothing to worry about any more. Look here, I've got half an hour's work to do and then we're having dinner. Would you like to go upstairs and take a bath and find some — some shoes and things? We've taken over the whole house, you can have what you want."

He found a frightened slave and gave him orders in an authoritative tone so that presently I was being shown the bath house and then conducted to a luxuriously furnished bedroom where whole suits of clothes belonging to some large and well-accommodated person, perhaps the Governor himself, hung in a closet. I sent the Negro away and shut the door.

I went straight to the mirror that hung over the dressing chest. I laughed aloud as my own reflection met my eyes. I hadn't looked into a mirror for ten years and I needed a shave just as badly as I had done on that morning in the cabin of the *Sheba*. I had shaved since of course, with Fergus's razor, but the last time I had used it was on that morning at Springhill before Tottie made his speech. So long ago now it seemed, though it was only three days. But how those three days had altered things. My mind reeled when I thought of it. I wanted to shout and sing and make animal noises of excitement and gloating. But I controlled myself and tossed Tottie's clothes into a bundle in the corner and found a razor and started to shave with a hand that shook despite all my care. The person in the mirror, so assiduously scraping his chin, was a stranger to me. I had no idea I was so big, or so brown, or so lean or so old looking. The last ten years had marked me more than half a life-time of ordinary living. My scarred back no eye need ever see. I need not see it myself unless I chose to crane and peer. But the deep lines between mouth and nostril and in my cheeks and forehead were there forever. And there was a powdering of white hairs in the mop of red that fell over my brow. And there was the stiff useless finger and the hole in my calf. Still, everything considered I had come out well. I was whole and sane, and I might so easily have been neither.

And I was free. And I had found a friend. I stood there naked in the middle of the big room and said, aloud, "I am free." Only for the erstwhile bondsman have the words any significance. The poor man may find himself rich, the sick man wake up well and both may begin planning the future and comparing it with the past. But the slave who finds himself free has no plans, no thoughts, no comparisons. He cannot get beyond the dazzling fact, "I am free." I hung upon that all the time until I was shaved and brushed and properly dressed in clothes that I took from the closet.

That evening, seated upon Glenranald's right after I had been led round from one to another of his friends, and the story of Boarswood had been repeated countless times and I had lost tally of the number of people who had kissed me upon both cheeks, I dined at a table spread with fair linen and lighted by candles and sparkling with silver. These hands, used for so long to no other tools than axe and hoe, shovel and pick, curved pliantly around the handle of a silver spoon. My stomach, accustomed these many years to coarse scant fare, took its fill of rich and delicate food, and after the harsh corn-brew the wines were like liquid jewels. It was a merry meal. The French were celebrating their victory and I was celebrating the more momentous thing — my escape and the meeting with Glenranald. There were toasts. "Today's Victory": "My friend Colin Lowrie who literally gave me ten years of his life": "The King of Scotland": "The King of France." And after that Glenranald took me aside into the room where I had first found him.

"Now," he said, "begin where we parted and tell me the whole story."

"First," I said, "you tell me things. I've been cut off for ten years you know. Is there any news from Scotland? My father and mother . . ."

"You didn't even know that?" His voice was heavy.

"I know nothing. Is it bad?"

"Of course, you couldn't know." He paused and I saw the white line come round his mouth. "They tried your father, Colin, for complicity in my escape. They dragged him down to Edinburgh and the poor old man couldn't stand the strain of the journey. He died as soon as he got there almost. In prison. God rest his soul." He crossed himself and I repeated the action mechanically.

"And my mother?"

"She must have been dead before you were over the doorsill by all accounts. I heard all this because Fraser of Frasersmote and Lesley of Strangcaundle couldn't get away. They took hiding in one of Fraser's shepherd's huts and were there six months before they got away. The excitement when they arrived — everybody crowding round for news you know."

"And Braidlowrie — the house?"

"Abandoned, like a lot of others. I'm sorely sorry to have to be the one to tell you these things, Colin. And I'm grieved about your people. It was all through me when you get to the root of it. And your ten years too . . ."

He paused and brushed his hand across his forehead and looked at me as though he expected reproaches from me.

248

"No need to be sorry," I said harshly. "My father and mother hadn't much of a life. So Braidlowrie's finished?"

"With Frasersmote and Strangcaundle and Blythlanger and my own Lavlossie."

"It's odd," I said slowly, "but it was always my ambition to rebuild that house, and get a little land together again. I don't suppose I'll do it now."

"We all have these ambitions," said Glenranald with a wry smile. "Mine was to try old Turnip Townshend's rotation of crops and see if I couldn't put Lavlossie on its legs again by farming. Instead, you see, I was fated to be a mercenary and fight the French king's battles for him. What are you going to do now, Colin? Would you care to throw in your lot with mine?"

"Do mercenaries make any money, Glenranald?"

"Not a sou. They live on the fat of the land one day, and starve the next. They make empires, but never fortunes. They sack palaces and die in ditches. But it's a grand life all the same."

"Not for me," I said thoughtfully. "I've got to make some money. And I've got ten years of misery to make up for. The only thing I know anything about is tobacco planting, so I must try that. Glenranald, will you help me to get to Virginia? I don't know why Virginia pulls me. Whenever I've thought about getting away, or a miracle happening, I've had Virginia in mind. I think there's something for me there."

"If you feel like that I have no doubt there is," he said, speaking equally thoughtfully. "Still, we could have used you. But let me think. Virginia, Jamestown.

One of our ships is going back to New Orleans with news of the victory in the morning. You could go in her. Despite the war there's still a good deal of trade between New Orleans and Jamestown. It should be a simple matter. Let's drink to your future. May you be rich and happy."

"It's strange," I said, voicing the thought almost as it came, "but when we left you, Janet and I, under that tree that evening, I had a kind of feeling about us, all going on our different paths. I wonder what happened to Janet. I never dreamed that my life would be like this, or that if ever we met again it would be here, or that your coming would mean so very much to me. It is queer, isn't it?"

"It's life," said Glenranald with a shrug. "But I do thank God that we came. When I think of you . . . a mere child . . . ten years a slave because of me . . ." He broke off and raised his glass. "I will give you a letter to a man who will be helpful to you in New Orleans, a M. Filsac. And you'll be ready to leave in the morning?"

I nodded, looking, not at Glenranald, but ahead, into a future agleam with possibilities. I was leaving St. Crispin's in the morning!

Two months later, after two voyages and a stay in New Orleans, all uneventful, and to me delightful, I landed in Jamestown. Hoarding my little store of money carefully, I sought out a cheap lodging. I found it in a hostelry called the *John and Pocohontas.*

250

* * *

I intended, once in Jamestown, to indulge for a little in that form of deferred activity known as "looking about me." I was just a little like a dog that has been kept so long upon a chain that when it is, by chance, released, it runs round in circles and makes no progress.

For ten years, indeed I might say for all my twenty-seven years, I had been ordered and controlled by minds and wills not my own. True I had had an undercurrent of life that was mine alone, no one had ordered me to help Glenranald, or to take Cassie, or to smother the baby, but my outer life, my time of rising, retiring, what I ate and what I did, had all been arranged for me. And although during the taking of St. Crispin's my wits had seemed unimpaired by their long time of disuse now that the whole of my life was in my own control again I found myself doing foolish things.

I found, for example, that the money I had taken from Tottie was very little to start life on. Yet in New Orleans I had ordered three suits of clothes, two pairs of boots, a great deal of linen. I found eating places and wine shops almost irresistible. I picked up a trollop in Quartier Sud and housed and fed her for days and gave her a broad gold piece at parting though she had given me less than a tenth the pleasure that I had had of Cassie for nothing. Within limits, and those imposed by greater age rather than experience, I was behaving much as I should have done had I landed, with a little money, in some such place ten years ago straight from the *Sheba*. But I enjoyed all the foolish things I did because I chose to do them and the very possibility of

251

choice emphasised the delicious fact that I was a free man. The desire for freedom in small personal matters amounted almost to mania. It was because of this that I was lodging at the *John and Poker*, as it was known to its intimates. Glenranald's friend, Filsac, had treated me with kindly hospitality in New Orleans, and had in turn commended me to a friend of *his*, a Mr. Preswade. I had presented the letter of introduction, and Preswade, with the instant hospitality to which I was gradually becoming accustomed, urged me to take up my headquarters at his house for as long as I wished. But this idea was repellent to me. I wanted to be on my own. So I thanked him and said that I might be in Jamestown for a very long time, or a very short one, my plans were so uncertain that I would not take the risk of upsetting his household. Then I must at least dine with him. And that I did.

The Preswade house was large and comfortably appointed, and the dinner was excellent. Mrs. Preswade was a faded woman who had once been pretty, and there were three daughters all fair and blue eyed who had inherited some of her looks. They all fussed and twittered round me in a way that should have been pleasing but which I found embarrassing and faintly alarming. They asked me numerous questions about the Filsacs. Had I known them long. Did I think Marie Filsac beautiful. Had I met her fiancé. Had M. Filsac tried to persuade me to invest in one of his wild-goose companies. They inquired into my own plans. Did I intend to settle in Virginia. Had I many friends in the state. I found myself giving awkward and evasive answers to these and similar questions.

From something, perhaps it was my acquaintance with the Filsacs whom they appeared greatly to esteem, or from my new clothes, they seemed to have gathered the idea that I was wealthy. Caroline, the eldest and most determinedly vivacious of the three, professed great disappointment when I confessed that I was not looking for a house in the town.

"You could have taken the Harrison house," she said. "It's quite the nicest house in the town. I only wish father would afford it."

"You'd love to have a stake in the Harrison house, wouldn't you, Carrie?" asked Julia with a hint of acidity in her voice. Caroline turned bright pink from the low frill of her corsage to the edge of her curly hair.

"I have at least been in it," she said.

"And would be now if old Harrison hadn't decided to send Thomas to England . . ."

"Girls, girls," expostulated their mother. "What will Mr. Lowrie think of you?" She turned her faded, apologetic smile on me and I gathered that what I thought of Julia and Caroline and Rosina was a matter of moment to her.

After dinner we went to the drawing-room where Rosina, after some apparently bashful hesitation, was persuaded to show me her paintings, which, her mother assured me, were considered to evidence great talent. I looked, with interest completely feigned, at the pale washy representations of various flowers and birds. After that Caroline seated herself at the spinet and rattled out several tinkling little tunes. Julie took up a graceful attitude and sang to some of them.

Then the questions broke out afresh. Did I sing. Did I like music. Was I fond of dancing. Had I visited the theatre at New Orleans. They'd heard that it was very good.

To all these questions I could only give answers that sounded like those of an idiot, unless they were understood to be those of a man who had spent his early years tending pigs and his later ones in a slave cabin. I hesitated to say that the only music I really like or understood was made by Negroes on their home-made banjoes, fiddles and drums. I could not say that to my mind the thin tinkling music was not to be compared with Timmy's rendering of "Lift Up Yo' Heart." The only dancing that I had ever seen was the barefooted shuffle and jig of the Thanking Days and Tottie's wedding. I grew more and more uncomfortable and wished that they would become discouraged and leave me to conversation with their father who seemed both well-informed and good-natured. But they were quite indefatigable. Finally Caroline said in her sprightly way, "Mr. Lowrie reminds me of someone."

"Sterman Lummis," said her father promptly. "I noticed it myself."

"Oh *no*," cried the girls, almost in unison. "Sterman isn't nearly so handsome! Is he, mother?"

"Is who what?" asked Mrs. Preswade who had been absorbed in her embroidering.

"Sterman Lummis. He's not nearly so handsome as Mr. Lowrie, is he?"

"Really," said Mrs. Preswade, poising her needle, "I'm afraid Mr. Lowrie will think Virginian manners very free after those of New Orleans. It is very confusing to have one's personal appearance so discussed. Don't you find it so, Mr. Lowrie?"

"I'm sure," cried Rosina, "that if somebody called me handsome I should be vastly flattered."

She looked at me in what I suppose people mean when they speak of "a fetching manner;" and I was utterly at a loss. Nothing in my experience enabled me to deal with this kind of small talk. Marie Filsac, the only young woman of their class whom I had met, had recently become affianced, and had treated me with reserve while I was under the Filsac roof. When I failed to produce the inevitable and obvious retort to Rosina's sally I thought the girls would have finished with me. But no, off they went again. Did I ride. Did I like riding. Would I ride with them some morning.

I sat there and watched them covertly. All young, all pretty, sprightly, vivacious, beautifully gowned and for me about as attractive as dolls would have been. Why was it? Under the light drift of chatter I searched for a reason. Even had I been what they imagined, a rich and eligible man looking for a house and a wife to grace it, I should never have chosen one of these. Perhaps, in my ignorance, I misjudged them. Perhaps under the frills and bows, the mannerisms and the sallies, there were real fleshly women whom a man might take into his bed. But I was not even interested to find out. They were, to me, empty and sexless. I was glad when

Preswade carried me off for "a quiet pipe" as he called it, in his own sanctum.

It was partly with an idea of making my position clear as well as through desire for information, that I said,

"Mr. Preswade, Mr. Filsac told me that you knew the country around here very well. I wondered if you would advise me. I have very little money and I want to start planting on my own, because I understand that. Is there land to be picked up cheaply anywhere in the vicinity?"

"None very suitable. Estates are always coming into the market, naturally, but fully developed and valuable. And for miles around the only unexploited land has been left so because it's worthless. If you really have very little money you should look around Fort Anchor way. Mind you, you then have to clear and build and wait to see how things turn out. It might be just as expensive in the end. Now what you really want," he stroked his chin, "is to find somebody who wants to retire and would take a sum down and retain an interest. I'll keep you in mind. I meet a lot of people in the course of my business, and I'll very likely hear of something . . ."

"That's very good of you."

"Good, not a bit," he said heartily. "I'm always glad to help anyone to start. I landed here myself in seventeen-eleven with ten pounds, now I've got one of the biggest export businesses in the state — in the country I might almost say. Get clear in your own noddle what you want and then go for it, is my motto. Always has been and so far it's only failed me once."

He paused, but the pause was not conclusive. It invited the question,

"And that was?"

He jerked his thumb in the direction of the drawing-room.

"Three girls," he said succinctly. "Can't be helped, of course, nobody's fault. And the worst of it is they're all such *girls*. If there'd been one of them with a bit of brain or interest in the business — and say what you will there *are* women like that — I'd have taken her in, damme if I wouldn't. As it is I suppose I'll have to sell it when I get too old to run it, unless one of them marries a likely fellow. And there the trouble is that the money and the business don't seem to attract the right sort. Likely young fellows prefer to strike out on their own. Now someone like you, with a bit of money to invest in the business to give him responsibility, and no nonsense about him . . ."

"How do you know I've no nonsense about me?"

"Watched you in there," he said with another jerk. "I always watch 'em. They're as silly as the girls, the ones that hang round most. 'La, Miss Carrie,' 'I swear, Miss Julie,' 'You're such a quizz, Miss Rosie.' Make me sick. Why, Rosie tries that handsome bait on everybody. They all bite. You just sat there looking savage and I liked you for it. 'Do you sing, Mr. Lowrie?' Do they want a man or a perishing canary? Tell me, have you ever known a man worth his salt who would stand up and sing the sort of piddling muck they do sing nowadays?"

257

I thought of Fanshawe, Glenranald, Fergus, and shook my head.

"Of course not. Look here. I've taken a fancy to you. Don't you go and do anything rash. Look around a bit and come here as often as you like and if you decide to put your bit of money into Preswade's I'll be real glad to have you. And you can have which of the little wenches you fancy most. Julie'd be my pick."

"Good God," I said. "You talk about doing anything rash. That's the rashest proposition I ever heard of. You don't know anything about me, never saw me until this morning. I might be the worst kind of rogue . . ."

"Don't you believe it! I've been out here getting on for fifty years and I've made my way. I know a rogue when I see one, and I know an honest man. Shouldn't have got far if I didn't. This place is civilised now, but it wasn't forty years ago. Why, my good man, the fact that after looking over my girls and hearing from all that twaddle about the Harrison house that you didn't look exactly like a beggar, you walked in here and said you'd only got a little money proves my case. A rogue would have hung round and hid that fact until one of the girls was yelping mad for him and it was too late to inquire into his circumstances."

"Maybe you're right. Still I don't think a rogue will do your girls much harm — with a shrewd father like you in the offing. Though I think you've judged me pretty hastily. I've done quite a number of things that you wouldn't think so startlingly honest."

"Haven't we all?" asked the man who had made his way in the world. "But it's what you are that counts. A dirty gold plate is better than a clean potsherd one, you know."

"More valuable, but not better if you've got to eat off it."

"Now we've got into parables, and I'm all at sea. Let me fill your glass. And don't forget my offer, and don't think I fling my girls at any stranger's head. I just try to make provision. After all, a father's duty, you know. We can't all breed Eulalia Fawcetts."

Hastily snatching at a chance to change the subject, I said,

"Who's that?"

"Ah, I was forgetting that you're strange here. Eulalia Fawcett owns Little Egypt. That don't mean anything to you now, but if you get into the planting business it will. It's the biggest plantation and the best in the state. It's way out beyond Fort Anchor. Eulalia's grandfather settled out there while the Injuns were still about. After he'd been there some seven or eight years and things were going nicely there was a little flare-up and he was scalped. His wife got away with Eulalia's father, who was a young boy at the time and Little Egypt was abandoned. Young Fawcett earned his living the best way he could, holding horses, sweeping yards, running errands, doing anything he could till he was about twenty. Then he went back to Little Egypt with a batch of rough boys that he'd picked up in the streets. They did all the work themselves, worked far harder than any slaves would have done, and it paid. Young Fawcett married a girl with money and bought out the rest of 'em. That is, he gave 'em a couple of hundred pounds

259

apiece and said, 'Thanks very much for all your hard labour, now quit.' Most of 'em ended back here in the gutter where they began. Fawcett had had all the guts and all the brains in that outfit, must have to have run 'em as he did, they were nothing but riff-raff once out of his hands. The girl with the money died without leaving any children, and Fawcett married again, a roughish girl he'd known in the old days. She didn't have any children either, and *she* died. By that time Fawcett was a rich man, and the next time he married it was a proper English lady who'd come out here with her brother who was one of the Governor's men. She took her maid with her because she couldn't fancy being waited on by a Negro. The English lady didn't have any children either, but the maid did, a girl, Eulalia. That was the joke of the whole countryside, four women and then a girl. Not that I didn't feel for him myself, I'd just had Julie, but then of course I hadn't tried — well you know what I mean. However, Fawcett, getting an old man by that time didn't seem to mind. He'd come in here sometimes with his wife and the maid, all dressed very fine and a nurse carrying the baby. He looked like those old fellows in the bible you know, wife and concubine all complete. He brought Eulalia up like a boy, took her everywhere, sales and all. When he died he left her everything. And to-day there isn't a cleverer, harder-dealing, shrewder planter in the whole of the country. And the rum thing is that she's a beauty too. When she comes in to a Ball, all the other women are fit to be tied with envy."

"She's lucky," I said idly. "And why isn't she married?"

"Because she's mad," said Preswade solemnly. "She's the maddest thing this world has seen since the Gadarene swine took a dive."

I looked at the clock. It was late enough to take my leave. So I refrained from asking what form the lady's insanity took. I'd been quite interested in her story but I had had enough of it. Bidding good night to the Misses Preswade I looked at them again with their father's words in mind. I might have the one that took my fancy. Blue eyes, wavy fair hair, smooth oval cheeks with the colour of youth on them, neat little waists and busts and hands and feet. Not a penny to choose between them. I tried to imagine one of them under a puff-ball bush: and suddenly decided that that was a good test, at least for me. Discard the pretty gowns, strip off the ribbons and trinkets, imagine the black dampish soil below the twigs above. Then if the idea was pleasing, she'd do, not otherwise. Amused by this thought I took my leave and made my way back through the still busy bustling street to the *John and Poker*.

It stood at the end of Port Street and was, to my eyes, one of the most pleasing buildings in the town. The spaces between the beams on its front were filled in with clay, hand-moulded into shapes. A little ship, an Indian head, a bird, a barrel, all crude, but with a reality in their rough moulding. The plaster had been recently washed over with a mellow tawny colour and this, with the dark beams and orange squares of the lighted windows mingled together in a scheme that was satisfying and right.

Port Street itself was a shabby thoroughfare full of small dark shops and warehouses, and the frequenters of the *John and Poker* might have been expected to match. But, because it was near the water and the warehouses, and because its ale was good, sooner or later one might see there all the prosperous merchants of the town. The tap-room was below the level of the street and people entering for the first time were betrayed because they fell in instead of walking. There was a worn and splintered counter at one end and behind it were barrels and shelves bearing bottles and pewter measures. Bits of the beaming and the curved doors showed that a ship's timbers had gone to its building, and it was seemly that there should always be sailors in the place and that the proprietor himself should be an old salt who wore a piece of black calico, neatly hemmed, over the spot where one of his eyes had been. His wife was a guttural Dutch woman, fat and placid, and his daughter who helped in the bar was fat and placid, too. Greta was never in a hurry, no matter how full the place might be. But the great attraction of the *John and Poker* lay in Sadie, the hired girl.

There was a strange blood in her somewhere. It had given her a most curiously shaped face, much wider across the prominent cheek-bones than anywhere else. Her forehead looked as though it had been pressed in at the temples. Her hair was unusual too, straight and black and so smooth it might have been painted into her skull, and gathered up in a knot at the back stuck through with coloured pins. Her eyes were the colour of rum and as clear and there were little darker specks in the liquid gold of them. Her mouth was not beautiful, it had wide, flat, rather pale lips and one could see where the colour that she laid on them stopped short of the edges. It was a sulky mouth too, and though it smiled readily it went back quickly into the sulky line.

I had noticed her, but not so minutely as this before the day of the dinner at the Preswade house, but that evening coming in and tempted by self-indulgence into taking another drink, I idly thought of my test for an attractive woman and applied it first to Greta and then to Sadie. And I realised that Sadie had passed with plenty to spare. She would be fine with all that black hair loosened and the bare earth beneath and the twigs above her. Fine. If only she had been one of Preswade's daughters my reply to his offer would not have been in doubt!

Maybe something of what I was thinking reached her. I have often thought that intangible things like desire and curiosity and hatred can be communicated without words. Anyway, tonight, after bringing my brandy, Sadie lingered by me, chatting and smiling as she had never done before. This brought me black looks from some of her regular favourites who began calling her and banging their mugs on the table. For a moment or two she ignored them, smiling at me more brightly, leaning towards me as she talked; then Josh, looking out through his one eye, called her and jerked his head. Suddenly meek, Sadie left me and went to attend the malcontents. I took myself off to my bed.

Next day I began my inquiries and found that what Preswade had told me was dismally true. Land prices were soaring. By the end of the week I had become assured that my ideas had been the foolish ones of a man who had no idea of the value of money. It dawned on me during the second week that I must abandon all idea of starting on my own. I must buy myself a small share in some existing business, otherwise I should find myself with my money spent, sinking to the level of a poor white, to the level of Tommy.

I met Tommy first on the day that I landed and he had come up to me, pulling his little cart behind him, to inquire whether he might tote my bags. I let him place them in the oversized barrow, and then said,

"I haven't the least idea where to tell you to take them."

"You a stranger, Mister?"

"Yes."

"What you looking for? Fine place or cheap one?"

"Cheap. But I also want to be comfortable. Do the two things ever go together?"

"You oughta try the *Poker*," said Tommy, turning the cart so that he could get into a position to push it.

"All right, I'll try it. I can always move if I don't like it. Lead the way."

So Tommy led me to the door of the *John and Pocohontas*, which was cheap as accommodation in the town was reckoned, and comfortable because Mrs. Josh was a skilled housewife and a good cook. I paid Tommy, and then, since the day was warm, treated him to a mug of ale. That, I thought, was a mistake, for since that day he had haunted me. I seemed never to go out or to come in without meeting him. "Morning Mister," "Evening Mister," he would say with a pull at the brim of his dirty old hat, and there was always ale in his eye. Then for two days as I went out on my round of search and inquiries I missed him and idly thought that he had found someone else to sponge upon.

But on the third evening he rose up as usual with his "Evening Mister" and this time he was inside the doorway, not leaning against it, and he had a table with a bottle and two glasses on it before him.

"Bin waiting for you," he said laconically. "You have a drink with me for a change."

He was covered with coal-dust and his left-hand was a shapeless swaddle of filthy bandaging. He had been drinking and his face was almost ecstatic. I looked at the bottle and realised that it was brandy that he was inviting me to share.

"There's no call to treat me to brandy," I said. "You've never had anything but ale from me. You can buy me a mug of ale now if you feel that way about it."

"Rum it was that night when I had the fever on me," said Tommy, in a reminiscent voice. "But what's the odds? Sit down and help yourself. I've had two days' work and a stroke of luck."

"Oh, what was that?"

Tommy thrust out his bandaged hand.

"Broke a coupla fingers on a chap's jaw. Talk about Samson's tool! If he'd had that chap's jawbone instead of a moke's he'd have got all the foreskins in Philistia."

"You mean you've been fighting?"

"Fight, it was a massacre. See, I got a job unloading a coaler and Big Dodder he got one too. I never was partial to that hunk of cheese and several times during the job we had a few words. Heaving coal don't improve the temper, see. Time we were being paid he cut up nasty about the amount he thought was due to him and the mate of the fellow who was paying us said, 'Better not have a row. Big Dodder is the roughest fister on the coast.' That got me savage so I up and said, 'Oh, no he ain't. I am.' Of course they looked at me and laughed and Big Dodder spat and grinned and I got hopping mad. The upshot of it was that they rustled up one or two other chaps of a sporting nature and collected a prize. Fifty shillings there was by the end as I'm a living sinner and Big Dodder and me set to. I let him hit me just once or twice to give the fellows a little show, they'd reckoned on that, then I thought of all the liquor fifty shillings would purchase, and got impatient. That was how I bust up my hand. Little Sister Bridget did it up for me. She didn't know I'd been fighting, of course, and calculated I'd hurt myself hauling, seeing the coal dust all over me. 'Poor fellow,' she says, sweet as a bird all the time she was tying it up. Drink up, Mister."

"I can't imagine you fighting, somehow," I said, studying the scrawny little man over the top of my glass.

"My appearance is rather misleading," he said pompously, "as many big fellows have found to their cost. I'll tell you another thing about me that you mightn't guess. I'm book learned. I used to be usher in a school."

"In England?"

"In Norwich, Norfolk, England. Horrible job it was too. Then an old aunt of mine — God rest her soul — left me a hundred pounds and I came out here to make my fortune. You know, Dick Whittington of the West. And I made it, sure, ain't I drinking as good brandy as the old *Poker* stocks!"

"Would you," I asked curiously, "do differently if you had your time over again? Stick to the ushering?"

"No fear. No bloody likely fear. I do enjoy myself. I bin enjoying myself ever since I stopped being sick on the way out here. I wasn't cut out for an usher. Mustn't smoke, mustn't drink, except on the sly. Mustn't fight, bad example. And me that had learned all that the Norwich Bludgeon could teach me, shut up all day with a lot of little pick-nose urchins and a cane and a book of dog Latin. Whereas now. Oh, I know you're thinking about my clothes, and the little cart and sponging drinks off good-natured people like yourself. Ah, but there's the secret. You don't begin to enjoy life till you've lost all sense of dignity, both your own and other people's. Too many people trade pleasure and independence and even honesty for the sake of dignity. And life ain't particularly dignified, you know. There's nothing dignified about being born or dying, or getting drunk or taking a wench, but they're all realer things than a clean shirt that'll be dirty tomorrow or a pocket full of money you can't spend as you like. At least that's the way I look at it."

"There's a good deal in what you say," I conceded. "But I must confess that money is important to me."

"Forgive me asking," said Tommy, leaning forward and tilting the bottle over my glass, "but have you got any?"

"I've got some, a little. I aimed to buy some land and start planting, because tobacco is the only thing I really understand, except pigs perhaps. But I've found out in these last few days that I haven't got half enough . . ."

"Easy enough to make some more if you've got some to start with. Why don't you start peddling on a big scale?" He wriggled forward in his chair and his small blue eyes, startlingly bright in his dirty face, gleamed with excitement. "I've often thought of it myself, but I've never had the money to get a proper start."

"How do you mean? Going round with a pack?"

Tommy laughed. "You wouldn't get far like that. No. You'd want a good, well-built cart with a cover and a coupla nice mules. Just think. There's dozens of planters — not the big ones, they get about more — but smaller people who don't get into town more than two-three times a year. They all got wives and daughters or a fancy piece that wants dressing. A cart of miscellaneous things, clothes and trinkets, perfumes, sweetmeats, things they can't make at home like tea and coffee, sugar, a book or two, some of 'em read, French slippers, new strings for harps, lamps. Why, I could go on all night. A cart of things like that would find a welcome anywhere it went. And would it pay? Oh Mister, would it pay? Nice life too, always on the move, seeing different people. I only wonder nobody's thought of it before."

"And has no one?"

"No, and I'll tell you why. Nobody'd think of it only a poor chap like me that hasn't the money to start with. Folks with money think of bigger things, like you and your plantation, see? This country's bin waiting for somebody in your position to grab a chance like that."

"It may be this excellent brandy," I said slowly, "or it may be your gift of the gab, but I begin to think you're right. Look here, you know this country and you've got wits. If I do it, will you help me?"

"Surest thing you know. Only Mister, there's just this. No domineering. If I feel like picking a fight, I shall do it. And if I feel like getting drunk I shall do it. And no recriminations. I'm warning you. Is it a bargain?"

"It's a bargain," I said, stretching out my hand. Tommy put his bony black paw into mine.

"I'll see you in the morning and see how you feel then," he said. "Sadie, Sadie, bring me another bottle."

In the morning, after I had breakfasted in my room, I went into the bar and found Tommy waiting. I had thought carefully over his plan through the long hours of a practically sleepless night and decided that it was worth trying. It appealed to me more than the suggestion put forward by Mr. Preswade which I had been considering more and more seriously as the days went by.

Tommy was surprisingly clean, though no more tidy than usual. The bandage upon his left hand was new and white. He greeted me joyously.

"I got an option on a wagon and a pair of horses. Will you come and look at them, or have you changed your mind?"

"Only to the extent of making it up. I'll come and look at the outfit."

I followed Tommy into the sunny street and through a labyrinth of lanes and alleyways into a yard. A fat man with a bundle of straw in his arms put it down and came to meet us, polishing his hands on the seat of his trousers.

"This is the gentleman upon whose behalf I made the inquiries," said Tommy in his most impressive voice. "And that, Mister, is the wagon, see?"

I saw standing across the yard a wide flat wagon, fairly new and very stoutly built. Its tarpaulin cover, stretched over iron hoops, was new and white.

"It looks a very nice wagon," I said to Tommy, forgetting that the owner was within hearing and the bargain still to make.

"It does not," hissed Tommy, with a vicious elbow in my ribs. "It's too small for our purpose and too lightly built, but I thought you might like to look it over before seeing the others." A pointed glance warned me not to ask "What others?"

"Why," said the fat man, "you talk like somebody what don't know nothing about wagons. If you was aiming to move down to Carolina that wagon'd be as good as new when you got there."

270

"We're not aiming to go to California," Tommy retorted with a great deal of the dignity that he forswore the night before, "and if we were that wagon would still be too small and too lightly built. Will you see the horses now, Mister?"

"Might as well look at them," I said with a casualness copied from Tommy's. But when the fat man had opened the stable door and led out the horses that were evidently awaiting inspection, my reaction was genuine enough.

"I couldn't possibly buy those. They're only fit for the knacker." They were indeed the sorriest animals it had ever been my misfortune to behold, thin and drooping of neck, bony of rump, prominent of rib and dull coated. It seemed miraculous that they should still stand up and hold together: ridiculous to think of them pulling that or any other wagon.

"There's plenty of work in them yet," said the fat man.

"Maybe. But I'm not the man to get it out," I said brusquely. "I'd be ashamed to be seen on the street with them for one thing." I was turning away and should have left the yard had not Tommy seized me by the elbow, and drawing me a little away from the horses and their owner, poured forth a sibilant speech in my ear.

"Their legs are all right, and their teeth and that's all that matters, Mister, see? All they want is feeding up for a week or ten days. The run of their teeth on oats and a little linseed oil and you won't know 'em. I'm no fool where horses are concerned, and that's a good pair. A worse horse, if you can understand that, would have been dead of starvation. They got guts."

"Yes," I said, "and precious little in them. Still, have your way. And do him down if you can. I hate a man that starves things." I thought for a moment of Tottie.

"What do you want for the whole outfit?"

"Twelve pounds," said the fat man promptly.

Tommy broke into a peal of laughter.

"Do we really look that raw? Come along, Mister, I've got another wagon in my eye and I think you're right about the horses."

"The horses are worth that alone," said the fat man. "You're getting a present of the wagon."

"And you're the fairy god-mother who's giving it to us," jeered Tommy over his shoulder.

"Well damn it, say ten, if you're so hard up." Tommy tilted his hat and scratched his head ruminatively.

"I wanted the gentleman to see the other wagon. And anyway ten is too much. Five pounds is generous for the wagon, and a pound a piece is what the knacker wouldn't give you for the nags. And nobody else would buy them, sure. I'll give you seven pounds for the lot."

"Split the difference," said the fat man.

"What do you say, Mister?" Tommy appealed to me.

"You know best, Tommy. Personally I think the horses would be a liability, even as a gift."

Tommy straightened his hat and went on haggling. Eventually he settled that we should give eight pounds ten for the lot, but that that should include stabling without food for the horses and shelter for the wagon for a fortnight while we got ready for the road.

"I'll see to the food, bring it with me and stand over 'em while they eat it, otherwise that fat-gutted shark would feed it to his own. Was that a bargain, Mister, was that a bargain?" He skipped with excitement. "Eight pounds ten, and in a fortnight's time I wouldn't take twenty pounds for the outfit. I mean you wouldn't. You must excuse me if the first person singular pops out now and then. I've what you might call identified my interests with yours."

"That's all right, Tommy. In fact I appreciate it. What now?"

"Corn chandler's; and then what about checking over what we want for stock?"

With irresistible energy he dragged me round from shop to shop, warehouse to warehouse, bargaining shrewdly over every penny before he allowed me to pay it and showing — though I didn't realise it then — remarkable foresight and imagination over the things he thought would be saleable and those that he ignored.

The fortnight went swiftly. Three times I received invitations from the Preswades and each time refused upon the plea of pressure of work, but I added to the third refusal that I would call and see Mr. Preswade in his office upon the following morning. On that evening Tommy came into the tavern to drink with me and asked suddenly,

"Mister, is all that money spent?"

"Not quite." I wondered what he wanted. We had agreed that we had bought rather more than the wagon would carry and I had given him money to replenish his wardrobe some days before, though I could see no evidence of his having done so.

"Then we ought to get us guns. Pistols too if you can afford 'em. Mind, if we sell out we'll be returning through pretty rough country with our pockets full and we don't want to take risks. Shall I see to it?"

"If you will. In the morning I have to say good-bye to someone. Then how about starting out?"

"Suits me," said Tommy. "Talking about saying good-bye, have you said it yet to Sadie?"

I had forgotten Sadie in the rush of preparation.

"Well, no. I didn't suppose she'd break her heart if I left without saying anything."

Tommy laughed.

"Some people don't know their own luck. That girl is made for you."

"I hadn't noticed it. But of course I'll say good-bye to her. And I'm coming back, you know."

In the morning I paid Josh and arranged to leave one of my bags behind. I shouldn't want my best clothes on the wagon. I went upstairs again to fetch the one I was taking and found Sadie making the bed.

"You going?" she asked. I nodded.

"Where?"

"Lots of places. Tommy and I have started a pedlar's cart."

"A pedlar's cart?" she repeated incredulously.

"Yes." She let fall the sheet she was holding and laughed.

"I thought you were a gentleman."

"Even gentleman have to live, you know."

274

"Yes." She paused, looking at me. "I wish I'd known."

"What?"

"About the cart — and that you hadn't any money. I've been kind of afraid of you."

"Well, you know now. What about it?"

"We've wasted a lot of time," said Sadie. I laughed.

"I've been very much occupied. But I'm coming back."

"How soon?"

I looked at her and suddenly I, too, regretted the waste of time that had resulted from her diffidence and my own preoccupation.

"Quite soon. A little sooner than I had expected, I think. Till then — good-bye, Sadie."

She came round the end of the bed and stood close to me, lifting up that oddly attractive little face. I stooped to kiss her, but actually she kissed me, a long hot kiss, heady as Everett brandy.

"I'll be back," I said thickly, and dashed out of the room.

I found Mr. Preswade in his dusty warehouse and he led me into a slip of an office, crowded with papers and samples. He swept a pile off a chair and bade me sit down.

"I've been expecting you," he said. "I suppose by this time you've discovered that nobody has any land to give away."

"Yes. And since I made that discovery I've been busy buying a wagon and two horses, needles by the gross, ribbons by the mile, hats by the dozen and a million

275

other things." Ignoring his gasp of surprise I outlined the scheme.

"Well," he said when I had finished, "it's not a bad idea, but it's hardly your job, is it? Peddling, I mean. Am I to take it that you prefer that to a share in *my* business?"

"I never compared the two. This was just thrust under my nose and I took to it. I really came to ask you a favour."

"Go ahead."

"I wondered if you would keep the rest of my money for me. I don't want to carry it round."

"Of course I will. And if there's anything else I can do you've only to say the word. And how about dining with us today."

"I'm sorry, but Tommy is getting the wagon ready now. We're just off."

"Come and see me when you get back. And good luck go with you. I'll mind your money safely."

"I'm deeply grateful to you. And of course I'll come in. Good-bye."

I reached the door and then looked back to say,

"Commend me to Mrs. Preswade and your daughters and say that I'm sorry to have been so busy that I couldn't say good-bye."

"I will. They're always talking about you and I shall catch it for letting you go off like this."

"Not if you tell them about the cart." He laughed and I closed the door.

Once outside, I fairly ran to the yard where Tommy, ready to the last buckle and neatly dressed in a suit of blue cloth and a new hat far too big for him, sat on the front of the wagon behind two sleek shining horses that I should never have recognised.

"Well, we're off," I said, climbing up beside him.

"We're off," echoed Tommy with a grin. "Get up there. They didn't seem to have no names, so I've called 'em Castor and Pollux. I like to use what education I've got." In a burst of laughter we creaked out of the yard.

It was a brilliant autumn morning, to me, after ten years in St. Crispin's, intoxicatingly fresh, and as we left the low-lying town behind and gained the slopes, the air and the beauty of the painted countryside and the feeling of making a new venture went to my head. The stay in Jamestown had been an interlude. Now I was on the move again, and life was going on. I thought of many things as the horses pulled steadily and the wheels gritted round. Of Tottie, rotting now: of Glenranald, pushing on the war somewhere. For almost the first time I thought about Cassie and Timmy and Jacko, Madda and Sylvy, my friends. Who owned them now? Someone of Jimmy Standish's kind I hoped. I thought about Sadie — I had missed something there, but it wasn't too late. Then I thought of the goods in the wagon behind me, and of all the people who would buy them. Suddenly the sense of the amazing richness of life swept over me and I found myself singing, most inappropriately, but very happily, "Lift Up Yo' Heart," Timmy's old song.

"Feeling good?" asked Tommy.

"Grand," I said. "Lift up yo' heart poor nigger."

★ ★ ★

We worked the round for three years. Dusty summer roads, muddy winter ones, and tracks that were not roads at all streamed away beneath our wheels. We came to know to a nicety what goods were in demand, and what hung on our hands. We had our regular customers and came in time to be trusted with messages and letters and goods to carry from place to place. Sometimes we had passengers, too. Up and down, always on the move, sleeping beside the wagon on warm nights, inside it on cool ones, cooking our food over smoky fires made of sticks, we visited in those three years practically every outlying household in the state.

We drifted into Carolina and sold our goods on the rice plantations where we saw the slaves working up to their knees in water in the flooded fields. A very unhealthy part where we could have sold our drug stock ten times over. Once or twice we traded with evil-smelling Indians.

We saw new plantations carved out of the forests or meadows; we saw old ones change hands. We had countless small adventures and various reverses of fortunes. But on the whole they were three happy, healthy and profitable years. At intervals we returned to Jamestown, rested the horses, furbished up the wagon and replenished our stock of goods. Almost every time I was able to visit Mr. Preswade and give him sums of varying sizes to add to my store. And every time, without any exception, Tommy, who kept surprisingly sober on the trips, went on a three days drinking bout while I made up for lost time with Sadie.

278

★ ★ ★

At the beginning of the autumn which completed our third year we made such a return. We intended to stay for a week. Perhaps it was because we lived in such close proximity on the wagon and in such isolation, that during the first three days of every holiday, by mutual consent and without a word said, we never met at all. I went straight to the *Poker* and Tommy retreated to some headquarters of his own. But on a morning previously arranged we met, completely in accord, and started upon the business of buying our stock. This time it would be things for the winter, little fur tippets, candles, cures for coughs and colds, sets of chess men, boxes of checkers, playing cards. And there were all the ordinary things to think of as well.

We got in on a Friday evening, stabled the horses, found a wheelwright and gave him orders about the wagon, had a drink together at the *John and Poker* and parted with the understanding that we would meet there again on Wednesday morning. The moment that we entered the bar of the tavern, Sadie, in accordance with the now long-established custom, put down her mugs and bottles and went to put on her newest dress. She had several, all of silk, all of colours that I had chosen, and all paid for by me. Josh and his wife understood that there would be no more work for her until I had left town.

By the time that I had washed and dressed in my best clothes Sadie would be ready, her black hair sleek, the colour smoothly spread on her wide lips, her eyes bright with welcome and excitement. The evening would be spent in eating and drinking at the Potomac House which was a change for Sadie after the *Poker*, and there were dancing girls and other kinds of entertainments there. In the mornings we lay late and then walked out into the town looking at the shops and the people; or I would hire a gig and drive into the country.

Sadie was a pleasant companion, undemanding, easily pleased. There were other men who enjoyed that companionship when I was miles away, that was neither a secret nor a source of jealousy. I couldn't be jealous of her because I was not the least bit in love with her. She was the perfect completement to my roving life, always ready with a welcome, prepared to return passion for passion, and to bid me farewell with enough regret to flatter my pride and not enough to make me uncomfortable.

On this particular holiday we followed our usual programme. The only noticeable thing at first was that on the Tuesday when I drove the smart hired gig with Sadie, dazzling in a new mulberry-coloured dress and hat by my side, the Preswade carriage, with Mrs. Preswade, Rosina and Julia in it, passed us. I took off my hat and bowed to them, but all three, without the slightest sign of recognition, looked me full in the face for as long as it took for our vehicles to pass one another. I put back my hat and laughed. Sadie made no sound, and glancing at her I was surprised to find her face fiendish.

"Damned old bitch and her litter," she said when she felt my eye upon her.

"They're all right," I said. "I expect they're angry with me because I never go to see them."

"Because you're out with me, you mean. I don't expect to be looked at, don't want to be, but they shouldn't have passed you that way."

"I don't mind how they pass me," I said, with complete truth. "I'd a sight sooner they did that than that they should stop and ask me to dine."

"*Why* would you?"

"Because I'm like that. And because Miss Rosina would have some new paintings to show me and the others would have some new songs. That kind of thing bores me. Besides, you forget, I'm a pedlar, not very respectable."

"Ever seen a person you'd like to *marry*?"

"No," I said frankly. "I haven't. And that means no offence to you, Sadie."

"I didn't think it did. After all you'd have married me if you *had* wanted to, wouldn't you?"

"That's one of the things I like about you, Sadie, you don't have to have things explained to you."

"That's where we're different. You do. You need somebody to explain to you right now that you ought to do something about yourself."

"What do you mean, do something about myself? What?"

"You ought to do *different*. All the time you're away you're with old Tommy. He's all right, but he don't amount to anything. And all the time you're back here you're with me, and I'm all right, too, but I don't amount to nothing. It's all wrong to me."

"Well, it seems all right to *me*. Tommy's a grand chap. Educated too, you'd be surprised the things we talk about in the wagon. And you're pretty and smart and sweet and you suit me. What more do I want? One day, quite soon, if things hold out the way they are, and we don't lose the whole cargo in a flood again or anything like that, I'll have enough to buy some land. And that's the only thing on God's earth that I want at this moment."

"Then you're devilish lucky," she said in a queer voice.

"Why, is there anything you want?"

"Yes. I want" — she paused and then said rapidly, "one of those fur capes."

"You shall have it, tomorrow. Tommy and I start shopping tomorrow morning. Is there anything else? You can have what you like, within reason."

"Oh, I'm reasonable. No, there's nothing else."

We dropped back into our usual chatter.

And that night, just before I slept with my arm over Sadie's warm relaxed body, I thought again of my words. Some land, and enough money to start with, was all I wanted on God's earth. It was true. So I slept, and woke to a day when something else that I wanted was going to spring up before my eyes.

Tommy wasn't there in the morning. I waited till nearly noon and then went out leaving a message. When I returned Josh had a neatly folded note for me. "Come and see me, please. Have had an accident. Top floor at fourth house in Tanner's Yard. Walk straight in."

282

I asked the way to Tanner's Yard and set out. It was not far distant but it took me some time to find it because I missed my way in a tangle of alleys and backways. When I arrived I found that it was a three-storied wooden house, unpainted and dirty, with only a narrow footpath between it and the back of the tanning yards. The whole quarter stank of the unsavoury trade. I pushed open the door and mounted the stairs, following them as far as I could and coming at last to a half-open door from behind which came the sound of groaning and a clear gentle voice that said,

"There, it'll be better soon. Try to be patient."

I pushed open the door and entered the most dismal room that I had ever seen in a house; seldom even in a slave cabin had I seen such squalor. A huddled, lumpy-looking bed with filthy blankets filled more than two thirds of it. A broken chair was the only other furniture. A hole in the roof had let in water which had washed the plaster from the whole of one wall, so that the lathes stuck out like ribs, and the other walls were indescribably dirty. Tommy lay on the bed with one leg outside the blanket and his coat carefully draped over his thigh. The leg was bandaged and the person who had just finished the bandaging stood at the foot of the bed packing a few things into a little black bag. The black folds of her draperies and the white bands around her face proclaimed her vocation.

"Hullo," said Tommy, and groaned again.

"What have you been doing now?"

"Had an accident with a lamp and scalded my leg with hot oil. This is Sister Bridget. She's been doing it up for me."

I looked towards the little nun just as she finished packing the bag and raised her eyes. Across the huddled bed and the groaning Tommy our eyes met and held. I couldn't next day have told you what colour hers were, or whether she were thin or fat, pale or swarthy. I didn't really look at her at all. I just knew that here was something vastly significant, terribly important, something that I had never met before, something . . . but there are no words. Columbus, when the new continent rose out of the sea to meet him, was not so taken aback as I was at that moment. He had hoped and expected to find it there. I, coming in to see Tommy, and looking politely towards the little nun as he named her, had come face to face with something that I had never given a thought to, something I didn't know existed. I felt my mouth open in a gasp as the thumping of my heart drove all the breath out of my body. I wanted to cry out. To say, "Stop. All these years have been bringing us together, let me see what you're like, now that I have found you and recognised you by something that can't be seen. Don't go now."

But she lowered her eyes suddenly and I drew a breath and said, "Thank you for what you have done for Tommy." She bent her head a little and turned back to the bed. "I will come tomorrow," she said in a small smooth voice, and then without a sound of a footstep moved through the doorway and down the stairs. I sank down on the broken chair, as weak as though I had just escaped from some awful danger.

I pulled myself together after a moment or two and listened to Tommy's story of a glorious fight that had ended by someone throwing a lighted lamp into the fray.

"Oil and flames rushing up my leg like the devil. I've got a hell of a leg. I'd sooner have broken a bone. Mister, it'll be a fortnight before I'm fit for the road."

"And wouldn't a broken leg take so long?"

"Not likely. Why I was about on a coupla brooms all the time my leg was mending. But God, when I put this down on the floor the throbbing drives me crazy."

"Well, you mustn't put it down. And, Tommy, you mustn't stay in this place. Why ever do you come here still? You get plenty of money. What do you do with it?"

"I sort of gravitate here. I lived here for years and years and often I didn't pay. So now I can pay I still come. See?"

"Then why don't you get it cleaned up?"

"Ain't no one to clean it. I suppose you didn't see Ma Peck as you came up. Well, she owns this place and she's got elephantiasis in her legs. Her legs are bigger'n a barrel. She can't clean."

"Who looks after her?"

"Neighbours, or lodgers, and the Sisters."

"Ah, the Sisters. You know I always thought of nuns as being shut away in cloisters, walking in walled gardens full of dark trees and white flowers and fountains. I never expected to find one looking after an old rapscallion like you."

Tommy laughed and groaned at the same time.

"Quite a poet when you give your mind to it! Ah, but she don't know that I'm an old rapscallion. She's mended me up dozens of times and I always pitch a hard luck story about accidents. In a way they are accidents, so it ain't downright lying. She said to me today. 'How very unlucky you are, you poor man!' She belongs to a special order, the Bethlehem Sisters of Charity. They do a lot of good."

"And do you intend to stay in this hovel and let Sister Bridget look after you, or shall I get you over to the *Poker* and call a doctor?"

"No bloody fear. Thanking you all the same. Little Sister Bridget knows more about tending the sick than any doctor does. And these ointments and things they make, real stuff, you know. They've been making them for thousands of years. Don't you worry about me. I've got food and water here, and you'll bring me some grog I should hope."

"Certainly I will. But, Tommy — if you can't get downstairs — there must be things that you can't very well let a little lady like that do for you."

Tommy's face went almost black with fury; I could see what he looked like when he was picking a fight.

"Who said I couldn't get downstairs?" he demanded fiercely. "I been bed-ridden before now and I can manage. I don't expect any sewage service from Sister Bridget. What do you take me for?"

"All right," I said, "keep cool." I opened the door and then turned. "I'll come tomorrow and bring you some liquor. Anything else you'd like? A book?"

286

"I've got one," said Tommy, diving under the pillow and holding out for my inspection a little brown linen-covered volume. "She brought it. Lives of the Saints."

I laughed. "Well, you'll be in better company than you would be if you were on your feet, Tommy, no doubt about that. I'll see you tomorrow."

I made my way down the broken stairs, and out of the alley. Then, instead of turning in the direction of the *Poker* where Sadie awaited me, I set off walking countrywards. I walked while the moon rose broad and red and narrowed and grew pale above me. I walked until I was alone in the night and then I sat down under a tree and thought. I did not avoid or shirk anything, though I knew that in the judgment of all decent men my thoughts would rank as sin. I had looked across that tousled bed and fallen in love with a Bethlehem Sister of Charity as suddenly and inevitably as I should have fallen into unconsciousness had somebody hit me across the head with a bludgeon. It was not of my choosing. I had nothing to gain from this and I had already lost my peace of mind.

I had looked at the little black figure without a thought save of gratitude for her care of Tommy: would any man look beneath that habit for the woman who wore it? Nuns weren't women in that sense. Brides of Christ they were called. And as such they must be regarded with reverence and treated with respect. But the fact remained that I had looked at her and recognised something that I had, all unwittingly, been searching for all my years. And I didn't want her as I

287

had wanted Cassie, or Sadie or the trollop at New Orleans. That kind of thing could be found anywhere. I merely wanted to share — though that is not the right word — the peace, the purity and serenity of the little face whose features I had not even noticed.

Years later, remembering the whole affair with the clarity that distance lends, I came to the conclusion that a neglected and almost forgotten religious sense had, most contradictorily, played a part in the score. I had learned long ago that in me a spiritual sense was lacking, but just as a confirmed mystic may sometimes feel most violently a pull of the flesh, so a hedonist may lapse into mysticism, though in him the mysticism will be touched by earthiness and he may, as I did, imagine that he loves where he actually worships. Be that as it may, there was I, hard and experienced, thirty years old, sitting out under the stars thinking of a Bethlehem Sister when I might have been with Sadie.

Before I set out on the tramp back to the town I had settled with myself that this thing must be forgotten. Nothing could be done about it. I must shut away the memory of that moment — and after all it *was* only a moment in a life-time — when a face had meant something more than a shop-window. I would go at midday to the house in Tanner's Yard, when Sister Bridget's morning ministrations would be finished and her evening ones still distant. Certainly I must never see her again.

I climbed the stairs just at midday, with a basket of delicacies in one hand and a couple of bottles under my arm. When I was on the second staircase I was conscious of a new scent warring with the old ones; a pleasant scent that called up a memory of pain and firelight and a fat Negress being kind. Oldfield's kitchen at Tessimadi and the cook plastering my fingers and leg with something out of a pot. Aunt . . . Aunt Iley's ointment, that was what it was. I opened the door of Tommy's den and saw Tommy with his thumb in his mouth to stifle cries of pain, and Sister Bridget with gentle sure fingers applying the ointment to his leg which looked like a joint of raw beef.

Tommy threw his other hand into the air and pointed to the bottles, shaking his head wildly the while. I caught his meaning and shifted the bottles inside my coat. Sister Bridget did not look up and all that I could see of her was her little stooping back and narrow shoulders and now and then a hand moving. But the room was so small and my feeling so intense that something of it, I felt, must reach her. I tried to distract my own attention.

"How are you, Tommy?"

"Doing fine," he said, removing the thumb for an instant and then stuffing it back.

"Your leg is in a hell of a mess," I said. Tommy took his thumb out to say,

"Beg pardon for him, Sister." I felt myself turn crimson.

"I think I'll come back," I said uneasily and moved towards the door.

"I've almost finished," said the little subdued voice. So I stayed where I was, and suffered, in another way almost as much as Tommy.

When I put the bottles inside my coat I had put the basket of fruit on the chair, where it now stood, a patch of bright clean colour in the squalid grey of the room. I saw Sister Bridget eye it when she straightened herself from the bandaging and when she had packed her little bag she turned to Tommy and said,

"You won't eat all that your friend has so kindly brought you, will you?"

"No, Sister. Help yourself."

"There is a child sick along the yard. I'm going there now. I thought if you would let me . . ."

Rather incommoded by the bottles in my coat I laid out some of the fruit on Tommy's bed and handed her the rest in the basket.

"I'll bring some more tomorrow," said my voice, what time my mind cried, "Look at me, please look at me one second." But she kept her eyes down as she took the basket from me and turned back to Tommy.

"I've filled your water jug. Is there anything else?"

"Nothing else, thank you, Sister. Bless you."

"And you," she returned promptly. Then she picked up the black bag with her free hand and slid out of the room.

"Now," said Tommy, "give me a drink quickly. God, when I get hold of the bastard who threw that lamp I'll strangle him with his own guts. I'd no idea there was this much pain in the world."

I found the handle-less mug that he used for water and splashed out a generous measure of brandy.

"Why, Mister," he said as I handed it to him, "you're all of a tremble. Bad night last night? Or are you ill?"

"I may have a touch of fever. This place doesn't suit me very well. I think, Tommy, that I shall start out on Monday as we arranged, by myself. I'll go as far as Fort Anchor and back by Cheecawi. Maybe you'll be able to travel by then."

"I'm sorry to go sick on you like this. But see, if you ain't feeling too good yourself you shouldn't go out alone. Suppose you have got a fever."

"I'm all right. I say, Tommy, do they ever get out, break away, get back to the world?"

"Who?"

"Those Bethlehem Sisters."

"I should say not! You see to do work like this they take special vows I believe, because they have more temptation."

"Visiting folks like you, eh?"

"Visiting folks like me they run into folks like you, don't forget."

"It must be a terrible life for a woman. It seems to run counter to everything women really like, pleasures, and clothes and admiration." I heard my mother's voice saying, "No, not so much as a new dress," the bitterest thing she ever said.

"They chose it. And Sister Bridget, at least, looks happy. The one who works with her doesn't. She isn't so kind either. I have drawn her, in a manner of speaking, and I always get well mighty sharp then."

"They work in couples, do they?" Tommy nodded.

"Gimme another drink. I'm feeling better. Have you been out buying this morning?"

I settled down on the broken chair and told him what I had bought and what I had seen.

Next day when I went to see Tommy the leg was already dressed and he was sitting up in bed with a most woebegone expression.

"I got that Sister Claude this morning," he said, before I was properly in the room, "and she caught me with a bottle. Said I was poisoning my system and took it away, if you can believe that. She came so early and they move about like mice, don't they? I didn't have a chance."

"I had brought you another bottle. But maybe there's something in what she said. Perhaps I'm doing wrong to bring it."

"Look here, Mister. I'm nigh on fifty and for thirty years or more I've drunk as much as I could afford to, vile tack some of it too. I've had a cracked skull, broken both legs and one arm, had the small-pox and the flux and lost count of the fevers. And now I'm a man that can only be floored by somebody chucking a lamp at me. If I don't know my own system by this time I oughta. If you reckon to be a friend of mine gimme a drink."

"I'm persuaded if not convinced," I said, reaching for the mug. "You must be as tough as old leather. How's the leg?"

"Doing fine. And make no mistake, that amount of raw flesh would have been a ticket to glory for a lot of people."

"I believe you."

"How's your fever?"

"My what? Oh, my fever. Gone."

"All the same I think you'd better wait till about next Tuesday, then I can set out with you and you needn't come back for me. It'll be a saving of time in the end."

"You won't be fit to move by Tuesday."

"Who says so? The inflammation is all gone this morning, even old kill-joy had to admit that. By tomorrow I shall be growing new skin like a baby's and by Tuesday I'll be skipping about. Wait for me, won't you, Mister? I don't want to hang round here by myself for a fortnight. I'll get into some more trouble if I do. I'll get looking for that swine and picking a fight and I ain't quite ready for him yet."

"I'll see," I said. "I'll look in tomorrow and see how you are and we'll talk about it further."

On Saturday I set out to see him in a very muddled frame of mind. Half of me hoped that Sister Bridget would not be there, that she would have gone, or that Sister Claude had taken on Tommy's case permanently. The other half looked forward eagerly to another meeting and packed up a stiff blue cone of the sweetmeats that had been bought for the wagon as an offering to the sick child.

She was there, repacking her bag when I entered and my heart jumped a bit when I realised how nearly I had missed her, even while my common sense was sourly conscious that I should pay for the meeting in mental disturbance later on. I greeted Tommy, who was looking very cheerful this morning, and then said, "I've brought you a few goodies for that child you mentioned."

"Thank you." She spoke sweetly, but her eyes were still averted, and with a sudden leaping of all my pulses I knew that this avoidance was not accidental. She wouldn't look at me. Why? The answer flashed unbidden into my reeling brain, but before I could either accept or deny it she had taken the blue paper cone and gone.

"Never knew you cared for brats," said Tommy. "Here, look, she's left her ointment."

I snatched up the little jar and ran to the stairs. She had paused on the lower landing and as I gazed at her, unwilling to move until she did and wishing that she would stay there, where I could watch her, for a long time, I saw her open the paper cone, peer at its contents, take one between finger and thumb and pop it into her mouth. And then, still watching, I saw the look of childish pleasure on her face wiped away and replaced by an expression almost of horror. She spat out the sweetmeat and swept her foot over the place where it had fallen. Then she began to descend the stairs and I followed her. As I passed the wet smear on the landing I could have wept.

"You left your ointment," I said when I caught up with her. She turned and faced me, holding out one hand. I did not immediately hand over the ointment, I looked at her palm for a breathing space. It was glazed and crossed by a myriad little lines ingrained with the dirt of labour, the kind of dirt that no amount of washing will remove. It was like my mother's hands. I raised my eyes to her face, and it was as though my gaze had pulled a red curtain upwards from her chin to her forehead. All that could be seen of the small face was scarlet.

"Give it to me please." The quiet voice was slightly unsteady.

I said, "There's something wrong, you know, with a religion that doesn't let you enjoy the fruits of the earth."

"It is I who am wrong," she said gravely.

I placed the pot of ointment in her hand and she turned away swiftly. I watched her join a taller black figure and then I went back to Tommy with my heart full of anger and bitterness.

I would have given everything I owned, every penny of the money that was stored in Preswade's office, for a chance to talk with her. I thought of all the millions of women in the world, any one of whom might be approached by a man sufficiently determined to ignore class and colour and creed — and there was just this one who couldn't be approached at all. And why not? A nun's habit was only stuff; a nun's vows were only words.

Suddenly, in the middle of Tommy's chatter and his renewed appeals to me to wait until Tuesday for him, I thought, I couldn't talk to her, but I could write. I kept making noises to Tommy to make him believe that I was listening, and within myself I examined this new idea. It seemed, even to me, rather a terrible thing to do: not for the obvious reasons but because it might disturb her peace of mind. But suppose our lives did run along a given line as the Pre-destinationists believed, suppose I had met her, through Tommy's accident, because she was my woman, wouldn't it then be cheating life to go away, struck into immobile silence because of the clothes she wore? Cheating life, cheating myself, cheating her — and she loved sweets and thought it sinful to enjoy them!

Once again I suffered that rush of blood to the head that had given me that unholy sense of power on the night when I killed the baby. I wouldn't leave this thing until I was convinced that it was hopeless. Life was very short and there were many things in it that a man might not control; what he could do, that he should. I would at least make a bid for what I wanted. I left Tommy and sped back to the tavern where I locked myself into my room with the excuse that I had accounts to do.

I should have sat down to write a letter of proposal to the Princess of All the Russias with much less trepidation. I scribbled madly, read critically, crossed out and tore up, I heard the customers at the tavern come and go. Afternoon broadened into sunset and the evening came. Sadie knocked at the door. I opened it and stood in the doorway as we talked.

"Shall we go to the Potomac this evening?"

"I'd like to finish this," I said. "I want to know where I stand before I buy anything else."

She looked over my shoulder at the evidence of my activity.

"Then I think I'll go down and help. Pete Richards got home today and he'll be in presently. He promised me a present. You don't mind, do you?"

"I looked at her, and the surface of my mind framed an answer, "Of course I don't, Sadie. I hope he's brought you something pretty." The rest of me was far away, lapped away, sunk in a state of feeling that Sadie could neither reach nor disturb. I sat down again at the table and went on stripping my almost naked quill. It was late when I had finished and then not to my satisfaction, but it was the best I could do and must stand. I read it through.

"This letter, the writing of which is the most difficult as well as the most important thing that I have ever done, may possibly shock and offend you. I only beg that you will read it patiently, think over it carefully and then, if it displeases you, forget it entirely.

"Four days ago, in the moment of our meeting, you looked at me, and without any intention or desire upon my part I fell in love with you and knew with a surety past all question that I had never been in love before, nor should be again. After a great deal of thought I have come to the conclusion that I should be wronging both of us if I let the fact of your vocation prevent me from telling you so. If you are indifferent to me, or if your mind is so fixed upon unearthly matters that human love has no place in your life, this confession of mine will affect you no more than the breeze affects the mountain over which it blows. But if, on the other hand, there is the slightest doubt in your mind about what you ask of life, I do beg of you to give me an opportunity of seeing you and talking with you.

"You believe, unless I am mistaken, in the value of holiness, service, chastity and poverty, you have dedicated your life to these things and would doubtless, if the opportunity presented itself, endeavour to convert others to your view. And I believe that this life is very brief and that pleasure is important and that the good things in the world were intended for our enjoyment — and to that point of view I make this attempt to convert you.

"Trying to see myself with your eyes I realise that I am an irreligious and sinful man: by any standards I am poor and worldly and rough but such as I am I adore you. I want nothing in the world so much as a chance to convince you that I love you, to marry you and make you happy.

"Tommy and I are setting out on Tuesday. If you have any answer for me please leave it with him on Monday. I shall only go to see him in the late evening."

I wrote my name at the foot of the sheet, folded and sealed it. Then I wrapped it in a linen handkerchief and enclosed it all in stout paper which I also sealed.

On my way out I stopped in the bar and bought a bottle of rum. I felt a little awkward over giving Tommy the packet so I waited until the rum had thawed us past the stage where much constraint was possible.

"When Sister Bridget comes next time I want you to give her this and tell her to open it when she is alone."

"What the hell is it?" asked Tommy, proof in its insolence that the rum was working.

"Never you mind what it is, just give it to her."

"They ain't allowed to accept presents."

"I don't see why they shouldn't have a chance to. It's only a handkerchief. After all she's looked after you very well; and I may not see her again."

Tommy held the packet in his hand for a moment.

"She'll give it away again."

"I don't care a damn what she does with it. You do as I say."

Without another word he slipped it under his pillow.

I stayed drinking with him until very late. The next day, being Sunday, I drove Sadie into the country and tried my hardest to focus my attention on her and not to wonder whether the note had yet reached its destination and what its reception had been. We ate at the Potomac House, and there Sadie asked suddenly, "Are those accounts still bothering you?"

"No. Why?"

"Every now and then you look like you were thinking hard about something. I thought it might be them."

"You have to think occasionally," I said.

On Monday I called upon Mr. Preswade and spent a longer time than usual in his office, trying to fritter away some of the time that lay between me and the evening when I should know. I bought a bracelet and a pair of ear-rings for Sadie and then called to see that the wagon and horses were ready for the road in the morning. I had called upon the fat man on the day after Tommy's accident and so put the fear of God into him that the horses had been not only fed but groomed as well. Everything was in order and at last there was nothing for me to do but to go round to Tommy's. I could hardly breathe on the stairs.

He was up and dressed with his trouser leg taut over the bandages.

"I can hobble round," he announced with glee. "I been out. Sister Bridget says I've made another miraculous recovery. And I've found out the name of the bastard that chucked that lamp. He's got a day of reckoning coming to him next time I get into town. Oh, by the way," he fumbled in his pocket, "this is for you." He took out a tiny packet, unsealed and tied with a scrap of coloured cotton. It bore the marks of his thumb.

My heart-beat made my fingers unsteady as I slid it into my own pocket.

"There was no need for her to thank me," I said, savagely aware that my face had gone hot. "I've seen to the wagon and we're all ready to start tomorrow. Are you sure you still want to come?"

"Positive," said Tommy.

"Then I think I'll get back to Sadie. Shall we say eight o'clock tomorrow?"

"Suits me."

"I'll see you at the yard then. Good night."

I went out of Tanner's Yard and then paused. I must read this at once and it was too dark to do so in the street. I turned into the *Sailor's Return* and sat down at a table. A man in an apron asked me what I was drinking.

"I'll tell you in a moment," I said.

I slipped the cotton over the corner of the packet and spread out the sheet. For a second a hot mist obscured my vision and then I saw the delicate sloping script.

"Service to God our Father and to our Holy Mother the Church must be voluntary and whole-hearted or an abomination. Since the moment that I saw you first I have been caught in the coils of the most mortal sin — apostasy. I see no face but yours and think of nothing but you. I have struggled with prayer and fasting to forget you, but I am not able. I am damned already and no more fit to be a nun. I will meet you on Tuesday morning at the house in Tanner's Yard."

I gave a loud shout, for the ending of the note surprised me. Everyone in the tavern turned and stared at me. I pretended to have called the aproned man.

"Have you Everett brandy?" I asked him.

"Never heard of it."

"Bring me some other then. It doesn't matter."

But I could not stay still, could not wait while he fetched it. I threw down some coins on the table where I had been sitting and ran into the street. Back to Tanner's Yard to tell Tommy that we shouldn't be starting at eight — no! Let Tommy go and sit on the wagon and wait and wait for me, while I in that dirty, tumble-down room of his kept a tryst with my love.

Sadie was waiting for me, and for the first time I felt the weight of the chain that I had forged upon all these visits. Tonight, when nothing was further from my mind than Sadie and her supple urgent body, I was obliged, by some law that hadn't even a name, to go through the mechanical gestures of love. It shot through my mind once that this would be the last time, and I thought, poor Sadie. But why pity her? There were plenty of men to sue for her favours, men more adequate than I was being at the moment. Long after she was sleeping I lay awake staring at the darkness and limning upon it pictures of tomorrow's meeting. When at last I slept it was only to dream wild dreams in which I fled from unknown terrors along endless tobacco fields in company with someone who was Sadie, and then Bridget, and then a woman whom I didn't know at all.

I was glad when the morning came and I could put my things together while Sadie tapped backwards and forwards partly helping me and partly returning her clothes and trinkets to her own little room among the attics. She was always just a trifle sad on these last mornings, and she was now, though she could not have known what I did — that I should never come back to the *Poker* as her lover again. I gave her the presents that I had bought her, the fur cape, the little ornaments, and endured the long passionate kisses of leave-taking. Then I took up my bag and made hot-foot for Tanner's Yard. No time had been mentioned in the letter, but I knew roughly when the Sister's ministrations took them there.

I removed a few of the papers and rags that blocked the broken window and stood watching the entrance to the yard. I saw the two black figures enter, confer together for a moment, and part. My hands and feet were cold and miles away from me, my throat was constricted and my tongue stiff. When, at last, without any warning sound, she stood in the doorway I was paralysed and dumb, able only to stare at her.

For the first time I could study all that could be seen of her face, the soft pale lips, slightly parted, the hollow oval of the colourless cheek, the sweep and lift of the golden eyebrows above the childish blue of the wide eyes. I had a moment of nonsensical thought. She had been God's and I had taken her. I pushed it away and thought instead that she had been dead and buried and that I had called her to life again, like Lazarus from the grave. And still neither of us spoke.

At last I said in a queer grating voice that made the words sound brusque, "Will you come with me now?"

"Oh no. Sister Claude would know. And I can't come in these clothes . . ." Her voice, always so small, was now a mere frightened whisper.

"I see," I said. "Well, clothes are easily come by. I'll get you some. And I'll meet you anywhere you like to arrange, any time when you can come alone."

I saw the blue eyes close for a moment and then open wide again, and I noticed that her mouth wasn't quite steady and her hands were twining together in the shelter of the wide sleeves. It suddenly burst upon me that she was dreading the step she was contemplating. My heart went out to her.

"You know you'll be all right, don't you? I'll take such care of you."

She nodded and then said quite quickly and firmly,

"There's something you must see first." With swift unsteady fingers she loosened the bands and drapery of her head-dress and let it fall on to her shoulders. The bare shaven crown lifted itself above the folds. Below the smooth unsightly head the blue eyes stared out, wide, frightened and yet somehow challenging. The pity of it!

I said in a shaking voice, "It will grow again. Oh, my dear, my dear." I took two stumbling steps across the room and reached for her little work-worn hands and holding them together in one of mine, put my other arm round her and held her to my heart. Inside the clumsy heavy clothing her body was smaller even than I had imagined, and it leaned towards me stiffly, unused to caresses, utterly unlike the body of any woman I had ever touched before.

We stood like that for a long time. The mad hammering of our hearts sounded like Pluggy's drumming.

"Sister Claude will be wondering," she said at last.

"Then you must go. I'll get some clothes and . . ."

"And I'll come here. I'll slip away this evening." I dropped her hands and she arranged the linen about her head.

"I'm afraid I shall bring you nothing but ill," she said. "No good could follow so wicked a woman as I."

"You don't know the meaning of the word wicked," I said. "And I'll teach you to forget all that kind of thing. You will come. Don't let anything change your mind."

"I have no mind any more," she said, and went softly and swiftly down the stairs.

I watched until she had re-joined Sister Claude and they had gone from the Yard together. There was drama there, I thought. The two of them, so alike, except for size, to the outer eye and yet — the one on the brink of so momentous an undertaking, the other so unknowing.

I went along to the yard and told Tommy to get off the wagon.

"We're not going until tonight. And there'll be someone with us."

"A passenger?"

"Yes. A passenger worth waiting a day for."

"You're looking mighty elated," said Tommy.

"Well, it's rather a good passenger," I said. Tommy grinned.

I went back to the *John and Pocohontas* and leaned over the bar where Sadie, in her ordinary clothes, was polishing pewter. I cut short her exclamations of surprise and delight.

"I find that I have completely forgotten a whole order. Comes of having Tommy laid up. I have to take a woman a complete set of clothes."

"Everything?"

"Everything from the skin outwards. That's why I want your help. Can you put your things on and come out with me, now?"

"Sure I can. Glad to. But that's a queer order, isn't it?"

"She's going to be married."

"Oh, I see." Was it fancy or did Sadie look at me oddly?

She was soon ready and we went to the shops.

"Now," said Sadie, "how much do you want to spend?"

"No stint," I said, "you see, she's never had any nice things before."

"How big is she?"

"Little. Her head would come about up to your ear." It had come just to my shoulder and the thought made me feel dizzy. "Yes, to your ear. And she's small, you know, like a child."

"No figure?"

"I suppose not," I said, my eye falling on Sadie's bosom.

"Then she's lucky to get somebody to marry her."

"Tastes differ, you know." Indeed, they differ in the same man, I reflected.

"Is she fair or dark?" I hesitated. "I mean what colour is her hair, silly?"

What colour is her hair? God Almighty!

"Her eyes are blue and her skin is fair. But she'd got something on her head when I took the order. Blue I think, blue velvet and brown fur. But I'll deal with that kind of thing. You choose underclothes."

"How many?"

"Three of everything," I said recklessly. "And no coloured flannel. Fine lawn. And if there has to be flannel let it be very soft and cream-coloured. Is that clear enough?"

"Quite," said Sadie, and there was no mistake this time about the odd look. "Lucky is the bitch with the bright blue eyes."

"What did you say?"

Sadie repeated the words which had nothing exceptional about them, considering the ordinary run of her language.

"I object to that word used in this connection," I said foolishly.

"Much I care," Sadie retorted. "I will now enter this elegant shop and buy the bitch some fine lawn shifts." She held out her hand. "Gimme some money."

Repressing an impulse to slap the hand I laid some money in the palm.

All day, Sadie, who had been quiet and sad in the early morning, was in her most teasing and mischievous mood; one, I must admit, that I had often found delightful, but which in my present state of mind was maddening. She plagued me to tell her for whom the clothes were intended. Every customer whom she had ever heard me mention by name was suggested. Her questions, her innuendoes, her chatter and above all the queer knowing look in her eyes spoiled the pleasure that I was taking in choosing beautiful and suitable clothing for that loved form.

At last it was over and I had two parcels, one of spare clothes that could go straight into the wagon, the other, which contained a complete outfit, I intended to take with me to Tommy's room. I should stand outside that door while behind it she stripped off the dull and heavy garments of her vocation and donned the bright worldy ones of love.

I hoped especially that she would like the dress of deep blue velvet, the colour of the night sky, and the snug little cloak of brown fur to wear over it, and the hat, bonnety shaped, of the same velvet with a narrow band of fur under the brim. She should wear it all the time, until that poor head was covered again by the little soft curls that were, I was convinced, its rightful wear.

I took Sadie to a meal at the Potomac House and gave her, for her services, a pair of gloves, London made, fellow pair to those in the parcel. I left her at the door of the *Poker*. Her parting shot to me was,

"Well, good-bye. I hope you'll approve of the shifts. They've got true lover's knots worked on the yokes."

I managed to laugh and say, "I expect I shall have a regular trade in wedding orders, after that neat touch of yours."

I loaded myself with a supply of delicacies for the wagon and stored them inside with the spare clothes. I had reckoned that if we travelled all night as we had done before where the roads were good, we should reach Fort Anchor by the evening of the next day. We could be married there. Incredible thought. In a little over twenty-four hours, she would be my wife. I had chosen the wine and food with care. Fort Anchor might not offer much and the wedding feast must be worthy.

Tommy was asleep on the bed. I roused him.

"Tommy," I said, "you've often professed great gratitude to me. I don't ask you to prove it because I believe what you say, but tonight I want you to do something for me."

"Anything you say, Mister."

"I'm going now to fetch the wagon round. Then I want you to sit on it, just outside the yard here and wait for me. The passenger is coming here, and there's a bit of disguising to be done. We'll join you at the wagon. We may be quite a short time, or quite a while. I want you just to wait. And afterwards no questions, or recriminations, as you said yourself when we went into partnership. Will you do that?"

A gleam of knowledge broke upon Tommy's countenance.

"I believe this precious passenger of yours is running away from somebody. Contraband eh? Shall we have the law after us, or will there be just a fight?"

"Neither, I hope. Well, I'll go get the wagon."

I drew up by the mouth of the yard so that Tommy's back would be towards the entrance and the hood would prevent him from turning to see behind him. I half hoped that he would not recognise Sister Bridget in the new clothes, and wondered how he would take it if he did. He always spoke to her and of her with such reverence that I feared his reaction to my sacrilegious plan. However, that could wait.

He hobbled down and sat on the wagon seat with a bottle by his side and a rug over his knees. I carried up the clothes and laid them on the bed. I had brought the lantern with me, and now I lighted it and set it at the head of the stairs. Never had a day seemed so long, and now that night was running in I grew wildly excited.

Now at any moment I might hear, with ears made sharp by expectancy, that almost noiseless step, that whispering voice.

I waited quite patiently. It might be difficult for her to get away. I had no more idea of the interior arrangements of a convent than I had of those in Heaven. I could not imagine what slipping away from one implied, but I did not think that it would be easily done. And I was quite prepared to wait until Doomsday, if I could be certain that that dreadful dawn would bring her to me.

Presently it was deep night. I went down and spoke to Tommy who was smoking peacefully with the rug drawn up round his shoulders. The horses, with hanging heads, were dozing as they stood.

"Not come yet?"

"No."

"Well, it's early yet. Give him time."

I left him with the ashes of his pipe making a spot of light in the darkness as he drew at it, and went back and waited again.

Twelve o'clock passed. One. Two. Crawling hours. Surely now, in the heart of the night, anyone could escape if escape were possible. I thought of my own fruitless attempts. Had she that hunted feeling? Would she be frightened of the dark journey? How I would welcome her in and comfort her.

I stood up and padded softly about in the confined space, fighting off agitation. I thought of Tommy and the horses — but after all I had done all I could for their comfort dozens of times in the past years. They must serve me now.

At last the window turned grey and in a downpour of rain the dawn came. Then fear, which had been kept at bay with difficulty since midnight, sprang and tore me. She wasn't coming. Something had stopped her. That she had changed her mind I didn't even then believe. "I have no mind any more." Only this morning, in this very room, she had said that to me.

Then I went mad.

I clattered down the stairs of the sleeping house and out into the street. Tommy had thrown sacks over the horses when the rain started and was sleeping again with the rug over his head. I roused him roughly.

"Come on," I said, and untangled the reins from his hands. I roused up the horses and turned them round.

"Where are we going?" Tommy asked, still heavy with sleep. I made no answer, only urged on the horses with voice and whip until they broke into a ponderous trot, the fastest pace they could make with the wagon behind them. We rocked and clattered through the quiet rain-washed streets until at last the grey walls of the Bethlehem House rose blank and unbroken on one side of the narrow lane. I pulled the horses to a standstill and threw the reins to Tommy.

"The Bethlehem House," he said in an awe-struck voice. "What are you doing here?"

I jumped down and ran to the great iron-studded door with a small grill in its middle panel. A heavy iron bell-pull shaped like a cross hung beside the door. I seized it and pulled with all my might. I could hear its jangling, muted by distance, far away in the heart of the house. And almost as though that peal had been an awaited signal, another bell, muffled and menacing broke the silence, beating at regular intervals. Someone was awake and moving, and this door should be answered if I had to ring all day. I would have her out, despite all the nuns in the world, despite God or the devil.

After a long time the wooden shutter of the grille opened so suddenly that I was startled, and a wide pale face presented itself behind the bars.

"You have a nun who nurses people, a Sister Bridget, here?" I said in a questioning voice.

"What do you want with her?"

"A man she has been nursing is crying for her. He's in delirium and nothing will quiet him. He thinks she is the only person who can do him any good. I've brought my wagon to take her back because the case is urgent."

"Who is this man?"

"I only know that his name is Tommy Long and he lives in Tanner's Yard."

And that, I thought, can be confirmed.

"Wait here," said the face. The grille closed and I waited with my heart going like a hammer. When it opened again should I see her, with her little black bag in her hand?

A still longer interval, a quarter of an hour at least. They were getting her up from her bed. I pictured the whole thing to myself. She hadn't been able to slip away last evening and she had gone to bed — perhaps she had cried a little, and wondered what would happen now. Then she would wake. They would say "Tanner's Yard" to her and she would understand. She would dress, outwardly calm, inwardly elated. In a moment now I should see her.

The door suddenly yawned open. I caught my breath. It was only the large-faced woman, alone.

"Come in," she said.

I stepped across the threshold and the door crashed to behind me. It was dusky inside though there were windows, unglazed, all along one side of the passage. It smelt of night and of polish and of green things growing beneath the windows. I followed the woman, intensely conscious of the noise of my footfall in that silence, only broken still at intervals by the dismal tolling of the bell. My guide stopped by a door, midway down a passage, rapped upon it, turned the handle, said "Go in," and left me.

There was a tall narrow window straight ahead of me and in an iron stand three candles were burning, so the room was lighter than the passage or the streets had been and I blinked as I entered. Then I saw the only occupant of the apartment, a little old — very old — woman, huddled like a monkey in a chair with a high back placed against the window. In that queer light, half-yellow candle glow and half the grey of early morning, she reminded me of one of Fanshawe's images, squatting behind the cupboard door in the cabin of the *Sheba*.

Her voice when she spoke to me was a thin thread of sound, husky and weak.

"Young man, what do you want?"

313

I repeated my story. At the door it had sounded convincing but now the falsity of it shrieked aloud.

"Sister Bridget cannot return with you. She is dead."

All pretence dropped from me as I cried, "Dead! But that's impossible."

"Sister Bridget is dead," repeated the thin inexorable voice. "She died at ten o'clock last evening."

"I don't believe you," I said flatly.

"Listen." Upon the silence broke the note of the bell. "That bell tolls for her."

I crossed the space that separated us. I hardly knew what I said, what I intended to do.

"Where is she? Tell me. Tell me or . . ." I laid my hand on the elbows that rested on the carved arms of the chair. The little wizened face looked up into mine, unafraid.

"What will you do, young man? Though you tear me in pieces you cannot bring her back."

I said, "How can I believe you? She wasn't ill. I saw her on her round yesterday morning."

"In the midst of life we are in death; a thing that you should remember. Since you doubt my word, come with me."

She rose, slowly and painfully, from the tall chair and crossed the room. I followed. There was a door almost in the corner. She pushed the top and it half opened, like the kitchen door at Braidlowrie. I looked inside. The tiny room within was dark except for the light of candles that stood at the head and foot of a slab raised on legs, like a trestle-table. And stretched on the slab was the body that yesterday morning I had held in my arms and promised to care for forever. The face was not covered. In the quivering light of the candles it shone almost as white as the linen that framed it.

A great groan burst from me. The thin voice said,

"Are you convinced?" The wrinkled hand went to close the door.

"Leave it," I cried. "Let me at least look at her." The top of the door closed as though I had not spoken. I stretched my hand over the bent shoulder and pushed with all my force. It remained closed. I swung round on the old woman.

"How did it happen? Why did she die?"

"God took her."

There was a terrible finality about the three little words. The bones in my body seemed to turn to water. I thought again of the moment in Tommy's room when I had imagined that I was taking the dead woman away from God. Even just now on the doorstep I was determined to have her despite nuns, God or devil. Which of the three had thwarted me? I was shaking from head to foot with rage and fear and impotence. The old woman spoke again.

"You should envy her; she died repentant. Unless you would be cast into outer darkness forever you, too, will repent and do penance before it is too late, for the affront that you have offered to God in thinking that His affianced Bride was a fit vessel for your lust."

My trembling ceased.

"Lust," I cried. "What do you know of lust? I know what it is, and I know that it would never have survived the sight of that shaven head. Lust would have turned away. I, God help me, I'd bought her a bonnet to cover it. I loved her, I tell you, I loved her."

"Love has been made the excuse for many sins, and few so vile as yours," said the old woman relentlessly. "Go now."

"You killed her!" I said. "You killed her. Rather than she should break some trumpery vow whose hollowness she had realised, rather than she should escape this living tomb you sent her to her real one. You . . . you talk about sin and God and the sin of murder is on your own hands."

"Go now."

She turned and seated herself in her chair again. Nothing that I could do, nothing that I could say, would do any good. As she herself had said, though I tore her in pieces I could not make the dead breathe again.

I opened the door and let myself into the passage. The light was stronger now and there was the same scent of polish and of green things growing. The woman at the door opened it for me. It closed with a dull thud. I was in the street staring at the wagon. In the heart of the building the bell was still tolling.

Tommy was perfect. He drove all day without saying a word, and with a surprising delicacy did not take the road to Fort Anchor but turned towards Cheecawi. I sat beside him, staring ahead, silent and immobile as though I too were dead. Life had stopped. Even thought was so painful that after a trembling moment or two on the verge of screaming insanity my mind dropped backwards into numb blank despair.

In the early evening Tommy broke the silence to say, "Better camp, don't you think?"

I nodded, and went mechanically about the tasks of unharnessing and feeding the horses and gathering sticks for the fire. Tommy cooked, but I couldn't eat the food he set before me. I drank an incredible quantity of brandy without feeling in the least different. Going to the back of the wagon for a fresh bottle I came upon the parcel of clothing. Shifts with true lover's knots on the yokes. Shrouds and the cold earth and the crawling worms, oh my love! I laid the parcel upon the fire and watched the flames consume it. And as I watched the flames slipped and gave place to a trestled slab with a still white figure upon it. She died repentant — for what? And then I realised that there were all the hours of the night to get through, and all the hours of the next day, and the next night. An unending eternity of crawling hours, full of nothingness.

Suddenly I started up from the fireside.

"I'm very sorry, Tommy, but I can't make the trip. I've got to find something that I must do all night and all day. I can't just sit on a wagon, I've got to have some hard physical work. I'm going to walk back into the town and buy Lebanon."

Tommy said nothing for a moment, and then, in a quiet voice, the voice of the English usher, he said,

"Just sit down for five minutes and listen to me."

"There's nothing to say, Tommy."

"Maybe not. But let me try. We've been together a long time now. You should run *to* friends, not from them, when you're in trouble."

I sat down again on the horse blanket.

"She was dead, wasn't she?" I nodded to him across the fire, wondering how much he knew.

"They did it for the best, you know. I wish you'd told me. I could have warned you that she'd never get away. They were bound to prevent it, to save her soul. And they did it. And she's in Paradise now, God rest her."

"Don't tell me you believe that twaddle, Tommy. Stories made up like the ones nurses tell to children — if you're bad the bogey man will get you, if you're good you'll get a lollipop. That's not stuff for men. She'd have been in Paradise now, at this minute, with me. And they hadn't saved her. Her vows were broken at the instant when she said she would come with me. Do you hear that, Tommy? She chose *me!* She loved me better than she loved God!"

"Her body may have done. But that's finished now and the sweet soul of her is beyond the troubling of the flesh, where we're told there is neither marriage nor giving in marriage."

"Tommy," I said, "you make me sick. It's minds like yours that allow such humbug, such twaddle to flourish."

"Listen, Mister, what did you see in her? She wasn't pretty, not a patch on that Sadie of yours for looks. She may have been clever, but you didn't have a chance to find that out. What was it about her that you loved?"

"Something that had nothing to do with looks, Tommy. I saw it the first moment she looked at me. And yesterday morning she showed me her head, all shaved, poking up out of all that muffling like a tortoise. And all the while there it was looking out at me. I shouldn't have cared if she'd been a leper."

"Well, there, you've said it yourself."

"Said what?"

"That there was something quite apart from the body. What was that but her soul? And that something doesn't die with the flesh. If it can overcome the body's disabilities it can survive the body's death. And that part of her is still there, where you can join it some day."

"Oh Tommy!"

"It's true. Listen. More than a hundred years ago there was a man called Henry King. He loved a woman and she died. He wrote some verses about it. I can't recall them all to mind, but bits of them struck me very much when I read them. Listen —"

And then, in a quiet voice, not as though he were repeating something remembered, but as if he were stringing the words as he went along, Tommy offered me this for comfort.

> "'Sleep on my love in thy cold bed
> Never to be disquieted!
> My last good night! Thou wilt not wake
> Till I thy fate shall overtake;
> Till age or grief or sickness must
> Marry my body to that dust
> It so much loves; and fill the room
> My heart keeps empty in thy tomb.
> Stay for me there; I will not fail
> To meet thee in that hollow vale,

And think not much of my delay
I am already on the way.
Each minute is a short degree
And every hour a step towards thee.'"

"Well," I said ungratefully, "what of it? They're just words, put together so that they sound all right."

"It isn't the words," said Tommy, and there was a new, fierce note in his voice. "It's the thought. I've been holding on to it all day. I knew by your face what had happened when you came out of the Bethlehem House. And — and I was fond of her too, you know."

"You're an odd mixture, Tommy, what with your fighting and your poetry. You hang on to what you can. I've got to find something to do. If I sit on this wagon and think I don't know what might happen. Lebanon is the place for me."

"Lebanon is a cursed place. Go on, snort and sneer as much as you like. Nobody's got a pennorth of good out of it yet."

"Then it's time somebody did."

"Have you been thinking about Lebanon ever since the day we passed it on our first trip?"

"I believe so. In the back of my mind. There was something about that deserted house and the buildings and the drying sheds, just waiting to be used, and all that land going back to brambles and forest — it sort of caught me. I've had it in my mind all day, when I wasn't remembering."

I drained my mug of brandy and got up and tightened my belt.

"But you didn't mean it about walking back, surely. Wait till morning and we'll go back together."

"Tommy," I said, and I heard the hysteria in my voice. "I know you mean it kindly. But I want to walk and I want to walk *now*! You go ahead and make the trip. The wagon's yours and everything in it. And I wish you the best of luck."

"But Mister . . ."

"For the love of God, Tommy, leave me alone."

"I shall come to Lebanon when the trip's finished."

"All right," I said. "Good-bye."

I stepped out of the circle of the firelight and set my feet on the road back to Jamestown.

Left, right, left, right, one, two, one, two, mechanically stepping through the darkness, making rhythm in the silence.

"Pray soft fo' de young angel dat has just put its wings on. Gotta learn a lot in Hebben . . ."

"Sleep on, my love, in your cold bed
Never to be disquieted.
You will not wake . . . will not wake . . . will not
wake . . ."

PART FOUR

THE DERELICT KINGDOM

Three wagons crawled slowly out of Jamestown. I drove the first because it belonged to me. Three mules pulled it. The other wagons were hired from the man who drove the second of them. The vehicles were loaded now with everything that I could think of in the way of equipment and my store at Preswade's was empty. I owned an abandoned plantation, a wagon, three mules, two ploughs, three hoes, two hatchets, three spades, three lanterns, six buckets, a table, two chairs, some bedding, and a supply of food, kitchen ware, meal, corn, oil and tobacco seed. I also owned three slaves, big black Koromantees in prime condition that had cost me ninety pounds apiece in the open market. They were seated now one on the tail-board of each wagon. I had chosen them with great care, for we had Herculean tasks ahead of us and I wanted no weaklings whom it would trouble my conscience to press. I could have bought Mandigoes more cheaply, "gentle and tractable" as they were billed, but Timmy and Jacko and their wives had been of that breed, therefore I could never own a Mandigo.

It was no good turning towards Cheecawi now, Fort Anchor must be faced. We creaked through it and just before midday of the fourth day turned off the road and on to the estate of Lebanon, which was to be my kingdom if I could subdue it.

In Jamestown, in Fort Anchor, in any one of the scores of plantations one had only to mention Lebanon and someone would use the word "ill-fated" in less than ten seconds. Then someone else would say that the place was cursed, and another, less credulous, would correct that with, "Well, say unhealthy and unlucky and leave it at that."

On the morning when I walked into Mr. Preswade's office and told him that I wanted my money as I had arranged to buy Lebanon, he had said incredulously,

"Lebanon! But surely you know its history. My dear fellow, don't throw away your hard-earned money there."

I knew its history as retailed in the colony. It had been cleared and settled at the same time as Little Egypt and it had included a group of trees which were regarded as sacred by the Indians. That was the tale. I do not vouch for its truth. The cutting down of those trees had started the trouble in which the first Fawcett had lost his life. The owner of Lebanon and his newly married wife had been killed and both plantations had been abandoned.

The Indian trouble had been settled at the battle of Fort Anchor, and some years before the second Fawcett had been old enough to start his rehabilitation of Little Egypt, Lebanon had had a new owner whose slaves rose up one night and burned the house over his head. There were stories to account for that rising which were never told when ladies were present, and in their absence only with disgust even by the most hard-bitten planters. The next owner had been a wealthy man who had cleared the place thoroughly, rebuilt the house and the outbuildings, and then survived four completely unproductive seasons before, completely beggared, he had shot himself through the head on a night of full moon. And, the superstitious whispered, that night had been the very night of the festival of the grove of trees.

In the next twenty years, while Little Egypt, its nearest neighbour, flourished exceedingly and saw the reign of three Mrs. Fawcetts and the birth of Eulalia, Lebanon, in the same district, on the same soil, and with the same climate, ruined three men. Horn-worm in the tobacco, typhoid among the slaves, murrain among the cattle, all had taken toll. It had been deserted eight or nine years before by its last owner, who, impoverished and depressed by his venture, had retired to drink himself to death in the taverns of Jamestown, leaving a widow, the nominal owner of the estate, living in a narrow brown house in a back street.

It was significant that even in those early days when I was looking for a cheap piece of land, that not one person of all those I approached suggested, even jocularly, that I should tackle Lebanon. Nevertheless, when I did make inquiries, the widow was not what she called "giving it away." It was there, she said, and it cost her nothing. One day, when the stupid stories (she called them stupid though her husband's venture was part of them) had died down, someone would come along and offer her a fair price for it. When the country was opened up more, as it was bound to be some day, the land might be needed for building, or something like that. She was every day of eighty years old, so her confidence in the future was ill-founded; however, it prevented me from getting Lebanon at the bargain price which I had anticipated. But, just as, in the depths of my slavery, Virginia had called me, so now, in the depths of my misery, Lebanon beckoned. I had a strange feeling that nothing else would do.

So now my cavalcade, complete with a cow that plodded along behind my wagon, crept up the grass-grown track and came to a standstill before the empty house that had seen so many people come and go. It was, in size and build at least, the average long low house of the wealthy planter. It had been white, but the colour, as well as a good deal of the plaster, had been washed off by the rains of forgotten years. The veranda had been supported by wooden posts: some of them had perished so that the roof sagged, blocking the doors and windows upon one side. Most of the other windows had been overgrown by climbing plants and creepers. Indeed the first thing one noticed was the extraordinary lush fertility of the place. Bushes and tall grass lapped like a sea at the very steps of the house. Even the lopped trees that made the veranda posts had in places broken out with twigs and leaves. It was overgrown, and it was silent. The silence was not a mere absence of noise, it was a presence that could be felt, a positive thing.

But, I thought, springing down from my wagon, soon that silence should be broken, axes would ring, and shovels clink on stones. There would be sounds of mighty labour, and I hoped that Alexander, Lokoja and Shandy would be happy and sing about the place. It was autumn now, and by the first rains of spring I must have land ready for planting. Lebanon and the implements, the slaves and the animals had consumed my substance. I could now hold out until the first crop was ready, but no longer. If I failed I was finished. I was not like the gentleman who had sustained four bad seasons before deciding that his brain was fit only for target practice.

I saw the hired drivers look at one another with expressive grimaces, but the faces of the Koromantees remained stolid and blank.

"I'll go around and look at the buildings and decide where I want things to go. Then we'll get unloaded and you can get along," I said to the drivers. To the blacks I added. "You three come with me."

I knew quite enough about Negroes and their superstitions. If I left them alone with the drivers now things would be said that would not be forgotten as long as a black foot moved in Lebanon.

Whoever he had been who had reared those buildings, he had worked well. The ruin was all superficial, the dilapidations all of little things. When we had scraped away the weeds and little bushes from the doors of the sheds and looked in we found them almost all whole and water-tight.

"This is the stable," I said, "and we'll have tools in here, and stores here. Alexander, clear the well and get the top off. Be careful, it may be rotten. You others come and bring the wagons round."

329

I went back to the front of the house and was at once conscious of some kind of confusion in the atmosphere. The mules seemed restive and the drivers were down from their seats. There was something uneasy. It wasn't as I had left it. I looked in turn at the loads, the drivers, the mules. And then I knew. Without anything to go upon I knew that one of my mules had been changed for one of theirs. They'd just finished changing as I got back. I got into the seat of my wagon again and looked over my team. I got down again, I knew. My leader had had a nick out of his ear where one of his little playmates in vicious or frisky mood had had a bite at him. The leader I had now had perfect ears. The leader of the last wagon flapped a torn one.

"I'm glad you approve my judgment of mules," I said, "but I chose them to keep. Put that one back."

"What you talking about?" asked the driver with the nasal voice who owned the wagons.

"You know well enough. Put my leader back."

"If you got some notion of switching one of your beasts off on me it won't work, Mister. Come on now, we want to get unloaded and off this place before sunset."

"That mule with the nicked ear is mine. I've been watching it all these miles. Nobody stirs a foot off this place till this is settled."

I unhitched the strange leader off my wagon and gave him to Shandy to hold, and went to the last wagon to reclaim my own. Immediately the driver put up his fists.

"Touch him at your peril."

I hit him, he hit me. The other driver rushed into the fray and caught me a stunning blow on the nape of my neck. It shot through my mind even as I struggled, that this was the beginning of the Lebanon luck. I was losing my best mule for one that was, no doubt, faulty in some way, and I was getting a good hiding to salt the bargain. But even as I thought it there came a yelp like an Indian war-cry and the two Koromantees flung themselves forward. They caught the two drivers around the knees, just as Abraham had caught me that day in the street at Josepha. The two men hurled over, landed heavily on their faces, and the blacks sat down with lovely precision and force on the small of their backs.

I unhitched the mule with the nicked ear. Shandy had let the other loose before he rushed into the battle and for a moment the two hovered vaguely.

"Let them get up," I said, and the Koromantees with some reluctance did so. "Now watch where the mules go."

Nicked-ear wandered back to his place at the head of the front wagon and the other mule went back to his companions.

"Bring everything round to the yard," I said.

We unloaded the wagons quickly and the drivers climbed into their seats. I had paid them half their charges when we set out. I now gave them the other half. As he took the money the man who owned the teams spat down at the ground close by my feet.

"I suppose you think you're starting well, Mr. Bloody Lowrie, doing me out of my good mule; but you'll need all your luck before you're through with this place and its ghosts. Yes, ghosts," he repeated, raising his voice so that the Negroes, running in and out of the sheds should hear him, "Indian spirits and ghosts of men that have suicided themselves. Full of ghosts and bad spirits this place is."

The empty wagons went bouncing away.

"All that," I said, in a desperate attempt to neutralise the effect of the speech, "is only spiteful nonsense, nasty talk because, thanks to you, he didn't get away with my good mule. Don't take any notice of him."

"Dat's all right, Marsa," said Shandy, "We all don't take no notice of spirits, or Injun gods or ghosties. We all ain't no iggerunt niggers. We all is Mohammedans."

Good Lord, I thought, who'll eat all that pork? And what can I offer them instead? I looked at the squealing pigs that had been lifted, with their feet tied together, from the wagon, and wished that I had realised before the significance of the scraps of saffron stuff wound round the woolly heads of my retainers.

We got the tools under cover, the pigs into a shed, the cow into another, and the stores stacked neatly away. Then I milked the cow while Alexander watched me and since it was now growing dark I lighted the whale-oil lanterns and opened the door that led into the house.

Inside there was the musky scent of a house that has long lacked an occupant. The kitchen was enormous and had a great rusty stove and ovens that took up most of one wall.

"Run," I said to Alexander, "pick up sticks and branches while it's still light enough to see, then get some straw and light a fire in here."

Lokoja — whose name soon became Loko — and Shandy stayed and helped me to bring in the rest of the things from the yard. I unrolled my bedding in the kitchen. The fire would at least make the place seem inhabited. Then I opened the stores. I gave them dried fish and biscuit, some milk in a bucket and some fruit. Before they left me to go to the shed where they had taken up their abode, I said,

"Listen to me. We've come here today, just the four of us, to clear this rank place. It'll mean a lot of hard work for everybody. But so long as you do your best you'll be properly treated and properly fed. Later on I hope to get more hands, but the brunt of the beginning will fall on you. So for every pound profit I clear in the first five years you shall have a shilling apiece if I'm satisfied with you. Do you understand?"

"Ah does," said Alexander. "Ah'll 'splain it to them."

"Good. Now take your supper and turn in. We must be stirring at dawn in the morning."

They picked up the food.

"You may take a lantern," I said. "Alexander, see that it's properly put out."

"Thanks, Marsa, Good night."

I sat down on a chair before the fire and stretched out my weary limbs and almost immediately my lids were drooping. My last thought before thought was blotted out by sleep was that I had chosen my cure wisely, what with shopping and arrangements and sheer physical exertion I had hardly had time to think about my loss.

I think that only a man driven by a need to lose himself in labour, or by some compulsion outside himself, could have worked as hard as I did during the next three months. I wasn't as hard as I had been at Springhill, there had been no need for muscle on the wagon and mine had softened. I suffered agonies from stiffness during the early days.

I rose at first peep of dawn and stayed out of doors until it was too dark to see. The land that must be cleared by the spring was full of weeds and brambles and tough little seedling pines. We had cleared it by hand, ending each day with a bonfire so that the weeds might be thoroughly destroyed. And even the ashes from the fires had to be collected, for, mixed with sifted soil, they would make the beds in which the seeds would be planted.

I was fortunate beyond words in my Negroes who worked as though they were indeed my partners, not my slaves. I never saw a wasted moment. One night I was disturbed by the sound of hammering. Looking out I could see a light moving about in the yard. Blast them, I thought with the peevishness of exhaustion, they're knocking down a shed for firewood, and went out angrily. But Loko, who was handy with tools, was squatting on his haunches making a new cover for the well, while Shandy stood by with the lantern, shifting round so that the light might fall where it was needed. The sight of such industry shamed me and drove me to take a broom and sweep out my kitchen; to heat water and wash the accumulated dirty dishes and a shirt; to do the dozen or more small things that one so easily shuffles off when every ounce of energy and every thought are claimed by some big, absorbing task.

Even when the ground was cleared — not the whole by any means, but the amount that I thought we could clear and which could support us — the ground beneath the rubbish was sour and set. Still, the ploughs could get to work then, and it was like the dawn of a new era when Alexander and Loko, shouting to their mules, broke the first sod while Shandy and I followed in the tracks with hoes to break the clods to powder. Now at least we could work upright after the long weeks of creeping and crawling. Now the mules, sleek and frisky after their long inaction, could shed a little of their sweat on the earth.

It was after the second day of the ploughing that Tommy arrived with the empty wagon rocking along the grass-grown track. He had a lump the size of an egg on his jaw and an eye in which purple, brown and yellow were richly mingled.

"Don't tell me," I said as I greeted him. "I can guess. You've dealt with the lamp thrower."

"I have so," said Tommy, clambering down stiffly. "If he walks again this side of Christmas I shall be very disappointed."

I felt sick suddenly. I remembered so vividly the last time that Tommy and I had talked about walking after an unlucky accident. I wished that he hadn't come. I was going to be reminded, by the sight of him and the

335

very sound of his voice, of the little room at the top of the house in Tanner's Yard where even now, unless someone had taken it, the blue velvet was gathering the blue mould.

Later on, however, when the fire was alight in the kitchen and Tommy and I sat over a supper richly supplemented by things he had brought with him in the wagon and I was listening to an account of the trip and of the fight with which he had celebrated his return to Jamestown, I found myself enjoying his company. The evenings and the nights had been lonely and despite myself I had sometimes become conscious of the silence and the distance and the darkness separating me from my kind. It was so quiet at night there in the big empty house, so void of comfortable human noise, that after a time the silence seemed to be made up of stealthy sounds. The great bare rooms at the front of the house took on a character of their own, and several times I was driven by a queer nervousness, quite alien to my nature, to take a lantern and walk through the dust of the passages and apartments, brushing away the strings of dirty cobwebs as I tramped along, assuring myself that they were mere empty rooms; endeavouring to fill the house with my living human presence. There were nights when I stood at a back window and listened and was glad when I could hear a stray voice or a shred of laughter from the shed where the Negroes lived.

And there were nights when a more subtle enemy attacked me; times when I brooded over the history of Lebanon and wondered whether, in years to come, I should be known merely as one of its victims . . . "And after that a fellow named Lowrie thought he'd take it. And do you know what happened to him? . . ." I could imagine the lowered voice, the gloating eye, as somebody recounted my story. What would it be? At such moments there was no question of the emptiness of the rooms. The great silent place was full of alien spirits, watching and waiting, waiting and watching for the time when they could reclaim the kitchen where my hearth was lighted, the yard where my livestock stirred, the fields that my labour had broken, for their own.

But Tommy with his black eye and battered jaw, with his pipe going and his glass at his elbow, with his odd conversation, half-academic, half-dockyard jargon, was proof against nervousness and depression and the spirits to whom they gave birth. I thrust away the memory of our parting and the manner of it and succeeded in accepting him for what he was, a pleasant human companion, and I was conscious of a lightening of heart when in answer to my question, "What are you going to do now?" he replied,

"Why, what do you think? Stay right here along with you. You can use me, can't you?"

"I can use you. And if you weren't useful I'd be glad of your company. But I wonder whether you wouldn't be wiser to stick to the wagon. That is a sure livelihood, as we've proved, and this isn't sure by a long way."

"Oh well, time enough to take to the wagon again when we've failed here," said Tommy with the comfortable carelessness of the constitutionally improvident. "And this being the end of the trip and no stock to renew, do you know what I'm going to do with the money?"

"No."

"Buy you some furniture for a couple of those other rooms."

"Oh no, you're not. If you want to put any money into this outfit let it be on necessary things, not fripperies."

Tommy looked at me balefully out of his battered eye, and I caught a glimpse of the characteristic wilfulness that had guided his life. "'Smy money. You gave me the wagon, didn't you? And I can't resign myself to seeing you live like a pig."

"I don't live like a pig. I clean this kitchen quite a lot."

"Maybe. But you can't go on living in a kitchen with your bed next to the stove. It isn't right. It doesn't look well."

"Tommy," I said, "I've lived for a long time in far worse places than this. If I choose to make myself at home in my own kitchen I don't give a damn how it looks."

"Well, I do," said Tommy stubbornly. "Next week I'm going into town and bringing back some furniture. And between then and now I'm going to devote myself to some house-cleaning."

It was on my tongue to say that he was a fine one to talk about domestic arrangements considering the hovel that he had made his headquarters for so many years. But that little room mustn't be mentioned, mustn't be remembered. I made no protest when next

338

day Tommy set about the house with a broom and a bucket of water, and when, after some day's absence he returned with a load of good plain furniture, I allowed myself to be moved out of the kitchen and took up my abode in two of the rooms in the front of the house, big square rooms with panelled walls and views over the tangled wilderness that had once been a garden.

Tommy installed himself in the kitchen and a room opening off it. They were soon as muddled and grubby as his room at Tanner's Yard had been, but my apartments were kept spotless, and every evening when I came in from the fields I was greeted by a tub of hot water, a clean shirt, clean socks and some kind of hot meal. It was heavenly luxury after the weeks I spent fending for myself, but it irked me a little. I felt that all this effort ought to be spent out-of-doors. I did once pluck up courage to voice this opinion to Tommy and had the reward of seeing him fly into one of his rare rages.

"I came here voluntarily and what I do I do voluntarily. I ain't asking for anything but my food, and if I don't perishing well earn that by being a civilising influence in your life I'll just take the wagon and go. Now then, take your choice."

I said meekly, "Don't be silly, Tommy. I appreciate all you do for my comfort. I only thought . . . well never mind what I thought."

"You thought you'd rather have another fieldhand, didn't you? Well, I ain't going to be one, see? I'm getting on in years though you mightn't notice it. Now get into that tub before it's cold."

★　★　★

One morning when Alexander and I were taking our turn with the ploughs and Loko and Shandy were sieving soil and wood-ash together for the seed beds I saw a stranger on horseback ride up the track. I called Shandy and handed the plough traces to him and walked up to the house. I stepped through the broken fence just as the stranger dismounted.

"Mr. Lowrie about?" he asked curtly as soon as I was within hailing distance.

"My name's Lowrie," I said, taking in at a glance his neat good clothes, the quality of his horse and the arrogance of his thin brown face.

"Oh, mine's Newlyn," he said, and held out his hand. I refrained from the instinctive action of wiping my own upon my breeches before I offered it, though I was conscious of the state of heat and dirt in which I had been found.

"Will you come in?" I said. "There's no one to take your horse, I'm afraid. I'll tie him here." I twisted the rein around the broken fence and led the way into the room where I lived.

"You'll think me a nuisance, disturbing you like this, but I felt I must just look in on you. We're neighbours after a fashion."

I could see him studying the barely furnished room, the uncarpeted boards with a couple of rugs flung down on them, the uncurtained windows.

"You're a brave man, you know, Mr. Lowrie, tackling a place like this."

"I don't know about being brave," I said, "mad is probably near the mark."

"Have you planted before?"

"Yes. I've done ten years of it — in the islands though."

"I see."

A silence fell. The only thing that I could think of to say was, "Where is your place?" and I was just about to say it when the door opened quietly and there was Tommy with a bottle and two glasses set out on the big pewter plate that he used for cooking flat pies on. He set it down on the table with an air that would have done Phoebe credit and withdrew. I looked at the bottle. It was Everett. Where in the wide world, I wondered, had Tommy had that hidden?

The brandy broke the spell and when at last I did ask the question it sounded a little less like a gauche schoolboy's attempt at conversation.

"Oh, my place is called Bablockhythe. It had some outlandish name when I took it, but I renamed it in memory of dear old Oxford." He smiled slightly and raised his glass. Oxford bred and proud of it, I thought.

"Well, here's luck to your undertaking. You've got an uphill task I'm rather afraid. I trust you didn't take this place in ignorance."

"No. I think I know everything about it."

"Well, knowing everything may help you to avoid doing some of the things that others have done before you. Have you plenty of labour?"

"I've three Koromantees — very good fellows."

"Three?"

"Three."

A look of astonishment crossed his face and was gone.

"Well, I won't delay you any longer. I'm sure you're grudging every second." He drained his glass and rose. I went out with him to his tethered horse.

"Pray let me know," he said as if from an after-thought when he was mounted, "if there is anything that I can do for you at any time. And if you care to ride over to my place it's by the ford."

"I'm afraid I shan't be free to pay visits for some little time yet," I said, with a glance at the wilderness about me.

"I suppose not. Good day."

"Good-bye," I said, and turned back to my ploughing.

My second visitor was as unlike Mr. Newlyn as it was possible for a man to be. He drove up in the middle of the afternoon, a fat little tub of a man with a face like a bladder of lard that had had a pursy mouth, a snub nose and two little eyes drawn carelessly upon it with a brush. The two grey ponies that drew the low carriage were as fat as he and they began placidly to crop the grass the moment they drew to a standstill. Their master rolled himself out on to the ground, helped himself to a pinch of snuff, sneezed, drew his handkerchief across his face with a flourish and stood waiting for me to come up to him.

"Aha, Mr. Lowrie, isn't it? My name's Goddy. Don't let me stop you, don't let me stop you."

"I'm almost ready to stop, and I'm glad to. Come in."

Once more I offered my bare house for a stranger's inspection. Once more Tommy, with almost uncanny precision, appeared with the brandy and the glasses.

"Aha, Everett. So you're a judge of brandy, Mr. Lowrie. You know I've been thinking about you ever since Newlyn told me that you were trying to work this place with three niggers. 'E did say three. Now tell me, 'ow much do you look to have under cultivation by the spring?"

I told him.

"So little? Still, I suppose for a start. Not bad for a start. Much capital?"

"I beg your pardon."

"I said, much capital? I mean 'ave you got enough to carry you over?"

"Sufficient, I think," I said stiffly.

"'Ow much did you give for the place?"

Too taken aback to think of parrying answer I told him that, too.

"Ooh, too much, far too much. Ruinous. And 'ow far are you forward. Beds ready?"

"We're at work on them now."

"Good, good. Look out for 'ornworm when the time comes. Very prone to 'ornworm this place is. I always think things like that belong on a place. I 'avent 'ad a case of 'ornworm at Ipswich in twenty years."

"You're very fortunate," I said. "Where is your place?"

"Beyond the ford from Newlyn's place. Bablockhythe, you know. Fancy sort of name don't you think? I call mine Ipswich, that's where my people come from. Little town in Suffolk you know. Where do you come from?"

"Scotland originally."

"Done any planting before?"

"Ten years in the islands."

"Which island?"

"St. Crispin's," I said.

"On your own?"

"Not exactly."

"Know Standish there?"

"Fairly well. He's been dead some time, you know."

"Yes, a pity. Good fellow Standish. What made you take to planting?"

"What makes anybody? The necessity to earn a living. Let me fill your glass."

The questions ceased for just a moment, a merciful moment while he drank, then wiping his mouth on the back of his hand he renewed the onslaught. What kind of tobacco did I intend to grow. Did I play tennis or chess. Was I married. Or betrothed. Did the little man who had brought the brandy look after me entirely. On and on and on. It was worse than work to a man already weary. And once I found myself thinking of the Misses Preswade, and had a fantastic vision of a meeting between them and Mr. Goddy. What a scene! A subterranean gurgle of laughter shook me at the very thought. I felt, as he was leaving, that I preferred his haughty neighbour, Newlyn; he lacked the vulgar quality of curiosity at least. But as the little man heaved himself into his carriage and tugged his ponies' heads up from the grass he said earnestly,

"Look 'ere, let me lend you 'alf a dozen men till the autumn. I could spare 'alf a dozen and never notice. 'Taint quite right or fitting for you to be working like a field'and."

"It's very friendly of you, Mr. Goddy," I said slightly taken aback by the generosity and obvious sincerity of the offer. "But hard work happens to be just what I need at the moment. And anyhow I took this place with the idea that I'd either break it or be broken and I've got to do it alone and in my own way. Thanks all the same."

"Right you are, but the offer stands if you ever get into a 'ole. And sometime when you're less busy, come over and see me. I've got a French-trained nigger cook, and I can promise you a good dinner."

The fat little ponies wheeled round. The fat little hand fumbled for the whip and then poised itself, arrested.

"You'd do better to plough the other way of that field, ridges'd drain better."

The whip descended and the equipage trundled away. Later on I learned, without surprise, that my second visitor was invariably called Busybodygoddy — all one word.

For a time after that I had no more callers. I knew why. Newlyn and Goddy had learned enough to show that I was not a social asset to the community, and there was a certain amount of prejudice against a white man who, although technically a planter, worked like a fieldhand.

The winter passed. The seeds sprouted gaily in their beds. The spring rains fell, soft and warm; and immediately Alexander, Shandy, Loko and I were swept away in the tide of labour of setting out. Every day I made a thousand holes in the top of the ridges and set out a thousand little shoots, pressing the soft earth firmly around the thread-like roots. I urged on the others. I sent Tommy down to Fort Anchor to buy chickens and any day that saw four thousand plants set out ended with a supper of roast fowl for everybody.

And once the setting out was done, when there was a little time before the need for hoeing became urgent, we had more land to clear. And the days were warmer now than they had been while we cleared in the autumn. Still, there was a world of difference between working here and working at Springhill. The thought of the result spurred me on. I did not go into the house until the gathering darkness made it impossible for me to see what I was doing, or until weariness reached such a pitch that I could do no more than push one foot in front of the other.

Going back one evening in such a state, with the thin shirt glued to my body with sweat and my face and hair as wet as though I had been ducked in a pond, I saw something pale moving near the gap in the fence that divided field from garden. Involuntary and unwelcome thoughts of Lebanon's ghosts shot through by labour-drugged brain, but as I made my way to the fence the pallor took on form and solidity and showed itself to be a big white horse, restively moving, and trying, by tossing its head, to break away from the

346

insecure anchorage of the broken fence. I thought, oh my God, another caller!

I looked at the front of the house and saw by the pale glow of candle-light from the uncurtained windows that my sitting room was occupied. I turned off abruptly and made my way, grudging every unnecessary step, round the house and in at the kitchen door. Tommy was bent over the oven, basting the fowls, for at this zenith of labour he cooked supper for all of us. There had been certain protests over the arrangement at first, but reason and obstinacy upon my part had won.

"Who's in the front there?" I asked. Tommy looked up with a completely expressionless face and said in a flat voice,

"A Miss Eulalia Fawcett."

"Well," I said, "you let her in, you must get rid of her. Tell her I'm dead, it's damn near true. I can't see anyone, least of all a lady, tonight."

"She," said Tommy, with a surprising degree of bitterness in his voice, "is one of those females that can't be told anything. She came galloping up about quarter-hour ago and I tried to send her along to the field so's you could get rid of her so. But no, she must come in. Calls for candles as though the whole bloody place belonged to her and settles down to read a book."

"Well, go through, there's a good soul, and say that I can't possibly see anyone."

"I'm not going near her any more. She's got the evil eye or I never saw it. You go and get rid of her yourself."

"Is the water hot?"

"Is it ever not?"

"Then I'll wash and put a clean shirt on."

I trod as carefully and quietly as possible up the uncarpeted stairs, washed, put on a clean shirt, changed my breeches, and out of deference to female company, put on the coat that had hung untouched in the cupboard since the setting out started. I combed my hair, regarded my hands and gave them a second scrubbing that did little to improve them, and then, with an unaccountable feeling of defiance, clattered down the stairs and into my sitting-room.

While I closed the door behind me, and for the second I took to cross the floor, the occupant of the room sat still within the circle of candle-light, holding a book close to her nose. Then, with a single movement, she looked up, closed the book with a little snap, rose from the chair and stood with her hand held out. I crossed the room and took the hand in mine.

"I'm sorry not to have come before. I've been away," she said in a slow deep voice. "We know one another's names, don't we?"

"Do sit down," I said. "I'm sorry that you've had to wait so long. I came in so filthy that I had to do something about it."

"You work very hard I'm told. That's why I felt I must come. It seems such a coincidence that Lebanon should be started again just as my father started Little Egypt. He worked with his fieldhands. I suppose you're past the stage of cricked back and blood-rushing-to-the-head."

"What do you know about cricked back?" I asked.

"I once did three weeks setting out. From curiosity. I wanted to see whether it was fit work for women. Black women *are* women, you know, though the fact is often overlooked."

"And what conclusion did you come to?"

"Well, making every allowance for the fact that perhaps they are nearer a state of nature than I am myself, I reckoned that half a day was quite enough. The women at Little Egypt knock off after they've planted four hundred. How many can you do?"

"A thousand!"

"Can you really? I never managed more than six hundred and fifty myself, except once. I did seven hundred one day when everything seemed to go properly. You know those days?"

"And the other sort!" I said. She laughed.

There was a little silence, but there was nothing uneasy about it. This was quite a different visit from the former ones I had received. I remembered what Preswade had said about her being mad. Perhaps what she had just said about planting was enough to prove her madness to people like Newlyn and Goddy.

I looked across at her. She had taken the two candles down from the mantel-shelf and put them with the two others on the table in order to read better and by the gathered light her face looked oval and pale and her hair seemed to be tumbled loosely about her neck. Then I noticed her eyes and thought of what Tommy had said. In this soft light, when ordinary pupils would have been expanded, hers were mere pin points of black in the palest eyes I had ever seen in a human face. And they had a mad look. I was staring at them now, and they were returning the stare, but they weren't seeing *me*. For a moment I had a queer feeling of not being there, or of being transparent. I moved uneasily and then stood up.

"I'll get some more light," I said.

"Yes do. I do like to see the person I'm talking to, and I can hardly see you at all."

The idea of going into the kitchen put the thought of hospitality into my head.

"I was just going to have some food. Would you care to have some too? It'll be very rough and we're short of cutlery but if you don't mind that I'd like you to stay."

"I was hoping you'd ask me."

Tommy took the arrangement calmly, but grinned maliciously when I began routing about for candles. "So would I," he said. "I'd want a whole chandler's shop if I'd got to sit with that one!"

"Don't be silly," I told him. "She's all right. The most sensible person that's come here up to now."

"And that's not saying so much. All right, you go and sit down and I'll serve it up the best I can. Aren't you glad I drove you out of this kitchen?"

"Not specially. I think she'd be quite at ease anywhere."

I gathered a handful of candles and went back to the room where my guest had returned to her book.

"What is that very absorbing volume?" I asked as I held the new candles to the old and watched them flower.

350

"It's rude to read in other people's houses, I know, but I'm always doing it. It's only 'Macbeth.'"

"Sometime king of Scotland. I remember my father making me read out of it. Do you *enjoy* reading it?"

"Enormously. I'm so sorry for him too. After all, he didn't *choose* his path, did he?"

"I don't remember well enough to venture an opinion."

"Well, I mean that at the very moment when he met those three old women and they hailed him by his new names, his crimes were already committed."

Some vague knowledge of the story drifted back to me.

"One of them said, 'Hail to thee, King of Scotland,' and he went away and thought about it and then killed his king in order to succeed him. Is that right?"

"Roughly. But he didn't chose to kill Duncan. He just *had* to. And the old women knew that he would, it was all arranged, perhaps before he was born. That's why I'm sorry for him. He's gone down as the arch-murderer, the offender against hospitality and loyalty and he couldn't help it."

"He needn't have killed him."

"If you remember he tried not to. He came out of the room once. Fate was too strong for him."

"Oh, well, if you believe in Fate to that extent we're none of us responsible for anything we do. You don't think that do you?"

"I don't quite know. Look back over your own life. In how many affairs have you had full control?"

"In quite a number. And I came to Virginia of my own free will, and to Lebanon."

"I wonder," she said, "I wonder." She spoke slowly and kept those queer pale eyes fixed on me. "Actually I have no doubt that anyone with the gift of sight could have told you were coming here, perhaps before you were breeched."

I had a sudden memory of fat old Mrs. Thatcher. Water she had said, and blood, and no woman would get any good of me. Cassie — Sadie — Bridget. Ill-gotten money — Tottie's belt.

But that gave me such a helpless feeling, like being a straw in a gale, that I was compelled to deny the significance of it.

"Some things that you can't help happen to you. But the rest you choose. I chose to come here, for example."

"But why?"

"Well, perhaps in the case of coming to this particular plantation, circumstances took a hand. But in the case of coming to Virginia, I had all the world to choose from and I chose to come here."

"But why? I mean why did you want to?"

"That," I said, "is a question no man can answer."

"Perhaps not," she said, "but I have a shrewd suspicion that we *want* what it was designed we should."

"And who designs it?"

"Ah, now that is the question that no man can answer," she said, and laughed suddenly. And just then,

Tommy, entering with plates and bread and a bunch of cutlery in his fist, put an end to the conversation.

When she stood up to pull her chair to the table I noticed again that she was tall and very thin, and that in her costume there was another sign of the originality that passed for madness. She was wearing a long green coat, its collar faced with satin, and flung open over a blouse whose front frothed with fluted frills. The coat fitted tightly at the waist and was loose below, showing as she walked a pair of long full trousers, gathered at the ankle, like those I had seen in a picture in one of Fanshawe's books. Turkish? I couldn't remember, but Turkish seemed to stick in my mind. They were graceful, and doubtless convenient, especially if she rode astride as I somehow guessed she did, but odd.

Still, odd or not, I liked her. Never in my whole life had I been quite so instantly at ease with anyone. Conversation turned at last to slaves and their behaviour, their peculiarities and their treatment and I found myself telling her what I had never told to anyone in Virginia — that I had been a slave myself. I described life at Springhill and the fight at Josepha that had set me free. I told her about Fanshawe and Glenranald and Barlesci. And as I broke down the habit of silence it seemed suddenly as though I had never really talked to anyone before.

The candles burned low. The earliest lighted of them guttered and died. At last she said, with flattering regret in her voice, "Well, I must go, I suppose. You have to work in the morning."

353

I said bluntly, "I'm very sorry that I can't ride back with you. I've nothing but wagon horses and mules. But I'll walk a bit."

She put out a long white hand and just touched my arm.

"My dear, you'll do no such thing. You were half dead with fatigue when you came in, all that time ago. I don't mind the dark and I know the way. Not that it would matter if I didn't. I've an uncanny sense of direction."

Disproportionately elated I cried, "Do you know, so have I!"

She dipped into the pocket of the long coat and drew out a scarf of some thin green stuff and wound it over her hair, tucking the ends into her collar.

"We've got a lot in common I believe. I hope we shall see a lot of one another. Come up to Little Egypt on Saturday and stay over Sunday. I'd love to have you and show you all my things."

"We usually work on Sunday," I began, but even as I spoke something outside myself took control. "It won't do any of us any harm to have the day off. How far is it to Little Egypt?"

"About ten miles. But listen. I'll send a man over with a horse for you. Now don't be stupid, of course I shall. I've a dozen, probably more. Are you good or bad? I mean would you like a steady one?"

"The steadiest one you have."

"Good."

The pale horse stood quietly, apparently dozing until we were almost within touch of him, then he threw up his head, whinnied and began to prance. I helped her into the saddle and wondered at her lack of weight, she seemed hardly solid at all. She reached down her hand.

"Good-bye, till Saturday."

"Till Saturday."

The pale horse wheeled round, reared into the air and shot forward. I stood for a moment listening to the sound of his thundering hoofs muffled by the grass and moss on the track, then I went slowly into the house. A person, I thought, vivid and likeable, unusual, frank, impulsive, intelligent, beautiful. My mind was excited, eager to see Little Egypt, and to push forward the acquaintanceship. I had enjoyed the evening as I could scarcely remember doing before: but under the excitement and the memory of enjoyment some faint uneasiness was stirring. The fact was not flaunted, but it remained; Eulalia Fawcett was a woman, and I was not sure just then whether I wanted a woman in life at all, even in the capacity of a friend.

On Saturday, just after midday, a small oak-coloured Negro rode into the yard on a black horse, leading a bay. He stabled and watered them and then sat down with his back to the wall of the stable and slept. I worked on until about three o'clock when I went over to Alexander and told him to finish up everything properly and to take next day for a holiday. Then I went into the house, bathed, dressed myself in the best of the suits I had had made in New Orleans, waked the Negro, said good-bye to a cynically-smiling Tommy and set out for Little Egypt.

The horse was steady and perfectly behaved, and after a time I caught the trick of rising with him and so escaping the bumps that had made the first mile or two a mild form of torture, and after that I could take pleasure in looking about me, and seeing the evidence of spring in every bush and tree and field. We crossed the ford and I could see, by standing in my stirrups, the roofs and chimneys of Bablockhythe amid a smother of fruit tree bloom. The sight of them, and of the sleek neat fields, filled me with excitement. Here was prosperity. And it seemed for the first time that I was about to share it. I did not draw unfavourable comparisons between this and my own tangled, broken-down estate. The very bloom on Mr. Newlyn's fruit trees promised me something.

Little Egypt began with a wrought-iron gateway, proof of wealth in this land where iron was scarce and transport expensive. Inside the gates was a park, smooth green grass and great trees with sheep and cattle and deer browsing among the lengthening shadows. The roadway, level and weedless, turned twice before the house came into view. The moment I saw it I knew it for Lebanon's sister, but a sister how decked and cherished! So white that it seemed to glisten, so neat that not a leaf appeared to grow out of place. Swinging baskets full of flowers hung down between the veranda posts, stout lanterns raised upon stone pedestals flanked the steps that led up to the door.

I fell off, rather than dismounted, and the Negro led away the horses. Before I had mounted the steps to the door it was opened by a tall Negro with grizzled hair

356

who said, "Come in Mr. Lowrie, sir. Miss "Laly'll be here a'most immediately. She leave word you wuz to make youseff free with ever'thing same twuz your home."

"Perhaps your mistress was not expecting me so soon."

"Oh yes. She leave word 'bout you."

Moving majestically he crossed the shining floor of the hall and opened a door.

It was the loveliest room I had ever seen. The walls were panelled and painted white with faint gold lines picked out on the moulding. One wall was lined to half its height with shelves full of books. Two glass chandeliers, each holding twenty candles, hung from the moulded ceiling, a small bright fire gleamed at the back of an enormous hearth. The floor was bare and shone like glass save where brilliant rugs broke the glossy surface. There were various small tables, each with a burden of flowers or books or statuary. One drawn up in front of the hearth bore a silver tray with decanters and a box of cigars upon it. There was a comfortable chair on either side the table.

I walked around the room, looking at the books, the little decorative things scattered about, the pictures, for a long time. The white-haired Negro came in and lighted all the candles, looked at me apologetically, but did not speak. At last, selecting a book almost at random, I sat down in one of the chairs by the hearth, sniffed the decanters and found the brandy and began to turn over the pages. It was a queer little book, printed unevenly in very black type and scribbled over now and then with ink turned brown with age. I looked at the title page which informed me that it was —

A Book of Spells,
Collected, Printed and in many cases Tried,
By
A Person Interested
Whose Name,
Owing to the unreasonable prejudice upon the part of
The Ignorant who regard
Spells as the Prerogative of Witches and other
Associates of the Devil,
May not appear

The page ended with the word London and the date 1550.

The book seemed to fall open naturally at a page about a third of the way through. It was headed, "To achieve a wish that does not involve the death of, or disaster to, another person," and went on —

"This is commonly known as the Cherry-Blossom Rune and has been used in rural England since the cherry trees were introduced into the country in Roman times. Indeed it is thought that the first trees were brought over less in an attempt to grow the fruit in a climate not eminently suited to it, than to provide material for this spell.

"Procedure.

"Watch for the breaking of the first bud. Upon the third evening after take from the most western bough a spray of cherry-blossom. Holding it firmly between the two palms, having a care not to cross the thumbs, repeat clearly these words.

"'Mithras attend me, Fortune amend ye, my true wish send me.' Now repeat your wish, being careful to word it exactly as you would have it. (Many wishes have been fulfilled to the wisher's doleur on account of carelessness.) Then say, 'As this shall wither and that shall blow, as that shall stay and this shall go, what I have wished shall e'en be so.'

"This is an infallible charm."

Penned below in the brown ink were the words, "It is best to wear the spray upon the person for an hour or so, and then to drop it into a clear fire."

I was still poring over the difficult crabbed letters when the door opened and looking up, I saw Eulalia. I dropped the book hastily into the chair and went across the room. She held out her hand, with the rich lace of her sleeves dropping to the kunckles of it, and said, "So you came."

"Of course. Didn't you expect me to?"

She lifted the heavy clustering hair from her temples with one hand and pressed the blue-veined temple with her finger tips.

"This is Saturday then?"

"But of course. Have you missed a day?"

She shook her head and smiled slightly.

"I've had a lot to do, you know."

We had met under the chandelier nearer the door and under the bright light I looked at her closely. It might have been the face of someone just awakened from sleep, the face of someone who had not slept for days and was dropping from weariness, or the face of one who had been trying the "drowsy syrups" of the poppy or the hemp.

"You're very tired, aren't you?" I said. "Would you rather not be bothered with me?"

I shouldn't have minded if she had sent me packing. For this was not the same person who had laughed with me over our rough supper, imitating Newlyn's pomposity, Goddy's nosiness, and finding matter for mirth in my shortage of table ware. This was a stranger. But she pulled herself together with a shrugging of shoulders as though she felt a draught and said briskly,

"Of course you must stay. Wait a minute, didn't they welcome you properly? I told Joseph to look after you until I came back. Are you sure? Then it's all right, isn't it? What are you drinking? Brandy? Give me some."

She sat down in the chair opposite to the one that I had been occupying and leaned her head against the high padded back.

"Which book out of all that multitude did you choose?"

I passed her the glass first, then picking up the book from the seat of the chair, offered it for inspection.

"Well, I'll be damned," she said. "I searched everywhere for that book a couple of days ago and couldn't find it. Was it just on the shelf?"

"Yes."

"That's odd. Give it to me."

I put it into her hand, noting again the chilliness of her fingers. She held it to her nose, sniffed thoughtfully and then pushed it under mine.

"Smell anything?"

"Old leather," I suggested.

"Nigger!" she said decidedly. "Lisette again. She pokes into everything. She's the bane of my life."

"I should get rid of her," I said casually.

"I'd like to, but I can't very well. You see, she's my half-sister."

She laughed and drained the glass. And then the spell broke. Animation returned to her face.

"I'm delighted that you came. We'll have a lovely time. Shall we picnic tomorrow? Do you like food out-of-doors? Would you like to see over the house? Then the food will be ready. I expect you are hungry. For myself I could eat a donkey and a bushel of beans."

She jumped up from the chair, full of vigour. It was like watching a resurrection.

We went from room to room, all shining bright, all well-lighted, polished, full of lovely things.

"Did you inherit it all," I asked, "or have you collected these beautiful things yourself?"

"They were mostly my father's third wife's. What she didn't have sent from England she made him buy," said Eulalia without interest. "I don't care much for owning things, not this kind of thing. I like my things out-of-doors, things that work. I'll show you them tomorrow. All this," she dismissed the accumulated beauty with a wave of the hand, "can only be looked at, so what's the point in owning it? To have seen a thing is

361

as good as having it, don't you think? The best things, the sun and the rain, even life itself, *can* only be looked at."

"You say the queerest things."

"Do I? Well, you should be prepared for that; anyone who mentioned me to you would say I was mad. Maybe it's true."

"Somehow I don't think so."

"Thank you. But the rest of them do. I think it's because I'm very fond of having my own way, and because I'm interested in things outside growing tobacco — though I do that very well. I'm interested in life and death and what people think and why they act the way they do —"

"And in Fate, and superstition and witchcraft," I supplemented.

"Yes. And in medicines and drugs, and books, and astrology, in history and religion and mathematics. It sounds rather a jumble, but life is too short to spend it all looking through one little spy glass. I'm interested in food just now, and here is the dining-room."

She opened a door and disclosed a vast dark room in which a lighted, flower-decked table agleam with silver swam like an island. As we entered she pulled a thick silken bell rope and before we were settled in our seats opposite one another Joseph and a black girl entered with soup tureens and plates.

"Lisette," said Eulalia as the girl set the steaming soup before us, "next time you want to borrow a book, kindly tell me. Don't *ask* of course, just *tell* me. It might be that I should waste time looking for it."

362

The girl made no answer but as I looked at her with interest, I saw the startling malevolence of the glance that she shot at Eulalia's back.

"Don't wait," said Eulalia. And as the door closed behind them she said, "That is Lisette whom I was telling you about."

"She's very dark — for a half-caste I mean."

"Colour is an incalculable thing. I wish to God she'd never been born. She's a thorn in my side."

"Couldn't you provide for her? Give her some money and send her packing."

"I shouldn't be comfortable about her. She's dumb you see."

"I see."

"And half-witted about some things, though she's devilish sharp when she pleases. Whatever I gave her the first man she met would have out of her. No. She's better under my eye. I still think father might have been contented with four white women. Still, I suppose he was like me, acutely conscious that life wouldn't last forever and anxious to crowd everything into it that he could. Let's talk of something else."

Course succeeded course, such food as I had never before tasted, and the wines matched it. The accumulated weariness of the last months dropped from me as a withered leaf drops from a winter-threatened tree. I found myself translated, merry, loquacious, catching Eulalia's eye across the table and matching wit for wit. For the first time the full force of her beauty struck me, the pale thin skin, with the blue veins showing at temple and throat and wrist, the narrow dark brows that sprang in a clean line over the eyes that were like clear water, the full, red, voluptuous curves of the mouth and the thick curls of coppery hair that clustered around the broad white brow. A delicate, a flowerlike face on its slender stem of neck; a hungry, menacing face.

She said suddenly, "A week ago I didn't know you, except by Newlyn's entrancing description. Now I seem never not to have known you. I've never liked anyone so quickly before. Has that ever happened to you?"

"Once," I said, speaking before I thought, "I fell in love at first sight."

"How romantic. Tell me about it."

"I couldn't — it wasn't very long ago."

"I'm sorry. I've never been in love, yet. But this face has had five proposals made to it, and Little Egypt has had fourteen. I've never thought of it before — but — it's a little hard on the face, isn't it?" She laughed.

"I expect you've got it the wrong way about. I'm sure it must be."

"Why, do you like my face?"

"Speaking dispassionately, I think it's the most beautiful and quite the most interesting I've ever seen."

"The face thanks you. But please don't ever bother to praise it to me. I assure you the proposals to it flatter me no more than those made to Little Egypt. I didn't make either of them."

"Oh yes." I remembered Fergus' patient face, Mac's surly one, Tottie's mean cruel countenance. "Oh yes, we make our faces. Our thoughts grave them, our smiles mark them, our vices mar them."

"And are we responsible for our thoughts, our smiles or our vices? No, my friend. Can you control your thoughts? Can anyone? What we *are*, our essences, ourselves, have nothing to do with our thoughts or our vices or our virtues."

"This doctrine of non-responsibility seems to have a great hold on you," I said lightly. "But I always think of myself all in one piece."

"Lucky man — the blessed single-mind that we read of. But it isn't all in one piece. It's like a — like a mule team and a wagon and a driver. There's the body, inherited from all the people who have gone to its making. I like brandy for example because my father did and my hair is red like my mother's. Lots of vices and virtues come from the same source. Then there's the driver, Fate, who chooses the path and somewhere in the middle of the wagon, wrapped and pinioned, gagged and blinded, lies the thing that is what one really is, the part that has a separate life, impotent, borne along. Sometimes it longs to cry out — not that way — not that thought — don't let me have to do this or say that. Nobody hears it."

She stared blindly across the table for a moment and then said in a different voice,

"The port and the cigars are in my room. Shall we go there?"

We went back into the shining room. She crossed to the fire and lifting her velvet skirt, kicked the logs over with the toe of her slipper, and then, fumbling at the laces on her bosom, took something and dropped it into the clear cavern that her toe had exposed. Drawn by irresistible curiosity I crossed the room quickly and was in time to see, shrivelling in the heat but unmistakably, a spray of cherry-blossom.

I felt a chill between my shoulders.

She turned from the fire and began to talk about tobacco. We talked on, matter-of-fact and businesslike talk until it was time to go to bed. I learned a lot. She knew the trade and the market as well as anyone could do.

I lay for a long time within the silken curtains of my massive four-poster bed, thinking of bales and grades, of horn-worm and sorting, of Lisette and cherry-blossom and spells, and whether or no we controlled our destinies, and of a white bosom just showing above some creamy lace.

Next day, followed at a distance by the oak coloured groom with a mule laden with food and bottles and rugs, we rode over Little Egypt. The fields were empty but the gardens behind the neat white-washed cabins were full of busy Negroes. Lines of coloured washing hung drying in the sun. Piccaninnies played in the dust.

As well as the tobacco fields there were meadows and corn-fields and great stretches devoted to vegetables. One field, set out in even lines with fruit trees all abloom, was planted with bushes and vegetables in the open spaces.

"My idea," said Eulalia, pointing with her crop. "I thought it would save space and the leaves from the trees make the soil rich. They're dug in every year."

It seemed so simple and reasonable that the wonder was that no one had thought of it before.

366

We went down to the drying sheds where she pointed out that they closed, not with haphazard boards and sheets of canvas but with cane shutters which rolled and unrolled.

"I thought of that from seeing a roll-top desk. They close for the drying and open again for the prizing. It saves a lot of labour."

With the experience of ten seasons behind me I could appreciate that.

"I'm just starting a new idea. I'll show you when we get to the river," she said.

The land sloped towards the river and then the slope ended abruptly where the land had been cut away so that between the edge of the last sloping tobacco field and the river bank there was a wide field, level as a table.

"We'll have to walk down. Will you mind?"

We waited until the Negro came up with us, gave the horses into his keeping and then walked down the steep escarpment that divided the two levels.

The lower field was just mud, soft and squelchy and through it little shoots were making their appearance.

"Do you know what it is?"

"I've been into Carolina," I said, "it's rice isn't it?"

"I do like an observant person," said Eulalia, looking at me with approval. "Good cheap food rice is, and they've done so well with it in Carolina I didn't see why I shouldn't have some here. Look, down there in the bank. That's a lock-gate. We close it and the water floods the field. It has to be set under water you know. And it grows more to the acre than any grain known.

That's another of my mad ideas; it amused the whole community for months."

I looked at her with a certain amount of awe.

"You've got a most exceptional mind," I said.

"You should perhaps say exceptional opportunity. I can afford to experiment. Making that dam and levelling this paddy-field took a long time, a very long time. Most people couldn't afford to keep men at work on it."

"Most people would never have thought of it."

"Too many people either can't read or don't notice what they do. The moment I read about Carolina I thought of this. But I couldn't do it until I'd made arrangements with Newlyn. You see, when the gates are closed he gets no water."

"And what arrangement reconciled him to that?"

"I built him a reservoir. I suppose I'd have had to build one for everybody along the course except that just below his place the Cheecawi runs in. That was fortunate, wasn't it?"

I nodded.

"Let's get back to the trees, shall we, and have our picnic."

We scrambled back up the rough steps hacked in the face of the escarpment and rode until we reached the trees. There the Negro spread out the rugs and cushions, set out the food and uncorked the bottles.

"Tie up the horses, Jason, and then you may go. You can fetch the things any time before sunset."

Jason tethered the horses to low boughs, mounted the mule and vanished between the trees.

"Carve the turkey, will you, Colin? And don't mind me calling you Colin. I call you that in my mind so it's absurd to go on saying Mr. Lowrie, don't you think?"

"I've called you Eulalia in my mind ever since you had supper with me," I said.

Beneath the budding trees we ate turkey and pie and fruit and cheese washed down with Canary wine. Then Eulalia said, "Now, if you don't mind I'm going to sleep for a while." She plumped up a cushion, lowered her head upon it, put a hand under her cheek and slept straightway. I stayed still for a little time, looking at her, watching the shadow of her lashes on her cheek, the regular rise and fall of her bosom, wondering why, though I admired and liked her so much, I desired her not at all. Then I too put my head on my cushion and slept.

I dreamed that little Egypt was derelict and that Eulalia and I were working it alone. First we were planting rice in the paddy-field, up to our knees in water. Then we were struggling with the shutters of the drying sheds which refused to move despite our desperate efforts. Eulalia said, "We'll feel stronger after we've eaten. There's a donkey and a bushel of beans for supper." We sat down to this repast and had cleared the donkey to a skeleton when Mr. Newlyn arrived and Eulalia said, "Hullo, Mr. Newlyn. We've been having a picnic."

I struggled up out of the mists of sleep and there was Eulalia stretching her arms, and Newlyn, with his horse's bridle over his arm, was smiling down on us sardonically.

"So I see. Perfectly idyllic."

"It was lovely," said Eulalia. "I often think we were intended to eat our food out-of-doors, it tastes so much better."

I had risen to my feet and Eulalia stretched out a hand for me to pull her up. While I did so she said, "Colin, you know Mr. Newlyn, don't you?"

"Mr. Newlyn was my first caller," I reminded her.

"Of course. I suppose you've been up to the house," she said, turning towards him.

"Yes. Lisette wrote on her slate where I should find you."

Eulalia gave me a sidelong glance, full of meaning.

"I rode over to tell you that the Ball has been arranged for the sixteenth. My wife and I much hope that you will join our party. Stuart is returning on the twelfth."

I went to untie the horses, but I could hear Eulalia say.

"It's extremely nice of you, but I had thought of taking a party myself. Mr. Lowrie has promised to join it already."

"Already! But it was only decided yesterday. I rode over to ask you immediately."

"I heard last evening," said Eulalia sweetly as she mounted. "But of course, since you are so kind; if you insist Mr. Lowrie and I will join you."

I made my inexpert way into my saddle with my face aflame. How dare she? How dare she? And

Newlyn was hesitating. Blast them both for putting a man into this position. Without exposing Eulalia in a lie I couldn't even say that I had no intention of going to the Ball.

"Certainly," Newlyn said in a cold, furious voice, "we shall be delighted to include Mr. Lowrie. I didn't know that that kind of thing appealed to him."

"And has Stuart been doing grand things in St. Kitts?" asked Eulalia as the horses broke into a canter.

"He has done a good deal of business, I believe. Equally important he has made some charming and useful friends. Sir Robert has entertained him frequently."

"Indeed," said Eulalia, and I at any rate could detect the irony in her voice. "And has Sir Robert a pretty daughter to fall victim to Stuart's charms?"

"I think," said Newlyn darkly, "that you know well enough that Stuart's eyes are fixed elsewhere."

Eulalia laughed. The track narrowed just then and she rode ahead. There was silence until she turned and called over her shoulder. "You'll stay and eat with us, won't you? We shall be early because Mr. Lowrie has to get back to Lebanon."

"I shall be delighted." And having been reminded that I existed he turned back and said, "I see that you have broken your own rule about visiting, Mr. Lowrie."

"One's own rules are easily broken, given sufficient temptation," I said shortly.

For me the day was ruined. The man disliked me and I disliked him, but while I was willing to forget my dislike at the table of a mutual friend, he was not.

371

Throughout the meal he never missed an opportunity to make me feel an outsider. A dozen times Eulalia dragged the conversation back to a subject within my ken, and every time he shot off again with a discussion of something that had happened in the past, or of a local character whom I did not know. I was obliged for long stretches of time to sit dumbly listening. As soon as possible I announced that I must be going. The road was not very well known to me, and I must be stirring early in the morning.

"You're still engaged in your hard labour then?" Newlyn said, smiling.

There was nothing but "Yes" to be given in reply. I couldn't add, "I'm not ashamed of working with my hands." That was what exasperated me; every one of his darts was quite harmless sounding and sped with a smile, and in the presence of any woman but Eulalia, quite deadly to one's vanity.

"I'll come out with you," she said. "Mr. Newlyn won't mind being left for five minutes, will you?"

Once outside the door she laid her hand on my arm.

"Don't mind him," she said, "that silly grand manner of his doesn't mean anything except that he'd rather be living on an estate in England than planting tobacco in a colony. He has a cousin with a title of some kind and that, combined with the fact that he has had to make his own way, has warped his character. He's quite kind underneath . . ."

"I suppose it takes an English gentleman to be so damned rude so craftily," I said.

The bay horse stood saddled in the yard.

372

"How're you going to get this animal back?" I asked, and my voice was still ungracious because my equanimity had been ruffled.

"I don't want him back. I want you to have him."

"That's absurd," I said. "Why should you give me a horse?"

"Because I like you. And I hope you'll come to see me often."

"You make it extremely awkward for me, don't you? And," I remembered my other earlier grievance, "look at all that nonsense you told him about the Ball. I've never been to a Ball in my life. I can't dance."

"You could learn."

"Maybe I could, and maybe I don't want to." I knew that I was behaving like a sulky, ill-natured boy and that knowledge made me more angry. "Look here, I'll send Tommy back with the horse in the morning."

"If you do I'll shoot him. Not Tommy, the horse. I tell you I don't want him."

"If I can't send him back then I'll walk home," I said furiously.

"Then I'll shoot him now."

I laughed and walked to the horse and began unhooking the little bundle of my things that hung on the saddle. A shot rang out, earth spouted a yard or two from my feet. The horse leaped. I jumped round and there was Eulalia with a little silver-mounted pistol smoking in her hand.

"Do you believe me? I tell you I don't want the creature. Get on him."

I took her by the wrist. "You *are* mad," I said wildly, "but you're not going to be mad with me. Give me that thing."

We struggled together for a second and then she put both her hands on my shoulders.

"I'd give you more than the horse, Colin, you know that. Take him please, as a token of — shall we say esteem?"

The pale eyes mocked me as she said "esteem," but before I could reply she had dropped her hands and was groping with her right for mine — a farewell handshake. Lisette, Joseph and Newlyn had come through the back door of the house. Consternation was on all their faces.

"What is it? I heard a shot," Newlyn gasped.

"Of course," said Eulalia easily. "I saw a rat. Missed it, I'm afraid. Well, once more, Colin, good-bye. I'll ride over some evening this week. Thank you so much for coming."

I rode back to Lebanon in a stupor. I couldn't forget the look of mockery, self-mockery, with which she had spoken the word, "esteem." She had meant far more than that. And the touch of her hands on my shoulders, the clasp of her fingers before they fell from mine had all been eloquent. I tried to consider the matter calmly, to convince myself that my imagination was deceiving me, that Eulalia was impulsive and unconventional and a little strange. But that uneasiness which had stirred in me on the night of her visit would not be allayed so easily. This good horse between my knees was not evidence of esteem, or of strangeness or of impulsive-ness. He was a link, the means by which she had made sure that I could visit her. She had called me Colin before them all. She had made my inclusion the condition upon which she accepted Newlyn's invita-tion. All these things pointed to one fact: and yet I could not accept it. What was there about me, poverty-stricken, horny-handed, gauche newcomer that I was, to make a woman in Eulalia's position "esteem" me? I could find no answer. But suppose my suspicions were right, what was my reaction to me? Even more puzzling a problem. I like her enormously, I admired her and was deeply interested in her character. But there was no heart in my feelings for her. That part of me had died in the autumn. Four little words had killed it. "God has taken her." Emotion, for me, had flowered rapidly and richly within a week; it had been cut down suddenly and ruthlessly; nothing more could ever come from that root.

Quite suddenly as I rode anger came on me, I turned hot with it. I hadn't asked this problem to confront me. All I wanted was to work hard at Lebanon, make a success of it, get together some money and return to Scotland. A plain, simple programme. I wouldn't have minded if I had never seen a woman again. That short sharp love for Bridget had made it impossible for me ever to have another Sadie and it had made it equally impossible that I should ever love again upon the same plane. I must never see Eulalia again. Tomorrow evening I would write her a note — God knew how I could express it without being offensive — but I must try, and Tommy must take the missive and the horse back to Little Egypt. It was no good starting something that could only finish badly.

I found myself regretting Eulalia's sex almost as much as her father could ever have done. She would have been a fine and interesting friend.

All the next day I worked madly, losing myself and my trumpery problems in labour. Compared with the magnitude of the tasks before me the question of whether or not Eulalia had any feeling for me, whether or not we ever met again, seemed trivial and stupid. Dusk came and we were feeding the animals and I had just thought, now I must begin thinking of how to word this note and persuade Tommy to take it, when there was a sound of hoofs and wheels and Eulalia rode into the yard, followed by a light wagon driven by one Negro and having two others seated in the back. I ran to meet her.

"I hope you're not too tired," was her greeting. "I've come to give you a dancing lesson. This is the band."

And suddenly I thought of her theories about destiny and the futility of crying "Not that way." In another four hours that note would have been written and delivered, the whole thing ended — or would it? I looked at her, so lovely and so assured, and within herself so certain that she was following her appointed path. Perhaps she too had cried, "Not that way," and had not been heeded but was now being swept along on the current and taking me with her. I made some protests, but she ignored them, installed the three Negroes on the stairs and waited while I washed. And

376

then, in the empty hall I stepped and bowed, slid and turned, took her hand and loosed it as she directed me.

If I had suffered from one of my recurrent attacks of seeing myself from outside, I should have been overcome by self-consciousness; or I should have been so amused at the figure I cut in my serviceable clothes, offering my horny hand to a lady, mincing and prancing, that I should have been unable to continue. But I had quite enough to occupy my mind as well as my hands and feet.

At Springhill I had become susceptible to Negro music. And now, as in those old distant days, I found my weariness dropping from me, the rhythm of my blood quickened and changed. It became impossible for me *not* to dance and even more impossible to ignore the fact that Eulalia was dancing with me in a manner more suited to the Little Pasture than to a stately Ball-room. When the length of our extended arms was between us she looked at me seductively from under those long lashes. When we came together she pressed so closely that I was conscious of her warmth and the perfume that came from her clothes and hair. The very clasp of her hand disturbed my flesh. I noticed that with a shock which I flung off, and reached for the hand again to repeat the experience. The Negroes were playing "White Man's" music, but they managed to infuse into the light, tinkling tunes something of their own wild rhythm, so that involuntarily I thought of the orgies of the Thanking Days. Eulalia, or the fate that drove her, had been wise: the music was fighting for her. A tired man can march behind a band when without it he would be supine from exhaustion: a coward can go into battle behind the skeeling pipes and never guess from what source he draws the courage to go forward. And many a man has taken a woman from the false desire that music has aroused in him.

Between this new, languishing Eulalia and the music of her Negroes I was undone. She paused at last as the tune ended, and still leaning against me, looked towards the stairs.

"That will do. Fetch in the basket and then you can go home. Tell them that no one is to wait up. I shall be late." She looked at me as she said the last words, and I, out of my new madness, thought — yes madam, you shall be late as you like. "Wait just a minute," I said, "Can you play, 'In the dark night, when the moon is dead?'"

Six black eyes rolled at me, startled. What could a white man know of that song, they asked.

"Can you?" I repeated. They nodded.

"Play it then."

There was no response, the black eyes had shifted and were fastened on Eulalia.

"Go on," she said sharply, "play what you're told."

Upon each face the puzzled look turned to one of scornful tolerance. Obviously we didn't know what we were asking, and the words were not demanded. They began to play so hastily that the timing went wrong and they had to start again. I took Eulalia by the arm and drew her into my room, leaving the door half open so that the strains of the wild music might follow us.

"I think," she said, with a kind of bold nervousness that loosened the last thread of my control, "that the moon is dead tonight." She held out her arms.

"In the dark night when the moon is dead . . ." Bridget is dead, love is dead, but the mouth under mine is warm and open and amorous . . .

"And need no bed . . ." An hour ago I didn't either, but I didn't ask this thing to happen to me. She did, and I suppose she knows what she's doing. She's not a young girl.

"Another night, another night." Damn it, let the future look after itself. This is the kind of thing that flares up suddenly and dies as quickly, like a leaf fire.

Out on the stairs the musicians completed the tune for the third time before Eulalia drew away from me and dropped limply into a chair.

"Tell them that that will do."

I went into the hall.

"I've never heard it played better. Your mistress says you may go now."

One of them shambled back with a little hamper tied with thin cord. I waited until he had gone and then bolted the door. Not that there was anyone to come in.

We were both in that elated, almost tremulously excited state that comes between the wakening of desire and its fulfilment. I saw her fingers shaking as she untied the cord. The little hamper was full of dainties, fruit and cakes and sweetmeats. There was also a squat dark bottle that she handled almost lovingly.

"Some monks in France make this. It's the best thing that the Catholic Church ever produced."

I felt my mind shy, like a horse when a rag flutters from a hedge. And just at that moment my eye fell upon the sweetmeats laid out on the little silver dish. Squares of soft candy. God Almighty. Those dusty stairs, the little groping fingers, the wet smear where temptation had been trodden underfoot. Oh, my love. Alas that the mind should be more constant than the body. Desire, bladder-like, deflated. I looked at Eulalia. Impossible now, after that long embrace, to send her away. Why rob the living to honour the dead? I brushed aside the plate of candy and picked up the bottle.

"I hope to God it's strong," I said. For not reason, and not kindliness, not the memory of that passionate mouth or the throb of the music, nothing but intoxication, could see me through this.

"Now can you possibly understand," came Eulalia's cool voice through the darkness and the confusion, "why men insist upon virginity in their brides? Could any state be less inviting?"

"It wasn't that," I said. "For the love of Heaven don't *talk* about it."

My mouth was full of the sour after-sweetness of the liquor I had drunk. My palms, my throat, the backs of my legs were clammy cold. My mind was full of shame and anger. I dreaded the moment when I must make a light and face her. I had yet to learn that Eulalia and embarrassment could not occupy the same room. She rose up with a dissertation upon a new idea she had had for draining a sour field. She interrupted her dressing to illustrate to me her meaning.

"Imagine that this bed is the field . . ."

I didn't listen much.

You might have thought that we were two strangers, whiling away in conversation a chance meeting in a tavern. But just before she mounted the pale horse she turned and kissed me. There was no doubt about the kiss.

And so began a period with an atmosphere and flavour, which, looking backward, I find difficult to describe. Out of it there emerges only that certainty that I was held in a kind of spell cast by Eulalia's personality. Often enough, in shame or anger, pique or pride, I would part from her, determined to see her no more; but the determination never outlasted the mood that engendered it. And out of all my time at Lebanon the happiest hours were those spent in her company. Not that they were invariably pleasant.

I might ride over, eager to see her, wanting to talk to her, wanting her. I might find her in any mood, loving, sternly sensible, ridiculously nonsensical, or withdrawn into a state of lethargy that I was more than half assured came from the use of some drug, though that she stoutly denied. Those were the worst times, for then I had neither physical nor intellectual intercourse with her. She would lie on a sofa, pale, cold to the touch, overborne by some dark onslaught that had neither name, nor cause, nor remedy. Even her voice would be muted. It was impossible to believe at such times that this was the woman who was capable of such merriment, such energy, such temper and such passion.

I would doubt then that she had any feeling for me whatever. The fact that I had ridden ten miles after a gruelling day in the sun-bitten fields was not enough to draw a smile or a word from her. But these moods would be gone almost before my anger had been dissipated and she would be over at Lebanon full of talk and plans and vigour again — but never with a word of apology. She had a way, too, of breaking off a conversation, a meal or a love passage and saying with a vague lost look, "I must go," or "You must go," according to where we were. In everything concerning her personal life she was erratic to the point of eccentricity. I've known her to rush into Tommy's kitchen, crying,

"Give me a crust, a thick one. I haven't had anything to eat since yesterday or the day before. I forget."

She would stay up all night, reading or doing accounts, and then go to bed for two days. Remonstrances called forth the spuriously reasonable retort,

"Eat when you're hungry and go to bed when you're tired. God didn't *order* us three meals and eight hours sleep in every twenty-four, did He?"

But about other things she was consistent, far more so than most women. She never visited displeasure upon an innocent head. She would break off a furious tirade to me to speak gently to Joseph or Lisette. She excused Goddy's irritating inquisitiveness by saying that it was because he couldn't read.

"He can't get interest, romance, and scandal and excitement out of a printed page, as I can, so he pokes into the living pages." And that struck me as a curious and novel summing up of a damned prying old nuisance.

There was nothing under the sun that she wasn't eager to discuss or learn, and nothing within her ken that she did not thoroughly understand. Some of the things she said were so sweeping that they made my more limited mind reel and I occasionally wondered whether our failures (though they became less frequent and were in time forgotten) weren't in some measure due to the fact that I had a certain awe of her mind. She was never subjugated, never completely possessed. That mind remained aloof, pandering to the desires of the body that it lived in, but still critical and free.

In all practical ways she was overwhelmingly kind to me, would have lent or given me anything had my pride been less stubborn. She would give advice in hints dropped casually, and discuss the business of planting so that I learned a great deal almost without knowing it. Most women would have been smug about their superior knowledge in a man's sphere, but to Eulalia it was nothing. Her excellent brain she regarded as a thing apart; like her face, she wasn't responsible for either of them. Yet there was at the same time a tantalising femininity about her, and never was that more in evidence than on the night of the Planters' Ball.

I had succumbed to persuasion, and to the knowledge that by staying away I should leave the land clear for young Newlyn. So one day I said to Tommy,

"I want you to go into Jamestown for me. Go to Mr. Preswade and ask him the name of his tailor and ask him if he will tell the fellow that he'll be safe to give me credit. Take my blue suit and tell the tailor to make me the best suit he is able in that size. I want it for a Ball."

"For a what?"

"A Ball. On the sixteenth of next month. I also want silk hose and thin shoes with buckles. I think I'd better write to Mr. Preswade and ask him to help you."

"Don't mention the credit then, Mister."

"Why not? I can't pay until the autumn."

"What about the horses? We don't want 'em. The mules can do it all. You didn't count my staying and bringing the horses when you bought the mules, did you?"

"No. That's true. But the horses are yours, Tommy."

"Well, what's to prevent *me* giving you the credit? I know you and the tailor don't."

"All right," I said. "I'll be much obliged to you. But, I say . . . don't sell them back to that fat fellow."

"I wouldn't sell him my old —" said Tommy succinctly.

"I would," I said, "at a price!"

Tommy performed the errand well, and eventually fetched home the clothes, perfectly tailored in rich plum-coloured material. The coat had silver buttons and the buckles on the shoes were silver too. I rode into Fort Anchor and had my hair dressed and spent a long time on my hands. When I had finished they were clean, but I regarded with distaste the chips and scars upon finger-tips and knuckles, and the palms that were almost as hard as hoofs. They were undoubtedly a labourer's hands and past remedy.

The Ball was held in the Court House at Fort Anchor, and though it was little more than a barn it had been transformed by flowers and shrubs and flags into a fitting background for all that existed of fashion and gentility within a radius of forty miles.

Eulalia was radiant. I thought once, as I stood behind her, that the back of her neck, with the coppery hair drawn away from it into a mass of curls and coils on her crown, was lovelier than the face of any other woman there. A little gasp had run through the assembly, like wind running through standing corn, when she entered upon Newlyn's arm. Following them, with Mrs. Newlyn, a heavy sallow haughty woman, I was reminded of Preswade's words about all the other women being fit to be tied when she appeared. That remark had roused no premonition in me then, and now I was her lover. Strange thought!

As the Ball progressed and I had time to look about me I realised that had I been a stranger in Fort Anchor for the first time and known nothing of her except what she looked like. I should have wanted to dance with her, should have angled for an introduction. And I might, in such circumstances, have enjoyed myself more. For Eulalia seemed bent upon flirting with every man of the number who gathered around her, and especially with Stuart Newlyn, a tall languid youth in his middle twenties, with a poisonously good opinion of himself. Something went to my head when I watched her dancing with him in the same abandoned manner that she had used with me in the dim hall at Lebanon. I was angry with her, but him I hated.

Mid-way through the evening, when about half the company had crowded into the small, inadequate ante-room where supper was being served, Stuart Newlyn and I simultaneously claimed a dance. The music had already started, a tune I liked and I meant to dance with her. We stood there, the three of us, in the shadow of a palm, Stuart and I glaring at one another like two dogs at rutting time and Eulalia smiling at us both, thoroughly enjoying the situation. I put my hand on her arm.

"You promised it to me," I said.

Young Newlyn struck down my hand. I whirled round, but before I could do anything, and there was plenty in my mind to do, Eulalia had taken my arm.

"I think Colin is right, Stuart. I'll have supper with you."

"I'm in your hands," he said, and with a stiff little bow to her and another glare for me, took himself off.

"Young whipper-snapper," I said. Eulalia laughed.

"He can be rather a dear and he's been fond of me for years."

"That doesn't allow him to go about slapping his elders' hands."

"Now, if you're going to be angry you'll forget your steps."

"And if you're going to be coy I shall forget something else," I said fiercely. "I'll show you whether I forget steps." A turn coming just then, I swung her up so that her feet left the floor.

Stuart was waiting when the dance was finished and she took his arm. As they went towards the supper-room I heard him say — I was meant to hear — "Why do you encourage that clod-hopper, Eulalia?"

"Now which is the nicer word," said Eulalia with exaggerated thoughtfulness, "clod-hopper, whipper-snapper? Whipper-snapper, clod-hopper?" She laughed as she tried over the words and that was the last I heard.

But afterwards, amid the confusion of many men claiming and struggling into their outer clothes, Stuart Newlyn and I met and carried on the war. It was all about a very stupid thing. I could see my coat with a pile of others over it and being anxious to rejoin Eulalia I pushed forward to take it instead of waiting for it to be given to me by the Negro who was handing out the hats and coats and silver-headed canes that had been left in his charge. In doing so I pushed my elbow into the back of a man who was just settling his hat upon his head. He tottered forward a step, righted himself and would have made no more of the matter, for everyone in the room was pushing and being pushed. But just behind me, before I could even mutter that I was sorry, a jeering voice said, "Oh, you mustn't mind Mr. Lowrie, Flowerdew. He's always pushing."

I got heated immediately.

"What the devil are you talking about?"

"You," he said coolly. "You've been pushing the whole evening."

"Are you trying to tell me how to behave?"

"I think it's time somebody did."

"And you might profit by the same instruction, you uppity young cub. You might begin by learning that a ball-room is not the place to start laying hands on people. If you'll come outside with me I'll show you where, and how, it should be done."

By that time everyone in the room was watching and listening with interest. I heard somebody whisper, "Who is the big fellow?" and someone replied, "New man at Lebanon." Stuart Newlyn waited a second, eyed me slowly and then,

"I've no doubt you'd enjoy a good bout of fisticuffs," he said with a scathing glance at my hands. "But if you want to meet me you'll meet me as a gentleman should."

"Wherever, whenever and however you like," I said joyfully.

"Tomorrow then at five o'clock in the afternoon. At Indian clearing. Pistols."

"Good," I said.

By the time that I was up in the morning and dressed and in the fields I realised that I had been a fool, and the knowledge grew with every hour of the day. I paused now and then and wondered what it was all about. We'd both wanted to dance with Eulalia and we'd both done it; he'd called me Clod-hopper, and I'd called him Whipper-snapper. So far we were even. He had pushed my hand away and I hadn't touched him, and he had jibed me about pushing, therefore I supposed that I was the injured party, and should have been panting for "satisfaction." But I was bound to admit that I wasn't. I had arranged to meet him in a moment of anger, and now I was angry no longer, except with myself. The whole affair was so artificial, like the atmosphere and situation in which the quarrel had occurred. With all that I had of Eulalia what did it matter whom she danced with? Why need I announce my claim in the eyes of men?

I looked about me at the bright weather, the green shoots rising from the ridges, the smoke going up from the kitchen chimney, my blacks bent in labour. These were the real things, the things a man might fight for. I was going to risk my life for nothing. It was just like a swaggering young dandy to make an issue and force a quarrel all about nothing. People like that never had anything real or urgent to grapple with, therefore they made all this fuss about affairs of "honour." Ordinary folks, with a living to earn, returned insult for insult, jibe for jibe, and if they fought, fought in a rage as Tommy fought. They didn't risk their lives over a disputed dance.

It occurred to me that the word "clod-hopper" had been well-chosen. Perhaps I was that. Perhaps the long years of menial labour had bred in me a menial mind. Was it peasant-like to think that life was too precious to throw away in a trivial cause? But I still didn't want either to shoot or be shot. However, I was in it now. And since I must do, I must do it properly.

I put down my tools and went into the house to look out the pistol which Tommy had insisted should be part of our outfit. I set up bottles on a post in the yard and practised shooting them down. There was nothing wrong with my aim, the splintered bottles testified that.

"What're you up to, Mister?" asked Tommy, after he had watched some time from the kitchen doorway.

"I've got to shoot a man at five o'clock today." It sounded incredibly stupid.

"What for?"

"We had a few words."

"Oh, a duel."

"That's it."

"Got a second?"

"I've got till five o'clock. What do you want?"

"I mean a second to go with you, Mister."

"No. Ought I to?"

"Must have somebody to give the signal and drag the body home."

"Then you'd better come. And listen, Tommy. If anything happens to me the place is yours if you want it. But if you don't, turn the niggers loose, will you?"

"Nothing'll happen to you. That about the body was just a jape. The thing is to shoot first, Mister. It's speed that counts. Take another shot or two with that in mind and I'll wring out a little pity for the other poor bastard."

He pranced about the yard yelling, "When I say 'now.'" "When I whistle." "When I drop my handkerchief, oh blast I haven't got one. When I raise my arm then." "Now, when I touch my head."

Quite soon it was time for me to wash and put on my clean shirt and blue breeches. We set out for Indian clearing, the desolate piece of waste land where the grove of sacred trees had once stood.

When we arrived there there were two horses tied to a stump near the edge of the level green space and Stuart Newlyn and another young man were pacing out the ground.

Up to that moment I had felt that I didn't want him to kill me. Now I realised that I didn't want to kill him. Good God! he was his father's only son, and he thought the world of him. Somewhere in the world there was the girl whom he should marry, on whom he should get sons of his own. In the clear sunny light of the afternoon he looked young and handsome. Even his languid manner and drawling voice failed to move me to hatred as they had done last night. Suppose I killed him!

Suddenly I remembered Tottie, shot in the back as he ran. Ah, but Tottie had injured, bullied and abused me over a long period of years; and the world was better without him. I had had a real grudge against Tottie, he had offended me over vital things, food and clothing and labour. This quarrel was like those of the children in the market place. I wanted to go to him and say so — but that would be put down as an effort to save my skin, the clod-hopper's fear of anything but a fist.

Feeling old and battered and foolish I watched the formalities. I chose one of the long pistols which the other young man loaded and offered me with a flourish across his arm.

"Your man can give the signal."

I dragged out my handkerchief and tossed it to Tommy who took it and turned his back. He was far more familiar with the procedure than I. I fixed my eye on the buff-coloured silk-clad shoulder. I'd wing him if I could. A little blood-letting would do him no harm. I moved my eye to Tommy. The handkerchief fell; my finger moved. Simultaneously I saw Newlyn's pistol fall, his right arm wag helplessly, and felt a searing pain across my cheek and ear.

Tommy snatched up the handkerchief and ran towards me.

"Another inch and it'd of been through your eye," he said through his teeth as he dabbed me. "Did you *aim* at his shoulder?"

I nodded.

"You are a first-class bloody fool, Mister, and no mistake. He's a killer. You can see it in his face."

"Well, there's no harm done, though I think I've lost a bit of ear."

"You have so. The lobe's gone. But I bet his arm's broken. Let's go see."

I returned the pistol to the velvet-lined box that lay on the grass, and straightened myself.

"Do you think it's broken? Would you like to come up to my house? It's near you know."

"The idea of calling upon you, Mr Lowrie, may occur to me when delirium sets in, not before."

"All right," I said. "Bleed all over the state if you've a mind to. It's all one to me. Though I fail to see what grudge you have against me now."

I was so relieved to be through with it and so little damage done that I couldn't realise that he was annoyed because he had failed to kill me.

Tommy and I walked back to the house and left the pair of them fumbling about, tying up the arm with neckcloths.

"I hope it's so that he never holds a pistol again," said Tommy savagely. "Four nicks in the butt I saw, and him so young. You might have been the fifth, Mister."

"Well, he risked his life each of those times, Tommy, remember. I must say I feel a certain admiration for people who risk their lives so easily in such little causes."

"Never been in any real danger, that's their trouble."

"I was thinking the very same thing this morning." Presently I left off dabbing at the groove on my cheek and the base of my ear and let the blood clot over the wounds.

By the time that I rode to Little Egypt next time there was nothing to show for it except the absence of my ear lobe. And Newlyn himself had been over to see Eulalia, and in a mistaken attempt to impress her had given her a very sorry account of Stuart's state. I was very jubilant and Eulalia said "Poor Stuart" with sympathy that was more ironic than mockery.

After that life resumed its usual pattern. It was like music made by two instruments, a drum and a fiddle. The work was the drum, steady, not varying, marking the time, the bedrock of the tune; and the affair with Eulalia was the fiddle, uncertain, frisky, variable, the trimmings of the melody.

The tobacco plants grew tall, so that as we stooped over our hoes we were lost to sight among them. We searched the leaves for signs of hornworm, we snipped off flowers and superfluous leaves. The crop had every appearance of being excellent. The legend of Lebanon's curse dropped into the background of my mind.

All through that summer I was happy, so long as I didn't allow myself to look backward or to think of Bridget. I looked forward instead. Looked to the day when I should sell Lebanon as a flourishing concern, and turn homeward to my real job at Braidlowrie. Sometimes when I thought of it the question of Eulalia reared its head like a snake, but I trod it down. Before that time came one of two things would have happened. She would have tired of me, and that was more than likely with a nature as violent and erratic as hers, or time would have clarified my emotions so that I could either love her or leave her. At the moment it seemed that I could do neither. Sometimes, when I hadn't seen her for a while, or when she was in a charming mood, witty and kind, I did almost love her. But something was always lacking. And sometimes things happened that repelled me and almost broke the spell.

Once I thought we had finished for good and all.

The tobacco leaves were just on the turn. Harvest would be upon us at any moment. I had been over to Little Egypt for the evening meal and after it we had talked of many things, idle rambling conversation of the kind that is only possible when people are well attuned.

394

I remember thinking how much I *liked* her; how much I should have valued her friendship even if that had been all I had of her. I enjoyed evenings like that most of all, I think, for they didn't make me think about love, or Bridget, or whether I was wronging Eulalia — or failing her.

On this evening she said something about the autumn, how sad it was. "It seems to be the end of everything, just as spring seems to be the beginning. Do you mind it, Colin?"

"I hate it," I said. "I always shall. The worst moment of my life was in the autumn."

"The day you were taken to Springhill?"

"No." And then out of the confidence bred by the evening's happiness I was suddenly telling her about Bridget. It was a foolish thing to do. And it was bad for us both. It insulted her and harrowed me.

When I had finished, and the scent of that corridor was in my nostrils and the sound of that bell in my ears and I saw the blue velvet laid out again on the bed, she said very quietly, ominously —

"You love her still, don't you?"

I longed, decency and affections made me long, to deny it, but all I could say was the truth. "Something remains, or something is gone. I couldn't say which."

She put her long white hand to her throat and gripped it as a man might his enemy's. Her voice when it came was strangled.

"So that is what is between us all the time — the stink of a corpse! A little slut, willing to break her vows for the first man who asked her."

I felt as though I had been hit, heavily, in the face.

"Damn you," I said wildly, "I'll never forgive you for that."

Half my anger was with myself for having told her, for having trusted her to understand. I hated us both. I went straight out, left behind me the horse that had been her gift and walked to Lebanon. It took me over two hours but I walked with frenzy, with passion, driving my feet into the ground, rejoicing in the aching of my limbs, the hot sweat of my body. Nothing was sacred to a mind like Eulalia's, I thought furiously, nothing was sacred.

I wished with my whole heart that I had never set eyes upon her, never listened to the mellow voice, never — and this was most important of all — never admitted that here was a mind of unusual penetration and power. For having admitted that one must accept the unpleasant fact that the offending speech had lifted, just for a moment, a shutter upon a deadly possibility. That was what made it so offensive.

I reached Lebanon at last and the hard walk and the hard thinking had left me exhausted. I had a curious feeling of emptiness. As I undressed and lay down upon my bed I had a moment of mental clarity. I thought this is what age will be like, not caring violently any more. One spent one's capacity for caring passionately as one travelled the years, just as I had spent my anger on the journey home to Lebanon. For the first time in all my years I realised that one day, I, I, Colin Lowrie, would be old. Old, cold, not caring any longer and then dead. And when I laid my bones to "rest in de cold clay" Bridget would be forgotten, and so would Eulalia and all the other people who had bound my life. I saw myself suddenly shooting like a comet down the years — and then darkness. Did it matter that I had loved Bridget and she had died, that Eulalia had spoken ill of her? How could it? I had my sudden first warm feeling for Eulalia when I saw her, not as the young, beautiful, capricious mistress of Little Egypt but as a frail human being of flesh and blood, growing older every day and going in the end to her grave. Tomorrow, I thought, turning upon my side, I will make my peace with Eulalia who after all is only a poor fellow pilgrim. And with that resolve I slept.

But in the morning, though I could remember the mood, and the resolve to which it had given birth, I did not feel the same at all. I thought, if I forgive Eulalia too readily I shall place myself in her hands forever. And though one day we shall both be old and eventually dead, at the moment we are young and very much alive. If I start treating people as though they were potential corpses there'll be no end to the things I must bear from them. No. Eulalia insulted the memory of the woman I loved beyond everything else, and she must apologise first.

And in this mood I set about gathering my harvest. That was real and remained after everything else had altered — the struggle, the labour and the sweat. The rest were only the trimmings. For three weeks we worked in a frenzy, gathering and racking and spreading the leaves. No word came from Little Egypt, and I had another warm feeling towards Eulalia when I thought that she too was busy with her harvest; she was like me, she knew what was real. Once the harvest was finished she would think of me and apologise, and I should go to her. We'd meet like friends after an absence.

The apology came sooner than I thought. One evening as I was serving out rations in the half-light there was a clatter in the yard. I looked out and there was the bay horse nosing at his stable door. No one was with him. I went out. He greeted me with whinnies of pleasure, but I ran past him and looked along the track to see if I could see who had brought him. But no one was visible, so I returned to the yard and, fondling his nose, led him into the stable. A white paper, folded and sealed, was attached to his saddle. I put it in my pocket and went indoors.

Tommy had lighted the kitchen lantern so I sat down beside it on a corner of the table, broke the seal and read the lines penned on it in black erratic letters.

"You said you'd never forgive me, and if that is true I am the most miserable of women. It was an unforgiveable thing to say, but I was stung into saying it. Whoever came between us, even if it were the Virgin herself, I should speak ill of and injure if I could.

"I seem to have so much and have really so little that I care about that I cannot bear to lose anything. And I care about you more than anything in the world. I'd rather have you again, even with that ghost between us, than live in this hell of loneliness.

"What could she have given you that I can't? What was she more than I am?"

The question ended the page. On the other side was written, "Please come." And that was all.

The saddle was still warm when I lifted it down and laid it again across the sleek brown back.

I had expected to find her flat, extinguished, hollow; but I was not prepared for the unlighted room, or to see, when candles were brought at her hasty order, the tangled hair, sunken eyes and cheeks, the pallor.

"I didn't expect you so soon. I thought tomorrow perhaps, or never."

"I said, 'Have you been ill, Eulalia?'"

"Ill? Of course not. I'm never ill. Why do you ask that?"

"Have you looked at your mirror lately?"

She blinked at me. "I don't know. Really I can't remember. What does it matter?"

"Look here, Eulalia. Have you got yourself into this state because of us — because we quarrelled?" And I had imagined her busy about the harvest!

"I don't know what you mean by 'this state.' If I am different from when you saw me last, I suppose it is because of that," she said petulantly.

"But it's so stupid," I said harshly. "You've wasted to a shadow. Are you trying to destroy yourself? You lived before I came. If I went away you'd still have to live, you'd have to eat and wash and do your hair."

"If you have come here only to shout at me, please go away." Her voice was cold. And she had written me that note, begging me to come, begging me to forgive her.

There was a long, awkward silence. The candles were now burning brightly and I could see the disorder, the tarnished beauty of the room: thick grey dust on every shining surface: dead flowers brown and drooping in the vases: a tray of untouched food on the table by the sofa where she lay. The room had not been touched since the night when I flung out of it crying that I would never forgive her. What on earth had the household been thinking?

I was conscious of a feeling of irritation. She had managed subtly to put me in the wrong. I was the offended and I had come hotfoot on receipt of her apology, prepared for a scene, not a deadlock of this kind. I had imagined that she would cry and repeat her apology and that I should comfort her, say that it didn't matter any more, and eventually take her in my arms. But this situation was beyond my handling. There was more in it than the meeting of two people who had fallen out and were now prepared to fall in again. Below the surface it was a war between two alien personalities which could neither agree, nor ignore one another, which could not even war openly. There was conflict in the very air. From a long way off the thought came to me that the difficulty arose from the lack of genuine, normal feeling in us. If I had loved her that ravaged face and neglected hair would have moved me to passionate pity, not to irritation. If she had been in love with me, after the normal fashion, the sight of me arriving so suddenly would have roused her from her apathy. Oh God, I thought, why did I ever start it?

I said with all the gentleness I could muster,

"Eulalia, go upstairs and do your hair and change your gown, while I get this room tidied and order us some food. I'm very hungry. Your note arrived just as I was giving out the supper rations and I didn't stop to have any, or to wash myself. So go and make yourself grand enough for two, will you?"

I was almost childishly relieved to see a faint return of interest to her face. She got up slowly and pulled the bell rope. Joseph appeared with a promptitude that led me to suspect that he hadn't been far from the keyhole.

"Have candles taken to my bedroom and the dining-room, and food ready in a quarter of an hour. And get this room set straight, fresh flowers and the windows opened." It was the old masterful voice and it did not change when she turned to me and said, "Come up with me: you can talk to me while I do my hair."

Slightly dazed I followed her up the stairs and into her room. I sat down on the cushioned window seat while she dragged off the tumbled gown and threw it in the corner, splashed vigorously in the water that was brought by a little spindle-legged Negress, and then arrayed herself in the dress that she had worn at the

Ball at Fort Anchor. She laid a lacy shawl over the shoulders of the gown and sat down before the mirror to struggle with the tangled clusters of hair.

"I think I could do it better," I said.

"Please do."

I took the brush in one hand and with the other clumsily lifted a lock at a time and brushed it until the old shining look returned to it. When I could draw the comb from forehead to the end of each tendril without encountering a snarl I laid down the brush and put the comb into her hand. As I did so I lifted my eyes, which had been bent on my task, and met her gaze in the mirror. Out of that restored and resurrected face the pale eyes stared at me from the shadow of the glossy hair. We looked at each other for a long moment, during which I was conscious of the ticking of the clock by the bedside, the scent of the perfume that she had opened while I was brushing, the warmth of a tendril of hair that still lay across my hand like a copper-coloured snake.

And once again a chill ran down my neck. For although she was looking at me fondly there was speculation in the glance — and unmistakeable triumph.

She began to comb her hair around her fingers.

"And how is the crop?"

I started. "Pretty good," I said.

"Mine is excellent, I'm told. I haven't seen it myself."

"Yes, I expect it is." I thought — if you wanted to grow snow-drops in Hell I suppose you'd do it.

"There, that will do," she said, withdrawing her finger from the last shining curl. "And now for some food. I am literally starving."

At last, full fed, we were back in the shining room all restored to beauty and order. No wonder capriciousness flourished where service was so prompt and unquestioning!

"I'll have brandy," said Eulalia, speaking to herself as she hovered over the silver tray of decanters and glasses.

Four little logs of apple-wood crackled and blazed from the back of the hearth. Their heat was unneeded and unnoticed but the sight and sound and scent of them was pleasing. The fresh flowers filled the air with their varied, delicate perfumes. Eulalia sat down with a rustling of silks and looked at me with shining eyes over the rim of her glass.

"There," she said at last, stretching her long slim arm to replace the glass on the tray, "now I feel equal to anything. I suppose it has never occurred to you to propose to me, Colin?"

The uneasy feeling that had lurked in me for months came to a head and found expression in a great jolt of my heart, but I managed to say calmly, "Propose to you. How could I? I've nothing to offer you."

"There's yourself, you know. Still, if you won't do it, I must. Will you marry me?"

"No," I said bluntly, "I won't. It wouldn't be a suitable match for one thing."

"Why not?"

"You know perfectly well why not. Our respective positions, the difference in our possessions. It's ridiculous."

"What does that matter? I don't treasure my goods. You can have them. Possessions are nothing. They should never be allowed to come between people who love one another. The thing is, do you love me, Colin?"

I thought hard. This was a crisis. A mistake now and God knew where we should end. I said,

"Eulalia, if I were under torture I couldn't give either yes or no to that question. You've been very frank, so I will be, too. What I feel for you I cannot understand. Ever since I've known you I've been in the same unsettled frame of mind. I do like you intensely, more than I've ever liked anyone. You're beautiful and clever and forthright and kind. Sometimes I'm more at home with you than I could possibly be with anyone else. This last three weeks I've been too busy to think about my feelings, but tonight I was so glad to get your message that I rushed straight out of the house without even washing my hands. But all the same — I don't *think* I love you. Wait just a minute. Don't be either hurt or offended at that. It's not due to you at all. I told you about Bridget. After that I don't think it's *in* me to love any more. I have been in love, and I know it's something quite apart from appreciation of mind or desire for the flesh. You can only understand it if you've known it."

"And you didn't even want me that night: the night they played the dead moon song?"

"Oh yes," I said, "I wanted you. Make no mistake about that."

"That's beyond my poor comprehension. I can't understand."

"I don't suppose any woman could. They're more in one piece than men. They don't distinguish, as men do, between the whole attraction and its component parts."

"You'd forget her in time," said Eulalia, dropping the argument. "I could make you forget her."

"I believe you could."

"Then why not let me try?"

"For a million reasons. Mainly because in the effort you'd eat me up alive. You always call the tune. This very evening you've had all your own way. From the moment I came through that door you were on top of the situation. And you know it. I know it too. Eulalia, I think you should have chosen a booby! Maybe you thought you had. There's another reason too, a more tangible one. I don't intend to stay in America all my life. As soon as I have made enough money I intend to go back to Scotland. There's a house and an estate there that have belonged to the Lowries for generations. To set it up again is my real work. Your home is here, and your work."

"I'd sell out too, and go with you."

"You think you would. But my dear you don't understand what it would mean. You're a Queen here. You rule, you possess people body and soul. You'd be lost. While I rebuild Braidlowrie I shall live in a hut, a sty."

"A dead nun, and a heap of stones," said Eulalia softly. "What adversaries!"

"It's a question of time, my dear. Paltry as they sound, they possessed me first."

" 'The first shall be last and the last first,' I believe we are assured," she said with a little laugh.

"Of the same vintage as 'the meek shall inherit the earth,' I'm afraid. I've never seen the meek get anything."

"Oh but they do, you know, they do! In the final issue it is the ploughshare that remains after the sword has been broken. The peasant endures while the king dies in battle. I've read enough history to know that. Enough to make me wonder sometimes about the slaves of ours."

"What about them?"

"Whether, not in our generation, or the next, but in one not so far ahead, the meek black will not inherit the earth that he has tilled."

"It'll be a pretty earth," I said, remembering the cabins at Springhill.

"The earth won't mind. Nature has no favour for cleanliness and fine manners and pocket handkerchiefs."

The discussion, thus set rolling, gathered momentum. The solemn chiming of the tall clock in the hall recalled me to a sense of time and place.

"I must go," I said, jumping to my feet.

"Well, come over on Sunday," said Eulalia. "Thank God we can still talk about things."

Where was the woman who had written that letter? Had any suitor since the world began, accepted a refusal with a long, prophetic-sounding discourse upon the future of slaves?

Next morning, staggering out still half blind with sleep, I looked over the field where all day we should be cutting the thick stems and watching the towers of leaves fall in orderly line, and stood still in amazement. It couldn't be frost and the heaviest dew could never shine so whitely. I broke into a run, reached the field and brushed my hand across the nearest leaves. Mildew! Every leaf on every plant smitten with the plague. I turned and ran to the drying sheds. Perhaps the leaves already gathered had escaped. Mildewed every one. For no reason, with no warning, out of the night this unaccountable thing had struck. Where the white foamy growth was brushed away the speckle of it remained, like the cover of an old book housed for years in a damp cupboard.

The first indefinable scent of autumn was in the air as I stood there that early morning. Later the day would be mellow and warm, harvest weather, sweaty weather, but at the moment the air was like tonic. The sun was rising above the lemon and grey strata of clouds in the Eastern sky. The slaves, upon whose door I had hammered in passing, shambled out into the light; their pale palates and lolling tongues showed as they yawned. The smoke of the fire that Tommy was making rose straight into the sky.

I saw all these things with my eyes while my mind took in the knowledge that I was ruined. Lebanon, like a wild beast that fawns upon its tamer until its hour comes to tear him, had struck at last. For almost a year, through a complete round of seasons, through clearing and planting and hoeing and garnering, it had held its hand, lulled me into a sense of false security, waiting this hour. It was no myth then, the story of Lebanon. Nobody had ever had a pennyworth of good of it — and I was not to be the exception.

The Negroes began to yelp around me. I waved them back with my hand.

For this we had risen early and late taken rest. For this we had knelt and cut away the brambles that rent our flesh, uprooted the seedling pines and torn away the creeping, tangled weeds. For this we had ploughed and planted, dug and hoed, sweated, panted, ached and endured. That this evil thing, in one short night, might make mockery of our labours.

I said at last, "Go get your breakfast. There's nothing we can do now."

I walked, with stiff legs that moved automatically, into the kitchen, where Tommy, blowing at the fire, looked round at me, startled.

"I ain't missed an hour or anything, have I? You're not back to breakfast, are you?"

"I might as well have my breakfast. We're ruined, Tommy."

"What's ruined us?"

"Mildew. Every blasted leaf in the fields and the sheds is covered with it. I've never seen anything like it in my life."

Even at that moment I was compelled to observe, with a sour amusement, the effort with which Tommy restrained himself from saying, "I told you so." Everything but his voice said it.

He cut several slices from a side of fat bacon and then said, "The mules could pull the wagon. We'll sell the new wagon you bought when you came here, and the blacks and the tools, buy a little stock and take the road again. Eh?"

"I suppose so. There's nothing else to do. We can't stay here, that's certain. We've got food till November. We'll let the niggers eat it as hard as they can and rest up before they're sold. They've been good chaps in their way."

The three black faces rose before me, so alike to the casual glance, but to me so individual. In the background I saw the market and the slave block. Who'd buy them? Someone like Tottie or Oldfield.

"Flaming Hell!" I cried in irritation because my past still tied my hands. "I shan't be able to bring myself to sell the poor bastards, Tommy. And unless I do we can't stock the wagon. They're worth the thick end of three hundred pounds."

"Why'n't you borrow some money? Enough to carry on another season. That Miss Fawcett'd lend it like a shot."

"I don't doubt it. But I wouldn't put a penny of anybody else's money into this outfit. I've lost my own and that's enough. Let's have some food. I'm going to take all that — ing rubbish out and have a fire after I've eaten."

I took a savage satisfaction in watching the mildewed leaves shrivel and burn. We each tended a fire and the four thick columns of smoke rose into the air and drifted westward, not the sweet-smelling smoke of burning tobacco, but the acrid, autumn-scented smoke of burning leaves mingled with a subtle flavour of corruption. Following the drift of the smoke to the west I thought of Little Egypt, and was suddenly curious to know whether the blight had struck there, or at Ipswich, or Bablockhythe. And once the question had occurred to me I must know the answer. I did not wish Goddy or Eulalia any harm, though I should not have mourned unduly over a slight misfortune befalling Newlyn, but if the blight were general I could have borne it better: perhaps discarded the notion that Lebanon — or I — had been cursed.

I saddled my horse and rode out on the track to Little Egypt, leaving the Negroes with the fires. When I neared the ford I rode slowly and looked at the fields around Bablockhythe. The ordered activity in them assured me that Newlyn's fields were untouched. They were being gathered in the normal way. My throat felt hot and full as I watched the loads being dragged into the sheds. It seemed impossible that a few miles away my own crop was smouldering into ash. But it had always been so. Before Bablockhythe was planted, before Ipswich was carved out of the forest, Lebanon and Little Egypt had started out as neighbours, as the only cultivated places in the wilderness, neck to neck they had started, and look at them now.

I sat there, turning over my bitter thoughts, when I heard a splashing in the ford. My horse pricked his ears. I turned my sick eyes towards the ford and saw

Eulalia's big pale horse scramble up, the silver drops showering from his legs.

"Hallo," she called. "I was coming to see you. Have you been having a fire?"

"Yes. You saw the smoke I suppose. I've just burned up a year's hard labour. It stank to Heaven."

"Blight?" asked Eulalia gravely.

I nodded. "Have you got it?"

"No."

"And Newlyn hasn't," I said, waving my hand towards the busy fields. "And I don't suppose Goddy has either. The people who warned me about Lebanon were right, weren't they?"

"These things happen. We once lost a crop on the whole of the eastern side and the west wasn't touched. The line was as sharp as if it had been ruled. Goddy's all right, as a matter of fact. He's been to see me this morning. Look at my face."

She pushed back the veil that hung from the brim of her hat to her shoulder, and on the thin white oval of her cheek four long red lines, with little globules of blood starting from them at intervals, glared.

"Goddy didn't do that!" I cried incredulously.

"No. Lisette. Look, shall I ride back with you, or will you come back with me? We're about half-way, so it makes no difference."

"I don't want to go back."

"Then come back with me and have a good strong drink. You look as though you could do with one."

She wheeled round her horse and I followed her through the ford in silence.

411

"Now," I said, as we drew level on the track again, "what has Lisette been doing?"

"Well, Goddy called once or twice while I wasn't . . . seeing anyone . . . you know . . ." She glanced at me out of the corner of her eye. "He saw Lisette and she apparently wrote a lot of most obscene rubbish on her slate and showed it to him. About you and me. She actually wrote that I couldn't be seen because I was being confined. How is that for a story? To Goddy of all people! He came over this morning to offer me his services. If you refused to make an honest woman of me he would either compel you to do so, or make it so hot for you that you'd be glad to leave the state."

"The bitch!" I said. "What on earth did you say?"

"At first nothing. I couldn't. I laughed so much that I could have screamed from the pain in my ribs. Goddy being all fatherly — peeping about furtively all the time to see if he could catch a sight of the little newcomer. God! It was the funniest thing I've ever heard, dreamed or read of. I said, 'I hope you haven't been spreading this ridiculous nonsense, Mr. Goddy.' And he said, 'I've been endeavouring to rouse public opinion.' Public opinion — his face — pomposity on two legs — and peering all the time — believing —" She broke of in a shout of laughter, bowed over the horse's neck and shaking so violently that at last the animal turned its head, stretching its neck in an attempt to look at her with a limpid, startled eye.

"Of course," she said, still spluttering, "Goddy was richly funny, but the whole thing isn't, very. The stupid story is all over the countryside by this time. And I was indoors for three weeks — and I haven't been to a public function since that Ball at Fort Anchor. I expect they'll all believe it, and since Goddy couldn't see the body they'll think I buried it in the midden. Really, I know I shouldn't laugh, but I just c-can't h-help it."

She went off into another peal.

"And Lisette, what did you say to her?"

"Told her to bring her slate to me, and cracked her over the head with it. She knew why. Her head must be iron. The slate just flew into a hundred bits and she didn't even stagger. She curled up her fingers like a cat's claws and ripped them down the side of my face."

"And are you going to keep her after that?"

"No. That is a little too much. She's going into Jamestown. The Bethlehem Sisters will look after her, if they're paid."

It wasn't until afterwards that I realised how the words had slid past me.

"And what are you going to do about this story?"

"What can I do?"

"I don't know."

"I'm so thankful that you didn't say you'd marry me, last night. They'd have taken that as proof. I can only deny it if asked and otherwise ignore it, and go on being friendly with you. I think that if we behave as usual, people will conclude that it must be wrong."

"But we can't," I said, suddenly remembering. "I've got to get out of Lebanon. I've failed to grow a crop and every penny I had was sunk in the place."

"Well, Hell! Can't I give you some?"

"I wouldn't take it. I wouldn't put any more money into that place. It's cursed."

"What will you do?"

"So far as I can see there's only one thing *to* do. Make what I can of the tools, one wagon, and perhaps one mule and go with the other wagon on the road again."

"And your niggers?"

"Turn 'em loose."

"You'll have to do that properly. Otherwise some swine'll claim them before they can turn round."

"I'll do it properly."

"I suppose," said Eulalia thoughtfully, "that no one would buy Lebanon."

"I wouldn't like to count on it. Would you?"

"No. Well, anyhow, you'll be here until when?"

"I've food and oil to last until November. We'll all lie on our backs and eat and get fat. And if you like I'll come and see you every day and look love-lorn and announce to everybody I see that I've asked you to marry me countless times but that you scorn the idea."

"That would help. You see, their poor little minds couldn't imagine a woman refusing to marry her seducer, could they?" She was smiling into my face, on the brink of laughter again. And then, all at once, the blind look came down like a shutter.

"It was silly of me to ask you to Little Egypt," she said. "I've got to go into Jamestown. I'll take Lisette in myself and kill two birds with one stone. You ride round to Ipswich and get your drink from Goddy. Tell him the

414

sad story and then go home by Bablockhythe and say the same. Good-bye."

She struck the pale horse a light blow and he leaped forward.

"But Mr. Goddy, of course it isn't true. Wouldn't she marry me if it were?"

"Of course, you're no match for her."

"Admittedly. But in the circumstances, supposing they were what you say, wouldn't she forget that?"

"Yes, yes. I suppose so. That Lisette must have been mad. Where did you say she was being sent?"

Echoes of Eulalia's hearty laughter in my ears.

"But Mr. Newlyn, of course it isn't true. Wouldn't she . . .?"

How Eulalia will laugh when she hears how they swallowed it!

We reckoned from four to five days for the journey to Jamestown and back if you travelled light, so it would be some days before I saw Eulalia again. Apart from feeding the animals there was now no work to do on the plantation and I couldn't bear the sight of the fields, so I slept most of the time. I was asleep on my bed in the afternoon of the fifth day when Tommy woke me with the information that a man was asking for me and was waiting in the sitting-room.

"Wha's he want?" I said sleepily.

"To see you," Tommy repeated patiently.

I held my head under some cold water, combed my hair and put on my coat. Somebody, I guessed, who had heard about my misfortune and come to see if he could drive a hard bargain over my slaves. He'd get a flea in his ear!

A small neat man stood by the window in my room, mopping his brow with his handkerchief and gazing with open disgust at the neglected garden. He wheeled round as I entered and composed his face.

"My name's Anderson," he said, holding out his hand, and then withdrawing it from mine to resume mopping his head and face. "I've had a very hot walk. I'm not used to walking and I was obliged to leave my carriage quite a way back. I didn't think your track would do my springs any good."

"No," I said. "It's hardly fit for wagons."

I pulled forward two chairs and after he had seated himself I asked,

"Now, Mr. Anderson, what can I do for you?"

"You *can*, if you will, sell me this place. The question is, *will* you?"

"Sell it to you," I said, trying to keep the stupefied amazement out of my voice, "what makes you think that I want to sell it?"

"I don't think so. I don't for a moment suppose you want to sell it. I came here in the hope that I might *persuade* you to do so."

"Have you taken a fancy to it or something?"

"I may as well be quite frank with you. My grandfather was the first person to settle here, Mr. Lowrie. Ever since I was a boy I've had a hankering for the place. It's only lately that I've come back to Virginia

416

and been able to do something about it more than hanker."

"But," I said, fumbling in my mind for a memory, "I thought the first settler was scalped with his wife . . ."

An expression of anger crossed the neat little face.

"They had a child, perhaps, and perhaps the child escaped, and perhaps that child was my father, and finally perhaps I know best about that. And I want to buy Lebanon."

"And have you come back to Virginia rich?"

"Moderately. Why do you ask?"

"Because unless you're rich Lebanon is not the place for you."

"You set a high price on it?"

"It sets a high price upon itself, Mr. Anderson."

I hesitated, studying the neat little figure, the honest-looking face, no longer young. I thought, perhaps he feels about this place as I feel about Braidlowrie. I had an impulse to tell him — Lebanon has ruined me and many men before me, it's a cursed place. And I had another impulse to name a price, the price that I had paid, take it if he would pay it and cut my losses that way. And then despair, which had never been far away from me in the last few days, tipped the scale. God's eyeballs! What could a few hundred pounds do for me now? Turn me into a pedlar again. To Hell with it. There is such a thing as honour and it seems to be about all I have left.

"Listen," I said harshly. "This place, for some reason or another, is damned. I forget how many men have gone through that door beggared, but I'm just another at the end of the line. This year I've lost every plant I had from mildew. There isn't a speck on any other leaf in the district. If you're wise you'll forget your ancestral home and your grandfather and keep your money in your pocket. People warned me and I wouldn't listen. I wish to God I had. Now I'm warning you."

"But surely," he said gently, "all this is superstition."

"That's what I said."

"And now you think that the mildew proves the superstition to be well founded. But that may be just a season's bad luck. If you could stay on . . . And anyway I don't want to grow tobacco. I intend to breed horses."

"They'll all break their legs, or eat their own young."

"Come, come, Mr. Lowrie. This is the most original way of spurring on a buyer's appetite I have ever encountered. I'll name my price."

He named one that made me fall backwards. It was about five times the amount that I had given the widow for the place.

"It's a crazy price," I said.

"It's the most I feel justified in offering you."

"Merciful Heaven, I'm not trying to string you along. If after what I've told you you think it's worth so much I can only thank God, fasting, that insanity takes such remarkable forms. You can have it."

"At once."

"At this minute if you like. Wait a minute."

I rushed through into the kitchen.

"Tommy, Tommy," I yelled. "There's an ancestor worshipper in there who has bought the place. Do you hear me, Tommy? Bought it. Is there anything to drink in the house?"

"'Bout a quart of rum, that's all."

"Get it."

I took him by the arm when he re-appeared from the store with the pewter-plate tray and dragged him with me into the room.

"Mr. Anderson, this is Tommy, my partner. Let's drink to your ownership of Lebanon. Perhaps after all we carry our own luck with us. May yours be wonderful."

The little man raised his glass with a curious smile.

"I have persuaded you to sell it, and that is all that matters for the moment. Will you meet me in Fort Anchor tomorrow to conclude the business?"

"Gladly," I said, and raised my glass.

A few minutes later I watched him teetering down the rough track to his carriage. I gave him time to get off on to the road, and then I got out my horse and raced over to tell Eulalia the glad tidings.

A tray with a coffee pot and a bowl of sugar stood on the table by the hearth; a pair of gloves and a hat lay on the sofa where they had been thrown so carelessly that the plume of the hat was broken, and Eulalia, with a cup in one hand and a saucer in the other, was marching up and down the room shouting a lot of names and figures to the wizened gnome-like creature who helped with the Little Egypt accounts. He held his quill between his teeth while he turned over the pages of two stout ledgers and shuffled his way through a mass of loose papers.

"Come in," she said when she saw me. "Sit down and have some coffee. I've just finished. Now, have you checked all that? And it's all quite clear. Tell them to transfer it at once. Get the letter written and let Jason take it tonight. He can change his horse at Flynn's place and ride straight through. It won't hurt him for once. He's got to be in Jamestown by tomorrow evening. Give him some money for a bed tomorrow night. I'll sign the papers as soon as you've written them. Be as quick as you can."

The little creature gathered up the papers and the books, screwed down his ink, planted his pen behind his ear and hurried away.

"A bit of business arose while I was in Jamestown," said Eulalia, sitting down suddenly. "Isn't it maddening to have to fumble round with formalities when you want to do something all in a hurry?"

"I've had some business, too," I said. "I seem to have sold Lebanon."

"Sold it, I hope, not given it away."

I told her about Mr. Anderson's eagerness and the fantastic price he had offered.

"Good," she said, "good. And now I can mention something I've been thinking. I hoped you might sell it, because I've had such a good idea. Come in with me and take a share in Little Egypt. I've a hundred experiments I could try if I had someone to help me, and a little more money."

"Since when have you needed either help or money?" I asked sceptically.

420

"Since I heard you had the money," said Eulalia, and laughed. "Seriously though, I meant it. I think we should work very well together."

"I don't," I said firmly. "We've had too many personal relationships."

"You don't mean that, do you?"

"I do indeed. Besides, now that I have, or shall have, the money, I have other plans."

"And what are they?"

"I sound," I said, after a moment's hesitation, "rather like those old men who set to sea in a bowl. But I *think* I'm going back to Scotland."

Eulalia's face went deathly, but she said promptly,

"You can't. You won't have enough money. I presume that by Scotland you mean Braidlowrie. That's right, isn't it?"

"Of course."

"Well, you won't have enough for that, will you?"

"I've been thinking. All the way over here I've been thinking hard about it. I haven't enough to go back and do what I planned. I admit that. I hoped, when I ran away, to go back, one day, very rich, and buy back the land and rebuild the house, make it the Great House of Braidlowrie again. That was a boyish dream. 'When I was a child I thought as a child,' you know. But within the last couple of hours it has come to me that I can go back and buy the homestead and a couple of fields perhaps. I can work there as I've worked at Lebanon. You see, Eulalia, I've been ten years at St. Crispin's, three on the wagon, a year at Lebanon. I'm over thirty, my best years are going. I seem doomed never to make a lot of money. If I wait until I do, I shall be too old to put my best into the job that *is* mine out of all the jobs in the world. If I go now, however humbly, I shall be there, putting my sweat into my own soil. And though perhaps you may not understand this, I feel, I know, that there will be more satisfaction for me in mending fencing and tilling an acre at Braidlowrie than in doing anything, however interesting or exciting, anywhere else."

"So you're going away," said Eulalia slowly. And just then the gnome opened the door and entered. He put the papers, ink and quill before his mistress and took up a waiting position behind her chair.

Eulalia ignored the pen, the ink, the papers. She jumped up from her chair, strode to the window, flung back the curtain and stood there, staring out.

Through the silence came the sound of the clock in the hall, the soft noise of the slowly burning fire. The little man stirred uneasily and coughed behind his hand. Eulalia didn't move.

"Madam," said the gnome at last, "Jason is waiting."

Eulalia growled without turning.

At last, driven to some interference I said, "Eulalia, don't let my affairs upset your own."

"Satan take you," she cried whirling round on me. "Your affairs *are* mine."

She left the window, crossed the room with hurried nervous steps and thrust the quill into the ink. Then she paused for just a second and looked at me. The quill scratched and sputtered suddenly across the bottom of one page, another and another.

"Cranmer," she said, and flung the quill violently into the heart of the fire.

"Tell Jason to go quickly and send Joseph in here to me."

Joseph appeared immediately.

"Take away this rubbish," she said pointing to the coffee tray, "and bring some brandy. Be *quick*."

When the brandy came she splashed it out so that it flew out of the glasses and mingled with the inkspots that had rained from the fiercely driven quill. She thrust the glass towards me and picked up her own.

"To Braidlowrie, Colin. You've worked fourteen years and made human sacrifice for it. I hope it will repay you."

"I can't understand you," I said heavily.

"You can't understand anything."

She emptied her glass, refilled it and emptied it again before I had reduced mine two inches.

"I was brought up all wrong," she said at last, drunkenly. "My father wanted a boy and didn't get one, so he brought me up like one. Big mistake. I always had my way. I always make a bid for anything I want. And women don't work well that way. I suppose if I'd been all soft and feminine you'd have stayed and helped me run the place. 'Poor Eulalia, she's so helpless.' Helpless hell! There's nothing I can't do, except make the one man I want love me."

I said, weary and ashamed, "We've been through all that. Suppose I did love you — and sometimes I'm damned near doing it — the other day when you laughed at that story that would have sent any other woman into hysteria, for example — suppose I did? You want me, and I want Braidlowrie. What on earth would you do about that?"

"Sell out and go with you."

"Then do it," I said recklessly. "I've explained to you all about the past and the future. What you see in me passes my understanding entirely. You elude me, even in bed you elude me and reduce me to — well blast it, you know, you're there. But there's some kind of link between us that's going to be difficult to break. But for God's sake think it over. Think what you'll be giving up. I won't even have a name in Scotland . . ."

"I'll think it over. Hadn't you better go now?"

"Yes. I suppose so. I've got to meet Anderson in the morning and make all the arrangements about setting my fellows free. I'll come over the day after tomorrow. And Eulalia —"

"Yes?"

"While you're thinking over the matter, remember that if you decide to come I can at least promise that I'll be faithful to you. I haven't much to offer, but that I can."

"You're a very faithful person aren't you, Colin? To a dream. To a memory. Very faithful."

I spent the next two days at Fort Anchor transferring Lebanon to Anderson who arrived with the money in his hand, and arranging about Loko, Shandy and Alexander. I gave them fifty pounds apiece and they parted from me with tears. Where would they end, I wondered. But I shuffled the thought away. I had done what I could.

★ ★ ★

When I got back to Lebanon Tommy had a message for me. I was not to go to Little Egypt for a week. It would take so long.

"Say it again," I said.

"That one they call Jason just rode over and said, 'Tell Mr. Lowrie not to call on Miss Eulalia for a week. It will take so long.' That was all."

"It sounds funny, but I think I understand. Now Tommy, what about you?"

"What about me?"

"What are you going to do?"

"What do you think?"

"The best wagon and the mules and the road again, eh? We'll go into Jamestown tomorrow and fill up with stock. How's that?"

"If we were folks in a book," said Tommy, meditatively, "I suppose I should stick to you. And if you were going anywhere but across the water I would. But I've crossed the Atlantic once and to tell you the truth I don't feel I could face it again. I hope you don't mind my saying so."

"I'd mind more if you wanted to come," I told him. "The wagon is sure and easy. There's nothing but hard work and penury ahead of me. I'll even have to change my name. Nobody will want a Lowrie in Scotland."

"You're one of those folk who have a destiny," said Tommy, suddenly the usher again. "And they're the only ones who have any story. The rest of us just drift."

"Let's pack up then and drift into town. Do you think that prancing steed of mine will condescend to pull the spare wagon?"

"Compulsion will do a lot," said Tommy.

So we put the ploughs and the hoes, and the bed into the big wagon with the mule team, and the chairs and tables into the smaller, and set out from Lebanon for the last time. It had been a halting place and a lot had happened there but I left it without sorrow.

We jogged into Jamestown, leaving the roof and chimneys of the Bethlehem House upon our left, and made for the old stabling place. Tommy went back to Tanners Yard and I went to the *Sailor's Return*. I didn't want to see Sadie.

We spent two days refurnishing the wagon and selling the rest of the stuff. I had to stay with Tommy during the shopping because he had an obsession that he was costing me too much. I had to do all the ordering. And though every shilling meant one less for Braidlowrie I had to discharge my obligations.

During the buying I ran into Preswade who hailed me with pleasure.

"I hear you've got rid of Lebanon. What now?"

"I'm leaving Virginia," I said. His face fell.

"You know that disappoints me. I mostly get my way as I told you. And I've always had a notion that you'd think better of my offer one fine day. Julie married in the spring — one of those la-di-da young dandies. I've got him in my office now, less use than a toothache. But Carrie's still free, and she's the eldest, you know."

"She'll present you with somebody suitable one day," I said. "The odds are surely against your getting three toothaches. And anyway I'm Jonah. If I'd joined you all your ships would have foundered and all your goods rotted."

"You sound a bit sour. What did Lebanon do to you?"

"Oh nothing. Lebanon was splendid. It raised me the best crop of mildew ever seen in these parts."

"Well, I warned you, remember. Still we won't mention that now." He coughed a little. "Look here, you sound rather disheartened. If you're in any trouble, short of money or anything . . . I can let you have . . . old friends you know."

"It's extremely generous of you," I said gratefully. "But as a matter of fact, I'm all right. I sold Lebanon well."

"Who to? A lunatic?"

"No, a fellow called Anderson. He would have it. I warned him too."

"Anderson," he said, wrinkling his brow. "A little, soft-spoken fellow, very neat?"

"Sounds like the same."

"But my dear man, he hasn't got enough money to buy a sausage mule. He's a kind of go-between. He'd do anything for twopence. I use him quite a bit. He'll go to sales and bid to send up prices, that kind of thing. He's quite clever." He pondered for a moment. "I bet you anything he's bought it *for* somebody. Now who

427

could want Lebanon on the quiet?" He pondered again. "Did you get your money?" he snapped.

"Yes," I said, "good minted money. So I don't care if he bought it for Satan."

"For that matter nor do I. I was only interested in thinking who it could be who wouldn't buy it openly. Or would buy it at all if it comes to that. You may think yourself damned lucky."

"I do. I shall probably go down to history as the one man who made a profit on Lebanon. You'll be proud to have known me."

"I'm glad to anyway."

"Well," I said, "I must get along. Good-bye, Mr. Preswade, and thank you again for all your kindness to me. I'll always remember you."

"And I'll always be sorry that you're not with me. Good-bye, my boy and good luck."

There was a little sadness about leaving someone whom I had liked and whom I should never see again.

The part of the conversation that had dealt with Anderson and his money slipped away from my mind. I never even wondered about it. It was not until months later that it suddenly flashed through my mind again and I understood. Eulalia's sudden departure to Jamestown on the day that I told her about my crop's failure . . . she hadn't meant to do that, because she had asked me to ride home with her. And the papers that she had signed so fiercely after I had told her what I meant to do with the money. God, what that signature must have cost her when she knew that she had given me the means to leave her. But not a hint, not a sign.

Except the word "Cranmer." After I understood I took some trouble to find out about Cranmer and learned that he had written something he didn't want to and so had burned his right hand.

It was too late when I understood all this to do anything about it, except humble myself before the thought of a woman who *could* and did sign those papers.

At the time, as I say, I thought about Anderson not at all. I just thought about the unpleasantness of final leave-takings.

The parting with Tommy was worse. He snuffled a bit.

"Look here, Tommy," I said. "If the day comes when you can't man the wagon, or change your mind about the Atlantic, come to Scotland. You'd better write this down, Braidlowrie, Crosslochie, Inverness. I shall be named Collins. You'll remember that because of my first name. I may not be there, I may not succeed in getting it back. But I shall not be far away, and I'll leave messages at the manse and the inn and anywhere else I can think of. And I'll always have a welcome for you."

"I guess I'll come now," said Tommy uncertainly.

"No," I said. "Come in a year's time, or two. You'll settle down once you're on the road again."

"Maybe I will. And God bless you, Mister, wherever you go. I won't forget that you took me out of the kennel . . ."

He choked. "And look here, suppose things go against you . . . I'll always be at Tanner's Yard see . . .

and if it's my last crust . . . Good-bye. Come up Beelzebub, get *along!*"

The mules strained forward. The last I saw of Tommy was a large red handkerchief, the last I heard was a snort.

I fetched my horse and set out on the two day journey to Little Egypt.

It was autumn now, the damp weather that Fergus had always dreaded; the trees had shed their coloured leaves and the sky, where it showed, was pale and cool.

I rode heavily, aware of a sadness of a finishing phase. Mother had said once, comparing English with French, that there were some things in French that could never be satisfactorily rendered into the other language and one of the things was, "Partir, c'est toujours mourir un peu."

Virginia had given me my love and taken her again. It had taken four years of my life, and it had given me the woman towards whom I was now riding. It had nothing else for me, but the sight of the people to whom it was home, whose orbit it was, saddened me. Life would go on here, busy and prosperous, troubled, happy, centred, while I tossed on the sea again and faced another life in another sphere. That was how the world looked to those about to leave it. "This will go on and I shall not be here."

Still, I was taking my chosen path, and whatever Eulalia might say about us not choosing our roads or our destinations I knew that I had been free to go or stay. I thought that confidently, and then something deep within me wondered. Had I, as a small boy with the swill-pail in my hand, not so much chosen as recognised and accepted my fate? Who could answer that? Not I. So I wondered instead what Eulalia's choice would be. I had no clue to that. And I hardly knew what to hope. I might think at one moment, "I wish she would come." But which she? The one who laughed so easily and merrily, the energetic, busy one, full of ideas and arguments; the absent, withdrawn one who lived a life in a region of which I knew nothing; the fierce masterful one, the one who seemed to hate everything, to hate herself and me? With which could I build Braidlowrie?

A kind of creeping excitement shook my bones. My mind swung on a see-saw. At one moment it seemed that if I left her behind the wrench of parting would be unbearable and the future black. At the next I pictured what our life together would be: uneasy, full of uncertainty, quarrels, maladjustments.

I stabled my horse at the pretentiously named Fort Hotel, which was a wooden shack with a swinging sign and some stables, and engaged a room. But the moment I was within the confined space with the rest of the evening and the whole of the night to get through I was seized with something amounting to hysteria. I went down to the bar, had a drink and then said, "Have you a horse I could hire?"

"No, don't own one."

"Does anyone?"

"Flynn. You passed his place about a mile back. He'll be abed."

"Then I'll wake him. And I'll fetch my own horse tomorrow."

"You'll pay for your room too."

"Naturally."

I walked back through the gentle rain to Flynn's, roused him with a handful of pebbles at his window and within a quarter of an hour was on my way to Little Egypt.

It was autumn, it was raining and it was early morning. I was reminded of such another.

The big house loomed pale in the darkness. Not a light showed. I was wondering whether I dared disturb its sleeping stillness when a window opened with a crash and a voice, Eulalia's voice, called through the darkness, "Who is there?"

"Colin. I'm sorry to come at such an hour, but I couldn't wait."

"I'll be down at once."

I tied up my horse and threw my coat over his back. By that time the door had opened on an oblong of faint light. I went in. Eulalia closed the door, opened her own room and began to light candles from the one she carried.

"You weren't asleep, or you couldn't have heard me."

"No. I was planning what to say to you when I saw you. But I didn't plan it like this."

She had put on a long velvet robe, furred at neck and wrist and hem, over her night attire, and the heavy hair fell on her shoulders. She pulled it round her and shivered.

"Has it turned cold? This fire hasn't been dead long, I sat up late. But all day whole flocks of geese seem to have been walking over my grave."

"Get something more to wear. Or if you like tell me what you've decided and then go back to bed. I can lie down on this sofa for a little while. It'll be morning soon."

"Are you really anxious to know what I have decided?"

"So anxious that though I'd taken a room at the Fort Hotel — for which by the way I had to pay — I left it, borrowed a horse from Flynn and came on here to find out."

"And do you mind? Which way I've decided?"

I looked at her and suddenly all the shackles fell from my mind. It was as though the whole of the past had dropped clean away, other people, our failures and differences and quarrels, and there was only the future and us. Myself, sane and certain at last, and this lovely shining woman with the strong mind and the gallant heart. I said humbly,

"I've so little to offer you. You will have to give up so much. But I hope you'll come with me, Eulalia." She began to laugh, not the merry sputtering laughter with which she had recounted the story of Lisette and Goddy, but a low trickle of laughter that had bitterness in it, and self-mockery and hatred.

"You would come back in that mood," she said at last.

"What do you mean?"

"Listen. The first day that I saw you, Colin Lowrie, I loved you. I thought that here was a person who might understand me, to whom I could show things, who could share the things I cared about. I loved you because you were handsome, because you were considerate to your slaves and didn't mind hard work. They sound silly reasons, and I suppose really they had nothing to do with it. Something in you called out to something in me. I didn't want it to happen. I told you, our real selves can only cry out 'not that way,' they can't avoid even a certain disaster. I didn't want to love you, but I did."

I took advantage of the thoughtful pause to say,

"Why do you make it sound all so far away in the past? The past doesn't really matter any more, I realised that tonight. We've got the future to think of."

"But we have no future, that's just it. You have one and I have one but we haven't."

"You're not coming with me?"

"No. I sent that message asking you not to come until after a week because I couldn't make up my mind. But now I know. When it came to a choice between Little Egypt and you I knew that I couldn't choose you. It's odd because I never loved Little Egypt until I was on the verge of losing it."

"You said once that we had a lot in common. I began to love you when I thought about never seeing you again."

"That," said Eulalia, bringing her hand down sharply on the edge of the table, "is what is wrong with us. It always has been wrong. We're far too clear-sighted and

434

far too frank. Instead of fumbling around with significant glances and half-finished sentences we've always spoken our minds. I told you I loved you, you told me that you didn't love me. Now we've changed our cries, but we're still out in the daylight of thought and love can only flourish in a kind of half-light. Isn't that true?"

"I don't know. What I do know is that you're trying to tell me that you don't love me any more. That's it, isn't it?"

"I suppose so. I blame Lisette, too."

"Lisette?"

"She took my book, just when I wanted it. I wanted to work the cherry-blossom spell on you, and I couldn't find the book. I got the wrong spray or I used the words wrongly, or something. It didn't work — and I've never known it to fail."

"For the love of Christ," I cried, "are you an enlightened, intelligent woman, or an old crone fiddling with knuckle-bones? Spells be — ed. I'll tell you the plain truth. You fell in love with me too soon, while I was still in love with a memory and I've fallen in love with you too late, after you've fallen in love with little Egypt. If I give in and stay here will you marry me?"

"No. I've had you once when your heart was elsewhere and that's an experience that I don't want to repeat. You get back to your Braidlowrie and do what you were always intended to do."

"And that's your last word?"

"On that subject, yes."

"It's for all our lives, remember."

"I know. Listen, I'll tell you something. When you first spoke of going back to Scotland I was shattered. I had hoped — and planned — so differently. After you had gone that night I thought about it and realised that you were right, terribly, terribly right. Love, even when it is mutual, is a tricky thing, liable to change. We make a lot of it because for some reason it has caught the fancy of the ballad mongers and the dealers in words. 'All for love and the world well lost.' Everybody thrills to words like that. It's very important to the human race that there should be children to carry on in the world — though why really I don't see, the world would be a far nicer place without any people in it. And in order to get children people have to go to bed together, and before that can be done with any grace they have to desire one another. That's all love is if you strip it down to essentials. And the time will come, I told myself, when we shall be two old people, when love would be indecent between the old bodies we'll have then. And I should begin to mourn for my kingdom, my interests, my experiments, my slaves. So I took the long view, Colin, and chose Little Egypt. That's why I can't let you sacrifice Braidlowrie."

I sat baffled for a moment before this glimpse into a mind at once so clear and so perverse. Then I stood up, went over to her and dragged her to her feet so that the furred gown fell open, and when I clasped her to me her bosom was warm to my breast. I kissed her, mouth, eyes, hair, the white hollow of her neck. She sighed, pressed closer to me, returned my kisses.

"There," I said at last, breathing hard. "Dismiss that with a few of your words."

Tears gathered in her clear eyes.

"Are you coming?" I asked. She shook her head and the tears splashed over.

"You'll not disturb my peace of mind that way again."

"But I want you, Eulalia, I want you."

"I wanted you. I know all about it, my dear. It passes. Come here."

Taking me by the hand she dragged me across to the window and pushed aside the curtain. Dawn had broken in the East and the world lay grey and flat and untenanted beneath the light.

"It's a new day, Colin. A time for fresh beginnings."

"I've made so many," I said heavily.

"But not this one before."

We stood there, still hand in hand for a long time, while the light broadened and the brilliant sunshine that so often ushers in a day of rain fell first on the tree-tops, gilding the bare twigs, and then at last on the soil of the empty fields. I tried to look forward. Suppose I stayed. I could persuade her to let me stay. She had drugged her love, thought it dead, written its epitaph, but it would wake. And hers would be the victory. Because she had been strong and chosen her acres she would have me too. I couldn't face it. It was oddly like the threat of emasculation. I must be strong, too, and follow my more ancient love. Perhaps then I might know victory. But looking at her face as she watched the brightening light I doubted it.

A long finger of sunshine touched the window-sill and as though it had been a signal our hands fell apart.

"Your horse is at Flynn's," I said. "I'll get a lift into town or walk. I don't think there's anything else to say."

"Except farewell. Fare very well."

"And you." I said from a throat that was suddenly full and hot.

"I shall remember you."

I couldn't speak again.

I lifted the damp coat from the horse's back and slung it over my shoulder, mounted, wheeled round and rode away without looking back. I had a feeling that she watched until the drive turned and I was hidden. The horse, with his head to his own stable, moved swiftly. The clouds that were chasing the sun caught and swallowed it. The fine rain started once more. "A dead nun and a heap of stones. What adversaries!" she had said. The dead nun had died for a second time at the moment when I had abjured the past, but the stones, the stones remained. I lifted my head so that the rain fell on my face. I thought suddenly of the fine rain of Scotland, blotting out the hills. I thought of the birch trees dripping their first green over the primroses by Breckny Pool, of the heather on Carnspur at the turn of the year. And below these trivial thoughts lay the consciousness that I was returning to Braidlowrie.

"Jacob worked fo' his gal . . ."

Seven years and other seven; exactly as long as I had worked. And I had chosen, not the house of flesh but one of stone. I shook off the mental picture of what Eulalia would do, how spend her days, her energy, her passion now. By my own tardiness and half-heartedness I had lost her. By my own choice I had gained my freedom. The wrench had been painful — but so had other things that I had lived down and forgotten. I must forget again.

But I knew that there is no forgetting. My mother, my father, Glenranald, Janet, Fanshawe, Jimmy, Cassie, Tottie, Sadie and Tommy — and last of all Eulalia, even those dimmer figures, black and white with whom I had laboured, had been woven into that curious experience of consciousness that we call life. Even Mrs. Thatcher was not forgotten, it was she who had said, "Ye'll come at last to ye'r journey's end, but not the way ye think to."

It struck me, as I brushed the rain-drops off my face, that that might be said of all of us, of every one of the teeming, toiling millions who pursue the unpredictable path.

Also available in ISIS Large Print:

The Villa in Italy

Elizabeth Edmondson

An irresistible invitation to a magical place

Four strangers are summoned to the Villa Dante, a
beautiful but abandoned house above the Ligurian
coast. Each has been named in the will of the intriguing
Beatrice Malaspina, but not one of them knows who
she is or what the connection might be. Delia, an opera
singer robbed of her voice; George, an atom scientist
unable to face what his skills have created; Marjorie,
a detective novelist with writer's block; and Lucius, a
Boston banker whose personal life is in chaos.

As they wait to find out why they're all there, the villa
begins to work its seductive magic. Amongst the faded
frescoes, overgrown garden and magnificent mediaeval
tower, four determined characters slowly begin to
change — the sorrow of their wartime experiences
growing into hope. But the mysterious Beatrice has a
devastating secret to reveal that will affect them all . . .

ISBN 978-0-7531-7890-4 (hb)
ISBN 978-0-7531-7891-1 (pb)

Golden Days

D. E. Stevenson

The green and golden beauty and the eternal atmosphere of "Avielochan" is the background of this delightful story. Mrs Tim goes to the Highlands of Scotland and is involved in a plot to rescure a naval officer from the toils of a siren; but, alas, the best laid plans "gang aft agley".

The characters are skilfully drawn, from the fierce Mrs London with her heart of gold to the garrulous Mrs Falconer who always gets things wrong and whose muddled stories of her girlhood make excruciatingly funny reading.

The house party amuses itself with picnics and fishing excursions and is suitably thrilled by the flourishing ancestral feud of two rival clans, which has its origin in the dim past.

Mrs Tim observes her fellow men and women with sympathy and humour and records her observations with a racy pen. The result is an attractive and witty story of an unusual character.

ISBN 978-0-7531-7612-2 (hb)
ISBN 978-0-7531-7613-9 (pb)